THE DARK CRUSADER
Copyright © 2021 by Jackie Ivie

ebook 978-1-939820-92-1
Print 978-1-939820-93-8

Printed in U.S.A.

Cover Design and Interior © format by

THE DARK CRUSADER

VALOR AND STEEL · 1

JACKIE IVIE

DEDICATION

*To Nancy, for everything you do
and have always done for me.*

.

CHAPTER ONE

ad 1254

"*HARAA'IQ!*" Cassandra cracked open leaden eyelids and blinked. Flickers of red and yellow flames could be seen, but it was blurry. Indistinct. Dull throbs of sound filtered through the haze, adding sound to the sight. A shout of "Fire!" came again. Cassandra struggled to lift her head from the pillow. It was all too much effort. Her eyes shut again.

"*Princessa!*"

There was only who knew her royal title. Cassandra willed her eyes open, ordered her fingers to tense on the woven mesh surface beneath her. Nothing worked.

"*Princessa!* We must hurry! Quickly now! This is your chance. No one is looking! What are you waiting for?"

She focused blearily on the man who knelt beside her. Even if her mind ordered, it nothing responded. Shouts and all manner of screams grew louder, pricking her ear with fear-filled words.

"Hurry! To the tunnels!"

"It's the *kafirs*! They've come!"

"How? And how many?"

"They've overpowered the guards! Quickly! Get to the tunnels! Everyone!"

Shouts resounded, more words about infidels, while continuous thumps from a gong reverberated through the floor. The last sent the slightest tingling sensation through her palm. *Thank the Saints!* She wasn't completely numb… and it might not be permanent. Cassandra narrowed her eyes. Tried to think. From her vantage, she watched palace guards spill into the scene, adding to the pandemonium.

Palace guards?

In the harem?

They herded the women enmasse, along with children and slaves. It was now impossible to make out words in a plethora of languages amidst an uncountable volume of dialects. There was too much background noise. It all blending into a cacophony. Flames chased shadows that raced through the smoke-filled chambers. A span of material used for decoration fell, before turning unrecognizable as flames devoured it. The situation was dire. Cassandra struggled with her body. Uselessly.

"You must come! Now!"

The eunuch, Emin, spoke at her side again, his handsome face full of worry. Cassandra met his glance. Blinked.

"What is it? You don't move."

She managed a frown. He lifted his head away to look over his shoulder. They both watched as an incinerated section of palace ceiling fell into the pool, hissing and sizzling before sinking from sight. The sounds had changed, too. No longer could she hear the gong, screams, or shouts. Now there was the roar of flames, the crashing of destruction. The pool water bubbled and steamed, adding even more opacity to the scene.

"Selique? She did this?" Emin asked at her shoulder.

Cassandra managed a cough. It burned her throat but she welcomed the sensation.

"That one was spawned by the devil and nursed at a hog's breast! You should know better than to have anything to do with her."

She gave another smoke-filled cough.

"Here! I've a covering."

He held one of the thick woven curtains that were used throughout the harem chambers. Cassandra had a hard time seeing him.

"E...min!" Her whisper hadn't much sound. He knelt beside her again.

"Grant me permission to touch you."

"Emin!" Another cough wracked her frame.

"I cannot touch you unless I have permission."

Cassandra hadn't much sensation in her body, but enough to feel the stone beneath her heating up. Flames licked at the very steps Emin was going to race down...and he talked palace protocol?

"Yes!" The word was hissed. Her throat hurt. Her lungs now pained. Actually, every aware portion of her body was painful.

He bent, deftly swaddled her in the curtain, hoisted her across one shoulder, and then he was running, his feet churning through flames and dancing past rubble. Upside-down, Cassandra watched it happen. Her head bobbed in vicious throbs of ache. Her shoulders swayed in concert. But then he stopped, rocking her outward and slamming her back. Her forehead smacked against him sending a pulse of pain through her temples.

"Where is it you think you are going?" A deep voice asked.

"There is...fire. There is a big fire!"

Those lessons Cassandra had given him were providential. Even said with an accent, she understood the broken Frankish words Emin used, matching their inquisitor's language.

"Right of plunder goes to the victor," the unknown male continued.

"Victor?" Emin asked.

"Aye. And that would be me. I am the victor. Toss your load in the wagon. Yes, that one. Don't tempt fate, lad. I've a very hungry sword."

Emin swung her. Cassandra got a glimpse of black-coated chainmail covered with a blood-flecked cloth and black hair. Then she slammed against something, and knew absolutely nothing.

CHAPTER TWO

WHAT WAS THIS? She'd overslept? Consciousness came slowly, like a slight beam of light in the deepest cavern. Cassandra lay unmoving as she considered. She felt odd. Disembodied. A chance thought drifted up through the fog in her mind.

Had she been poisoned? Was that it?

She licked dry lips with a drier tongue. Tried to open her eyes. If this was death, it wasn't what any of the religions prophesied. More likely this was the aftereffects of drugging. She'd been drugged by a jealous rival. Could Selique's assassin even now, be approaching to check on his handiwork...a blade held ready to plunge into her unguarded back?

This wasn't like her. She should react, not simply somnolently ponder things. Nothing felt normal but she'd have an easier time puzzling it if the creaking and rumbling noises would cease. She'd never felt so disoriented. Vulnerable. Stupid.

Her stupidity amazed her, adding bitterness to recollection. She'd attended sup with Selique.

There hadn't been an option. No one declined the current favorite. So Cassandra complied, spent the time in complete attentiveness, murmuring platitudes, vacuously smiling and chatting, playing with the food; pieces of cheese, figs, morsels of perfectly seasoned mutton. But she'd been foolish. She'd sipped at the woman's juice!

Selique was the sultan's favorite and the woman jealously guarded the position. She had nothing to fear from Cassandra. She wanted an escape from the silken prison, not further imprisonment. As one of the more unusual women in the harem, she always kept her hip-length, magenta-streaked hair under concealing head-scarves, her eyes downcast, her features hidden...most especially her pale, unblemished skin. Yet, despite every effort to the contrary, she'd caught the sultan's eye.

And from that moment, she was on borrowed time.

Emin had told her such a thing was her destiny. She was too beautiful. She was bound to attract the sultan's favor. Beauty was a curse she'd rather not suffer. It wasn't her fault she took after her father. Spoken as the most handsome man in the Asen II kingdom of Bulgar, he'd wed a Candia Duchy princess from the island of Crete, been granted a small principality on the very edge of civilization, given the duty of protecting the civilized world from barbarians. He'd built a castle. Fortified the town.

And died trying to hold it.

Cassandra gasped.

What in the heavens was wrong with her?

Nothing was gained from remembering the slaughter that brought her into a *Mamluk* Sultanate's harem, turning her existence into one of alertness. Tension. Hiding. Trying to escape the notice of powerful women and jealous shrews, where gossip destroyed, a small move could be perceived as a slight, innuendoes carried penalties, and any meal might be the last.

Like last night...

Wait.

Something more than a drugging had happened. Something immense.

Cassandra frowned. Searched her memory. It seemed surreal. Had there been an attack by Western crusader knights? Was it possible Emin had actually helped her escape in the confusion that followed? Just when every filmy piece of material she'd been given to wear felt like iron bands?

But - if that were the case - why did it feel like she was in physical bondage right now?

The moment she thought about it, every portion of her body began throbbing with ache. Cassandra tried shifting position. The drapery material was wound tightly about her, and her right ankle was locked in a twisted position. A bejeweled anklet bit into skin. She tried again to move. This time she gained a sharp pain through her head and a chest that burned with gasped breaths. Nothing else changed. She was imprisoned by dead weight, each gasp pulled through hair strands. That was strange. Her hair had been braided and secure beneath an ornate headdress. She squirmed and shimmied. Groaned and wrestled. If she could just get an arm loose, she'd brush hair from her face. Then maybe, every inhalation wouldn't be florid with heavy perfume.

The situation was untenable.

Carpets and silks and all manner of other items smashed until her lower legs spiked with each heartbeat. Cassandra set her teeth and squirmed for long sweat-inducing, heart-pounding moments, succeeding only in wedging herself between two unyielding bolts of material and the wooden slats of a wagon side. That was a trade-off. Despite the continual throbs of cramped limbs and scented hair that infused each breath, she had access to fresh air. She inhaled as deeply as allowed by the mass surrounding her.

And endured.

The night lengthened, bringing chill and dry, dust-filled air. Cassandra slept when she could, doing her best to ignore aches that multiplied, along with the emptiness of her belly, and overwhelming thirst. This wasn't freedom. This was just another prison, walled with treasures and wagon slats.

And time wore on.

They continued through the night. The sky was a lavender shade when she next woke. Cassandra forced open eyes drier than any desert. She was exhausted. Numbed. Semi-conscious. That's why she missed her opportunity when the wood shimmied and stopped moving. Wheels were wedged. The animal that had pulled the cart was unhooked. She heard muffled banging and clanging, more than one guttural oath. Sounds of horses whickering.

This couldn't be her fate. She was not slated to die of thirst surrounded by plunder from a palace. Someone else could lie amidst riches, her body dry and wizened and mummified...but not her. And such thoughts were absurd. Surely they would check the cart. Check their plunder. Catalogue items.

It grew lighter, the sky taking on a pre-dawn hue. The goods about her felt somehow heavier. Cassandra closed her eyes, prayed for oblivion again. And that's when she heard them.

"My laird. A moment?"

A cultured voice spoke near her feet, startling her. He spoke a language she'd learned from a Celt woman in the harem, but with a strange dialect. That made translation challenging but not impossible.

"One moment? From you?"

The response sent an undeniable reaction. Her heart leapt, her eyelids snapped open. Her throat tightened. It was the man who'd claimed victory. She recognized his voice instantly.

"We've a new man in camp. With a wild tale. Says there is a woman with us. In that cart."

"A woman?"

"'Tis unlikely. I ken. There's no wench within leagues of this purgatory. Can't be."

"Bring him here."

Heart-pounding moments of time passed before Emin next spoke in his high-pitched voice. Rapidly. Emotionally. He used the Frank language. He wasn't proficient, especially when agitated. The words were jumbled and hard to follow. The cultured-sounding man translated.

"Well. You heard him. Still claims he brought a woman. From the harem."

"Check."

Carpets were lifted, weight displaced. A bolt of fabric rolled across her, one was removed from her side. Cassandra shakily hauled in a deep breath, grimacing as it hurt. She didn't have a choice, however. Staying hidden meant death. Somehow she managed to swivel toward them, sitting hunched over. The drapery shifted just enough she could see.

Dawn lit the area, sending fingers of golden light through the hills. It touched on the top of a spike-tipped tent before filtering onto the group of men she faced. Most wore hoods, their faces shadowed. It didn't hide their started expressions. Unpleasant shivers raced up her spine and over her scalp, adding to her misery. Her heart thumped erratically throughout her chest. She hadn't a hint of moisture with which to swallow. Each blink scraped while her eyes watered defensively. Every breath hurt. Long stray strands of hair stuck to her face. She might have brushed them away if she wasn't swathed in drapery, and if her limbs obeyed. Then again, she might just pull more of her braid loose. She wasn't veiled, but most of her face was covered.

They weren't all crusader knights, although some wore armor beneath tabards that carried the cross emblem. They all looked filthy. Weary. Blood-covered. Armed. She couldn't tell quantity. This was bad. She faced a motley crew of death dealers and she couldn't even move?

One of them cleared his throat. "My laird?"

"Silence."

She knew the leader instantly. He regarded her from their midst, without expression. He stood taller by at least a hand span. He'd shoved his hood back. She hadn't been mistaken earlier. He had lengthy black hair. Ends of it caressed his shoulders. His facial hair was a match, all of the black making his eye color unavoidable. They were vivid blue. Ice blue. Cold. And hard.

He turned his head to look down at Emin. The eunuch had always seemed immense but not when placed beside the blue-eyed man. He might have spoken but the leader forestalled him.

"No man steals a woman." An arm toss was sent her direction as if clarity was needed. "They are to use and discard. Those are my orders. For a reason. Now...you have given me a problem." He pulled in a large enough breath it lifted his torso before he let it back out with a gust. He sent commands as he turned away. "Henry. Take her to my tent. You," he gestured at Emin. "Come with me."

She wasn't given the option of walking. That was pure luck. She wasn't capable. Sensation was returning to her limbs and with it came unbelievable pain. Spikes of agony speared her as one of the knights pulled her across a bolt of fabric and slung her over his shoulder. Cassandra gritted her teeth, but a cry escaped. The man didn't even break stride. She railed at herself. She couldn't afford to show weakness. Not now. Not with freedom so close! She had to be a worthy negotiator. Strong. Flexible...yet imperious. She'd always plotted escape. She had it already planned and paid for. An attack on the summer palace was providential, the chaos perfect.

If only she'd had the sense to keep from drinking Selique's juice!

All was not lost, though. By some stroke of fortune she wore her most impressive jewelry, a headdress, golden collar, matching girdle, armbands and anklets. She'd donned them for the sup. Just a portion was enough to buy her and Emin's freedom. She had bargaining to do, her wits to keep about her. Some luck. She needed more than an aching body that resembled sand-putty. It wasn't an auspicious way to think on her next move.

It wasn't much of a tent, either. Nothing resembled a sultan's tents. Those had been the size of palace gardens, constructed of dyed textiles, the floors covered with skins, soft pillows and rugs. They were divided with opaque, filmy curtains into smaller areas, for privacy...to house the chosen women, such as Selique.

Or Cassandra.

She shivered involuntary. The knight didn't seem to notice. He tilted sideways to set her down. Her legs were still afire as blood returned, but they didn't buckle. He didn't wait to find out. He simply let her go and backed out. A dark length of material fell over the doorway closing her in, and that's when she got her first look at what a leader of these men called a tent.

An unlit blackened samovar sat at one side of the door. Weak daylight percolated through coarsely-spun, dun-colored walls. There was no decoration to soften or mute the uneven texture. Cassandra wondered if the weave was intentionally worked roughly, or if it was simply the mark of poor workmanship. Not that she cared. Either way, the effect was dull, drab, and uninspiring.

Against the back wall a small wooden chest rested, large enough to sit on, or place a tray atop. A thick roll of material was beside it. The floor was covered with a rug in shades of gray flecked with black. There was nothing more.

Cassandra's lip lifted. If this was the extent of their dyeing, weaving, and woodworking skills, she probably looked like a creature of myth, wrapped as she was in drapery with vivid peacock blue tones about her face followed by every shade of green, yellow and then orange, until it ended with a dark red in the puddle at her feet. It wasn't supposed to be used as clothing. The strands were too thick, the weave stiff. It was scratchy, smelled of smoke, and completely unsuitable for clothing.

And she wouldn't part with it for anything.

The door flap swished as it lifted. Cassandra turned to face him. Her legs wobbled, but supported the move. She couldn't do a thing about her pulse.

He should have designed his tent with more height. The top of his head grazed the material, lifting it as he entered. It set him free as he reached the center. Cassandra instinctively backed a step. Dimness made him loom threateningly large. It also turned his expression into something sinister. He folded his arms, and regarded her silently for several moments.

"*Parlez vous Francais?*" he asked.

She nodded.

"*Bien*. You may begin," he said.

She'd already heard the impressive range of his voice, but in his tent, it stunned. Deep. Full. Menacing. Cassandra jerked. The palace drapery didn't hide the reaction.

"With…what?" She had to clear her throat mid-question. Her voice wasn't strong or imperious. It hurt, too.

"Who are you and what is your value?"

"I'm…no one." *Value?* What did that mean? In this world, women had little value. Surely he knew that.

"I didn't quite hear that."

Cassandra sought enough moisture to lick her lips but had to forego it. Dark dots danced through her vision. She watched them fade and dissipate as she looked up at him. Despite lack of sustenance, a night of drugged sleep, and an obstruction in her throat, she thought her words had been audible. And the tent wasn't large. He couldn't help but have heard her words.

"I said—"

He put up a hand, stopping her. It almost reached where she stood. Cassandra backed another step. She didn't know how much area she had left behind her. It probably wasn't much.

"Before we go another moment into this, let me give you some foresight into your situation."

He untied the knot at his throat and pulled his cloak off, folded it as though it was freshly laundered, not stained and filthy. Tossed it onto the trunk. Cassandra watched him in silence.

"I do not like games. I never have. I suggest you cease playing them."

She didn't know how to answer, so she pressed her teeth on the tip of her tongue and waited. He lifted an arm into the space between them and slipped straps from metal spikes along the bottom of his wrist, opening a gauntlet that reached his elbow. He pulled one finger loose, then another, until he had the glove off. He flexed his hand as if the leather had stifled.

"Let's begin again. Who are you, and what is your value?"

Cassandra forced her feet to stay precisely where they were and locked her knees. He needn't know how they shook. He removed his other gauntlet. It didn't diminish his size. He was immense. Either hand could close about her throat with little effort. And squeeze the life force right out of her.

"Your answer?" he prompted.

"I...I am nobody, and—"

The hand he put up to stop her this time was bare. He clenched his jaw and his eyes narrowed.

Lush black eyelashes shadowed his eyes. The shadow reached his nose as he lowered his chin. Cassandra swallowed audibly. This was horrid. And her wits were deserting her.

"My name is Rhoenne Guy de Ramhurst. I am known as the Dark One. Perhaps you have heard of me."

Cassandra shook her head.

"'Tis said I'm feared. Reviled. I give no quarter. Expect none. I take. I maim. I kill. Without remorse. Without regret. I have no emotions. I could give you to them."

He motioned with a head jerk over his shoulder, denoting the camp outside. She gasped. One side of his mouth lifted, as if he found it amusing, but only enough to waste half a smile.

"Or I could keep you in here. With me. Safe. And un-accosted."

"By you, as well?"

He took a step toward her. Cassandra backed until there wasn't space left. Two steps. That's all she'd had. She leaned into a tent, making it bow slightly with her weight. She wondered if it would be able to support her if she fainted.

Fainted?

Her back stiffened. She may be facing death, but she was still the Princess Cassandra Alexandria, youngest daughter of a Vottenavia prince. She had little use for fainting. She'd never been weak. It was against family. Creed. It was against everything she'd endured in the eight years she'd been a prisoner.

Unfortunately, it was exactly what her entire

body was suffering right now.

He hadn't come any closer. The knowledge helped. She replayed his words through her mind. He didn't play games. He had no emotions. He didn't care what happened to her. Wasn't that what he'd said?

He spoke again, forestalling her thought process.

"You worry without cause. I have need of a woman, I take one. You? I don't need." He smirked. "Or want."

Oh no.

If he said another word, she was going to cry. Cassandra fought the emotional onslaught, tightening every muscle at her command. Tighter. Tears wouldn't gain anything save disdain, and probably get her tossed from the tent. And they were senseless. He didn't need her? He didn't want her?

So much the better!

Another emotion filled her. One she recognized. It fed anger into her blood and strength through her limbs. She narrowed her eyes, sent back any thought of tears, and regarded him as he was her. Without expression. Without emotion.

"Ah. Good. We finally understand each other," he remarked.

She nodded.

"So answer me. Who are you?"

"Cassandra Alexandria. Of the kingdom of Vottenavia."

"You are not one of them?"

She shook her head.

"Why does the eunuch find you of such value?"

She shrugged, lifting the drapery. The jeweled breastplate she wore moved beneath it. She watched his glance flicker there before returning to her face. If anything, his expression hardened further.

"I am the sultan's favorite," she lied.

"Were you now?"

She nodded.

"No longer."

"You killed him?" she asked.

"I didn't say that."

"He isn't dead?"

"I didn't say that either."

"Is he...a prisoner?"

"I don't take prisoners."

"Then what am I?"

"A mistake of nature," he answered.

"My...she must have hurt you terribly," Cassandra answered, without one iota of forethought.

She didn't see the move but it wouldn't have mattered. He had her throat in one hand and had lifted her. The dots were back, larger and darker than before. She'd been right about his hand encircling her throat. She knew she'd also been right with her comment. Some woman had hurt him. She could tell it by a flare deep in what had to be the most intensely blue eyes she'd ever faced.

Strange.

Death was supposed to possess black eyes.

Cassandra closed hers and swallowed despite the pressure on her throat. He lowered her until the tips of her toes touched the rug. And then he waited. Unmoving. She pulled in a breath that shook, eased it out, and opened her eyes. The dark blobs in her vision slowly cleared away. She almost wished for them back. He was so close she could see each individual lash, especially since he had his head lowered until their noses almost touched.

"Undress," he said.

Her eyes went wide and her gulp against his thumb couldn't be missed.

"Now?" she asked with a whisper of sound.

He moved his head down, and then back, before returning to looking at her.

"Will you...bargain for it?" she asked shakily.

His face hardened. He opened his fingers with a rough gesture, freeing her. Then he spun. The door flap shifted, and he was gone.

CHAPTER THREE

CASSANDRA MOVED TO the trunk before her legs collapsed. Every limb shuddered, her heart raced like a caged thing, her eyes smarted with instant tears. She had moments. She daren't waste them. She needed a weapon. Anything lethal. She wasn't going to be ravished. She'd die first.

Her body still wasn't functioning properly. She pushed crumpled stiff drapery down beneath her arms, ignoring where it scraped skin. Shoved his discarded cloak aside. His trunk wasn't locked, but the clasp gave her trouble. Several heart-pounding moments passed while she worked and twisted the metal. And finally, the hasp dropped open and she flung the lid back.

It rocked back to smack her fingers.

That hurt.

Cassandra stifled the instant wash of tears and dove into the contents. He had garments on top, fashioned in the same dull shades as his tent. Some folded. A few squashed into balls. She rifled them, searching for something solid. Anything. And quickly! Her fingers closed on a hard object, pulled it out, and nearly flung it aside in irritation. It was a wooden crucifix, plain and smooth-edged. Worthless as a weapon. She shoved it back in, pushed more material to the sides, and found treasure.

It was a dagger. She pulled it out clumsily, uncaring if it sliced anything. Success hit as a rush of heat, followed by a wave of thrill. The hilt was fashioned to resemble entwined vines... or perhaps it was snakes. It was ornate, almost feminine. That proved his people possessed some skill in metalworking. The blade was thin and extremely sharp.

Her evaluation of the weapon didn't take but a moment. Time was too precious.

She wove the weapon's blade into the back of her girdle with one hand, while the other pushed down on the mess of items in the trunk. She shut the lid, tried once to re-clasp it before giving up. A toss sent the cloak back where he'd put it. Then she stood, pulled the drapery back into place about her, and turned to face the doorway. She had one gasped breath of time before the door material was shoved inward.

It wasn't the knight.

Emin stumbled and fell to his knees. Bent forward, his forehead pressed to the floor rug. He looked weak. Completely cowed. Light glimmered on his bald bowed head as the door flap fell into place behind the knight.

There wasn't much room in the tent and their captor's presence somehow overtook it all. He stood just inside the door, lifting the roof with his height. He'd crossed his arms. Spears of daylight percolated through the loose weave of the tent, each one dancing with dust motes. The light showcased the riveting quality of his eyes, and something far worse. Something unexpected and completely unwelcome to Cassandra.

He was handsome.

Excessively so.

Despite years in seclusion, Cassandra had experience with male beauty. The *Mamluk* Sultanate was full of handsome men. She'd actually seen some. The harem had latticed walls with numerous small openings. Men often visited the Sultan's court. Whispers would fill the harem if a handsome man was spotted, and the women would all rush to peek, including her. Not that she cared, but she'd learned early. Just as unusual coloring drew attention, unusual behavior did the same. So she'd looked. Evaluated. Tittered over handsome men.

But this man eclipsed them all.

And that was grossly unfair.

If the man sensed her train of thought, he didn't act it. He didn't give her any sign of any kind. He simply regarded her as if he had nothing better to do. It was unnerving. He just stood there. Waiting. Long moments passed. The light strengthened, heralding a day of oppressive heat. Emin shifted with a scuffling noise. The sound of her pulse got louder and faster in both ears. And still nothing happened.

"I...don't understand," Cassandra finally spoke.

"And you don't listen."

She couldn't stop an instant flash of ire. She tried to hide it with a practiced move, lifting a shoulder enough the jeweled piece at her bosom shifted. She watched his glance shift to her breast movement for the barest moment. His cheeks looked darker again. That was interesting. He pretended to be made of stone, but his flush might have just betrayed him. Sensual interest was something she knew...and could use.

"You seek to play games?" he prompted.

Cassandra shook her head.

"Oh. I misspeak. You call it bargaining."

He uncrossed his arms and slid a hand down his thigh. She watched him flip a leather thong loose to pull a large knife from its scabbard. She couldn't look away. He held the blade out, twisting to send flashes of light from a wicked, serrated edge. It made her hidden dagger resemble a sewing implement. He glanced down at where Emin crouched between them. Back at her.

"Last chance," he remarked.

"He means nothing to me," Cassandra lied. "He's a servant. A half-man." She made her words as insulting and sarcastic as possible. She couldn't prevent the tremble that accompanied them, though.

"Is that so?"

He bent to lift Emin's forearm. The move pulled Emin from his hunched position. The eunuch didn't even look up.

"I will start with a finger. When he runs out of them, he loses toes. Then, I shall start on limbs. You understand me, yet?"

Ice shot through her veins. Her face lost color.
She rocked in place, amazed she still stood. Emin
was so used to stifling emotion he didn't betray a
speck of it. The tent still reeked of fear.

"Wait."

Cassie pulled her arms free of the drape and
lowered it from her head, revealing the small
gem-encrusted circlet above her head. She felt,
rather than heard, the knight's indrawn breath.
She couldn't hear anything over Emin's words,
spoken in rapid Arabic.

"No, Highness! Please? Whatever it is he has
requested of you, do not do it! I am lower than
camel dung. I am nothing!"

"Emin, cease. Now."

Cassandra's tone stopped further pleas. She
pushed the drapery off her shoulders. It was stuck
in places with sweat and smoke-grime. Near her
waist, she found an edge, plucked it loose with
nerveless fingers, and slowly spun free. It took
two rotations. The drapery unwound and she
dropped it, forming a mass of fabric at her feet.
She looked down at what she'd just revealed.
Everything was crystal clear, completely focused.
She didn't even have her hair to hide behind.

Gold armbands encircled both upper arms. The
same metal formed the filigree collar that ended
just beneath her breasts. It was inset with multi-
colored gemstones in a floral motif. The bottom
edge was a series of points with a jewel dangling
from each tip. They were fashioned to dance
about, catching and reflecting light with every
move she made...including the act of breathing.

The girdle at her hips was even more spectacular. Flashes of color refracted throughout the tent as light touched on her.

Cassandra took a deep breath, looked up to face him...and found she couldn't. The tent behind him was safer. She didn't want to see his reaction or even if he had one. The pieces had been created and designed for a singular purpose – to enhance. The collar caressed and defined her bosom, the girdle did the same to her hips, and that piece contained more gems, more gold, and much larger gems that dangled from the points at her thighs. The pieces had been fitted to her measurements.

Exactly,

He grunted. She couldn't tell if that was a sign of pleasure or not. She took it as further command and lifted an arm, touching the catch of an armband. The metal sprang loose. She held it while unfastening the piece from her other arm. Gathered both bands in one hand. Held them out to him.

"Drop them."

She did. They bounced and rolled, one ending up beside Emin. The other circled to a stop near one of the knight's boots. Cassandra reached behind her neck for the collar clasp next and snapped it open. Pulling it forward released her breasts. The collar had defined and supported her. The gossamer material she wore beneath it was useless. His lips might have tightened, but his beard hid the motion and she was doing her best to focus elsewhere. She lowered her arms and dropped the collar onto the floor beside Emin. It made a slithering sound as links slid onto the rug floor.

She didn't wait.

The girdle had three clasps at the back of it. She worked them with one hand while the other pulled the dagger free. She swayed and bent, hoping the snapping of each clasp disguised how she laced the blade into the material that flowed from her headdress. It was the lone option. The dagger was priceless right now and the skirt material would tear with any weight. She was hot with a full-body blush, while icy shivers ran her frame. The combination made her fingers clumsy. Once she lost this girdle, she'd be almost fully exposed. Near-naked. Vulnerable. The skirt was comprised of little more than sheer panels, layered and slit throughout.

"*Princessa!* Please! I am not worth this!"

Cassandra jumped as Emin interrupted, his burst of words high-pitched and filled with emotion.

"Emin. Cease. He knows." Cassandra touched her glance to the knight momentarily before skidding it away.

"You told him?" Emin asked.

"I told him nothing. He knows you mean something to me. He knows I won't allow him to hurt you. He's using it. I would, too. Mourning will not change it."

She was too late. Emin began lamenting in a litany of moans about his failure to protect her. He was wailing when the knight shook him, using the arm he held. Emin didn't stop until the knife blade was at a finger. The knight didn't say a word. He didn't have to.

Cassandra dropped the girdle from nerveless fingers onto the swath of drapery at her feet. It landed with a slight thud. "There," she announced. "It's done."

"Your head covering?"

He moved the blade and pointed with it. Cassandra snarled and turned sideways to him.

He huffed something that could be amusement while she fumbled with the combs from her ears and slid the piece from her head, wadding it into a loose bundle before dropping it. The slight thud of sound as metal hit metal sounded loud in her ears. She didn't dare look to verify anything. She couldn't tell if he'd heard, or if he suspected. She wasn't warm anymore, either. She was exhausted. Dehydrated. Shaky. Weak. She only hoped she found the fortitude to grab the dagger before he tossed her from the tent.

She heard rustling. Shadows moved on the tent wall. Cassandra turned her head to watch the eunuch stand, with what appeared to be the knight's help. But that wasn't possible. The man was evil. Crusader atrocities were legion. And then there was his earlier descriptions to her. He'd been wrong. She'd listened. He'd said he was feared. Reviled. He maimed and killed, without remorse or regret. She hadn't believed it.

She'd been naive.

"Go. Eat. Rest. Stay from the others. They do not understand a half-man such as yourself.

You'll be called when needed."

Emin looked at her for verification. Cassandra met his glance for a moment and nodded before moving her focus back to the doorway. Emin bowed.

"He will do as you say," Cassandra said.

"I know he will," The knight answered.

Emin backed out. The door material skimmed across his shaven head and then fell back into place. The knight spoke again, his voice holding what might be a humorous tone.

"It works both ways, you know."

"What does?" she asked.

"My knowledge," he answered in Arabic.

Her heart fell. The air thickened, becoming harder to breathe. The crusader hadn't moved, but he'd gotten larger somehow. She wondered how it happened. And then she did something truly stupid. She moved her gaze to his. She realized the extent of her mistake as buzzing filled both ears. The other-worldly hue of his eyes held her captive. He was so very handsome. She wondered what he'd look like if he were shaven, his hair tied back from his face, his frame dressed in a blue silk tunic that matched his eyes....

Oh no!

What was she doing?

Cassandra tore her gaze away and looked down, completely mortified. She'd been embarrassed when disrobing for him? There was no description for what she felt now. She regarded the puddle of palace drapery, the pile of glinting treasure, her own near-nakedness.

"You have my thanks," he said.

Cassandra stiffened. "For what?" *Stealing?* The last word was unspoken.

"You didn't force me to make good on my threat."

"You didn't wish to hurt him?"

"I didn't say that," he answered.

"Then you wanted to hurt him?"

"I didn't say that, either."

"I don't understand," she said.

"I am not fond of attending confession. Your obedience saved me from it. For that, I thank you."

She watched him reach for her collar with one hand, the other one lifted her girdle. He already had her armbands between his fingers. He hoisted and dropped his hands as if testing weight. Her riches looked small in his possession. Insubstantial. And then an even worse horror happened. She pulled in a shaky breath as her eyes filled with useless stupid tears.

Oh no! She couldn't cry now. *Not now. No.*

He fished a bag from beneath his tabard and shoved her riches into it before secreting it back under his banner. Then he gathered her headdress, searching through the material purposefully, as if he knew she'd hidden something. It didn't take him long to find the dagger.

He may have glanced at her then. She couldn't tell through the blur.

"Was this for me?"

She shook her head, using a tiny gesture.

"Good thing. 'Tis of little use on a man, unless

you hit a vital spot."

"It was...for me," she whispered.

He grunted a reply, and stepped away. Out of view. Cassandra didn't move, not even to blink. That way the tears hovering at her lashes might somehow stay unshed and hidden.

"You leave this tent and I will not stay your fate. You ken?"

She didn't know the last word, but understood the meaning. It sounded threatening. It was a stupid warning, too. He'd taken every choice from her.

Even death.

CHAPTER FOUR

THEY HADN'T KINDLED a fire to warm the kettle of porridge. If they'd watered it down enough, it wouldn't be an issue. Rhoenne didn't know what they'd tossed into it this time. He didn't much care, either. He'd eat what they had when they had it. They all did. That's what a warrior did when on campaign.

Especially a losing one.

This, the seventh crusade, led by King Louis IX of France, was especially egregious, as if doomed from the start. There had been some warning two years prior when they'd started. The region they'd invaded was fraught with defeat, mainly due to *Mamluk* soldiers. *Mamluks* were former slaves, ruled by a slave-king. Hardened. Extremely disciplined. They won nearly every battle. The crusaders should have retreated months ago, before King Louis had been captured, and the men under Rhoenne's command decimated.

They hadn't a prayer of reaching Acre, the only crusader stronghold left in this miserable country. That meant once proud, well-equipped knights had been reduced to men slinking through the nights like common thieves, intent on escape and survival.

The ragged band of mercenaries that tagged along didn't share those goals. They were in it for the money.

And yet somehow – when Rhoenne least expected it – God had favored him.

Finally.

And now, thanks to the woman, he needn't waste time bartering their plunder for passage back home, either. In his bag, he had the means to bribe their way onto a ship, and leave these godforsaken shores. All he needed was the direction.

And a little luck.

Henry, his closest man, looked up as Rhoenne exited the tent. The knight reclined against one of the wagons, one hand resting lightly on his sword hilt, as though bored. The eunuch was curled into a ball at the knight's feet, his head and shoulders covered with Henry's cloak. The wagon created a defensible nest and a well of shadow, demonstrating the servant had chosen well. Rhoenne twirled the little dagger as he walked toward them. He nodded a greeting. Spoke in Gaelic, the language of the Scots.

"Trouble?" he asked.

"Piddling."

"How small?"

"Some of the mercenaries. One small victory, a spot of plunder, and...there you have it. Trouble. Na' much for handling pain, either."

"Pain?"

"I dinna' stop any from deserting, if that is your question."

Rhoenne considered him for long moments, until the knight elaborated. "Oh, verra well. Cease that. None perished."

"We lose any?"

"Ramhurst? *Nae.* We are still six."

Six. When they'd started with forty of the best knights from the French court and eight men from his clan. Rhoenne shoved the disgust back into the pit of his belly where it sat, pounding inexorably. As usual. He was used to it.

"Have you eaten?" he asked.

"*Nae.*"

"Come. Join me. We'll both partake."

Some of the men slept. Rhoenne stepped over cloak-wrapped bodies as they circled the camp center, keeping a watchful eye on his tent and the eunuch's recumbent form. Henry snagged a bread loaf from a dented basket without breaking stride. Rhoenne didn't know who'd thought to pilfer the palace kitchens, but he was grateful. Bread was a welcome change. Freshly cooked bread was ambrosia.

Their approach didn't go unnoticed. Two Ramhurst knights, and a like number of mercenaries, stood beside the food cart. Rhoenne caught some curious glances. He returned them with his usual stare. The offenders went back to their meals. Henry tore the bread loaf in half as they arrived, handing one to Rhoenne. He scooped out the center, smashed it into a large bite, and was chewing on it as he filled the bread bowl with fare that had actual chunks of meat in it.

"We have salt?" he asked.

"Most definitely."

Someone tossed the salt bag. Seasonings and spices were pleasant surprises from this crusade. As was coffee. Rhoenne fished out a pea-size lump of salt. Crushed it atop his meal. Used the little dagger to stir then shovel porridge into his mouth, chewing and swallowing quickly in order to avoid tasting. Today, that was unnecessary. There were cooked mutton chunks mixed in with the gruel. Some bits of date. Perhaps even berries. That was a welcome change. He wiped the blade on his tabard and stuck it in his belt. He was swallowing a mouthful of soaked crust when Henry spoke again.

"You've worked up a healthy appetite. Care to enlighten me?"

"On what?"

"You have the lone woman in camp. Surely there is some tale to relate. Some...advice to give, perhaps?"

Rhoenne ignored the knight's wink. Took another bite of his soaked bread bowl. Chewed it. Swallowed. "I still wear my armor, Henry," he finally replied.

"That must have been difficult," Henry replied.

One of the men chortled. Another bit off a laugh. Rhoenne took another bite of crust. Chewed.

"Is it that bad?" Henry prompted.

Rhoenne swallowed, speared his man with a

sidelong glare that usually garnered him silence, if not solitude. "What?"

"Your woman trouble."

"Have I ever had woman trouble?"

"Only with the quantity of them we continually need scrape off of you. Ceaselessly. Although, since there are more than enough for all, it is a chore I cannot rue."

The knights snickered. Rhoenne narrowed his cheeks in thought. "I think you've spent too much time at the French court."

"You were there as well," Henry pointed out.

"True," Rhoenne shrugged. Took another bite. Chewed. Had it swallowed before Henry spoke again.

"You should allow me to assist you with your latest burden. Surely the woman is hungry?"

"I do na' ken. Nor do I care."

"Then allow me to provide her with a meal."

"*Nae.*"

"Her servant can, then. I'll have him—." Henry stopped mid-sentence at Rhoenne's head shake. "Not even him?"

"I do na' trust her."

"When did you ever trust a woman?"

Rhoenne grunted. Pondered it while Henry waited. "Good question," he finally replied.

"So...in the meantime, you'd see her starve?"

"Cease pestering. I will see to it."

"You? Personally?"

Rhoenne smirked. "Oh. Good. You do listen."

"She must be comely...this woman."

Rhoenne's shoulders fell. "Henry FitzHugh."

"I am eaten up with curiosity and you are my best source of information. Her servant is useless."

"You pestered him, too, did you?"

"Only because I know how close-mouthed you are. It is a Ramhurst trait. Or so, I've been told."

"Did we steal any spirits?" Rhoenne asked, changing the subject.

"They do na' drink such. We have beer, though. Here. Hold this. I'll fetch you a draught."

Henry held out his half-eaten bread bowl. Rhoenne looked down at the skim of grease congealing atop it, looked back toward his tent.

"I can fetch it myself."

"Well...ask something of me. I am your closest man. I trained and fought for the position. I stand ready to serve. And yet I am ignored. For hours, it feels."

Rhoenne blew a sigh. "How soon can we reach a town with a seaport?"

"A seaport? That depends."

"On...?" he prompted waving a hand for emphasis.

"Many things. The path, for one. Euan and Grant are on that assignment as we speak. They should be back afore sunset. Mayhap sooner since they're *nae* longer afoot. Horseflesh makes a vast difference. In the meantime we must assess our situation. We have wares now. Lots of wares. Travel with wares takes time. Wagons cannot go as quickly as a horse can. Speaking of...horses require rest. Waterholes. Grazing. In hindsight, taking so much might not have been in our best interest."

"Your reasoning?" Rhoenne asked.

"Our victory creates issues, my laird. We now have wares to transport. Horses to feed and water. Not only will both slow us down, but we are now a target. Beyond all that of course...is the matter of the woman."

"Yes. The woman."

Despite everything, Rhoenne's tone altered. He was afraid it was noticeable. Henry's next words verified it.

"This is interesting. I may have to factor in even more time."

"For what?"

"Your apparent interest. In yon woman."

"Surely you jest."

"Allow me to go visit her."

"What good will that do?" Rhoenne asked.

"It will do me a lot of good."

The Scots about them snorted. Rhoenne's expression went blank. He had the last of his bread bowl swallowed before he answered. "Finish your meal. We've provided enough entertainment this morn."

"Where are you going?"

"To get some beer."

Rhoenne was already halfway to the cask, easily spied on a wagon bed, due to the three men prostrate beneath it, snoring drunkenly.

"What about your woman?" Henry whispered the words at his side.

Rhoenne frowned. "She is not *my* woman."

"Best not let anyone hear you say that. Claiming her is the lone thing controlling them...and protecting her. You ken?"

"I am na' dense, withal your opinion to the contrary."

"Actions speak louder than words, my liege... and your actions speak plenty. There is a woman in camp. *One*. We did na' even see any women last eve. Actually...we have na' seen one in so long a time, I forget. So. There is a woman in our midst. Alone. You do na' seem to want her. You think the others don't take note?"

"They have to go through me first."

"Aye, and afore that, they must get through me. I guard your back. Why else would I forego a delicious meal and my rest in order to watch the morning sun rise on your tent door?"

"To say nothing of whetting your insatiable curiosity about the woman."

Henry sighed. "You know me too well. So. Tell me. Is she comely? Spare of flesh or voluptuous?"

"Henry." Rhoenne lowered his voice ominously. It usually worked.

"I need this information for my assessment. We're in a land that trades in humans. A woman has value. A comely one will fetch a verra nice price at the slave market."

Recollection of how he'd left her flashed through Rhoenne's skull without reason or an iota of warning. He banished it as his tankard filled. "She is comely enough, I suppose."

"You suppose?"

Rhoenne grunted.

"You are na' sure? What does that mean?"

"It means I am cautious. Nothing more."

He spent the next few moments draining his tankard. Henry was waiting for him to finish. He was refilling it before the knight spoke again.

"Cautious? You dampen all sense of triumph, Ramhurst! We happened upon a small, lightly guarded palace last night. Without plan or forethought, the attack we mounted was somehow victorious. We now have all manner of goods to sell. Enough to buy passage from these god-forsaken shores! You also managed to acquire a woman. I would ask why you, but I already ken. Women have but to see you and they adhere like warm porridge does to the belly. Yet, what do you do with such good fortune? Preach caution. I vow we cannot be from the same clan."

"That palace belonged to the *Mamluk* sultan."

"So?"

"The woman is from his harem."

Henry whistled beneath his breath. "Harem? Did you say—harem?"

"Aye."

"Well. That explains everything. She has obviously ravished you. No wonder you are out-of-sorts."

Rhoenne choked on his next swallow. The beer burned his throat. "Will you pull your mind from the bed sheets for a moment and use your head!"

"Just tell me it was pleasurable. Is that too

much to ask?"

"Will you cease?"

"I've heard the tales of these harems, as have you. She probably has all manner of knowledge on tupping. Sensual pleasures. Orgies."

Henry's eyebrows lifted suggestively several times. Rhoenne closed his eyes. Reopened them. Scowled.

"I did na' touch her." An instant remembrance of her throat in his hands made his scowl deepen. "Much," he added.

"You are inhuman. Somehow, you were gifted with a harem woman. Such a gift was bestowed without warning. Out here...in the middle of nowhere? I add now that you have the only tent for privacy. And you claim you did na' even touch her?"

"Women mean nothing to me. You ken as much."

"Ramhurst—."

"Actually, I misspeak," Rhoenne interrupted. "They mean trouble. Nothing but trouble."

"I have already offered my services to assist."

"'Tis *nae* jest. You listen but you do na' ken. She is from the *Mamluk* sultan's harem, I tell you! *That* is the issue."

"I still do na' ken."

"He will come for her!"

"Is she truly so beauteous?"

Rhoenne scowled. "The trouble is na' her face and form but her treasure."

"Treasure? You mean she's a maid? Well, why dinna' you say so earlier?" The knight licked his lips. "This improves her value immeasurably."

Rhoenne grabbed the smaller man's shoulder with his free hand and bent close enough he could hiss words through set teeth. "Must you twist every word I utter this morn?"

"Forgive me. I admit to a bit of jubilation over our victory, a loosened tongue, and an intense interest in your woman, which – now that I ken she hails from a harem – has only been sharpened. 'Tis my duty to assess and advise, my laird. Gathering facts is a necessary part. Despite my attempts at levity, that is what I have been about this morn. I vow it."

Rhoenne released him. Stepped back. "Did we post guards?"

"Two."

"Add more. Rotate them. We will sleep in stages."

"You truly think he'll come for her? Surely he'll reason that she'd be ravished by now...and. Well. They call us infidels. To be killed on sight. We are still at war. We routed the sultan's men, destroyed his home. He may na' give chase... unless he is in love. That is a possibility. There is much a love-struck man will do. He will even kill—! Oh. Blast my tongue! You said I would be flailed alive, or face banishment if I—."

Henry cut his words off. Rhoenne was breathing hard. That was one indicator of emotion. The tight fists he'd made were the other. Henry looked at him, then down at his half-eaten meal. Back up to Rhoenne.

"I should...go back to the others," Henry

offered.

"Too late," Rhoenne replied.

Henry swallowed. "Forgive me. Again. I have rarely had my own tongue so betray me. Do you wish to carve on me now? Or...later?"

"Neither, if you cease the buffoonery."

"Verra well. You wish complete seriousness this morn? All I can infer is the woman has bitterness to her features and a tongue to match. You say she is a treasure. I shall have to bow to your judgment. It must be true. Otherwise, why would you worry? You truly believe the sultan will come for her?"

"She is na' the treasure. She had a treasure. *That* is why he will come for her. He may be on our trail already."

"Grant went that direction. He'll send warning."

"Good thinking." Rhoenne gave a shadow of a smile.

"This treasure? 'Tis vast?" Henry asked.

Rhoenne nodded.

"How vast?"

Rhoenne tipped his head, considering. "Enough to leave without these wares and these wagons and most of the horses."

"Leave it? All of it?" Henry's brows rose.

"Aye."

"The mercenaries may balk."

"We do na' need them. Gift it to them."

"We are going home?"

"Aye."

"Thank the Father! And the Son! And the

Holy Mother, Mary!"

"Inform me when Euan and Grant return. We move as soon as they report. Tell the clan. Be subtle."

"So now I am unsubtle? I suppose I deserve that. First a buffoon, and now loose-lipped."

Rhoenne regarded his man for long moments again. Henry finally relented, and looked away first. "Oh. Verra well. I shall attempt subterfuge. 'Tis that vast? This treasure she has?"

"Aye."

"May I see it?"

Rhoenne shook his head.

"Because of the woman who wears it?"

"She *nae* longer has it."

"You took it?"

Rhoenne shrugged. "I have it, yes."

"She just gave it to you? Ah! My faith is restored. I knew you had a tale for me."

"Not much of one. I threatened her with the eunuch."

"I see. You used your 'heartless Dark One' pose."

"'Tis *nae* pose."

"You forget. I have known you since childhood, Rhoenne."

"I do na' recall childhood."

Their glances met again. Henry broke eye contact first. Cleared his throat.

"Fair enough. I forfeit. I shall cease pondering the vagaries of fortune while recalculating our journey."

"Try getting some rest, as well," Rhoenne said.

"Will we be taking the woman with us?"

Rhoenne's breathing stopped. He regarded his tent for long moments, while his heartbeat grew loud in his ears. Taking her with him was problematic. Leaving her or the eunuch was unmerciful. The mercenaries weren't a chivalrous lot. There wasn't one among them he'd trust.

"Afore you remonstrate with me, I have a reason for my query. Does she ride? Will she require assist? How about her man? I will need to make allowances and add time to my assessment."

"I am na' decided."

"Would you like an assist with the decision?" Henry asked.

"I believe I need another bread bowl. With porridge. Salted."

"Another?"

"'Tis for her."

"Are you perchance requesting...that I fetch it for her?"

"Rouse her man. 'Twill be simpler."

"Simpler?"

"The last thing I wish is anyone to think I am open to sharing. You ken?"

"Wise words, my liege," Henry replied. "Verra wise."

Strange.

He felt a lot of things. None of them was wise.

CHAPTER FIVE

THE WOMAN WAS perched atop the wooden chest, elbows on her thighs to support her face in her hands...a picture of abject misery and complete defenselessness. She didn't look up at his entrance, not even when he'd reached the center of his tent and stood looking down at her. Rhoenne regarded her for several moments while the weight in his belly didn't even shift, despite her obvious attractions.

She hadn't taken the time to cover herself. She could have used the mass of multi-hued fabric that swathed her lower legs, his discarded cloak, or she could don a spare shirt from his trunk. He knew she'd rifled it. That begged the question of why she sat with so little covering. Her attire seemed crafted of mist. It skimmed every curve, making it impossible to avoid noting how womanly she was.

Rhoenne regarded the picture she presented, pondering the reason behind it. This woman knew she was in the midst of a horde of armed men. Men, drunk on victory. Battle-hardened. Dangerous. Volatile. Yet here she sat, posed.

Near-naked. Extremely vulnerable.

Was she crazed, extremely foolish, ready and willing...or did she have plans to manipulate the situation? He decided on the latter. Her possession of the dagger cancelled out the first three. Rhoenne had enough experience with women to know they schemed and manipulated. She was probably a master at both...and she possessed additional skills that weren't difficult to deduce given her previous status – harem woman. She could incite lust, foment passion... create sensual enticement. Rhoenne didn't have any first-hand knowledge but just as Henry had remarked, he'd heard the tales, usually spoken after bouts of drinking, accompanied by a lot of lascivious gestures. This was an evil land, where a man could claim multiple women...all at once if he wished.

All of that went through Rhoenne's mind as he watched her at her pose. If any other man saw her like this, there would be trouble. Probably bloodshed. Most likely, that was her intent.

Women!

Rhoenne cursed the word. He'd been untruthful earlier with Henry. It was obvious. He definitely had woman trouble.

Pinpricks of sunlight touched her, flecked throughout with the lazy floating of dust motes. The light turned streaks in her dark hair a burgundy shade. He hadn't noted that earlier. Her hair was long. It looked thick, too. She wore it braided down her back. It ended on the rug floor behind her. He knew she was comely.

Her hair only added to the sum total.

He should probably alter his opinion. She was much closer to beautiful. Dark–haired, with fair, flawless skin. Despite being slight, she was perfectly formed. Extremely womanly. All of it easily discerned at the moment. None of that was odd. The *Mamluk* slave-king had his pick of women. The man obviously had a good eye.

"Are you thirsty?" Rhoenne asked.

She jerked, lifted her head, and speared him with an expression that cancelled out any thought of vulnerability. If she still possessed his dagger, several parts of his anatomy would be in danger. Her look promised it. Rhoenne's lips twitched.

"I asked if you thirst," he repeated, and held out the tankard toward her.

She licked cracked, dry-looking lips. "Water?" she asked.

"*Nae.* Beer."

She made a face, but accepted the almost-full mug. Her hold was shaky, and the moment she had the drinking vessel to her lips, she was chugging liquid thirstily. He grabbed the bottom as he realized it.

"Wait. Wait! You must sip it. An empty belly may...revolt."

She lowered the tankard slowly, met his eyes, and sent an effect akin to a lightning charge right through him. Rhoenne's breath whooshed out, a high pitched note zinged through his skull, and – in spite of the impossibility – the ground shifted. Rhoenne swayed but caught it instantly. His legs bent, his right hand grabbed for his sword hilt.

Every muscle went tense, every instinct alert and wary. He stayed in that position for uncountable moments, taut as a bowstring, ready to respond.

Absolutely nothing happened.

She regarded him throughout, her eyes wide. He wasn't certain of her expression, but she no longer looked vulnerable, disdainful or remotely posed. She looked startled, even a bit alarmed. Her lips gapped. She breathed rapidly. The movement emphasized the size and shape of her barely-covered breasts. Rhoenne flushed as he realized it, attempted to avoid noticing, then tore his gaze away to make it a certainty. He blinked several times until the section of tent behind her head came into focus. He let go of her tankard. Stood. Pulled in a large breath that was audible.

What — by the saints — had just happened?

Rhoenne Ramhurst wasn't one for flights of fancy. He didn't waste time on whimsy or day-dreaming. Life was too short. Despite how the church preached, he didn't believe in sorcery, the occult, or any of the dark arts.

And he wasn't about to start.

Such nonsense was for the soft-minded and weak-willed. Rhoenne was the exact opposite.

He'd heard the stories, however, tales of decadent potentates who kept paid sorcerers at their courts. They were rumored to deal in all manner of black magic arts, fortune-telling, alchemy, necromancy, and more. Was it possible he harbored such a woman? And she practiced on him?

This easily?

No.

Rhoenne narrowed his eyes and glared at the porous texture of the tent wall. He didn't believe in mysticism. He scoffed at the existence of banshees, *poucahs, gobbe-shites,* or any other mythical creature associated with his beloved Highlands. He sure as hell wasn't going to accept such nonsense in a foreign land on enemy territory. There had to be a simple explanation. There always was. This one was easy to decipher.

He needed rest.

He'd delayed it far longer than he cared to reckon this time. The Dark One was said to be indefatigable. Tireless. He slept with his eyes open on occasion. He could go days without rest, and usually did. That alone could cause a man to feel a bit off-kilter, could even have him imagining a shift of the elements. Besides, nothing appeared changed. There was no swaying motion as if earth movement had occurred. No alarm sounded. No sounds emanated from outside that he could tell.

Rhoenne concentrated. Listened to his breathing and the thumping of his heartbeat through his ears. Everything looked the same, even the dust motes filtering through the needle-fine bits of sunlight allowed through the weave of the tent walls.

That settled it.

He'd been too long without rest.

That was one thing he could change. He reached over a shoulder and slipped a button loose on his cross-embroidered tunic.

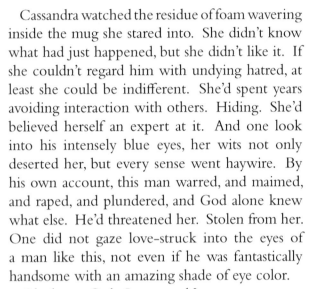

Cassandra watched the residue of foam wavering inside the mug she stared into. She didn't know what had just happened, but she didn't like it. If she couldn't regard him with undying hatred, at least she could be indifferent. She'd spent years avoiding interaction with others. Hiding. She'd believed herself an expert at it. And one look into his intensely blue eyes, her wits not only deserted her, but every sense went haywire. By his own account, this man warred, and maimed, and raped, and plundered, and God alone knew what else. He'd threatened her. Stolen from her. One did not gaze love-struck into the eyes of a man like this, not even if he was fantastically handsome with an amazing shade of eye color.

Oh, dearest God. Love- struck?

Cassandra reeled inwardly. She hadn't just thought that. Oh no. No. Never. She'd rather perish by her own hand. For that, she'd need the little dagger back, or something as deadly. He had other weapons. She'd just have to locate and pilfer another one. Cassandra took a sip of the brew as she considered. The mug was heavy. It took both hands to lift it, and one to hold it steady atop her knees between sips. She took another drink, lowered the tankard, and was just swallowing as his crucifix-bedecked tabard flitted through her view. She choked, starting a coughing fit.

He didn't seem to notice.

She'd recovered and was wiping a forearm

across her eyes as he bent to place the now-folded, blood-specked gray banner almost reverently on the floor rug, next to the mass of fabric at her feet. Cassandra dared a glance upward. He wore a blackened chain hauberk. A thick leather belt held his sword at his side. Several knives were stuck into the belt. She spotted her dagger. A thin strap of leather scored him from shoulder to hip, attached to the bag that held her pilfered jewelry. He removed his belt, wrapped it about his knives. Lowered it to the other side of his tunic just out of her reach. The bag was lifted over his head next, He wound the entire thing into a lumpy mass, and set it on the opposite side of his belt.

She looked from the bag to him. Back to the bag.

Hmm.

Cassandra took another sip of beer. Resettled the mug on her knees. Looked back up. His hauberk had been made of smelted iron links, laced together, but it wasn't much for cover. The weave was see-through, and the thing appeared molded to him. Chainmail clearly defined a very large and extremely fit male. Alarm sent shivers along her arms, across her shoulders, and right to the crests of her breasts. Nipples stirred into awareness against gauzy bodice material that felt thick and scratchy. All of it startling and completely unwelcome.

Luckily, he wasn't paying the slightest attention to her. His focus was on something well above her head as he lifted an arm and started opening metal hooks down his side, separating them by feel. His movements sent shadows across his chest, his upper arms, and his abdomen. Another rush of shivers flew over her skin, garnering the exact same result, and one addition. She could feel her cheeks warming.

As if she blushed.

Cassandra sent the order to ignore him and look elsewhere. She looked down at the mound of colorful material still encasing lower legs, moved her gaze to the items he'd placed beside it, his tabard, weapon-filled belt. The bag. Then to the bed-roll. The tent door was behind him. Her gaze slid quickly past, attempting to ignore the man obstructing the view. The samovar was next. And then she was back to the mass of palace curtain around her feet. It was useless. The tent was small, there wasn't much to look at, and he took up most of the room. Aside from which, this Rhoenne was a truly stunning specimen. He eclipsed every male she'd rushed to the wall to peek at, point to, and then titter over. He even surpassed the eunuchs.

Cassandra halted her own train of thought, instantly dismayed...and yet, who was to know? She had years of long, empty hours and nothing to fill them save her own thoughts. She'd observed the eunuchs often. Spent time assigning and debating attributes. That's why she'd befriended Emin. He was one of the largest. Strongest. Most fit.

Except when compared to this man.

Cassandra swigged another mouthful of the

beer, swallowing quickly. Her nose tickled, bringing an urge to sneeze. She barely held it back, but jerked with the motion, while a slight sputter betrayed her. She was being silly. She had some experience with observing large, fit males. Any reaction right now was odd, implausible, and completely senseless. This Rhoenne was just a man. He didn't have any ability to affect her.

He's just a man, Cassandra.

Her gaze went back to him. A flurry of goosebumps ran her skin, ending with the tightening of her nipples again. Another rush of heat hit her cheeks. All of it unbidden. Unwanted. Yet undeniable at the same time. There was something happening here, something that went beyond proximity to a handsome man with a fine physique. She'd never experienced anything like this. She didn't know how to stop it. And then he worsened it immeasurably with a deep breath that enlarged his chest, and flexed the chainmail.

Cassandra quickly looked back to her drink. Lifted the mug. Took a large swallow. Another. She'd never imbibed beer before. She usually drank water, fruit juice, or tea. Sometimes coffee. But beer seemed innocuous. After all, it was the drink of the masses. Every non-Muslim outside the palace walls drank it – the poor, laborers, slaves, even the soldiers. It was extremely unpleasant at first, but the impression changed. She tilted the mug to get the last bit, pulled the empty tankard from her lips and held it in her hands. He'd warned beer might revolt in her belly? What a strange admonition. That was the farthest thing from what was happening. She felt slightly giddy, completely flexible, and all-over relaxed.

"You ever drink beer afore?"

His deep voice startled her. Cassandra slid off the trunk, but caught it with a hand to the tent wall. She wasn't in time to stop a giggle. She slapped her free hand to her mouth while the mug settled into her lap.

"Wondrous."

The word was hissed. Whatever he referred to, it didn't sound wondrous, yet even that was funny. Sounds of merriment trickled from behind her hand as he plucked the tankard from her lap. She watched his lower legs move the two steps to the door. The flap of material lifted partway, allowing a flood of bright sunlight in. Her eyes narrowed in defense. Emin's voice filtered through the opening.

Emin.

The eunuch mustn't see her like this.

It took a bit of effort, but Cassandra regained a seat, glancing down at thighs easily discerned through her skirt. Perhaps that was the meaning of his 'wondrous'. She should change it. She brought skirt panels up from the sides, alternating them atop her thighs. That didn't help much. She was still visible, and the design left her legs completely exposed. She smoothed the panels back out again. Now, she looked even more naked. She reached down for the wad of curtain, and everything rotated crazily. Cassandra gasped and sat upright, her heart pumping furiously, as she watched the view cease moving. She'd never felt so loose and uncontrolled. What a horrid realization. She laced her fingers together atop legs she pressed together. That helped a little. She turned her hands over and spread her fingers apart, noting traces of henna on her skin and nails. Her hands needed washing. All of her could use a bath. In a harem pool...

"Here."

He shoved a bowl made from bread into her hands. A cream-colored mass was settled within it.

"Eat."

She lifted the bread. Sniffed. Wrinkled her nose.

"Now."

The word wasn't a request. Cassandra ran a finger along the edge of the bread before tearing a section from it. She nibbled, then smiled. "Oh. This is good. You know how to bake bread." She tore a larger piece of the crust away.

"No. We know how to steal."

"Steal?"

"It's from the palace."

"Oh. My. My. *My.*"

Her voice lowered on the last word and it pulsated through the enclosure with the way she'd said it. It was his fault. He was the one who'd bent forward to shimmy out of the chainmail, revealing a thin tunic. The garment was badly frayed on the edges. Stained. One side had a long tear. The material hadn't been dyed or ornamented. It was the same dull shade as the tent. And it might as well have been painted onto him.

He stood to his full height and regarded her without expression.

"You need to finish."

"With...what?"

Confusion colored the response. This was all too strange, he was entirely too engrossing, and shivers had turned into a rivulet of sensation, ceaselessly rippling along her skin, lifting goosebumps. And worse. He looked as though he not only knew what she suffered, but the reason for it. He spoke his next words to the area directly above her head.

"Your porridge."

"Porridge." It wasn't a question.

"You are not hungry?"

"I am...not sure," she replied.

"Cassandra."

"Emin told you my name?"

"You told me."

"I did?"

He huffed something that sounded like annoyance.

"Listen. I do not know what you are used to, but I already told you. I have no need. Or want. You ken?"

"Oh."

She'd never felt quite this aware, and stimulated, and provoked. Disembodied. Slightly dim-witted. How was it possible to become someone different in the span of time it took to drink a mug of beer? Was it the drink? Or could it be a result of her recent past? Being drugged. Nearly suffocated. Forced to submit to revealing herself. Or...was it due to her complete inexperience with men? She had no one to advise her. No one she'd even speak to. She never had.

But if nearness to a man sent bizarre sensations that confused and annoyed, the nonsensical words he spoke did worse. Was he speaking of sup? Of course she was used to eating. To prove it, she lifted the entire bowl to her mouth and tore a large chunk from the edge. The contents had leached into the bread, revealing it was overly salted, but not inedible. She swallowed the bite then tipped the bowl and started slurping. She had the contents emptied when she heard a slight groan. Cassandra lowered the bread and looked up at him inquisitively. His expression was grim. His lips thinned to a slash. His jaw set. His eyes were an even brighter hue than before, if such a thing was possible. Her mouth didn't work properly. She slipped a stray bit of porridge from her lips into her mouth. Licked at her fingers.

"I warn you. Do not do that again."

Cassandra tried to regard him with the same soberness he was using. It failed miserably. She couldn't seem to control her own facial expressions? "Do what?"

"I only have one sleep-roll," he informed her.

"You do?" *What did that have to do with sup?*

"And I sleep alone."

He grabbed the hem of his linen tunic and peeled the garment up and over his head. The remnants of the bread bowl fell from her fingers.

Cassandra didn't hear it, feel it, or even watch it. She'd never seen such a span of lightly tanned flesh, so rippled with muscle. He had an array of marks and scars, some vicious-looking, others no more than thin, light-colored lines. They didn't detract. Quite the opposite. He looked every inch a virile male, from the hardness of his chest and abdomen, to the dark line of hair leading to the waistband of his chausses...

Cassandra reeled in place. She didn't know how to control it. She was actually amazed she still sat on his wooden case. This Rhoenne was beyond jaw-dropping. She couldn't conceive of what would have happened if he'd been glimpsed by the harem. It would have been riotous.

There was a brown leather patch sewn at the front of his chausses, right at the juncture of his thighs. Exactly at her eye level. She tried to look away, but nothing on her body obeyed. Cassandra slammed her eyelids shut, gritted her teeth, and then she realized what he'd been telling her. She reopened her eyelids. Looked up.

"You sleep alone," she stated.

"Aye."

"Where am I to sleep?" she asked.

He shrugged. Since there wasn't any material on his upper body, she got to observe how his skin looked as it moved over sinew and muscle. Her mouth dropped open again. She couldn't find one thing to change it.

"Wherever you wish." He motioned with his hand to the tent space. His motion encompassed the door flap.

"I...can leave?" She hadn't considered that.

"Of course. The men await that very thing."

"They do?"

"There's a woman in camp. Under my protection. My possession is the lone thing standing in the way. Of course they're waiting."

"I...have Emin."

She tried to sound convincing. It didn't work. She sounded unsure. And small. He inhaled a huge breath. Exhaled. She didn't think anything could be more disturbing than watching him shrug. Now she got to find out she'd been wrong.

"How many can he take without a weapon?" he asked.

Her ears heard melodic notes, akin to singing. His question was indistinct. It took a few seconds to comprehend and reply. "Oh. He will need a weapon. You should...give him one."

"I don't have to give him anything. I don't have to do more than the obvious."

He lifted the roll thing, unstrapped leather ties, and unfurled it, turning it into a pallet with little thickness to keep a body from feeling hard ground. It was in the same drab color scheme he favored, although there was a black cross embroidered on every corner.

"You'd have him fight without a weapon?" she asked.

He'd crouched, smoothing out the wrinkles of his bed before reaching for the wad of jewelry-filled bag. He settled it at the top of his mat. Near her feet. He looked across at her then, the motion putting a small line into existence across his forehead. Cassandra's heart swooped to the pit of her belly. She actually felt it.

"*I* wouldn't be doing anything."

He looked away and stretched out on the mat, slid down onto his front, defining all manner of muscle in his back, his thighs, and even his calves. There was no disguising it. His chausses were knitted. They clung to him.

"But you would. You just said—"

Cassandra's voice stopped. Her mind was a moment behind. He flipped onto his back, settled his head onto the bundle of bag, and then slanted his glance to look up at her again.

"I said you are free to leave. He is free to defend you. That is what I said. That is what I meant. And I am going to sleep now. You may do as you wish."

And then he shut his eyes.

Cassandra looked around his tent again, taking much more time than before. The room spun crazily if she moved her head too quickly. There truly wasn't much space. She put her arms out to gauge it. One hand reached one side of the tent. If she stretched, she'd reach the other side. Since he'd placed his sleep-roll directly down the center, he took up most of the floor. He looked even more immense in a prone position. His boots reached the door flap. He wasn't leaving her any room.

"Debating your options?" he asked.

"Yes," she replied.

"You won't last long. Don't scream too loudly."

Her silence must have revealed her puzzlement,

for he explained.

"I speak of your escape. And ravishment. Don't scream. I need my sleep. I just spoke on it."

"I wasn't escaping," she replied.

"No?"

"I was wondering where I could fit."

He shifted, making a bit of room on the pallet right next to him. Cassandra did the only thing she could think of. She swiveled away, and that just rotated her right off the trunk.

CHAPTER SIX

TIFFNESS SENT NAGGING discomfort, making her shift. She didn't want to awaken. The dream was too real. She was abed in the castle. Warm. Safe. Cassandra snuggled her cheek further into rough fabric that scratched unlike anything they used at home, or in the sultan's harem.

Her eyelids opened. She blinked. Focused. Remembered. She was a crusader knight's captive now. She slept, propped against his trunk, atop the rainbow-hued drapery. She was cuddling a mass of material in her arms. She stared at it uncomprehendingly. Strong daylight no longer filtered through the walls, giving little indication of time of day. It didn't mute what she saw. It truly was his cloak cradled in her arms.

That was disconcerting.

Cassandra sat upright, set the garment from her, and looked at a surface that wavered before solidifying into a tent wall. An ache throbbed in her head, her eyes burned, and her throat needed something to ease the parched desert feel. If this was the result of quenching thirst with beer, she'd just as soon forego it. She was going to forego a lot of things...just as soon as she escaped this crusader's control. She had to use her wits, though.

All was not lost. In fact, she might have gained.

It hadn't happened how she'd wanted, but she'd escaped the harem. She was outside the palace walls. She was uninjured. Emin was somewhere outside. She still had her anklets for funds. She had a voluminous cloak for concealment. She might even have access to weaponry.

Cassandra moved her glance despite how it hurt her head.

She'd been right!

His belt still wrapped around multiple knives. It was on the floor right beside her. The little jeweled dagger was easy to remove. Best of all, she was alone. She had to be. Cassandra held her breath and listened. There wasn't a sound to be heard above the beating of her heart.

She rose to her knees, donned the cloak, tying the straps at her throat. She settled the hood atop her head. The garment was enormous, but that was beneficial. She plucked up the dagger next, then turned around and barely kept the surprise from sounding. She couldn't prevent the fall. Her hands barely missed his head, while the dagger skittered to the door, stopped by the tent flap.

She wasn't alone at all.

The knight was on his back atop his sleep mat, still taking up most of the floor, his head pillowed on the jewelry-filled bag, his arms crossed atop his chest. Then his eyes opened. And Cassandra froze.

Long moments passed while she hovered, her heart smacking her chest with a rapidity that pained. Every nerve alert. Tensed.

And then he just shut his eyes.

Seconds passed before Cassandra moved ever so slightly, settling back onto the drapery pile. She waited for her heartbeat to return to normal before working to control the shaking that overtook her next. She was so grateful for the cloak! The material was thick, warm, protective, the combination calming panic she'd never admit. And it was senseless. He'd told her she was free to go. He just hadn't known of the anklets, nor that she'd filch his cloak and a dagger.

The entire time, she didn't take her gaze from him. It was incredible. She could barely make out the movement of each inhalation. His exhalations were just as hard to spot. He slept like the dead.

Well. That fit.

He exhibited as much emotion as a dead thing, too.

The instant thought sent a stab of amusement. She almost vocalized it, then sobered. Time was wasting. He wasn't disappearing. If he caught her, she'd just lose the cloak. She might be able to snag up the dagger without his knowledge. Either way, she'd risk it. Cassandra gathered her nerve, crawled toward him, and just like before, he opened his eyes. Cassandra stopped. Watched. Waited. His eyes were open, but nothing about him changed. His gaze was vacant. There wasn't any sense of recognition. He didn't seem aware, or even act awake. How was such a thing possible?

She wondered if this could be a reflex action, something they worked at. These knights could be trained to sleep like this, able to open their eyes at any hint of movement. They might need such a skill to defend against an enemy...or frighten any unsuspecting females in their vicinity.

She smirked and moved, barely shifting the air with the movement. Little particles of sand floated about. She waited until they calmed. Rhoenne didn't budge. His eyes remained open yet unseeing. She slid a foot into place beneath her; put her weight on it. Nothing changed about him.

She couldn't stay long in the position, though. Her leg was trembling before she got the other foot beneath her. The effort made her pulse pound, sweat broke out on her forehead, and her breath was shaky, but she was finally crouched, and there was no sign that he'd heard or sensed anything.

She slid along the side, staying clear of any contact with the tent wall that might sound like fingernails grazing along fabric. Easing her toes alongside his mat, she reached the point where his pallet met the door flap.

And he still hadn't moved.

Cassandra reached out a hand behind her for the dagger...and it wasn't there! She motioned with her fingers, stirring air. She still couldn't feel it. She clenched her teeth, turned her head, saw where the blade rested. But the move made her wobble.

She toppled.

Fingers brushed his ankle.

And the next instant hard arms wrapped about her midriff.

A moment later, she was on her back. The cloak had opened, too, rendering it useless. She didn't have time to cry out before the crusader was atop her, holding her in place by the sheer weight of his body. He had her hands trapped right between her breasts, smashed there by his chest. His heartbeat was strong against one palm.

Oh no!

Cassandra was about to do the one thing she'd promised to never do. She was going to cry. It was going to be loud and vicious, too. She fought rising sobs, her eyes filled with tears despite how she scrunched them shut. She held her breath. Tensed her body. She dredged up every bit of disgust and revulsion. She tried everything she knew to send the emotion back and nothing worked. The best she managed was silence. She choked back sound as unpleasant shivers coursed her skin. Adding to the ignominy, she knew he watched all of it with those blue, ice-cold eyes of his.

And then he changed everything.

What had to be lips touched hers, tasting, then nuzzling, tipping her head slightly with each motion. His lips were satiny hard and unbelievably warm. Surprise and confusion raced through her, followed by a rush of intense heat. Any urge to sob strangled to a halt in her throat, while the unpleasant shivers of a moment earlier somehow became rivulets that carried something akin to enticement and thrill. All of it hinting of wonders she hadn't any idea existed.

His lips pressed inexorably against hers. He nibbled. Caressed. Sucked. The kiss deepened. Each breath came quick and sharp at her nose, alternately stealing, replacing, and conjoining the available air. Cassandra felt herself slip, then it became a freefall, allowing free rein to the sensations. Her spirit soared. Her senses careened, each one heightened and sharp. She'd never felt anything like this. It eclipsed the joy of listening to perfectly composed and orchestrated music, outshone any long soak in warmed scented water, easily surpassed every oiled massage she'd ever had. This was the most delightful experience in her life.

He tilted his head and took all of her mouth with his and Cassandra's mind went on complete hiatus. Her body surged against his with primal instinct, and she started sucking at his mouth with motions he'd just taught, mingling tongues. Taste. Moans. Thrill after thrill coursed over and through her, teasing of pleasures she couldn't comprehend and yet thoroughly wanted.

A raw groan swelled through their entwined lips. It came from him. It grew in volume as it deepened, filling the enclosure with sound that reverberated off the tent walls. Remnants of it hovered for uncountable measures of time, imbuing the space with an audible mix of yearning, craving, and desire. She would have joined in, but he took all the air.

But then he moved, yanking his mouth away, lifting his head, pushing his chest from contact with her, to stare down at her with wide intense blue eyes from less than a hand-span away. Cassandra lips were still pursed. Her breathing panted. Her body pliant and willing. And all of it had halted as effectively as if she'd been doused with iced water.

He was definitely awake now. At the same time, he looked befuddled. Bewildered. There was no doubt he was aroused. The patch of brown leather that covered his groin was heavily swelled where it pressed against her upper thighs.

"What...are you doing?"

Threat filled the words. His tone promised something dire. It didn't remotely match how the strength of their every breath shoved their bellies into each other.

"I was leaving." The words didn't have much sound, and they were a lot lower-timbered than usual.

"Then why accost me?"

Cassandra blinked several times. Stared. "Me?" she finally responded.

"How oft must I say it? I have no need. Or want."

"But you are the one...atop me," she answered and the last words were whispered.

He bit out a curse, but she was guessing since it was in his language and she'd never heard it before. He pushed away. From there he rose to stand at the edge of his sleep-mat, his head lifting the tent top while he studiously kept from looking down at her. And if he thought he portrayed emotionless indifference, he was going to need practice. There wasn't any portion of him that looked unmoved. Bared skin glistened with moisture, he heaved each breath, and his groin patch was distended to an impressive size.

She blushed.

As if he'd known her train of thought, he turned sideways, putting truly impressive buttocks on view as he pulled and fussed with the front section of his trousers. That was intriguing, frightening, stimulating, and a thousand other mysterious things that someone should have explained to her much more succinctly. She'd had the lessons. When she'd first arrived at the harem she'd been schooled. Older women handled the instructing. *Her primary purpose was not in creating desire, but fulfilling it.* A kiss was nothing more than a gesture of devotion. When, and if, the sultan favored her to his bed, she was to keep uppermost in her mind that she was there for one purpose – his pleasure. If he allowed a kiss, she could expect a meeting of the lips as a prelude of the divine pleasures he would bestow on her.

A meeting of the lips...?

Somebody hadn't been truthful because that description didn't remotely resemble what Cassandra had just experienced.

Her lips felt raw and swollen with aching fullness this man had sucked into existence, while her skin felt like she'd been rubbed with fine granules of sand mixed with honey, and it had fully dried to an continuous itch. Everything was ratcheted to a sensation of alertness and sensitivity to the point she vibrated with agitation. Her skin pinged with tingles, her breasts felt larger and heavier, her nipples were an irritation, and her lower belly had sparks shooting through it, although they weren't heated or strong like they had been. What the kiss had created was enjoyable and exciting, and full of the promise of more. None of her lessons mentioned anything about this.

She wondered what else they'd left out.

"Don't. Move."

He stepped over her. She heard rustling from beyond her head that could be her drape. Clanking followed that might be his chainmail or weaponry. Then thumps that could be his trunk. She didn't look. She was still encapsulating her experience with kissing, contemplating, and then memorizing it.

"Put this on."

One of his stored garments dropped onto her as he stepped over her again. He'd dressed. The newer tunic didn't cling to him like the previous one. The plain wooden crucifix dangled from a chain about his neck. He had his bag draped across one shoulder. She didn't have time to see more since he shoved through the door flap and left.

Rhoenne did a quick scan of the area as he exited the tent. Twilight crept over the hills, darkening the landscape and making it temperate enough to travel. It didn't hide where Henry leaned against the wagon, the eunuch beside him, nor did the gathering night conceal the forms of both Grant and Euan over by the beer cask wagon. They lifted tankards toward Rhoenne in greeting, but then ruined it with grins. Rhoenne turned back to Henry and the eunuch, lengthening his stride as he approached. He nodded to first Henry, then the other man.

"You." He motioned with his head back at the tent. "See to your mistress."

The eunuch bowed, touched his forehead with the fingertips of one hand, then took off at a jog.

"Henry. Come with me."

Rhoenne strode purposefully to where they'd hobbled the horses, circling the entire camp in ever-widening circles as if reconnoitering. His stride forced Henry to an occasional jog to keep up. Noting the man's trouble helped ease the anger pumping through him. That way it wouldn't be misused or misdirected. Rhoenne thought he'd conquered his emotional side. He'd subjugated it, along with the strange issues he had with sleep. He'd killed the ability to feel. Or care. He'd fought on the lists until every speck of human frailty got annihilated, along with his adversaries. Now, if emotion ever intruded, he used his wits. Time. Work. Training. If he needed a fight, it wasn't hard to find one. Avoiding a fight took skill. Uppermost was recognizing its source. And then eliminating it.

He knew what fueled this emotion. It wasn't

difficult to ascertain. It was the vixen in his tent. Because of her he'd had an episode of sleep walking, suffered arousal that still annoyed, stiffened with agitation through every muscle and complete frustration that sent a wash of red over his vision with every heartbeat.

And now he had to contend with insubordination?

The horses didn't match his mood. They were docile. Several mounts were saddled. Bedrolls and packs were strapped into place. The amount of horseflesh had been whittled down an appreciable amount. Two of the wagons were also gone. A dozen men milled about, Ramhurst clan among them. They all studiously avoided eye contact. The knights had shed their armor and dressed in the Arab burnoose robe for anonymity.

Rhoenne reached the far end of camp, turned as if to look over the situation and waited for Henry to catch up. He looked down at the man for long moments, while nothing happened save the whicker and whinny of horses, sounds of bridles shifting, a bit of conversing over by the beer wagon where the scouts lounged.

"How long have Grant and Euan been back?" Rhoenne asked.

"Not...overlong."

Rhoenne tipped his chin down to regard Henry long enough the man lifted his eyebrows. Sucked in his cheeks. Checked his hands, fronts and back. And then he answered, but it sounded like amusement laced the words.

"Oh, verra well. Long enough to partake of

sup. Drink a bit. Discard their armor. Change. As have we all."

"You were to fetch me the moment they arrived," Rhoenne said.

Henry nodded. "True."

"Then why dinna' you?"

"The sounds from your tent were...uh."

Henry stopped his explanation. Rhoenne regarded his man for another long span.

"Off-putting," Henry finally supplied.

"Off-putting?" Rhoenne asked.

"Severely so, actually."

Rhoenne felt a flush rise through his chest and jaw. He ignored it, letting his beard and the encroaching nightfall hide it. He waited long moments for his man to elaborate, but Henry just returned the stare. Rhoenne spoke first, but to say the man's name in a censorious tone.

"Henry FitzHugh,"

"If it helps, there is *nae* sign of pursuit from her sultan. At least...na' yet."

Rhoenne's shoulders relaxed slightly. He hadn't realized he'd had them tensed. This was all her fault – that vixen in his tent.

The unbidden memory of how she'd looked occurred to him. Not as he'd left her, covered with the tunic he'd dropped, but earlier, when she'd been beneath him. The film of color that constituted her clothing completely askew. Her perfect breasts heaving. Her eyes glistening. Her lips readied...

Rhoenne banished the recollection. His jaw tightened. He nearly gave vent to the growl.

"You just told me Grant and Euan have na' been here long. Yet, they already ate, changed, *and* reported?"

"Na' fully, but once I made a decision to... counter things, I made it a point of asking about pursuit."

"Counter things?"

"I doona' disobey you as a general rule. You ken as much. So, I debated my options."

"You were na' given options."

"True...but in this event I felt it prudent."

"Prudent." It wasn't a question and it was hissed between his teeth.

"Well. You see. I did approach your tent to awaken you. I was alone, yet Grant and Euan were within earshot. Most of the others as well."

"What the devil are you speaking of?"

"You have a great range of voice, my laird."

Rhoenne swore. Instantly. And viciously. Henry coughed. Sputtered. Then wheezed through his next sentences.

"'Tis a family trait. I believe one of your forebears was a troubadour...of some note, I might add."

"Must you?" Rhoenne bit out.

Henry cleared his throat. "This sounds like woman trouble, if I could be so bold."

"I do na' have woman trouble, and *nae* you may na'."

"May I infer that your woman is na' coming with us, then?"

"Would you cease putting words in my mouth? I did na' say that. And she is *not* my woman."

"Oh. Then...she is coming. Verra good. I shall have the horses prepared."

"I did na' say that, either."

"What is it you said then?"

"I did na' say words that led to any inference, one way or the other! That is what I said. And that is what I meant."

He put too much emotion on the outburst. He was also breathing hard. Both reactions were unacceptable. Rhoenne set about tempering them. He pulled his hands into fists, rolled them inward, working his forearms. He was debating dropping to the ground and doing push-ups when Henry spoke again.

"You are difficult this eve, Rhoenne. I will na' attempt to decipher the reason. I do not wish my head bitten off. I am merely ascertaining needs. That is my job. And since you are ever close-mouthed, I work with what I am given. You are not clear, or I am more obtuse than usual. I need the quantity of persons in our party so I can prepare the mounts."

Rhoenne contained a growl. "You are determined to be a thorn in my side."

"And you are more dour than usual. Verra well. You win. I shall cease attempting to gather facts and await your leisure. We all shall. Those who choose to accompany us, anyway. The mercenaries who did not wish it thank you. They are gratified and amazed at your generosity in bestowing the entire wealth of plunder on them...as is everyone else - except me, of course, but I ken the reason. We will be fifteen if your woman comes with us. Fourteen, without. Or less. That will depend on the eunuch. So. There you have the reason for my queries. The nearest port city is Batok. 'Twill be a healthy ride. We should start soon."

Rhoenne regarded his man for long enough anyone else would have fidgeted before filling the silence with words as they confessed. Henry simply waited. Rhoenne sighed and spoke first.

"Why waste time blathering about horses, then? Surely she rides. Or did her man tell different?"

"'Tis na' a horse for her, my liege, but for you. I have selected two that will suffice. Large. Strong."

"I have no trouble picking horses, Henry. And I am not that large. Carrying me will not weaken a horse."

"You will be riding double."

Rhoenne considered what he'd just been told. Actually felt a tingle of reaction somewhere deep in his belly. He swallowed before answering. "No."

"Then I shall be riding double."

"Once again. No."

"Forgive me, my laird...but I insist."

Henry didn't sound like he'd just issued a challenge. It was too dark to see him clearly but he'd lost any trace of joviality and sounded deadly serious.

"She is a harem wench, FitzHugh. A woman of low morals and less decency. "

"She is a woman and therefore deserving of chivalry."

"I do not need a conscience at this late date.

Nor did I request one."

"It sounds as though someone needs to deliver a good clout to your head," Henry remarked.

Rhoenne stepped back, instantly taut. "Your meaning?"

"I am willing to risk life and limb to step in and deliver said blow."

"You have twelve years of age on me, FitzHugh. I outweigh you by three stone, perhaps more. I am unbeatable on the list."

"You call me *auld*.? And slight? And seek to weaken me with odds?"

"No. I speak of your defeat...and a reluctance to deliver it."

"I am still willing to risk it."

"Good thing we are speaking symbolically. I would hate to have to do something about your words."

"Rhoenne. Please. You speak of my words, and I admit. I speak many that are nonsensical and jocular. 'Tis my nature. I would na' change it if I could. But hear these. This godforsaken country may have taken years of life from us. Our blood. And our sanity. But I will *not* allow it to take our honor."

Leagues of time could have passed as Rhoenne considered Henry's words, reflecting on their meaning. He couldn't remember feeling so chastised, even when his father had lived.

"Good thing it is too dark to see you clearly, FitzHugh," he finally remarked.

"Agreed. The darkness delivers a measure of courage when one needs it. Also makes it difficult to plant my face into the ground with one swing."

Rhoenne snorted. "Prepare the horses. We will be fifteen. I shall fetch the woman. I will take her up on the horse with me. And I will verra much blame you the entire time."

"Fair enough. We are in accord. Go. I'll alert the men, and then I shall rue the nightfall I just appreciated."

"I thought the journey was prepared. Horses readied."

"It is. And they are. I but rue lack of daylight as a lost chance to peek at this mysterious woman of yours."

"How many times must I say it? She is *not* mine."

"For the time being, she is."

Rhoenne sighed heavily. "Sometimes I wish your cousin had beaten you in the games. I truly do."

"Had Angus FitzHugh earned a position in your Honor Guard, you'd have had no end of troubles. And well you ken it. Angus has a wealth of brains but a dearth of brawn. Poor vision. His aim is off. His cooking skills nonexistent. His wit slow. His lack of luck legendary. His—."

"Enough already. I forfeit," Rhoenne interrupted, and if he had any ability to feel amusement, then that was what colored his answer.

CHAPTER SEVEN

THE GARMENT HE'D dropped on her was a tunic. Cassandra stood on legs that still shook, slipped the cloak tie apart and let it drop to the bedding mat with its own weight. She flipped the tunic into shape, found the bottom hem, and yanked it over her head. She shoved her arms through large armholes, pulled the front down. The garment was enormous and heavy. It fell without any help. She lifted her arms next, and pulled her braid out, working hand-over-hand until it was free of the material. If she wasn't literally racing against time, she'd have frowned over loose hairs that fluffed and sparked, while bemoaning the snarls. She'd have done something about it, too. Her hair needed attention badly. A washing. Oil. A good combing using one of the fine-toothed combs she owned.

Used to own, Cassandra.

The amendment added impetus to her motions. She didn't know how much time she had. She daren't waste a second. Whereas before she used to have all the time in the world, now she couldn't find enough. It was enough to make a former pleasure-loving harem dweller gnash her teeth. Then again, she'd never been a dim-witted pleasure-seeker. She'd have slit her own throat first.

The reason for her haste wasn't just the man and his unspecified return, although that was of import. It wasn't that she wanted to be well-covered from his gaze when that happened, either. The impetus behind such hurry was what she needed accomplished before he caught her. It was the weight still on each ankle. She didn't know if he'd seen her anklets. She needed them hidden before he returned. Finding a spot beneath this tunic wasn't going to be difficult. The garment was the equivalent of wearing an enormous grain sack, the neckline so wide the thing wouldn't stay on her shoulders. Any movement sent the garment's neck opening careening down an arm, or both. The bottom grazed her ankles.

She pulled the hem up. Balanced on one leg to unclasp and remove an anklet. She was just finishing with the other when the door wavered, signaling a presence behind it. Cassandra dropped her foot. Cold invaded her veins as the neckline fell off her shoulders, while the hem dropped onto her toes. And then Emin spoke, requesting entrance. Relief steadied and calmed as she granted permission. He entered and then he collapsed onto his knees before her. That's when the perfect hiding spot occurred to her.

"Oh. *Princessa*! I have been so worried! You are well? He has not harmed you?"

"Quickly, Emin. Take these." Cassandra held

out the jewelry.

His gaze went from the anklets up to her face. His expression one of astonishment. "He...left them with you?"

"He does not know of them! Here! Take them! Quickly."

He leaned back, and held his hands up as though the pieces might burn.

"What is it?" she asked.

"*Princessa*! You do not understand! You must give them to him!"

"This is all we have left. We will need it to barter passage!"

He shook his head. "No. Please. You must give them to him. You must do whatever he says! The moment he says it. You understand?"

"You are mad."

"They are leaving, Highness. They have been very secretive on their plans, and they speak a mix of languages, but I am used to such things, and so I listened and pieced together what I heard. They ride to Batok!"

"Truly?"

"Aye. But Allah has not been merciful, I fear."

"They are taking us to Batok! And the shipyard! How is any of that unmericiful?"

"They do not say what is to happen to you."

"What does that mean?" she asked.

"Forgive me, Highness, but I do not know if you are to go or be left behind. It appears they have prepared for either event. They now await his decision. None have the slightest idea what it will be. He leaves everyone in suspense while he considers. And he is as close-mouthed and obstinate as a mud-brick wall!"

"He'd leave me?"

Her voice cracked. She couldn't help it. Her heart decided it couldn't just skip. It could stop and send painfully hard beats once it restarted. She clasped her hands at her breasts and held them there.

"I do not know if he will or not," Emin confessed. "I admit...I had great hopes when we heard his voice earlier, but then he left this tent, sent me to attend you, and I am unsure again. I cannot say what his decision will be. No one can. Except...perhaps you?"

"Me?"

"Who else knows what has transpired between you and him?"

"Of all the rotten—! Lowdown!"

"*Princessa*! No! No! Please! I beg of you! You must not say such things! You must not even think them for fear they receive utterance. We may still be in time! You must do exactly what he says without a fight! What man wishes thorns when he takes a woman to his bed?"

"His bed?" Cassandra exclaimed.

"It is a matter of life and death! Those who stay behind...with the wagons? They remind me of wolves. Death would be more welcome! They would not be merciful, and I could not prevent them, although I will die first. Please, Highness. Please? I beg of you."

"You don't know what you ask."

"Is it truly so hard? Can you not think of him

as your new master...akin to His Excellency, the sultan? At least...for the time-being?"

Cassandra set her jaw. Regarded the eunuch. "This is unfair."

"The world is an unfair place, Highness."

"Especially for a woman," Cassandra said.

"For many," he replied softly.

Cassandra turned and stared at the door flap without really seeing it. She had just tasted freedom from an existence of manipulation and pretense! And now Emin wanted her to do it again? She hadn't full knowledge of what happened between a man and a woman but she'd spent years observing jealousy and passion and secrets and vendettas and hatreds...and what they did to people. That's how she'd whiled away most of the hours that droned on without end.

To those of a vacant mind, life in the harem was wondrous. To her, it was an encapsulated world of time that ticked by with the slowness of a weak drip. Sometimes women swam. Danced. Did needlework. Some painted. Some wrote. Others read. Some played music. Beautification and cleanliness were time-consuming events that everyone enjoined, but some women preened continually, poring over every real or imagined imperfection. Almost all of them toyed with emotions and fears as they gathered in small groups to shred each other. Gossip was the main recreation. Cassandra had been subjected to it when she'd first entered. She'd been eleven, bruised from her kidnapping and travel, fearful of her future. She hadn't known the languages.

But even then, she'd seen how they used words as weapons.

And then she'd tried to understand why.

She became adept at hiding. Keeping to shadows. Ignored. Dismissed as beneath notice. Few noticed her. She was considered odd. Unfriendly. Tiresome and boring. She learned the languages they spoke. Any and all of them. She didn't join a group, and she didn't spend time with the outsiders – the unpopular women who banded together in defense. No one realized she studied them. And then she'd test herself. Every day there was some event to observe, usually more than one. She'd watch situations being set up. Calculate the reasons behind it. Guess the end result, and watch them play out. Check her accuracy. She'd gotten very good at it.

That's how she'd known this Rhoenne had been hurt by a woman.

She didn't know to what extent, but it made him declare he was heartless. Hard. Cruel. He'd had a lot of practice at it. He was very good. The emotionless hard personae he'd assumed was almost ingrained.

And Emin begged her to try to please him?

The man would detest her if she tried.

It may already be too late. There were too many variables at play. She suspected if she'd spit words of hatred at Rhoenne or heaped abuse, he'd leave her without a backward glance – because that's what he expected of a woman. If she'd been pliant and soft and seductive, he'd also leave her behind, because he'd guess the act of seduction was to save her skin – which he also expected of women. Disinterest such as she'd shown him may have been her best tool.

...except for that kiss.

Oh my.

His response had been unguarded and raw, showing something she instinctively knew he didn't want seen. He was very good at his emotionless demeanor, but it wasn't perfect...and she'd been a witness. The man was living behind a facade. She didn't know what he'd do to preserve it. Emin was wrong. She hadn't fought anyone.

The Dark Knight was fighting himself.

She truly didn't know what might happen next. She didn't know what had made him like he was. She didn't know if she wanted to know. She didn't even know if she could face him. That kiss had changed everything in her world. She'd never felt so wild. Stimulated. Aroused. Enthralled. Excited.

And terrified.

If he'd felt just a small measure of those emotions...? She might get left behind because of that.

All because of a kiss.

Cassandra shivered anew at the memory. Blushed. She faced a volatile situation with no right answer. Surviving a harem sounded easier. At least she'd had hundreds of women to hide amongst.

"How long is this trip?" she asked finally.

"Two nights. Less. More. It depends when we leave, and what dangers we will face. Then there is the voyage ahead. This crusader seeks transport from these shores, as well."

"We have our passage paid."

"A man who will take bribes from a shrouded harem woman with no chance of escape will sell his own children."

Cassandra frowned. "Why didn't you say so earlier?"

"Hope is an endearing quality."

Endearing. Strange, she'd never thought of herself in concert with that description. "Then we definitely will need these." She lifted the anklets.

"*Princessa.* Please. We will be under the protection of a strong man. He will handle things like funds."

"You are a strong man."

"Not enough for one as beautiful as you."

"You have been among women too long, my friend."

"Yes. Most of my life. But you are most beauteous. You have mirrors. You know I do not lie."

There was no reasoning with him. Lots of things determined status in a harem, although the real power resided in the sultan's mother. Following her came the great wife, then the lesser wives. And then the concubines, starting with the current favorite. Catching the sultan's eye was of paramount importance, and all knew he wished a beautiful face and pleasing form. Cassandra wasn't blind or stupid. The harem was peopled with women from multiple lands.

Almost all of them could be considered beautiful. Emin was extremely biased. He had been since she'd befriended him.

"Shouldn't we hide just one of these? For emergencies?"

"And if he finds out, what then? He will have no qualm about tossing both of us overboard."

"Emin—"

"It may not be onerous. He is much younger than His Excellency. In his prime. More fit. Much more handsome. Probably a tiger when he—"

"Cease that. I am not blind." Cassandra interrupted him before he got any further with his descriptions, sounding exactly like a woman would. And a lot like she had.

"He is not such a bad master, Highness. He sent me to see to your needs. I will help you prepare. You need to be ready before he requires it."

"So, now I have to anticipate his needs? This better not get much worse."

"Would it truly be so bad? He seems fair, if a bit harsh."

"You compared him to a mud-brick wall earlier, Emin."

"No!"

Cassandra almost smiled at his horrified look. "Calm yourself. It was a figure of speech no one will ever hear from my lips. And I completely concur. So. Tell me. Did he give you leave to fetch me something to eat? And drink? Something... that isn't beer?"

"I will return with such. But first I shall see if there is anything fit for you to wear."

"You don't like my new gown?" She spun. The tunic didn't twirl with her, and it gapped worse at the shoulders once she stopped.

"Why would you dress thusly? He will not find you of any interest. You do injustice to a pig."

Cassandra laughed. "He was the one who ordered me to wear it."

"No!"

His horrified look was back. That was really amusing.

"Oh, indeed. This is what I am commanded to wear. I need a belt of some kind, though. Could you see if there is something I can use? A rope, maybe? Or perhaps I can fashion one with my head scarf...although it might be too colorful. Oh! And sandals. I cannot run about barefoot forever."

"I do not understand these infidels. Oh. Wait. Perhaps he wishes to hide your beauty from all others. I take it back. If that be the case, he shows uncommon sense."

"If you start extolling his virtues again, I will banish you."

He stood. Bowed. "You wish a length of rope. Food. Water. Sandals. Is that everything?"

"Yes."

He nodded. Bowed. The door flap swished and he was gone. Cassandra went to check the wooden trunk. There wasn't anything left in it. Nothing to use for a belt. Or shoes. She shut it

again.

"Water. Bread. Stew. Eat quickly, *Princesse*."

Emin's hands materialized beneath the door with items. Cassandra didn't need to be told twice. She was at the door before the door flap finished swaying. The water was cool, a bit brackish, and absolute heaven to her throat. The spicy stew dazzled her tongue. They needed a lighter hand with their use of seasonings, but if she added a piece of bread to each bite of stew, it was quite delicious. Filling. And warm.

"Rope."

A length of hemp slithered beneath the door flap next. Emin was more resourceful than even she realized, but he'd brought a rope long enough to circle her several times over. Cassandra wound the rope twice about her waist, crossed it between her breasts, looped it over her shoulders, across her back, around to the front and tied it at her waist. Ends trailed to her knees.

The door swished again.

"You've found sandals, too?" she enquired.

"Sandals?"

Cassandra gasped, looked up, and instantly her glance skittered back down. She had her answer to one thing. She couldn't face him. She could blush, though. And stay tongue-tied and silent. She'd always been hidden and quiet, but why, when she needed her voice most, was it absent?

The knight didn't say anything. She dared another peek. He stood just inside the door, lifting the top of the tent with his head. He wore a burnoose. He had his arms folded, while regarding her with narrowed eyes. He didn't look happy about anything. She looked back down again.

"I...am barefoot."

She stuck a foot out for proof. The henna marks were fading from her nails and skin, but it was easy to see she didn't go barefoot as a normal course.

"You have no need of sandals."

Oh, God!

She knew instantly that he'd made his decision.

He was called The Dark One. Hard. Heartless. Emotionless. He was proving it right now. A man with 'dark' attached to him didn't care if she was savagely raped. Tortured. Then stoned. Or worse. The color alone branded a man hard, and cruel.

The reason he'd come personally was because he needed to demonstrate – to himself - that if he could face her while condemning her, then there was no pretense. No façade. He could go about his way unscathed. Further cement his personae. Continue his quest for vengeance against her gender. To right whatever wrong the mysterious woman had done to him.

She was as certain as if he spoke the words.

Oh, why had she spent so many years researching and reading human behavior? She'd rather be ignorant of what people did and why. But...if that had been the case, she'd never have plotted to escape the harem. She wouldn't have been at Selique's sup. She'd have been assured a long life as a pampered pet even if the boredom was life-sapping.

But she would never have to deal with this level of hurt.

Tears flooded her eyes...stupid useless things. Cassandra stiffened her back and held her breath and sucked the emotion back into oblivion. It was one of the hardest things she'd ever done.

"You are standing on my cloak."

Her limbs were frozen and stiff, as if she'd aged instantly. Cassandra backed a step on legs that shuddered. Another. Tried to remain standing. And she wondered why God had helped her escape the harem and spared her a death by fire at the palace. Both sounded better than the fate that would soon be hers.

"Must you take forever? You were supposed to be dressed."

Cassandra looked down at the rope-decorated tunic. "I...am," she choked out.

He reached down for the cloak, pulled it from beneath her toes. The anklets rolled out, and clanked together as they hit his boots.

"More? You had more treasure on you?"

"An...kles." The word contained a sobbed note despite the hold she exerted. But he didn't seem to notice or care about that, either.

"I see."

He bent and picked them up. She heard rustling as he secured them in the bag. She didn't move her view from the toes of his boots.

"I can't believe any man put that much gold and gems on one woman, even if she was his favorite."

Cassandra nodded. She could tell him the truth, but he was leaving her. What would it ever matter?

"Are you going to come here, or make me come and get you?"

"What?"

Surprise held her immobile, eyes wide, mouth open. She'd been wrong? He wasn't leaving her?

"You question me? Still?"

She daren't answer. She was filling with something akin to incomprehensible joy. She thought she'd burst. He kept his gaze on his hands as he shook out his cloak to swirl it around her shoulders, deftly securing the ties at her throat. He pulled the hood over her head, grabbed one side of the front opening to haul it across her torso, and brought the other side over to cocoon her. Fabric swathed her, head to foot. He left just enough room for her to see if the hood didn't droop.

And he was talking the entire time.

"I am *not* taking you from this tent and up on a horse with me unless you are completely and totally covered. For that we need my cloak. I should think it obvious. And I cannot believe I am explaining myself. Now. Ready? No more wasted words? No more argument?"

She nodded her head inside the hood. Then she shook it. Then nodded again. The cloak didn't move, but he must have seen or guessed her answer. She couldn't speak. She was singing soundlessly, dancing without movement, and laughing with abandon.

Inside.

Where it wouldn't show.

"*Women!*"

He made it a curse word and then he completely stunned her. Rather than sling her over his shoulder, he bent and lifted her, one arm beneath her knees, one behind her shoulders. He pulled her close, his arms hard. Strong. A shaft of something speared her. Cassandra was atremble with it. She'd never experienced anything like this before, either. And then he moved, ducking his head to shove beneath the door, then walking with sure strides, the entire time carrying her like she was something precious, rather than chattel to be transported. To Cassandra, it resembled floating. She was radiant with relief and glee and hoped the swaddling hid it.

Emin joined them. Rhoenne spoke. She already knew his voice was impressive. Hearing it with her ear pressed to his chest was an extraordinary experience.

"Why aren't you mounted?"

"I was fetching sandals."

"She won't need them."

"Yes, Excellency."

At the title, Rhoenne huffed something that didn't sound like pleasure, and there was a definite hitch to his stride before it resumed. Several steps later, he stopped. Cassandra lost the support of his arms as he set her atop a horse. If she wasn't aglow with emotion, she'd be frightened. She'd ridden in her youth, but never sideways, in front of a saddle, or with her limbs plastered in place.

The only steadying influence was his hand on her waist. There was enough light in the vicinity to see quite a number of horses, most carrying a rider, some with large packs. Cassandra averted her gaze. She turned her head to the right, back the way they'd just come.

Toward the light and noise.

The camp was set up in an area surrounded by dunes. At the moment it was lit by torchlight, loud with celebratory sounds including shouts, laughter, and more than one crash. Wagons, piled with goods circled a fair-sized center space where a bonfire was burning. Quite a number of men were milling through the area, whistling. Ranting. She heard more than a few shouts regarding their departure. And some that contained slurs about women that sent a stab of fear.

Thank you, God. Thank you.

Cassandra sent a silent prayer winging to the heavens before turning her head back. The knight was before her, cinching something beneath the horse's belly. His left hand was still about her waist, holding her in place. The burnoose he wore made him appear even more massive. His shoulders were really impressive. The cloak hid how she licked at her lips, but not what might show in her eyes. She turned her head before he noticed. Focused on the horse's mane between its ears.

"Is that a woman or a carpet, Ramhurst?"

The man with the cultured voice spoke. She didn't know which man he was. She didn't check.

"You are annoying, Henry."

The answer was spoken right beside her ear. Cassandra jerked. His hand tightened as he caught it.

"*Moi?* Annoying? I merely comment on what seems to be an overly deft manner of...packing."

There were some snorts and snickers from those about them. The knight gave a heavy sigh.

"I have cause to wonder if the poor woman can breathe," the man continued.

"My problem. Not yours. Start riding."

"We are all mounted save you, my laird."

Cassandra made things infinitely more difficult by turning to face him. He had his left foot in the stirrup, his leg crooked, and an extremely defined thigh on display. The burnoose had been gathered up, so it was no help. The glance he sent toward her was even less helpful. Cassandra met it. Lost her breath.

"And so we stand about and await your pleasure. As usual," the man continued.

"Henry."

"Yes, my laird?"

It must be true. It seemed like they all waited. And watched. Rhoenne reached his arm over the horse, grabbed the saddle behind her and lifted, pulling the entire thing slightly askew. She lurched forward, his arm stopped it, before he swung his other leg behind her and slid into the saddle. And then he pulled her close to him.

"There. We are aboard," he announced.

"Very good. Graham?"

A lone whistle split the night from somewhere out of sight beyond a dune. The horses farthest away started first, and then the next, acting like pearls on a chain that had tilted. Their turn came, the horse started up, and Cassandra slid again. His left arm tightened, pulling her closer to him, settling her buttocks into his lap.

Oh my.

The cloak hid the blush, but didn't stay the heat of it. She needed to recall her evaluation earlier. The best way to deal with the knight, Rhoenne Ramhurst was with disinterest. Regardless of how he held her in his lap, cuddled against his belly and chest. Another blush filled her with heat. It was accompanied with a lot of shivers.

From the experience thus far, this journey was going to be difficult.

CHAPTER EIGHT

THIS WAS NOT a good idea.

The woman had her nose against his upper chest, her every breath sending light puffs of air onto his throat where his beard didn't quite reach. He looked down at her. The cloak wasn't enough cover. Although still wrapped about her, it had long since loosened. He'd slighted her earlier, mainly because disinterest and avoidance only worked if you ignore something. He'd have to concede one thing for a certainty. She was an amazingly beautiful woman. It was little wonder the sultan had hidden her away in a harem.

"Cassandra", he whispered to himself.

The hood was open enough he could make out long lashes that sent longer shadows down her cheeks, perfect unblemished skin, and lush kissable lips. Her hair was a source of scent. It had been perfumed. The aroma was flowery and entirely pleasant.

And then she shifted again.

Rhoenne tightened his abdomen, the move pulling him upright. She was a restless sleeper, constantly changing position. Each time he'd expect her to awaken but time and again, she'd settle back without a break in her deep, even breathing. He'd never known anyone to sleep with such abandon, nor in such indefensible positions. At one point, she'd been draped forward across his right arm, numbing it with the weight of her upper body. The numbness had been his fault, however. He could have moved her. Another time, she'd been sprawled before him, her head on the horse's neck, swaying to and fro with each step, her legs balanced on one of his thighs, her feet jutting out into air. She seemed to have an innate ability to plant something into his nether region with each move as well, usually with just a hint of warning. An elbow. A knee. A heel. Sometimes it was a softer portion of her frame. Just now, she was curved into a ball with her head on his left thigh and her legs on his right, it was a section of her buttocks that was shoved into his mid-section. That sent a disconcerting twinge through his lower belly. He ignored it. Everything about her was disturbing. Despite the thick barrier of material about her, he swore he could feel every inch of her.

The only thing worse than allowing her to use him as a sleeping mat, was having her awake. He'd had three hours of that experience already. Every time she'd shifted, he'd been consciously made aware of it. And her. She'd stiffen oddly. His belly would react, sending reaction he had no choice but to notice because he had to staunch it. She'd finally relax into him again. He could go back to ignoring how it felt to have a woman against him. And ponder on why he had to feel anything. He wasn't used to any of this. It had been a relief when she'd finally slumbered.

Perhaps he should have put her on the horse with Henry.

He looked back up at the line of men and horses. There wasn't much to see although a pre-dawn hue was just starting to lighten the horizon, sending long fingered shadows from sand dunes and clumps of scrub brush. With luck they'd be at the oasis Euan had discovered by mid-day. If the men Euan met with at that oasis spoke true, they'd reach Batok within two more days. They were still somewhere in the land called Egypt, where sand and sun blended together, and false images shimmered in and out of existence. It was hard to judge distance. It was hard to do a lot of things. Such as dealing with having a woman in his arms.

He silently swore.

Rhoenne had to consciously force his thoughts to something else. He had bargaining to do. Passage to arrange. The ocean voyage might take two sennights or more to reach the first Christian kingdom. Depending on where, it might take another month to reach his home.

And Tyneburgh.

Tyneburgh was a Highland paradise with burns that ran cold and deep and filled with salmon aching for a fisherman's hook, glens filled with trees and rocks and sheep. The valleys held crofts peopled with industrious clan. The land claimed three lochs so cold they stole a man's breath, and sometimes so warm that mist wrapped the waves. Ramhurst land. His land. He hadn't been back in years. Since the fateful day—

The woman shifted, halting thought again.

Rhoenne instantly tightened his abdomen. The move pulled him straighter. And all she did was shimmy against him with pinpoint accuracy, sending a lot of trouble through his groin, up his belly, and into his chest. Rhoenne sucked in his cheeks. Consciously had to tense and wait for the sensation to die.

This was such a bad idea.

He had little experience dealing with prolonged physical contact with anyone. He'd ponder if and when, but he already knew the answer: *never*.

It was better to look toward Graham, who'd assumed the lead. There wasn't much of a path, and even when they happened upon one, they'd skirt it. This country was fraught with danger. Even without armor and tabards, the crusaders didn't resemble local lads. Red beards covered too many cheeks, while two clansmen were towheads. They'd have gone beardless but a shaved face was cursed with sunburn and whipped with sand pitting, beside being more noticeable. With his dark coloring, Rhoenne could easily pass as one of them if nobody looked at his eyes. Those came from his Norman great-grandfather and namesake. And this line of thought didn't help at all.

So he changed it.

The journey would take six sennights. Give or take. With luck, he'd be back at Castle

Tyne, facing what had to be faced. Rhoenne consciously had to ignore a twinge through his belly. *Damn everything.* He was The Dark One. Feared. Reviled. Remorseless. Emotionless. A shell of a man. Thinking of his home was just self-defeating. He sure as hell didn't need the regret and guilt that accompanied it.

Rhoenne blinked and focused on the group again. The horses were roped to each other, keeping the line uniform and together. It also made it convenient to doze without risk. Most of the others were in that state, sending occasional snores and grunts into the night. Rhoenne remained wakeful, as was his wont. That left a lot of time for introspection. He was in the midst of the line, since he was the weakest link. He rode double, and he had the added problem of a female. No doubt she'd be completely useless if danger struck.

This was not honor.

This was a bad idea.

To maintain their pace and still gain rest, the lead riders changed. They'd done it twice thus far. The leader would move to one side, fade back toward the end, and get replaced. A group of riders could cover a lot of territory this way. Ramhurst clansmen were old hands at this. They'd learned this method a long time ago. It was the best way to avoid a skirmish. Escape an errant band of Sassenach soldiers. Return from reaving against a rival clan. Or sneak back from a jaunt into town that would see them whipped by their sires if they'd been caught.

And he hadn't thought of that in years.

Rhoenne smirked. Regarded the men again. He didn't know why some mercenaries wished to accompany them, rather than share in the spoils back at camp, but he figured every man had reasons. Sooner or later, they'd get known. It wasn't his problem. He had enough of those already.

From the front, a brisk whistle split the air. The lead horses had halted. Graham was around a bend, and couldn't be seen. Almost instantly the Ramhurst clansmen were armed, off their horses, and ready to spring into action. It was an impressive response, honed from two years in this hell-hole. The mercenaries were slower, but within moments, they too were battle-prepared. All looked drowsy. The eunuch had dismounted as well, but he stood beside his horse with a quizzical expression on his face. Rhoenne alone was still mounted. He'd stopped his horse. No one saw the motion to snag two knives from his belt. He held them at his waist, hidden by the cloak Cassandra wore. Other than that, he hadn't moved. He looked over the group without expression. Cassandra's current position was beneficial. He didn't need an arm or hand to hold her in place. She didn't even pause in her breathing.

"Ramhurst!"

Henry's harsh whisper came from his right side. Rhoenne turned the horse a quarter turn. Nodded slightly at the man.

"You don't dismount?"

"I'm waiting," he responded also using a whisper. Not due to any danger, but he was trying to keep Cassandra asleep and unaware.

"For what?"

"Another whistle. One means alert. Two for action. You ken the signal."

Henry groaned. He wasn't the only one. The others stood from their crouched stances, returned swords to scabbards, arrows back to quivers. Bows back to saddles. It was amusing enough to smile, but Rhoenne remained expressionless.

"You." Henry motioned one of them. "Jog up there and see what all the fuss is about."

A couple of Ramhurst clansmen took off. Men started rubbing at bearded faces. Stretched and yawned. Some separated from the group to relieve themselves and returned. All soundlessly. Then Henry spoke, but it was a bit louder than his whisper.

"Well. We are awake. Might as well break the fast. We fried gruel into cakes. Who has the pack? My laird? You wish one?"

"Aye." Rhoenne reached and accepted a misshapen flat pancake. He munched and swallowed a bite and was ready to bite off another one before Henry spoke again.

"You wish one for your woman?"

Rhoenne almost answered to reiterate once again that she was not his woman. Something stopped him. There was a distinct silence about them as if the men not only waited for his answer, but found it of immense interest. And he instantly knew that was what Henry had intended. He took another bite instead. Chewed reflectively and at length as though the cake was tough as well as dry.

"Is that a *nae*?" Henry asked.

"'Tis early yet," he answered, still using a light whisper. "She still sleeps."

One of the men returned, slightly winded. He gave his report in snippets that didn't have much sound. Cassandra continued slumbering as a dead weight on his legs, which was much preferable to having her awake.

"We've got vultures ahead. Circling. Just over the next rise."

"Vultures," Henry returned.

"Aye."

"Right. I'd better go check." He looked to Rhoenne for a nod of approval. "Who's with me?"

Euan and Iain volunteered. Henry and the other two slipped horses loose, jumped into saddles and left. Graham and the other man remained out of sight around a dune. One of the mercenaries spoke up.

"So. Looks like we've got us some time to stand about. What do you think we should do?"

"You want to keep your voice down," Rhoenne remarked. "I've got a passenger."

"We are aware of your passenger. Aren't we, men? Very much aware."

The man spoke again, but he'd lowered his volume. Rhoenne narrowed his eyelids. Regarded them without expression. Felt his heart rate quicken. His muscles tighten. Gut clench.

Surreptitiously, his left hand moved the hilt of one blade and then the other as he positioned them between his fingers.

"Serkan. Right?" Rhoenne asked.

"That is my name, yes."

The mercenary still spoke in a low voice, but there was a challenging tone to it. Rhoenne had known the woman was going to be trouble. And just look. Here, it was. The odds against him were not overwhelming, even with the handicap of Cassandra. But then he watched his odds vastly improve, while they didn't even notice.

"You want to show us the woman now?" Serkan had a distinct swagger to both his tone and mannerism. It was probably bolstered by the men around him.

Show? That wasn't what was being requested, and everyone knew it. The question of why these particular men had accompanied the crusaders to Batok was getting answered, and he should have known what it was.

"She's sleeping," Rhoenne replied.

"Well...she wouldn't even know if we sneak a peek then, would she?"

There was the smallest hint of movement to his thigh as if the weight resting on his legs reacted. Rhoenne considered it for a moment before answering. "You appear to have forgotten something."

"What would that be?"

"You are going to have to go through me," he informed them conversationally.

"There are seven of us. And only one of you. I

think the odds are in our favor. You agree?"

"I think you'll need to recalculate your odds, Serkan."

"You cannot take all of us."

"Maybe. Maybe not. But you might want to check out her man. He's behind you. I don't know whose bags he pilfered for weapons, but he looks like he'll decapitate most of you before I even get off the horse."

It was difficult to say that without a hint of the amusement bubbling under the surface. They spun as a unit. Rhoenne used the time to get his left hand from behind Cassandra. Knives poised. He watched Emin slash the air menacingly with a sword in each hand, showing he knew how to use them, and quite well. The eunuch had tossed off his robe, exhibiting a physique that promised pain, he had several knives tucked under his wide belt, and his expression was murderous.

Serkan and a few of the mercenaries turned back to Rhoenne. The others didn't take their attention off Emin. All of them looked desperate and confrontational. He'd accepted the inclusion of mercenaries a fortnight ago because there was safety in numbers. He'd wondered how far they could be trusted. Well, that question was settled and he should have known the catalyst would be a woman.

Wasn't it always?

"Now...don't be this way, *komutant*."

"You call me commander now? How...odd," Rhoenne remarked.

"We were just joshing with you. We didn't wish

anyone any harm. Least of all to your woman."

"Of course not," Rhoenne agreed.

"We simply—. It has been a long time for us. And you have the lone woman."

"So?" Rhoenne replied.

"What do you expect us to do? Ignore this?" Serkan was still their spokesman.

"I don't care what you do. I'm going to sit here and enjoy my cake. This lovely sunrise. Wait patiently for the information I requested my men to bring back. You should worry more over what Emin will do."

"Him? What can he do? We are still seven. And you are...one-and-a-half."

A different man spoke contemptuously. Rhoenne twisted and flung one dagger at the speaker's chest. The other one went into Serkan's throat. They all heard gurgling as it found its mark. Emin decapitated the closest man with one swipe. That was impressive. All three bodies sank to the sand. Serkan's body twitched non-rhythmically for some time before stilling.

"Make that four," Rhoenne said in the silence that followed.

The four tossed down weapons and went onto their bellies, arms out. Emin looked over the prostrate men and up at Rhoenne. Then, the man crossed the swords before his chest and dipped his head.

"You need any help with them, you let me know," Rhoenne said.

"I need no help, Excellency."

Rhoenne nodded.

Blood, betrayal, and breakfast. All before sunrise. He truly detested this country.

Rhoenne folded and smashed the remainder of his cake into a massive bite size. Shoved it into his mouth. Chewed. He had it swallowed before leaning forward to whisper in the vicinity of Cassandra's ear, near his left knee. She had to guess he'd suspect. She was shuddering in place. No amount of cloaking covered it. He didn't know how she planned on ending her farce of sleeping, but he figured he'd save her the trouble.

"You need to relieve yourself?" he asked.

She jerked. Slid. He snagged her with an arm, brought her up to his chest. And held her there. She was still shaking. Rhoenne's arm tightened subconsciously. That surprised him. He spoke through the hood.

"I will be moving you. No argument."

She nodded, her head against his throat. Odd warmth spread throughout his chest, unbidden, unwarranted, and completely unwanted. Rhoenne lifted his head in dismay. He held her to him and dismounted. She wasn't particularly heavy, nor was she unwieldy. Emin stood, feet apart, arms folded. Swords held in each hand, blades up. He made a convincing guard.

"We'll be right back. You have trouble, you chop heads."

"I will have no trouble, Excellency," the eunuch replied.

He smiled wickedly. Rhoenne almost returned it before settling for a grunt and nod. He walked to the other side of the horses, set Cassandra on her feet, waited for her to find her balance. The hood tipped back. He reached for the tie at her throat. And then he made the mistake of looking into her gaze. The sun was just peeking over the horizon, touching her eyes with pale yellow light and making them glow. Rhoenne's heart gave a mighty thump, his breath snagged, the weight in his gut sent a warning spark. His knees even wavered. He was locked in place. Spellbound. Rapt. The entirety of it surprised, dismayed, and then it angered.

He was not the type to be bowled over by a woman's beauty.

Hell sounded better.

Rhoenne ripped his gaze from hers, turned his head aside, gritted his teeth, and unwound the cloak by feel. Once freed of her, he held it out creating a circle of privacy around her.

"Be quick."

The words were harsh. It was the best he could manage. Chivalry was a farce. Honor right behind it. He was mentally devising a fitting punishment for Henry when she cleared her throat.

"Finished?" he asked.

"Yes."

Rhoenne worked at covering her again, doing his utmost to ignore everything about her. He avoided anything to do with another glimpse at her face or into her eyes, but he couldn't help noting the swell of her breasts...the smallness of her waist. It was impossible to overlook, since she'd done the damnable deed of lacing a rope about herself in order to highlight her curves.

He swaddled her with ruthless efficiency before hauling her up into his arms again. The tight wrapping would be problematic before long. The sun wasn't fully up, and already it heated the air. He didn't care. Not right now. He could easily see why the men in this country kept their women covered or hidden away.

Cassandra kept her nose against his throat as he carried her, making him even more aware of her and what his body experienced about it. There was absolutely nothing he could do to stop or even temper it. He strode past where the mercenaries sat in a huddled group overseen by Emin. Nobody had done anything about the bodies of their fallen comrades, although the line of horses had moved as far away as their reins allowed.

Good.

At least his reputation for killing without remorse or regret was beyond reproach.

Rhoenne had just set her up on the saddle when Henry appeared from around the dune, Euan and Iain at his heels. Rhoenne kept his palm on the small of Cassandra's back and turned to his man. Worked to keep a flush hidden as Henry stopped before him.

"You had trouble?"

"Not much. What did you find out?" he asked.

"I should have left clan here for you."

"No need. What are we looking at?"

"The woman?"

Rhoenne sighed heavily. "Henry. Any trouble is past. Now, report. What do we have?"

"Recollect the deserters I spoke on?"

"They didn't get far I see. Dead? Robbed?"

"Aye. Wagons and horses are gone, too."

"You note any missing hands? Disembowelment? Mutilation of some kind?"

"What manner of man would do such a thing?"

"One with a prior claim of ownership. Pronouncing judgment."

They both glanced at where Cassandra perched.

"The sultan?" Henry asked.

"None other. He's a *Mamluk*. You heard about the final battle of *Fariskur*. Did they sound like civilized men to you?"

"Hmm. True. Well. I cannot say about mutilation. The vultures make quick work out here, my laird."

"They have any clothing?"

"Stripped bare."

"We may be in luck, then. Either way, we've got two days and nights ahead of us and less chance for rest than afore. Mount up."

"What of them?"

Henry pointed to the four defeated mercenaries. Rhoenne looked them over dispassionately.

"Leave them. We take the horses. Supplies. Weapons."

"We leave them nothing?"

"They had my fate set. I'm being generous. They've got a fair walk to the oasis or a longer walk back. Not my issue."

"Fair enough. What of him?"

Henry pointed at Emin. Rhoenne twisted his lips to stop the smile. The eunuch knew what they pondered. He looked even more dangerous somehow.

"Emin has taken possession of some weaponry. I approve. Handle any replacements. We've got spare swords and knives now. These barbarians do make good steel. Now, cease wasting time and words. The days do not lengthen, nor does my patience expand. Mount up."

Rhoenne put his foot in a stirrup, lifted into the saddle, looped an arm around Cassandra and yanked her back against him. He heard her gasp. He meant it to look as possessive as it undoubtedly did. He only wished it didn't feel so right.

He instantly amended the thought.

He wished it didn't feel like anything at all.

CHAPTER NINE

THEY REACHED AN oasis late afternoon.
Cassandra couldn't recall a journey as miserable. If she'd still worn any kohl from the harem, it would have run off. She was miserably hot, itchy with continual rivulets of moisture that plastered the gauzy material from the harem to her skin, sapped and somnolent from heat, dry-mouthed with thirst. This, despite the three times a man had ridden close enough to hand Rhoenne a goat-skin bag filled with water, and he'd allowed her to drink most of it before quenching his own need. This experience didn't bear any resemblance to how she'd traveled with the sultan.

She'd journeyed into another world.

When the harem traveled, women were escorted under guard into lavishly appointed, horse-drawn covered sedan carts, lined with padded silks and filled with pillows. Curtains were drawn, sealing the women in, making a luxurious cage. Every need or desire had been anticipated and fulfilled. There were other carts in the caravan, loaded with food. Drink. Sundry items that included musical instruments, writing implements, reading material, and everything needed for adornment: Garments, jewelry...cosmetics.   Soldiers and eunuchs provided escort and protection, some mounted, many afoot.   Slaves ran alongside, bearing all manner of refreshment. Fruit baskets. Sometimes figs, dates, pistachio, and other nuts. Flagons of cool fruit juice. Pots of brewed tea. An assortment of cheeses. Breads. Freshly grilled skewers with succulent chunks of lamb, beef, goat, and the usual green peppers, onions, and eggplant. Sometimes, they'd even been offered pastries stuffed with dates or figs.

Sun may have beat down on the coach but the interior was dim, the air perfumed. If it got unbearably stuffy, a slave would be brought inside, to wave an ostrich or peacock fan on the occupants. They'd always seemed grateful for the chore. She'd wondered at that. What creature would prefer a cage to freedom? Now, she wasn't so sure.

She wasn't certain of much anymore.

No one had sufficiently described the dangers of life outside the harem walls. She'd read some of the romantic poems, listened to the stories. It was a way to while away time. She'd thought the prose overly descriptive, ludicrous, and trite. Now she knew the stories were complete fantasy.

None of them had any resemblance to this experience. Constant riding. Little food beyond a dry cake to nibble on and then suck into swallowing consistency. Brackish tasting, warm water. A back ache developed from staying in one position all day. Her backside felt bruised and sore. Numbness intermittently claimed arms and legs. Each inhalation contained suffocating air filled with the odor of her once beautifully oiled and perfumed hair. Except for when the knight offered her food or water, Cassandra kept the cloak closed. The alternative was peering through waves of heat that burned her eyes, and reflected light so bright it pained.

Perhaps there were valid reasons women coveted a position in a harem. It didn't seem possible, but she might need to rethink her every assumption, even the most entrenched ones.

That was a frightening proposition. Almost as scary as experiencing this strange world she'd been jettisoned into. She'd likened harem life to a never-ending pursuit of nothingness. A prison with silken walls...but still – a prison. It was dangerous, too. Although placid on the surface, Cassandra had observed malevolent female machinations. She'd witnessed death. Poisoning was common. But never had she listened to death dealt with such horrifying efficiency as it had been this morning. Violence such as that would never have occurred in her presence before. No man would have been allowed close enough to warrant it.

No wonder Emin spoke as he had! Now she knew what he'd meant when he told her he wasn't strong enough to protect her. He wished to stay with this knight? She could well see why. Until her lot improved, she shared the sentiment. So Cassandra leaned against him all day, suffering without complaint. It wasn't due to weakness or a sore backside. Being with Rhoenne Ramhurst meant safety, and in this world she resembled a newly hatched chick.

The analogy should have been amusing.

It wasn't.

She wasn't used to going without stimulating her mind for this long, either. In the harem, there was always a way to mute the life-sapping quality of each day. Something of interest happening. Something to put her mind to. A new language to learn. Now she had a comparison. Time droned on, the horse kept a back-aching sway, stifling heat plagued her, and she had nothing to temper it save the boredom of her own thoughts.

And fears.

And worries over what this Rhoenne might do.

Or not do.

The group rode in virtual silence the entire day. Steady. Constant. It came as a surprise when they halted. Then one of them spoke.

"Well. Well. What have we here," someone announced.

"Looks like we've got a settlement ahead, lads."

"That is not a settlement, Grant. 'Tis a hole in the ground. A couple of trees. A mud brick hut. A penned goat. Oh. My mistake. They've got two goats."

The speaker had to be Henry, the man with the cultured voice. He possessed wit and a quick tongue, as well.

"This is it? A hole in the ground?"

"That is a well," another man pointed out.

He had a higher-pitched voice than the others, making it easy to pick his out.

"Are you telling us we've reached your oasis, Euan? Finally?"

"So I got lost. I'm not the lone one."

The high-pitched voice belonged to Euan. Cassandra made a mental note.

"That what you call it? Lost? We backtracked at least twice."

"Three, if you count the mirage." Henry said.

"Henry." Rhoenne spoke. Throbs of bass notes went through her ear. Cassandra started. He huffed out a breath that might have been amusement at her reaction.

"My laird?"

"Go. See if there is a charge for water."

"Bargain us a meal while you're at it."

That was the first speaker, Grant. Cassandra made another mental note matching voice to name.

"What if they can't cook?"

"It's got to be more edible than the slop we make." Euan's high-pitched voice came again.

"What should I use for funds? Have we...gold, perchance?"

Rhoenne sighed hugely, moving Cassandra too. Henry was saying something with the reference. Something only he and Rhoenne knew. And now Cassandra. She'd bet he'd been told of her jewels.

"We have a lot of extra horses," Rhoenne replied.

"And they are expensive to keep. I'm going to

need a lot of gold for that as well."

"Why don't you go see if anyone at this oasis would like the chore instead?" Rhoenne pointed out.

"Ah. You want me to trade horses. Good plan. Smart."

She heard sounds that equated with horses being separated and herded.

"Well. Our Rhoenne is smart. That's why he's the laird." Grant remarked.

"He's the laird because his father was laird. And his father before that. And his father afore that. And afore that—have I reached the first earl yet?"

Cassandra reeled in place without moving, her eyes wide. Rhoenne Ramhurst was an earl? *An earl?* Her mind repeated it in stupefaction. He was a nobleman? She knew what that entailed. She came from royalty. Her father had been a prince! Noblemen were sworn to a code of chivalry. They embodied courtesy, honor, courage, and a willingness to protect the weak. And this Rhoenne had actually considered leaving her to monsters?

And still might?

"You're shaking."

His quiet observation halted every thought, turning her reaction into a heated ball that surrounded her heart and then squeezed. She couldn't believe she'd actually found him handsome, and struggled with a response to his kiss. She knew to look beneath the surface. The prettiest face sometimes hid the most evil. Rhoenne Ramhurst may be the most beautiful man birthed. But his soul didn't match.

If he even had one.

"You need a rest?" he asked.

Did she need a rest? She needed decent food. Cool water. A soft sand scrubbing followed by a bath in tepid water. A massage with warmed oils. Her hair combed out by someone patient enough to work out all the snarls. And she needed it oiled and then re-braided. But mostly, she needed distance from him!

"I need...a bath," she finally answered.

A soft chuckle rumbled through him. "Well. That will not be happening."

She would have stiffened if her back wasn't a mass of ache.

"You are not entertaining, lass. Not that I particularly care. I just want you to know."

She sucked in air, but was saved further response by another announcement from one of them. She couldn't assign the name.

"Hark! Henry returns. He's not bringing horses. Looks like a good sign."

"We are getting a rest? Finally?"

"Apparently," Rhoenne answered.

"A long one?"

"Long enough to fill water bags. Stretch legs. Eat," Rhoenne replied.

"Sleep?" Someone asked.

"Sleep in the saddle. We've got time to make up."

"Or we can just go sleepless, like you do," Henry must have joined them, since that was his remark.

"Oh, he sleeps. I've seen it. It's the way he wakes that you need to be wary of."

That sounded like the one named Grant, but she couldn't be sure. And despite everything, Cassandra actually felt herself blush.

"How I sleep, or if I do, isn't going to get us food and water." Rhoenne's reply accompanied how he tensed his legs, shifting to start the horse. And Cassandra felt every bit of it. "And we have added worries now."

"How so?"

"We just painted a bigger target on our backs."

"We did?"

"We bartered with prime horseflesh. The sultan's palace was just destroyed and plundered. You know how rumor spreads on the air out here. Don't tarry overmuch. And we don't want to get lost again, either."

Any camaraderie or joking was instantly quelled. Cassandra considered it as they approached the settlement. Rhoenne Ramhurst was morose. Enigmatic. The man could put a damper on a celebratory feast. No wonder they called him dark.

The horse stopped again. Rhoenne jumped from behind her, gaining her an instant shiver. She hadn't realized how hot it was between them.

"See to your mistress." He was walking away if his voice was any indication. Cassandra lifted a finger and opened the cloak a slit. The men hadn't been succinct. The horse had stopped beneath a grove containing more than two trees. A bit of green shrubs and wild grass was beneath their feet as well. The horse bent his head and started plucking at it.

"Highness? Will you grant me permission to touch you?"

"Yes. Please. And Emin?"

He'd reached for her, but stopped at her query, calmly waiting with his head bowed deferentially.

"Thank you," she solemnly said.

He lifted his head, straightened, and then gave an enormous grin, his white teeth flashed against his swarthy complexion, and she could have sworn he flushed. The cloak hid her answering smile.

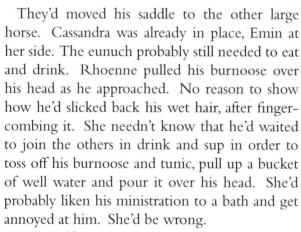

They'd moved his saddle to the other large horse. Cassandra was already in place, Emin at her side. The eunuch probably still needed to eat and drink. Rhoenne pulled his burnoose over his head as he approached. No reason to show how he'd slicked back his wet hair, after finger-combing it. She needn't know that he'd waited to join the others in drink and sup in order to toss off his burnoose and tunic, pull up a bucket of well water and pour it over his head. She'd probably liken his ministration to a bath and get annoyed at him. She'd be wrong.

It was self-preservation.

He was traveling through a sun-baked desert, and he needed a cooling off. That was insanity at its finest. So was her request for a bath.

A bath?

There was no way he'd allow Cassandra to take

off one layer of clothing. She was definitely not disrobing enough to bathe. The thought alone was troublesome. Nothing made it dissipate. It required a bucket-full of water to handle. The realization irked. Irritated. And angered. And that made him scowl.

Emin looked over at his approach. Nodded sagely. Then sprinted for the far side of the tree grove. He'd obviously delayed his own needs in order to protect Cassandra. Such loyalty was laudable, and interesting, given his skill and present company. He had to sense the Ramhurst clansmen were the most trustworthy men alive, and neither man living at this oasis looked like they'd be trouble, even if they were inclined to add more wives to those they already claimed.

The eunuch would need to grab a skewer or two, quench his thirst, and do it rapidly. The others were already assembling and roping together the dozen horses they'd selected for the continuing trek.

They had two more days before they'd reach Batok. Or one night and tomorrow. Rhoenne didn't know for certain. He hadn't studied it, and he wasn't inclined to care. He was only grateful. Having a woman accompanying his every move, preying on his mind, was problematic.

Problematic?

It was hell.

He looked up at her shrouded form sitting sideways in front of his saddle. She really looked little. Lost.

"Did he bring you water? And sup?" he asked.

She shook her head. Rhoenne swore beneath his breath. "I'll see it fetched."

"Wait."

She lifted an arm, stretching the cloak, and easily defining her curves. The small waist. Nice buttocks...

Rhoenne cursed silently this time.

"Your man, Henry brought them."

That must have happened while Rhoenne was rinsing off. The man needed to be horse-whipped. Rhoenne regarded her for a long moment.

"You know his name?"

She nodded.

"Don't think to use it."

"Use...what?"

"I know exactly what women do. And how they use it. And I'm telling you in advance. Don't try it. Not on my men. And especially not on me. I'm immune."

She lifted a hand up through the tie at her throat to tip the cloak hood back. He expected her to be glaring hatred at him. Instead, her expression was serene and completely inscrutable. But her eyes!

He already knew she was stunningly beautiful, but her eyes were beyond description, easily her best feature. He'd labeled them green. At the moment, they looked like deep wells of molten gold. Luminous. Ever-changing. He didn't know what was going on, but he got an instant impression that she not only knew his every secret but she knew the panacea, as well. Rhoenne had to lock every muscle to keep eye contact with her and ignore a heavy buzzing that filled each ear. The thump of his own elevated heartbeat. The instant parched feeling of his throat. His voice was harsh, the words clipped.

"Oh, good. We understand each other. Once again."

She lowered the hood without answering one way or the other. Then she turned her head aside as if to look over their horse's head. It was an obvious effort to dismiss him. And that would have to do. He'd done what he set out to do. Put her back into the same category in which he held all women. That way he could handle her frame against his again. Held close. All night. He pulled in a huge breath. Looked at his right hand actually shake. He disguised it by reaching around her to grab the other side of the saddle, ignored the softness of her hip against his forearm, and lifted himself up and into place. The hard saddle bore a small uptick of rolled leather at the back, a knob of leather at his front. Rhoenne settled into place, before wrapping his left arm about her, to pull her into a secure berth between his legs. She was stiff and unyielding the entire time.

Rhoenne almost smiled.

"Someday I hope you'll explain this to me."

Rhoenne lifted his head at the soft words. It took a moment to awaken, another to comprehend. Cassandra had her knees tucked up beneath her, and she was snuggled against his chest. And he'd had his chin atop her head.

"All these dark hours. Awake. With naught to do...save ponder."

Henry spoke again, the words soft, almost whispered. Rhoenne turned his head to the right and then looked down. Henry rode alongside, but he was a smaller man, and his mount was a good hand shorter than the horse Rhoenne rode.

Rhoenne mentally shook himself. Blinked on the realization.

He'd dozed?

"I mean, you were ever this way. Even as a lad. You wouldn't stay in your tower chamber. We'd post guards, yet you managed to evade them more times than not."

"Henry."

"Remember the time we discovered you atop the dovecote? Your father was preparing for a clan war before we found you. And none could decide how you'd managed to climb there while fully asleep. I oftimes pondered what you saw in these long, dark hours."

"Henry," Rhoenne cautioned again.

"My laird?"

"What do you want?"

"Oh. I am having difficulty sleeping. And I knew you would be wakeful. So..."

"You decided to converse with me about nonsensical things," Rhoenne supplied.

"More or less," Henry agreed. "Perhaps you could help?"

"With what?"

"This mystery. I cannot fathom what it is about

these night hours that would keep a man awake... unless he is on guard duty or leading a group of wanderers through danger-infested deserts, such as Grant up front there."

"I like the solitude," Rhoenne responded.

"Ah. Solitude. I have found that if one is of prickly temperament, large stature, and frightens off all save the most brave of souls, one usually earns solitude."

"If you have a point, make it and have done."

"I am just musing aloud. You know, at one time I actually wondered if mayhap wakefulness could be a learned skill...because of worry over what might ensue."

Looking down briefly, Rhoenne muttered, "brave words, my friend."

"True. One thing I have discovered about this. It is easier to be brave if it is a dark, moonless night, one is atop a horse, and the object of one's pointed remarks cannot do much except glare."

Rhoenne sucked in his cheeks. Considered Henry's words. He should take offense. Think of a cutting reply. But something about the woman asleep in his arms made it difficult to even think about umbrage. He'd been regarding his man with a baleful look. He was surprised Henry called it a glare.

"Does she have a name?"

"Who?" Rhoenne asked automatically.

"Your woman."

"She's not—" Rhoenne stopped his own protestation. "Her name is Cassandra. Cassandra Alexa-something." He was afraid his voice warmed on the name.

"So...is she bonny?"

"Henry."

"Oh, come now. It's the midst of the night. Everyone sleeps. I have little to occupy myself, except ponderings over why you fear sleep enough to forego it. The least you could do is satisfy a poor old man's curiosity."

"You are lucky I'm atop this horse with a woman asleep in my arms."

"True. So conceded. So...is she?"

"Is she what?" Rhoenne asked crossly.

"Bonny."

"Oh. Yes."

"She's bonny, eh?"

"Yes."

"How...comely?"

"Henry."

"You are the one who just whetted my curiosity. You could have kept telling me to mind my own business, but no. You had to tell me she's comely. Well. Now I am very curious. So. Tell me. Is she as beauteous as France's Queen Margaret?"

Rhoenne sighed audibly.

"When she was younger, of course," Henry added.

"I believe I already commented that you spent too much time at the French court," Rhoenne informed him.

"Not more than a year."

"Closer to three."

"Didn't feel that long."

"That's because we've been out on crusade for

almost two years, as well. Put it together."

"We've been away from home a good five years. That does not bode well for a homecoming. Is that what you're trying to say?"

Rhoenne didn't reply. He didn't like the answer.

"So. Are you going to tell me?"

"Tell you what?"

It was Henry's turn to sigh, but his was exaggerated enough to put many a court jester to shame. "How comely your Cassandra is."

"You are very persistent. I'll give you that."

"Ramhurst. I am your most trustworthy man. I would never betray a hair on your head. I've devoted years of my life to your service. Good years. Long years."

"Is that supposed to mean something?" Rhoenne asked.

"I'm seven and thirty. Nigh two score. *Auld* age is around the corner. 'Tis time I settled down. Found a wife. Have a few bairns. Raise a few sheep. It would behoove me to find a...comely woman in this plan. Yes?"

"Don't even think about it."

"Think what? I merely muse on my future plans, and you get all prickly and possessive. And it's not as if you want her...although, if you did return after an absence of five years with a woman in tow – and a comely one, I think Aileen would drop dead with the shock."

Rhoenne's back clenched. The rest of his muscles weren't far behind. His belly burned next. His skull took the equivalent of a hammer blow. Then his chest joined in, feeling as if his heart was squeezed in a vice. He had to wait until the sensations ebbed enough to answer noncommittally. Even then, he didn't trust his voice.

He held Cassandra's sleeping form against him to lean left, searching with his right hand beneath his burnoose for the bag. He eased the drawstring open. Fished out one of her anklets. Brought his hand back out. Then held it out to Henry.

"What is this?"

"Take it. You'll be handling the bargaining."

Henry took the piece. Twisted it. Available starlight twinkled on the gems and gold. The man gave a light whistle of appreciation. "We will get passage easily with this."

"That is but a taste, my friend."

"A taste?"

"You wanted to know how comely she is. Well. Now, you know."

"Holy Mary, Mother of God."

"Exactly."

"So when will I get to see her?"

"Not sure. You might not."

"Rhoenne."

"Do na' take that tone again. I'm warning you."

"You are not thinking of leaving her in Batok... are you?"

"Me? I'm simply waiting to enjoy the long dark hours ahead of me. In solitude."

"Rhoenne."

"Rest easy. You have given me something to ponder, Henry. Your idea has merit. I need time to ponder it."

"Which idea?"

"Aileen. Dropping dead."

Rhoenne kept his voice perfectly flat and emotionless. It still contained a measure of hatred. He knew Henry heard it. The starlight didn't just make the jewelry glint. It brought out the whiteness of Henry's teeth with his smile.

CHAPTER TEN

THEY REACHED BATOK in the early hours of the second day. Horses had sensed it well before the men, their steps quickening while clansmen slumbered away. The road meandered around more and more impressions of settlement. Heat shimmered across the night air. They were well into this country's inundation period. A sliver of moon sent vague illumination onto leagues of fields awash in water, buildings in the far-off distance, shadowy hulks of ancient structures that littered the land. There was an enclosure around the city, although it appeared to have crumbled in places. It wasn't much of a city, and even less of a port, but two large-mast sailing ships were docked, while another one was anchored just offshore. The docked ships looked to be in the process of loading or unloading. The other apparently waited high tide.

Rhoenne turned his attention to Batok. It resembled every other port city in this part of the world. Low mud-brick buildings fronted the water. Other structures dribbled back in alternating squares that attached to each other, some larger, some taller. It created a zigzag maze they'd have to progress through regardless of the street they entered. He had the best path selected before they reached the open gates.

They'd secure lodging first. Then decent food and drink. He had coins in the bag. Not many, but enough to pay for their current needs. They didn't need the jewels yet, but he'd observed Henry digging at the anklet more than once, using a dagger to unseat gems that he secreted away. Henry FitzHugh was smart. Efficient. With his tanned face and dark coloring, he could pass for an Egyptian. Rhoenne could send Emin with Henry to assist with the bargaining, but that meant he'd have to contend with protecting Cassandra. And he'd already had enough of that responsibility.

Rhoenne glanced down at her. He'd kept verbal contact with her to a minimum. She'd returned the effort. But there wasn't anything he could do about the physical portion of this. Every little thing she did seemed calculated to make him aware of her. The days had been difficult. The night hours had become indescribable.

At the moment she slept with her head in the crook of his left arm, her buttocks in the space between the saddle horn and the horse's neck, her legs bent so her knees were jammed into his right side. The cloak was still attempting coverage, but there was no way to conceal the fact that she was a very desirable woman.

Very.

She stirred, as if she knew his thoughts. He

instinctively gripped her thigh with his right hand, stopping any slide. And then he had to deal with a sensation of warmth that blossomed through his chest as if his heart swelled. That sent an invasion of heat down his belly. Fiery trouble flooded his groin, creating a turbulence that he refused to acknowledge or accept. His thighs tightened in defense. His gut, chest, back, arms, even his jaw clenched for the same reason. And it was useless. All of it.

Nothing he tried physically managed to halt this from happening. Mental exorcising failed in even more vivid fashion. He kept silently repeating words, as if they'd create a shield between them. She was a woman. Women were the lowest of creatures. A vile plague. Adam had just been the first man to learn it, back in the Garden of Eden. Women were put on earth to torment and seduce and lie...

Damn it.

No matter what he thought of Cassandra, or how he tried to shove her into the category of scheming ruthless heartless woman, it didn't stop what happened. His heart would swell somehow. His belly would twist. His loins would thicken ominously. His muscles would attempt defense. He'd shudder, stifling things he'd never had to deal with. Not for this length of time, nor at this level. It had happened the last time he'd touched her. The time before that.

And the time before that, as well.

And the time before...

Rhoenne cursed again.

This was war. He refused to lose. Women were a disease. Dealing with one this closely and for this length of time was worse than battle. It was a curse. But it was his to bear. Stoically. And silently. Until he was victorious. Nobody need ever know.

"So. Rhoenne. You going to allow the lass to bathe?"

Rhoenne stiffened further at Henry's words, sucking in and exhaling air as he worked to stifle cravings that he refused to admit. He only hoped he kept it hidden. "What?" he finally responded.

"I am simply willing to put forth my name as an assist with said endeavor. You will consider it?"

"You will be busy bargaining. That ship looks ready to sail."

"We've got a day."

"What makes you so certain?"

"High tide is but an hour away, my laird. That ship would not be at anchor still if it were sailing this morn. I hazard a guess that it prepares to leave on the morrow. Therefore, I appear to have some time on my hands. As do we all."

Rhoenne grunted.

"So. Your lady will enjoy a bath. I would be willing to assist should you grant her one. You will think on it?"

More than he wanted to. Rhoenne cleared his throat. "She has her servant," he answered.

"Why should he get all the joy in life?"

"Because he has been gelded. And you are getting damn close to the same fate."

Henry sniggered. "I see."

"Why don't you ride on, find an inn, and get us a room."

"*A* room?"

"For her."

"It's a mite early yet, Rhoenne."

"So? Wake an innkeeper."

"That is na' the issue, my laird. Innkeepers do na' care about much more than coin. And, begging your pardon, my laird, but what we possess is worth much more than a rented room. We could purchase an entire inn with a couple of stones. It is simply a trifle early for the markets to open, and with them, a merchant willing to trade for jewels."

"What do you take me for, FitzHugh?"

"Must I answer that when you are most vexatious? I do value my head...and my loins. Despite my jesting. "

"I have coins."

"Gold dinars?"

Rhoenne nodded.

"Excellent. Well. Hand some of them over. I shall seek out lodgings. With access to a bath for your lady. Anything else you want me to arrange?"

A bath for Cassandra.

A flood of heat sent everything right back to battle-ready status. Rhoenne tightened his thighs so harshly it lifted him from the saddle and upset Cassandra's perch. He had no option but to snag her before she fell from the horse. He had her belly against his, her head against his shoulder, and a dose of liquid attention from her startled, opened eyes.

Oh.

He was in trouble.

"Good catch, Ramhurst," Henry tossed off as he moved away.

He didn't need Henry's laughter. Or his jibe. He needed something drastic. Perhaps even a woman. But one thing was certain. It wasn't going to be this woman. He was going to have to retreat for now. The battle may be lost, but he was not losing the war.

"Come along, Euan. Keep up."

Rhoenne strode down another alley, ducked beneath another awning that wasn't a problem for shorter people, and glanced back to his clansman. The streets were narrow, vendors filled both sides, crowds of shoppers moved about, and Euan hadn't ceased complaining.

Amid stuffing his mouth.

"You really should try one of the meat pies. Seriously, Ramhurst. You should take a bite. It's nigh heavenly."

"I already ate three at the last stall."

"True. But these have some sort of...spice. Oh. Look. Apples. And grapes! Can we just stop and get—?"

Rhoenne spun, flipped him a coin, watched the fellow catch it deftly, snap up a couple of apples and a cluster of grapes. Rhoenne caught a return toss of an apple, started munching on it as he turned back around and resumed walking. He passed an alley. It looked dim. Untraveled. He speared it a look and moved on. The rest of the street held another assortment of stalls, a rug seller, another spice peddler, pot merchant, and a jeweler whose wares glimmered in the sunlight looking a lot like her eyes.

Cassandra...

Rhoenne gave a silent curse and turned aside. Started up another section of the street. They'd built their city on mostly level ground, so it wasn't arduous to walk about, even at a brisk pace. He lengthened his strides, pushing past crowds that every marketplace seemed to spawn. Heavily veiled women walked, surrounded by attendants. Loud street hawkers pushed their wares. Discordant music swelled out of a side street. Sounds of an argument could be heard in another. And none of it did a thing to mitigate his problem.

Euan trotted alongside him, alternately chewing on a meat pie in one hand, and snagging grapes from the bunch that dangled from his other hand. The fellow was like a bottomless food trencher, despite his gangly frame. Rhoenne didn't know where he put it.

"You ken...if you tell me what it is you search for, I might could help you find it," Euan offered.

"A woman."

Euan stopped. Then he had to jog to catch back up. "Well, if that be the case, look about you, man. Women are littering your path. As usual."

Rhoenne turned about. Regarded the mass of humanity filling the street around them. Euan had been exaggerating, but not by much. There were a lot of women in the vicinity, several covered with all-encompassing black cloth. They quickly covered their eyes and looked away. Not so their attendants. Rhoenne intercepted more than a few looks. There were a lot of bold women trying to catch his glance, as well. Among them uncovered women - slaves, and probable harlots, if he wasn't mistaken. He didn't give any a second look. Not one piqued his interest. Most of them were gawking at him. Rhoenne felt a rising flush. He should have kept his hood up.

"It is ever like this around you," Euan remarked. "Must be nice."

"I don't look for just any woman," Rhoenne turned and started walking again.

"Oh. All right. What kind do you search for, then? Tall? Short? Fat? Thin? Auld? Young? Free with her charms? Tight as a maid? What?"

"I should have brought Grant," Rhoenne commented, and brushed past another group of shoppers clogging the street.

"He's keeping the eunuch company."

"He'd better be standing guard."

"That's what I meant. Would you mind not taking such long steps? You make me appear the size of a tot."

Rhoenne snickered. Looked down the next alley. It was darker and even more empty-looking than the last one. But then a shaft of sunlight pierced through the gloom, showing the distinct shadow of a crucifix, while an etched fish on a wall caught his eye.

Well. He'd wanted drastic. Looked like he'd found it.

"Stay here," he told Euan.

"And do what?"

"Keep any from accosting me."

"You've got a lot of women trailing you, my laird."

"Delay them."

"With what?"

Rhoenne handed him two coins. "Use your imagination. Don't you juggle? Play a reed? Tell a fine story? You just said it must be nice to have all this attention. Well. You now have it. Enjoy."

It was a small Christian church, constructed of mud brick. The outside had little save a small cross atop the door peak. The inside was candlelit and decorated with colorful biblical frescos. There were four short benches. An altar. A curtain blocked access to whatever lay behind. It was dark, quiet, and serene in the church, contrasting with the loud, busy enterprise of commerce just down the street. Rhoenne walked up the short aisle and drew his sword. Putting it tip-down into the dirt floor, he went to his knees before the altar. He said a silent prayer. And then he felt a presence.

Rhoenne lifted his head and looked across to where a diminutive priest stood beside the altar. Rhoenne got to his feet slowly. Sheathed his sword. The fellow was smaller even than Cassandra. He frowned at the instant comparison.

He knew plenty of petite women. Why did it have to be Cassandra that instantly came to mind?

"Welcome, my son. Have you come for confession?" the priest asked.

"No, Father. It's a bit late for that."

"It is never too late."

"Then it's too early. I am certain there are still sins I am destined to commit."

"You are a crusader knight."

"Is it so obvious?" he asked. It was an easily answered question. This land belonged to those of Muslim faith. The seventh crusade had been raging through the land for years. Rhoenne carried a western-crafted broadsword. He prayed in a Christian church.

"You seek passage from these shores? Perhaps even...with the Venetian ship at dock?"

Rhoenne went still. "Why would you think that?"

"Come with me. Please?"

The man lifted a candlestick, and walked to the curtain behind the altar. He pushed it aside and gestured Rhoenne to follow. Rhoenne considered it for a scant moment, then followed.

The room was little more than an alcove, containing a table. Stool. A cot. And the scrawniest woman Rhoenne had ever laid eyes on. She sat on the cot. She glanced up at him then quickly looked down to her lap. That one glance was enough. The woman's eyes were large and dark and tormented. They took over her whole face.

"This is Olive."

"Olive," Rhoenne repeated.

"We do not know her true name. That is what we call her."

"She's mute?"

"Her tongue was cut out."

Rhoenne felt the center of his back twinge. He had it covered instantly.

"She was left at our doorstep a month ago. Hauled off a slave trading vessel and left at death's door. We don't know why they cut out her tongue. She cannot say. She has regained her health now."

"This is health?" Rhoenne asked.

"But she is not safe here."

"She's safer here than out there," Rhoenne commented.

"No. In this country, no woman is safe. Surely you have learned that."

Rhoenne nodded.

"You must take her with you."

"Oh. No. No." Rhoenne shook his head, and repeated it. "No.

"If anyone sees her, she is doomed to reenter the life she barely escaped. Surely you know this."

"What makes you think I'm not her doom?"

"That, I cannot answer. I just know she will be safe with you."

"How do you know that?"

"The Lord works in mysterious ways."

"I have heard those words since I was a bairn. I begin to think they are a disguise for when a man has no good argument to offer."

"You came here for a reason, Crusader."

Rhoenne's lips twisted. He barely kept the smile from showing. "True. But it is not what you think."

The priest's downturned eyes said much. "Absolution does not come from prayers and confession, my son."

"What makes you think I look for absolution?"

"'Tis why you knights enjoined on a crusade and pursued war. You have been promised absolution by the Pope. I know the edicts."

"Maybe I came because I like killing," Rhoenne returned.

"Do you?"

Rhoenne smiled humorlessly to himself. "Or maybe I'm here because I heard of fabulous riches. Streets lined with gold."

"Have you found it thus?"

"Or...I might have come because the alternative was worse."

The priest nodded. "I see."

Rhoenne regarded the small man for a length of time, as though deep in thought. "Forgive me, Father, but the answer is still no. I'm sorry. I cannot help you. Or Olive."

Rhoenne turned to leave. He'd lifted the curtain before the priest spoke again.

"But, my son...surely you are in need of a handmaiden at this very moment? You have someone who needs served. Olive is very good with her hands. She is very patient. She is expert with a needle. Her skill at weaving is extraordinary."

Rhoenne paused at the door. Turned. "How

do you know this?"

"I only say the words the Lord puts in my mouth. I do not know anything."

Rhoenne looked at Olive's bent head. Back at the priest. Gave a heavy sigh. He was going to be in for a fine bit of ribbing from his clansmen, starting with Euan. He could already hear it.

"Does she have a covering?" he asked.

The priest touched Olive's arm and motioned her to stand. She was even more bony-looking when she did so. The priest then pulled the coverlet off his bed. It looked the equivalent of sackcloth. The fabric completely covered Olive. It didn't make anything about her look less emaciated or frail. The priest motioned for her to follow Rhoenne. Rhoenne bent down to look into her face. Waited for her to make eye contact. Had to wait for it to happen three times since she blushed the first two times and her glance skittered away. He tried to give her a reassuring expression. She acted like she understood. He nodded. Then he stood and turned back to the curtain. He didn't know what else to try. She'd either follow or not.

Rhoenne pulled two gold dinars from his bag, placed them in the offering jar as he left.

Euan had gathered quite a crowd. It appeared to be due to his juggling skills, which were considerable. When he saw Rhoenne, the three plates he'd been tossing and catching fell with a crash. As did the water jug he'd pitched too, splashing everyone in the vicinity.

There was a general bit of laughter and applause.

Rhoenne strode through them. He didn't look back to see if Olive followed. He was already regretting his decision. He felt like a dupe and a fool. He'd either just complicated his life into a nightmare, or he'd untwisted the knot fate had been mercilessly strapping about him. Either way, he had just gained another woman to protect.

Women!

Euan caught up and started complaining. Rhoenne looked heavenward for a moment.

"Thank the saints! You took forever. I had about run my gamut of tricks!"

"I saw no trouble," Rhoenne replied.

"You don't know how quickly a crowd can turn nasty, and—. Ramhurst? I think you are being followed."

"Really?" Rhoenne replied.

"Yes. Some bird woman. Wait. I'll shoo her away."

"No."

"You want a bird woman to follow us?"

"I bade her to do so."

"You did? Wait. Is this the woman you looked for?"

Rhoenne didn't answer. He couldn't. He didn't truly know anymore.

"Call me dense, but this does not look like a woman you would search out. Is she a relation of some kind?"

"No."

"A...rich noblewoman lost on these shores that we will ransom?"

Rhoenne regarded him for long moments

without breaking stride.

"Verra well. I have a vivid imagination. 'Tis why I tell stories. But I am at loose ends here. She is not rich. She is not a relation. She is not the woman you searched for—."

"I didn't say that."

"Then she *is* the woman you searched for."

"Do you have any coin left?" Rhoenne asked to divert him.

"Aye. Both."

"Good. Go get a honey bun. Get one for... her as well."

Rhoenne nodded with his head to the thin figure directly behind him. That bode well. She had enough sense to stay close. He noticed she was breathing hard and trotting, so he slowed his step as well as decreased his stride length. Both affectations were completely unlike him. He hoped Euan wouldn't notice and make mention. Rhoenne was doing his best to ignore it.

He seemed to be gaining woman trouble by the minute. Henry's comments would be unstoppable.

He was scowling before they reached the inn.

CHAPTER ELEVEN

A SNIFF TOLD HER too much.
    She'd never been this filthy. Ever.

Cassandra dipped her elbow into bath water,
testing the temperature. No longer hot enough
to steam the room, it still resembled heaven.
Temperature didn't matter. She'd embrace it had
it gone tepid. But she refused to enter it until
she'd prepared enough, and without at least one
attendant it was a time-consuming operation.

The moment Rhoenne had carried her into
this chamber, ordered her to stay, and then left,
granting her a measure of privacy, she'd been
working. He hadn't looked back to see her
nod, but she hadn't expected him to. She hadn't
thanked him, either. She should have, and would
have, if everything about him wasn't sending a
silent signal. She hadn't needed the warning.
She already knew he wanted nothing to do with
her, and that included her appreciation. So, she
bestowed it on Emin.

The man was a wonder, but she already knew
that, as well.

Cassandra had been effusive over Emin's first

offerings. Each time he knocked at her door begging permission to enter, he'd brought more. First, he'd borne platters of grapes, plums, dates, figs, cheeses, four kinds of breads – from coarsely ground wheat with bitter bits baked in, to tempting cinnamon twists iced with honey. With his next entrance, he'd brought two platters of skewers, perfectly seasoned and grilled, with alternating chunks of meat and vegetables. Following that, he'd gifted her with three kinds of juices in various jugs, a tureen of chilled water, and then even a pot of brewed tea, with a cup to partake as she wished.

Cassandra hadn't been able to do more than nibble at each selection, although she'd done it twice. She'd only sipped at the drinks. After the journey she'd just endured, she hadn't needed much sustenance before feeling overfull and replete. She'd shed the cloak the moment the door shut behind Ramhurst. Lifted the disgusting weight of what had once been beautifully arranged hair. Starting from the bottom, she'd barely managed to unbraid a hand–length portion before Emin had first knocked, his entrance putting her attention fully on hunger and thirst.

Once those were satisfied, however, she'd become aware again of the itch of unwashed skin, the odor of her unwashed body. The rope webbing she'd tied about Rhoenne's tunic felt solidified into place. It was also loose about her frame. Lush, womanly curves were desired in the harem, and while she'd been slight, she was voluptuous enough to catch the sultan's eye.

Now, she probably looked sickly and spare.

Not that Rhoenne Ramhurst would even notice or care.

The hint of reaction that stabbed behind her eyes at the thought was as disastrous as it was unbidden. She didn't *want* that man noticing her! She wanted the exact same thing he did – to be free of further interaction between them. And that thought sent a throb of what couldn't possibly be sorrow through her chest, while another stab of tears misted her eyes.

Far too stupid to consider, and wasteful of this interim of time he'd given her.

And then Emin had brought a tub!

Oh my!

Remnants of her feast covered the only sleeping platform, the lone table, and the tops of both stools in the room. There was just enough room for a large tub Emin had turned sideways to fit through the poorly-constructed door. Cassandra couldn't contain the reaction. Every hint of sorrow evaporated instantly. She'd clapped and jumped up and down with joy as he set the tub in the center of the room, leaving space to walk around it. She'd been working at the knots in her rope when he knocked for entrance next, bringing cans of heated water that steamed the small enclosure even before he'd poured them. He'd also taken out one of the daggers at his belt and offered it to her, wordlessly helping with the rope. She'd had to cut the rope in more than one place to get it freed and he'd waited, patiently watching. And then he'd held his hand out to retrieve the blade, as if he knew what she'd planned with Rhoenne's little dagger, and thought she'd still consider that option.

She'd never choose death. Not now, when she was this close to her objective! All she needed was passage to the Bulgarian court! Or any court that recognized the Vottenavian name. Returning to her life had been an eight year dream.

The tunic was stuck to her in the exact places the rope had held it, holding it even when the rope was gone. It was revoltingly stained, too. It would be worse when she finished, however. She only hoped there would be time to wash it in her tub when she finished. Hang it to dry. She'd have to do the same with her undergarments. She didn't have another choice. They were all she had.

The tunic had grown even larger, if that were possible. She pushed it off her shoulders and it fell. Then she'd exclaimed in dismay at the condition of what had been beautiful silk attire. The garments had to be peeled off. Cassandra had shuddered with revulsion, and then turned to securing her hair atop her head. The short length of rope came in handy then, and even without help she had it secured into a massive bun atop her head. Large and unwieldy enough to destabilize every movement, it was better than before.

And then she turned to the other supplies he'd brought.

She'd suspected it might take him time to procure olive or palm oil that had been whipped into a thick cream consistency. She'd also asked for a vial of lily extract, packets of powdered myrrh and cinnamon. She needed them to mix into the fragrant *Susinum* perfume that she favored. She should have known he'd be knocking with the items before she'd finished undressing. Cassandra slid behind the door before allowing entrance. Not due to Emin. He'd seen her body enough times it wasn't an issue. The reason for her shyness was the lurking shadow of a Ramhurst man who'd been behind Emin more than once. Cassandra didn't know what might happen if one of Rhoenne's men saw her nakedness. She didn't even dare pursue the thought.

She'd next sent Emin for a fine-tooth comb as well as Natron salts, ash, sandalwood, and lemon extract. The salts could also be mixed with ash, sandalwood and lemon for soap. She'd need more whipped oil however. She'd used most of it in the original vat to coat her body. Emin returned just as she'd reached the small of her back, and considered either leaving her back untouched, or coating the tunic and applying it with that. Emin had a flush about him, but he agreed to smear a handful of cream on her back and shoulders. He'd looked flustered when he'd left her that time. Cassandra was even more embarrassed. She'd covered it over by busily adding and mixing ingredients for both her scrub, and the soap. She'd dumped the ewer of water into the tub so the vessel could be used for the scrub. She'd moved food from the bread and cheese platter onto the fruit platter in order to use the plate for the thick soap mixture. She mixed and molded with her fingers to the perfect consistency. And then she set about coating her body with the scrub mix.

The Natron hadn't been just salt. There were fine grains of sand mixed in. That was helpful, actually. It would slough off the dirt even better. Cassandra rubbed as she applied it to her oiled skin, ignoring her back. She used the tunic to wipe it all off. The garment was a disaster of dirt and oil well before she worked it back and forth on her back and shoulders. She wasn't asking Emin for help again. He would probably thank her wordlessly the next time he knocked. She had a handful of soap mixture and was just preparing to slather it on a leg when the door opened.

Cassandra looked up. Her gasp of dismay was swallowed up by the door slamming and his instant oath. Rhoenne stood there, his jaw locked, his eyes narrowed, and breathing so heavily, the sound reverberated. Cassandra had a foot on the tub, her hand atop her lower leg, and nothing whatsoever to hide behind. After the initial glimpse of him, she quickly looked at a side wall. She didn't have to guess what expression he'd have about anything. He was livid. It sounded in his words, said between set teeth. She didn't have to ask about that, either.

"What...are you doing?"

"Bathing," she whispered.

"Why are you posing?"

Cassandra glanced up at him. Down at herself. *Posing?* "I'm not," she replied.

"Then why does it look like you are?"

She daren't move. In this position, she was barely shielding her nakedness. She didn't know what he expected her to answer.

"Who has seen you? Thusly?"

"Emin." She cleared her throat. Her words still sounded like a fearful whisper. She sounded like a child who'd been caught in disobedience. She couldn't shake the sensation, either.

"Who else have you shown?"

Shown?

Cassandra blushed. Fully and gallingly. She already knew what he thought of her, but having it put in words was callous. And frightening. And for some reason it sent her heart into palpitations that sent pain with each beat, too. She didn't dare delve into that affliction. She didn't trust her voice, either.

She shook her head. The hair mass wobbled. She put her free hand to it to keep it from toppling.

He didn't say anything for such a long time, the steamy enclosure that had felt warm and humid now chilled. It could be due to the removal of her scrub. But she doubted it. She didn't know what to do. Say. Think.

"May I...continue?" She spoke to the wall. She could upbraid herself about the little lost girl voice later. When she found her imperious side. And had some clothing for bravery.

His breathing altered. He gave a heavy sigh. She wished he quit doing that. It raised a lot of trouble all along her skin. All kinds of things she tried to refuse and ignore. Her belly tickled. Her breasts tingled. Her nipples tightened. All of it thankfully hidden in her current position. She darted a glance toward him. He was looking at the ceiling. And then he folded his arms and lowered his head to glare at her. Cassandra lifted her chin slightly and met his look despite how the odd shiver that flew up her exposed back.

"Not in my presence," he finally answered.

Cassandra nodded. Her hair wobbled forward dangerously. She shoved it back a fraction and held it.

"I brought you something. Something you need."

Cassandra blinked. She was afraid the surprise showed. Her shoulders moved back fractionally, and that move sent the mass of hair backward. Her chin tipped up and her body went sideways. She grabbed for her hair with both hands, lost her position at the tub and ended up crouched beside it. There wasn't a more ignominiously position she could have attempted. Tears of humiliation flooded her eyes. She couldn't prevent them.

"It looks like you could use some help," Rhoenne remarked.

"But—."

"I'm not offering. I am not allowing Emin to help you, either. And my men are not coming anywhere near you."

He opened the door. Cassandra peeked up to see that he'd only opened it a hands-width. She watched his shoulders move as he leaned into the aperture. The room was larger than his tent. He made it look miniscule.

"Come."

When that didn't appear sufficient, he twisted, reached out, and brought a figure in by a grasp of his hand on a shoulder. It was a slip of a woman, so thin she looked like her bones might snap. And Rhoenne manhandled her?

Cassandra squelched the instant upset as the woman lifted her head. Her cheekbones were sharp. Pointed. Her features pinched. And her eyes were easily the most terrified Cassandra had ever seen. They took over her entire face.

Rhoenne propelled the woman in front of him before he let go. And then he crossed his arms, and looked down at Cassandra with his usual enigmatic expression.

"You bought a slave woman?" she asked.

He shrugged.

"I thought Christians didn't deal in human trafficking." She couldn't help the note of censure, although she tried.

"I didn't like the alternative."

"Where is she from?

"Don't know."

"What is her name?"

"Don't know."

"She doesn't speak Frank? Or Arabic?"

"She does na' speak at all."

"She's a mute?" Cassandra asked.

"Her tongue has been cut out," he informed her without a hint of inflection.

"Oh, dear God," Cassandra's voice carried the horror. She rose. Instantly realized the mistake, and sank back down.

He hadn't noticed. He'd tapped the woman on the shoulder, and Cassandra watched as Rhoenne waved his hands and pantomimed washing, first his arms and belly. Then his hair. Then he pointed at Cassandra. And then he just looked heavenward in an attitude of defeat.

Cassandra couldn't decipher the woman's expression this time when she looked back down to Cassandra. Then the woman looked back up at Rhoenne. Back again to Cassandra. The dawning realization of what she was being tasked to do chased every bit of fear from her features. She looked stunned. Then inordinately pleased. She nodded. Took off the burka she'd been wearing, folded it, and draped it over the edge of the tub. And then she rolled up her sleeves. She lifted a hand next, pointed it at Rhoenne, and then the door, and then waved, looking exactly like she was shooing him.

Rhoenne's expression was priceless.

Cassandra had to duck her head before he saw any of it reflected on her face.

"I will na' be far," he remarked.

Cassandra sobered before she looked back up. Nodded. The smile wouldn't stay off her lips however. She watched him look there. Then over her head again. And then he gave his heavy sigh. She was probably in luck that he'd gone before her snort of amusement turned into laughter.

He was on this third tankard of ale before

anyone bothered him. He'd given the men leave from guard duty and strict orders to leave him alone. That was after he'd stripped down to just his jewelry-filled bag, taken a maliciously strenuous swim in the ocean, toyed with shaving before discarding the notion. Then he'd dressed in new Arabic-inspired long trousers, and a tunic with embroidered edging. It was a slim-fitting tunic that hugged his chest uncomfortably despite being the largest Emin had purchased. He'd sent the eunuch on a shopping expedition, to keep him from any further view of Cassandra, but also to purchase attire.

For her.

Rhoenne didn't care what style, what material, or what price. He just wanted her covered, the larger and more voluminous the outfit – the better. What had happened? All the knights now wore new attire, but at least a trunk had been delivered to the door of her chamber. And the skinny wench had taken possession of it after Emin knocked.

He knew the last because he'd been morosely positioned at the end of the hall by then. He hadn't left her unguarded, however. He'd added Iain and Graham to Grant's duty of watching her door while he'd swum. With the warning that he'd personally punish anyone who disturbed her.

Disturbed her?

What a farce.

She was not the one being disturbed.

Rhoenne took another quaff of beer. Swallowed. He'd already eaten as much as he could hold, finished his repast with a cup of thick coffee, and downed two tankards of ale in rapid succession. And all of it was an effort to keep his thoughts from straying...right back to her.

It was an impossible task!

Her image might as well be emblazoned on his eyelids. Exactly as he'd seen her. One shapely leg lifted, showing a curved hip, leading to a wondrously small waist. And the side of a bountiful breast that he'd had a very good view of. With not a stitch of material to mute any of it. Her skin had been rosy, with just a hint of shine...

Oh.

He was in massive trouble every time he shut his eyes.

And it was her fault.

The woman didn't show any sense. He was doing his utmost to keep from taking what she just continued offering. *Damn her.* He was doing everything possible to keep his primal urges at bay. She was obviously well versed in her craft. She knew exactly how to raise desire...to an incalculable level, and for an insurmountable time. His determination was being chipped away with every passing moment. Every descriptor he used for intestinal armor was close to failing. He was heartless. Cruel. Uncaring. Strong. Inhuman. And all of that turned to pudding every time he closed his eyes. He'd even begged God for help with what was becoming incessant relentless craving. Pure physical want. And massive need.

And what did she do?

Prance about naked.

"Ah! My laird! There you are! Standing in shadows. Wrestling with inner demons. As usual."

Rhoenne didn't just glare. He sent a promise of doom with his attention. It didn't work. Henry was immune.

"Do na' be so glum! I have great tidings! And I have heard of your foray into the markets as well. And your newest acquisition. I must say...I am surprised." Henry chuckled as if there was something laughable about anything.

"You do not want to bother me, FitzHugh. I am spoiling for a fight," Rhoenne warned.

"Really? How big a fight?"

Rhoenne growled.

"That big, huh? Well. You have no reason for such gloom. We have been successful beyond my wildest dreams! Look. Just look at all these dinars!"

Henry opened a large bag at his hip and lifted a handful of coins from it. Rhoenne glanced at the pile of coins then back at the knight's face. He took another drink of ale. Swallowed.

"Verra well. Do na' congratulate me. But I have managed to not only gain a measure of coin, I have secured passage within hours and we do na' even have to pay! Well. Except for the woman."

The woman...

Damn it.

The words sent trouble shooting straight to Rhoenne's groin. And in this attire, it wouldn't stay undetected. He should have donned the burnoose again, despite the heat of being indoors.

Rhoenne turned sideways, leaned a shoulder into a mud brick wall in a dismissive fashion. He crossed his legs defensively. Regarded her door even more sullenly.

"It will be a working voyage for us, but what man among us cannot sail? Except perhaps the eunuch, but he will soon learn, I have no qualm."

Rhoenne grunted.

"You doona' wish particulars?"

"No."

Henry continued on unimpeded. "That ship we saw at anchor? 'Twill sail with the tide. They'll send a skiff for us. It should be here after midnight. They'd have sailed this morn, but some of the crew took bad sick. The captain had no choice but to send them back ashore."

"So?" Rhoenne asked.

"So...they've had some sickness in port. Some fear 'tis plague. The ship captain can na' interest anyone in sailing with him. He is desperate. He is willing to pay us! He will na' even charge us for the lone cabin. For your woman...or both of your women, since Euan tells me you have added to your...uh. Stock."

"Finished?" Rhoenne asked.

"You are deuced dark this eve, Ramhurst. More so than usual, I mean."

Rhoenne growled again.

"You know...I think I'll go and find myself a nice tankard of beer, and some company that actually wishes my presence. You will be ready when we sail?"

"Me?"

"I meant your women. Will you make certain they are ready? I understand you have given strict orders that no one is to approach them. You may wish to rescind that...or alter it slightly. Allow the eunuch to help. He appears in need of an assignment. And he's not quite as fond of... solitude."

Rhoenne's chest felt tight. His eyes burned. His head ached. His gut was wrenched. And his groin was a throbbing problem that wouldn't recede.

"Final warning, FitzHugh," he returned.

"Try and talk some sense..."

The man tossed a hand in the air and strode away, his words fading along with him.

CHAPTER TWELVE

H ENRY'S JUBILATION HAD been premature. They'd been desperate. It showed. Getting aboard this ship may have been a quick solution, but it was not without peril.

Rhoenne sensed it before they raised anchor. The ship was a two-mast lateen-rigged *cocha*. They had a cargo of goods to sell in Venice, but it didn't change the nature of the ship, the captain, or its crew. This was no merchant ship. This was a slaver. He knew it in his gut. He'd hauled Cassandra aboard over his shoulder as if she had the value of a carpet. Emin was at his heels with the skinny wench trussed in the same fashion. While Emin stood guard that first night, Rhoenne reconnoitered. A trip to the hold verified it. The iron chains holding crates in place were affixed to the ship's ribs, and they had wrist-sized cuffs welded on.

Men willing to treat humans as chattel in exchange for gold were not just untrustworthy, they were dangerous. The captain claimed to be Muslim, but he didn't follow the strictures of his faith, nor did any of his crew. The man was a sot, the crew unruly. Any order given was obeyed with a surliness that begged punishment. The captain stayed too drunk to care. More than one crewman should have been tossed overboard for insubordination. The Ramhurst clansmen were outnumbered by more than four to one.

And Rhoenne had two women to protect.

Emin wasn't much of a seaman, but he made an excellent guard. He stood for hours with his back to the cabin door, wicked-looking weaponry gleaming from his belt, his stance unmoving and deadly. The door was only opened to allow for food and drink to be sent in, refuse to be handed out. Emin protected the cabin during the day. Rhoenne kept vigil at night. They'd developed a system. Emin would nod when he appeared. Open the door. Rhoenne did a visual check. If Cassandra wasn't already abed and sleeping, she did a good imitation of it. The servant woman would nod. And then he'd go about his night.

Two crewmen worked during the night, one kept look-out. The other worked with ropes and sails under Rhoenne's direction. The work wasn't arduous, even with an ever-present breeze. That was one good thing. The crossing would pass quicker, and the motion wasn't too stomach-churning for any with a weak belly.

But Rhoenne couldn't stay awake and watchful forever. He knew his limitations. He'd started taking short naps throughout the day, tying himself to a cot in the hold. The first sennight passed uneventfully. An eighth day. A ninth.

The cabin door opened on the tenth night. Just

past midnight. He didn't see it. He didn't hear it. But he instantly knew it. Rhoenne was atop the mizzen sail when he sensed what was happening. He reacted instantly. Instinctively he dove for a line, and thanked fate he'd wrapped strips of cloth around his hand to protect his blisters. The slide to the deck burned his palm even through the bandaging. He'd plucked a dagger from his belt before he landed, all within seconds, and without sound. He didn't have time for subtlety, however. He took the last yards with a full body lunge, rolled into a crouch, ready to kill. Quickly and remorselessly. And the skinny maidservant may have lost her tongue, but she had no trouble making a muted squeal before she turned and ran back into the cabin.

"What is it, Ida? What?"

Cassandra spoke from inside the cabin. His heart instantly palpitated. Rhoenne told himself it was the effects of his exertion and not the sound of her voice, then disguised the idiocy of that thought with a quick scan of the deck. There was a new moon above them, sending a little light onto the deck. Nothing looked amiss. No alarm sounded. The creak of masts, flapping of sailcloth, and slap of rope was the only sound... other than the harshness of his breathing.

"Did someone see you? Yes? Well...who?"

Cassandra spoke again. She was speaking a Slavic tongue. Rhoenne slowly rose to his feet. Tucked the dagger back under his belt. Stepped into the portal since Ida had just left the door open. His eyes had adjusted, making it possible to see where Cassandra stood, completely covered in cloth.

As if she was leaving.

"Oh," Cassandra addressed him with a flat tone. "It's you." Then she turned to the servant woman and spoke in Slav again. "Why didn't you tell me it was Mister Big, Bad, and Barbaric?"

Rhoenne barely kept the amused snort from sounding. He settled with clearing his throat. Lowered his voice to make it sound rough and intimidating. "You disobey?" he demanded.

"Don't be angered at Ida. Please. It was my idea."

"Ida?" Rhoenne asked.

"That is her name."

"She told you her name?"

"Of course not. I had to find out which language she understood and then guess until I got it."

"I see."

"She may be silenced, but she's not stupid."

"I never said she was. How many languages do you know?" Rhoenne asked.

The burka lifted as she shrugged her shoulders. "A few."

"Are you going to answer me?" Rhoenne continued.

"I just did."

"About your disobedience."

She tossed us a hand. "Oh. I didn't think it would matter. No one was around."

"I told you. I would be around."

"So you did," she told him.

He watched her turn around. Her shoulders looked slumped suddenly. She opened her burka. Gave a sigh. "You were right, Ida. It's useless. I am a prisoner, although I do not accept that beauty is the reason. I can't get a free breath or a glimpse of anything except the walls of this cage. I can't even gaze at the stars."

She looked so little. Sounded so wistful. Rhoenne's chest swelled with warmth as undeniable as it was massive.

Oh.

He was in trouble.

"Stars? You wanted to view stars?" he asked in the same language they'd just used.

Cassandra gasped and spun. It wasn't bright enough to see her face as she probably went over what she might have just given away. His mind had to see it for him. It was just as entertaining.

"You know Slav...too?" she asked.

"Aye. And *Rus.*"

"Well. Of course you would. You are just a perfect gaoler, aren't you?" She spoke crossly.

"You are being protected," he stated.

"I know. That's what I keep telling myself. It doesn't make it any easier to bear."

Rhoenne considered. It had been ten nights since they'd sailed from Batok. Nothing out of the ordinary had occurred. There were only two others up tonight, and he had a rough idea where they would be at the moment. One favored the galley and a midnight snack. The other usually fished from the stern, snagging several of the large fish that trailed in the ship's wake. Rhoenne had

been the only one high on the rigging. It should
be safe enough.

"That's truly what you were doing? Seeking
a breath of fresh air and a bit of stargazing?" he
asked finally.

"Yes."

"Come with me."

He held out his hand. She didn't move.

"What is it now?" he prompted.

"You...wouldn't toss me overboard, would
you?"

Rhoenne straightened. Frowned. "Why would
you ask that?"

"Please! If that is my fate...don't hold it against
Ida, as well. Please? It was not her fault. She's
been through enough in this life."

Her voice broke on the plea, and the last part was
whispered. Rhoenne was immobile. Stunned.
Not only at her words, but the genuine sincerity
she'd exhibited while she said them. She actually
thought him capable of tossing her overboard?
Worse, he couldn't fault her line of thinking.
He'd been punishing her for interrupting his life.
He'd been penalizing her for being born female.
He'd purposely tarred her with the same brush
reserved for Aileen and her ilk.

And with her plea, Cassandra changed
everything.

He'd suspected she was different. That's why
he'd fought it so hard.

The small ship cabin wasn't large enough to
contain the breadth of his self evaluation, and yet
too small to hide from it. Rhoenne Ramhurst

considered himself a reasonable man. Fair. Tough, but just. Right now, he felt almost bestial. He rarely experienced any kind of upbraiding anymore. Henry was usually behind it. This experience ranked up there with the worst of his life. He didn't know what expression might be on his face. He was actually grateful it was dark.

Rhoenne took a deep breath, exhaled with an audible sigh, then put his hand back out toward her again, palm up. And then he spoke. Softly. Solemnly. "Cassandra, take my hand. I merely seek to grant your wish. And assure your safety as I do so."

"You're...granting my wish?"

He nodded slowly. "Yes."

"Truly?"

"Are you trying to make me change my mind?" he asked in a teasing tone.

"Are...the stars out?" she asked in a hesitant voice, as if his words were still not to be trusted.

"Aye. And very brilliant."

He didn't realize he'd held his breath until her fingers touched his. The bandaging curtailed further contact, but just the touch of her fingers was enough to make his heart throb with an intensity that staggered. His knees even trembled. He very nearly took her hand to his lips to kiss her fingertips. He didn't know what vestige of common sense stopped him. He was only grateful.

There wasn't a level for the depth of trouble he was sinking into.

He'd been right about the starlight. It was

not only brilliant, it illuminated the shininess
of her hair, the small upturned nose, the glitter
of her eyes, wide and excited. And it hovered
on the curve of her soft lips, highlighting them.
Rhoenne stifled a groan as he led her to the rail,
backing until his thighs reached it. That's when
he noticed something obvious. He hadn't even
taken the time to cover her with the cloth. He
suspected the reason. He'd gone insane the
moment her fingers touched his.

"Is it thus...every night?" she asked.

"Thus?" he asked. He was amazed his voice
worked.

"So...vast. Look. The sky is filled with stars.
And the air! So..."

She tipped her head back to inhale a large
breath. And all the available light seemed in play
for her, the moon and stars working in tandem, to
bring out her perfection, turning her from mortal
to golden-hued goddess. And he was starting to
turn poetic. Just like a troubadour.

Good Lord.

He was shaking, too?

"Fresh," she finished.

"It's got a hint of rain," he explained.

"Rain?"

"We've had calm seas. Few clouds. That may
soon change. That is what you smell." He was
talking weather. But he could be saying anything.
His mind wasn't connecting properly. He should
be grateful his mouth worked.

"Well, I think it's divine. Free. Crisp."

Crisp.

He hadn't considered air with that description before.

"I'd forgotten how it smells," she continued.

"Air?" Rhoenne asked.

"I've lived in an incense-filled cage for eight years," she informed him. "Eight...lengthy years."

"You must have been very young."

"A child. But they like them young."

What she said was as disquieting as how she said it. In a calm, modulated fashion. Dead-sounding. Rhoenne felt his back clench like it had when he'd heard of Ida's mutilation.

"Did someone...sell you?" he ventured.

She shook her head, then turned her gaze directly to his. Since he looked down, and the moon was at his back, his face was shadowed. Her features might as well be spotlighted. Rhoenne caught a breath. Felt a whoosh of sensation. And leaned forward...drawn to incredibly lush lips. Pursed and ready.

For a kiss.

He caught the move at the last second, yanking his abdomen so tight, it pulled him back upright. And then he stood there, looking over her head, breathing hard, watching a sail flap with a slight breeze silhouetted against the star-filled night sky. And wondering when he'd lost all his wits.

"They overran the castle. My father...he went down amidst so many of them, I didn't see his end. My mother...and sisters? I don't know what happened to them. If they died, it...wasn't quick. I heard their screams long after I was tied and gagged and taken."

Her voice trembled. Rhoenne clenched his jaw so tightly it hurt.

"I did not know what women suffered...during battle, but I vowed to never let it happen to me. That is why—"

She stopped. He glanced down at how she'd bitten her lower lip. She'd also looked down. The light sent long shadows of her lashes onto her cheeks.

"You took my dagger," he finished. It wasn't a question. He already knew the answer.

She nodded.

He reached to his belt, plucked the little knife out, and held it to her, hilt out. She looked from the blade up to him, and at the contact of their gazes, every thought went flying right out his ears. Musical notes flitted through his ears, blending together to compose a melody. Rhoenne hadn't sung in more years than he could remember. And just like that, he started composing?

For how long he gazed into her eyes, he couldn't say. Music filled both ears. Beautiful. Soul-stirring.

She asked something. Her lips moved. He didn't hear or comprehend any of it. Rhoenne finally tore his gaze from hers and looked out at the endless vista of night sky again. He didn't know what had happened. He couldn't explain or interpret. All he could do was vibrate in place. And hope like hell she didn't notice.

"I said...'tis dangerous still?" she repeated.

"Oh. Aye."

He glanced back at her. She smiled and looked

away. It looked like a blush touched the tops of her cheeks, but it wasn't quite light enough to be absolutely certain. And that didn't even matter. Rhoenne vaulted heavenward. Touched the stars. Marveled at a burst of brilliant light. Spun in wonder...then dropped. Right back into his boots and well-worn Arabic attire, standing with his buttocks against a ship rail with a knife held in his outstretched hand. He shut his eyes for a moment. Reopened them. He was amazed he hadn't moved.

"Here. Take it," he said.

"But you are my protector. I trust you. And...I have Emin."

Rhoenne felt his chest fill with pride, despite the stupidity. "We cannot be everywhere. Please?"

She took the dagger and held it against her chest, blade down, the hilt separating her breasts. He needed to look elsewhere...and rapidly.

"But we've come so far. Surely...Candia is close?"

"You will not be safe there." Rhoenne spoke to the top of her head. It was a much safer focal point.

"Candia is a Christian kingdom. Part of the Venetian Republic."

"And you are too beautiful."

Oh, hell.

He did *not* just say that. No. He wouldn't. He didn't. Rhoenne could have bitten his own tongue. Beauty was a weapon! Hadn't he learned? Telling her he found her beautiful was tantamount to complete surrender. He wasn't just admitting he might have erred in his judgment of her...but he had to go and give her ammunition, too? What if he'd been wrong? And she was exactly like Aileen?

"The sultan's harem had hundreds of beautiful women. Haven't you heard it said that 'each was more beautiful than the last'?"

"Surely you have to line them up that way."

"What?" she queried.

"Beautiful women. If I say my clansmen are each larger than the next, I have to line us up that way, so it makes sense. Therefore, you can only have beautiful women that are more beautiful than the next...never mind. This is starting to hurt my head."

She giggled. His heart plunged to the pit of his belly and started pounding, blending in with the feeling of disgust he usually harbored there. Rhoenne shook his head to clear it. Spoke on the obvious. "Besides, you were the sultan's favorite. That puts you at the top of the line."

"Oh, dear. I did tell you that. Didn't I?"

"Are you now going to recant?"

"Forgive me. It was a lie, but not a huge one. I was not his favorite...not yet. Why do you think I had to escape?"

Rhoenne regarded her for a long moment. The music started fading from his ears. He swallowed. "You forget," he finally said. "I have the jewelry he put on you." And then he patted the bag that was anchored to his belt.

"He put jewels on all his women."

"All?" Rhoenne's eyes went so wide the air

hurt. His jaw dropped as well.

Cassandra nodded. She had a slight smile on her face as if she dealt with a half-wit. Rhoenne searched her expression for any indication that she lied. Still couldn't believe it.

"No man would put so much wealth on women. I refuse to believe it."

"Women are possessions to these people. Adorning them is the same as adding gilded accoutrements to a horse. Surely you know that? Their culture is rife with atrocities. Isn't that why we crusade against them?"

Rhoenne stilled, once again feeling every bit of gall from the defeat finalized by the battle of *Fariskur.* It overrode and colored the sensations and emotions he'd suffered since bringing her out of the cabin. The disgust in the pit of his belly was back in full force, as well.

"We lost this crusade," he told her, his voice bitter. "King Louis of France has been taken. We lost the last of *Outremer.* We barely hold the City of Acre."

She must have realized how his voice had changed, even if she didn't suspect the sensations he'd been experiencing since they'd left the cabin. She also sobered. Regarded him with the same lack of expression.

"But you survived," she told him. "And so have I. And Ida. Emin. That is what matters. I think I should go back in now. It...turns chill."

She shivered visibly. Rhoenne hustled her back to her prison.

Her cage...of safety.

CHAPTER THIRTEEN

D ARK CLOUDS GATHERED on the horizon, blocking the sunset. They'd grown darker as the day progressed. Rhoenne was the lone man watching the storm's approach with apprehension. The breeze grew to gusts of wind that snapped the sails, rattled iron and rope, and sent ominous creaks throughout the ship. He'd begun a continuous circuit of the ship as eve approached. Bow to stern. Starboard to port. Hull to the highest point atop the mizzenmast. His nod to any Ramhurst clansman was returned. The looks he intercepted from the other crewmen were expressionless and dark, which were not all that unusual. Rhoenne returned those in kind. More than one man had a sullen, malicious bent to his demeanor. That also wasn't abnormal, but it seemed more pronounced today. Rhoenne told himself he was being imaginative, but he couldn't shake the feeling.

He was too unsettled to rest. He assigned blame to the approaching storm and the strange aura of animosity the crewmen seemed to project. Their captain was useless. The man was drunk and snoring from the back of the galley behind the curtain he'd rigged since giving his cabin over. That was also completely normal for this voyage.

But something kept Rhoenne pacing. He was leery it might be to keep from pondering what might be the true issue at play in his life.

Because of last night...

Something had happened to him last night.

Something massive.

The thought sent all manner of annoyance through him. His heart rate quickened. His throat felt tight, the tunic even tighter. The garment had long-since torn open at the seam down his back and at both shoulders. Every move today seemed to rip it more. But then the worst sensation of all happened, and without a hint of warning. He'd chanced along the wrong section of deck. Without thinking. Or watching. Drawn near the spot where Emin now stood guard. Reached the area just outside the cabin door.

And a sliver of something rare and absolutely euphoric went right through his belly.

Rhoenne had stopped mid-stride. He'd disguised it with a move to the railing, and a sharp gaze out at the horizon. As if that helped. He didn't dare glance back at Emin. Rhoenne had too much to do with stifling a sensation he'd never felt before. Could it be because he'd been with Cassandra? Last night. Supposedly stargazing?

No.

Impossible.

The unease grew apace as the day progressed. Gusts became an unabated wind that snapped sailcloth and loose hair. Rhoenne pulled his into a queue and tied it back. It was too late to seek rest, even if he'd been so inclined, and it had been vacant. A silent crewman had taken up a position in the hold near where the sleeping cots were stretched and hooked as needed. The man had been whittling, while whistling a disjointed tune. He'd stop both whenever Rhoenne approached. If he looked up at all, it was to give a blank, indeterminate look. Rhoenne regarded him in silence if that happened. The fellow would always look away first, and return to his carving. And his whistling.

The day became a surreal span. Time alternated. A shard of something ecstatic spiked him every time he thought of last night and it was offset with an oddness that carried apprehension. Foreboding. And a feeling of disquiet he couldn't shake.

If he believed in magic, he'd swear he'd been bespelled.

The agitation did not ease with twilight. Flashes of lightning lit the sky intermittently in the distance. Thunder rolled across the waves. The very air filled in ominous omen. Rhoenne stood mid-ship, looking up, and considered reefing the amount of sail. The captain hadn't given the order – or if he had, it was ignored. But once the storm hit, pulling in canvas was going to be difficult, if not impossible. The first drop of rain splashed him.

"Ramhurst! There you are! Looking hale and hearty, I see."

Rhoenne looked over at Henry's approach. "Why would I na' be?"

"You did na' partake of the fish stew?"

"I never eat the slop they cook."

"You have fasted?"

"Does it look as if I fast?"

The man looked him over. Then shook his head.

Rhoenne gazed heavenward for a moment. A raindrop hit him in the eye. He blinked it away. Looked back down at his man. "I have to get the sails reefed, FitzHugh."

"Oh. Yes. Well. Do not let me stay you."

"That is exactly what you do! Now, go below and rest."

"I came to warn you to guard your belly."

"I have no issue with that."

"So I see. I simply try to ascertain how it is that you managed such a feat when every other man is laid low. Save Euan, but I think he has iron-clad innards."

Rhoenne regarded him for long moments. Another raindrop hit his cheek. He relented first.

"There are three men up at night. One is an expert fisherman. He has yet to disappoint. We have fresh grilled fare every night."

"Oh. Good. I shall go check the women."

"Na' so fast, my friend."

"I do na' attempt a peek at your women! I need to make certain they are well!" Henry didn't just look exasperated. He sounded it as well.

Rhoenne sighed and found himself explaining.

"I deliver fish to Emin each morn. He alone sees to their needs. The rest of the catch is delivered to the galley. For the fish stew they cook."

"Oh. Well, tonight the batch was bad."

"You appear fine." Rhoenne had his hands about the mast and a foot against it before Henry spoke again.

"I did na' partake. The approaching storm has me...worried."

"Worried?"

"You do na' sense it?" Henry asked.

Rhoenne considered his man. Debated options. He'd appreciate Henry's help when the storm broke, but the man needed rest. The last thing Rhoenne wanted was a worried, tired man once the storm broke. Rhoenne finally shook his head.

"No? Well, I have na' taken a ship through a storm afore. With a worthless captain. And a crew down with sick bellies."

"Do na' fash. We shall manage it," Rhoenne replied.

"What about the women? Have you thought of them?"

Had he thought about her?

Nonstop.

Rhoenne sighed. "Have you a purpose with these words?" he asked.

"You need to have Emin tie them."

"Have you gone mad?"

Rhoenne climbed. Moved a hand up. Found

a notch. Hauled himself up another half- body length. He wasn't tying anyone in that cabin. Cassandra already likened it to a prison.

"To keep her safe!" Henry called after him.

"She's in a blasted cabin, FitzHugh!" he yelled down.

"And she'll be bruised, Ramhurst!" the man shouted back.

Rhoenne slid back to the deck. Climbing was going to require concentration. Dealing with Henry required massive patience. He turned and regarded him obstinately. Henry looked just as obstinate.

"Why will she be bruised?

"Waves send cargo flying. You know that. You've seen it."

Rhoenne regarded him for a moment. Nodded. "True. Should the waves warrant such, I'll speak with the eunuch. Now. Go below with the others. You'll need rest."

"Rest? I know you say you are unworried, but there is a storm brewing and yet you climb rigging." Henry paused, then added, "...with a sword strapped to your back."

Damn.

The man was smart.

"'Tis my short sword. Good for hacking. I may need it. Now, get below. And that is an order."

"I already answered it." Henry returned.

Another raindrop hit his cheek. "I've climbed this nightly. There is *nae* cause for concern. Or worry."

"I'm your man, Rhoenne. I will na' save my skin should the storm break with you out here by yourself."

Rhoenne gripped the man's shoulders. Leaned down. "I will na' fail, Henry. But should that happen, someone has to get those women to safety. Someone honorable, smart, and strong. You ken?"

Henry looked him over evenly. Then nodded.

Rhoenne grabbed the pole. He'd gained footing on the first cross-piece before looking down. Raindrops were hitting in earnest now. Darkness had fallen. He could barely make out the deck below. Henry was nowhere to be seen. The first sails moved easily. Rhoenne pulled and secured line, the sailcloth sucked into place against the mast. He moved up. Did the same to the next piece. Looked over at the other mast. Rainfall was visible with every flash of lightning now. Rhoenne grabbed a line. Took a deep breath. And swung across to it. He smacked into wood below the cross piece, but didn't fall.

Rain had slicked the pole, making it difficult to grasp. Every move had an incremental slide downward to it, adding impetus to his climb for the mizzenmast. Rhoenne grabbed it with one hand, yanked himself up. Straddled it. Grabbed the line for a sail and started yanking, each pull bringing the cloth closer to the mast. The shoulder of the tunic gave over and ripped away. Wind whipped some of his hair loose. Rain dampened, then saturated. He shoved a forearm across his eyes to clear vision. He yanked on rope again. Again. And again. When the line wouldn't budge further, he knotted it. Then he sat for a moment, breathing heavily. The main sail was a mass of fabric adhering to the mast, flapping at the edges.

From up here, the world was rocking wind and stinging rain. If banshees existed they were at play, yanking at his clothing, pulling at his hair, doing their best to unseat him. Lightning lit the sky, showing the ocean surface writhing like a beast, while the ship looked like a small insect. Then it went dark again. Thunder tumbled through the air.

He slid farther along the mizzenmast. Found the line for the next sail. Started yanking. And that's when he heard the scream.

Rhoenne didn't hesitate. He jumped out, holding to the sail line, and swooped down to the deck, pulling canvas in a shredded mass along with him. The landing on his left side was brutally hard. A wall of heavy canvas fell atop him. Rhoenne rolled and clawed and kicked his way free. He didn't even notice the crash of wood that smacked into the deck behind him.

He should have known what was being planned.

He should have gone with his gut instinct.

He should have paid attention to danger signals.

This is what came of poring over a sense of wonder that hit him with every recollection of being with Cassandra.

Ambush.

His right hand unsheathed the short sword as he ran, while the left plucked daggers from his belt. He'd be facing at least a score of them. Maybe more. Excitement sent an edge to his movements. Heightened the thrill of combat. Rhoenne had never lost a battle, not until this crusade. He didn't like the taste of defeat. He wasn't allowing it again.

He didn't just have surprise on his side this time. He had strength. He had skill. And he had hate. He'd come on this crusade to eliminate these devils. He'd spent the past two years honing that skill. Rain slicked the deck, waves rocked the path, and darkness stole vision. Rhoenne wasn't hampered in the slightest. He was attuned, perfect focused, battled primed.

He knew exactly where they were, and exactly what they'd planned.

The entire deck before her cabin was packed with men. They were easily seen because they had a lantern lit in the cabin. The light came out in bursts that matched the sway of the deck, sending spears of light on a throng that crammed the portal, near bursting it with their fervor. Yelling loudly. Rabidly. Hungrily.

Like animals.

Rhoenne started hacking.

His right hand shoved the sword into the first man's spine. With his left, he slashed a neck. He spun, planted another blade into a chest, then kicked the body off his sword to free it. His next sword swipe took off a head. The movement of the ship was as nothing. Rainfall meant even less. Nothing impeded. Nothing altered. He dealt death with each motion. He barely heard Emin's angered cry. The sound added enhancement to an already altered experience. Rhoenne's heart rate ratcheted to a higher level; became a cadence of harsh beats. Loud. Strong. Remorseless.

He slashed through another man's torso, took off another head. Stuck another dagger into a throat and then ripped it free. Someone tossed a punch at him. Rhoenne cut off the offending arm. If the man screamed, Rhoenne couldn't hear it. He couldn't hear anything over the throbbing beat pulsating through him. Rhoenne plucked more knives free of his belt. Stuck one into the next man's eye socket. The other blade opened a throat. He shoved his sword into the next man's belly, wrenching upwards as he pulled it free. Black, wet mass spilled out amid a gurgling sound as the man fell. Rhoenne used his body as a platform, catapulting over a wall of them right into the cabin. And somehow he landed on his feet. Bestial-looking expressions turned to shock at his arrival before them. And everything halted...for a scant moment of time.

And then Rhoenne moved again. He stuck a dagger into a cheek. Felt a sharp pain in his side. Ignored it. The next man received a sword blow that nearly decapitated. Another one was disemboweled. He jammed the sword into a man's chest. His fall wrenched the hilt from Rhoenne's hand. He snagged more knives from his belt. Emin gave a renewed yell from behind him. The cabin was small, but Emin's cry was barely audible. Rhoenne had both arms moving rapidly, slashing and cutting in motions almost too quick to follow. He carved a man's face open with a dagger. Stuck another blade into a throat. Yet another man got two blades delivered into the sides of his skull, as Rhoenne rammed them right through his ears. He pulled more blades from the back of his belt shoving one into a man's gut. Another slit across a throat. The last few men turned into cowards, and fled. Rhoenne tossed knives after them, taking at least one down. Emin gave chase and they got swallowed up by the dark.

Rhoenne sucked for breath. Exhaled. Inhaled. Exhaled. His heart was a throbbing center of heightened exertion, stress, and thrill. He closed his eyes. Said a quick prayer. And turned around.

The lantern hung from a hook at his eye level. It sent flashes of light through the cabin in jerking motions. It touched on Ida's cowering figure, and just behind her was Cassandra. Her hair was loose, framing her. She held the little dagger at her breast, the blade inches away from her heart. Her eyes were wide with what was probably shock and horror. But she was alive.

And untouched.

Relief was a physical affliction. It weakened instantaneously. Rhoenne's heart gave a kick that nearly sent him to his knees. He wavered momentarily before steadying his legs beneath him again. He'd just achieved it as Cassandra barreled into him. And then she burst into sobs.

Rhoenne was breathing hard. Physically spent. And glorying with a sensation of such beauty, there was no equal. He had no comparison.

Tears stung his eyes. He put an arm about Cassandra, lifted her from the floor, and held her to him. Her unbound hair was a waterfall at her back, cloaking her. He started crooning. Saying nonsensical things. Speaking her name. Telling of her fearlessness. Her strength. Her resilience. He could never remember later just what he'd said as she cried hysterically, her face buried in his throat, her arms about his neck.

The room's rocking had increased. Rhoenne moved with the sway. Crooning words. Almost singing. Light splayed back and forth across the cabin. Ida walked around them. Rhoenne turned to watch her start shoving at bodies – and parts of bodies – with a foot, sliding them on the slick, blood-covered floor out the doorway. She was joined by Emin, who grabbed from the opposite side of the carnage, silently pulling and then heaving the dead over the side. And that was the scene when Henry and Euan rushed into the field of light, swords drawn, daggers ready.

And then their jaws dropped.

Rhoenne held Cassandra closer. Her weeping had calmed to hiccups, but her arms were still wrapped about his shoulders. Her hair trailed down her back and over his arm.

Henry sheathed his sword first. Euan followed then he started dancing from side-to-side while he stared up at Rhoenne with his eyes almost as wide as his mouth.

"Greetings, gentlemen," Rhoenne remarked casually. Cassandra stiffened. He put his other hand to her back to hold her exactly where she was. She didn't fight it.

"By the faith, Ramhurst. If I had na' seen this—." Henry's voice stopped.

"I had some trouble," Rhoenne said. "But 'tis past."

"How the devil—?" Henry's words ended again.

"I have na' known you to be speechless afore, FitzHugh. 'Tis highly entertaining," Rhoenne remarked.

"We'd have been here earlier if we'd known," Henry answered.

"Or if Emin had chased one of the devils into the hold sooner." Euan spoke up.

"Ah. That explains how you found out and why you have mounted a rescue," Rhoenne teased.

"Ramhurst." The reproof stained Henry's voice.

Rhoenne took a few moments to stifle the amusement as Henry said his name.

"Aye?" he offered finally.

"I am beyond words. I have seen you in battle. I was ever impressed. But this. This. I have never seen the like. How many did you take?"

"I do na' ken exactly," Rhoenne replied. "A score. More. Less. All. Most."

"How did you do it?"

"I do na' ken that, either."

"And you took *nae* injury?"

Rhoenne shook his head.

"By the faith, Ramhurst. If tales of your valor were na' already the talk of the glens, they would after this."

"Only if someone were to speak of it," Rhoenne returned.

"Well, I will," Euan remarked.

"Euan. Come with me. The laird will be better served if we check the ship."

"You think there might be some still hiding?" Euan asked excitedly.

"Possibly. But we need check for issues. We are facing a storm. We have an *auld* ship full of cargo. From the looks of things, we've got a mast down...and now we've got less crew. A lot less. 'Twill be a long night. A powerfully long night." Henry's voice continued on unabated as they faded from hearing.

"Emin!" Rhoenne called.

"Yes, Excellency?" The eunuch's bulk filled the doorway.

"Go to the galley. Bring me a bottle of whatever the captain has been drinking."

"Yes, Excellency."

The man took off at a trot, barely missing Ida's arrival with a bucket of water. She poured it on the blood mess, matching the motion to a roll of the ship. That method swept liquid out the door. That was impressive. As was her second and a third bucket flushing. Rhoenne's legs were feeling the strain simply by holding Cassandra and maintaining an upright stance.

"I'm...going to put you down now, Cassandra."

Her head shifted as she nodded. Rhoenne went to the cot. Fell, more than sat, with her on his lap. The structure was hard. Narrow. Prison-like.

"Ida?" he spoke to the maid when she'd finished swishing with a fourth bucket of seawater. She was instantly before him, still holding the bucket. "You need to find your mistress something clean to wear."

"They didn't touch me," Cassandra whispered.

"You're..." Rhoenne gave a sigh before continuing. However he said it, she wasn't going to like it. "Covered in blood," he finished.

She looked down at herself. Gave an exclamation that was filled with horror. It matched her shudders as she crawled from him, placing her back to the wall. She tucked her legs up beneath her. Her hair shielded her, but he watched her shake her head from side to side and it sounded like she barely kept from gagging.

"It's na' that bad," Rhoenne told her.

"This blood! From all those men!" Her voice rose.

Rhoenne grabbed a shoulder of his tunic and finished tearing one side open, ripping the sleeve off. He rolled the material around his fist, making a pad. He looked at her. She appeared to be trying to push further from him, even as the wall fought it. He shook his head.

"No, sweet," he said softly. "You are covered with my blood."

Then he lifted his arm, took a deep breath and located the puncture wound along his side. He pressed the wadded material to it, and lowered his arm to keep the pressure on. And then he realized what he'd just called her. Cold washed through him, sending unpleasant shiver in its wake. All he could hope was that she didn't note it. And cover it with something else.

"Your hair is down," he said, frowning at his disingenuousness. That was the best he could manage? A remark over hair?

"Ida...brushes my hair. Nightly. After a sponge bath."

"Ah." He shut his eyes. Yanked them open almost immediately. He wished she hadn't mentioned the bath part.

"You're injured," she said.

"Oh. Aye."

Cassandra pulled away from the wall. Moved closer to him. "But you told those men—. Henry. I don't understand. They would have helped."

"'Tis but a scratch."

The padding had saturated. Rhoenne could feel it. He watched her glance there and back to his face. But she didn't meet his eyes.

"That is not a scratch."

"I've had worse."

"Why did you lie to them?"

"Harsh words, woman," he returned.

"Tell me why you didn't speak of your injury."

"Penance," Rhoenne replied.

"What?"

She scooted to the edge of the cot. Right next to him. Pushed a lock of hair behind her ear. Strands trailed her arm. Pooled into a mass of darkness onto the bed between them. What blood he'd smeared on her dress was drying to a brown shade.

"This was my fault. All of it. I am to blame. A

score of men are now dead. You were almost—."
He scrunched his eyes shut. Shook. Reopened
them. "If I had not taken you stargazing, this
wouldn't have happened. Any wound is penance."

"Then it's *my* fault," she told him.

"No." He shook his head. The room seemed
to move with it. That was odd. "I knew what
they were like. I knew the risk. And I still
took it. Ida?" The maid was before him again
almost instantly. "You found fresh clothing for
Cassandra?"

She lifted a shapeless-looking dress. "Good.
Give me the old one. I need more padding. And
I don't know who allowed you a lantern in here
on a night like this, but I am grateful."

"Emin brought it.   Ida was...frightened,"
Cassandra told him.

"I see. Well. It's as fortuitous as it is enlightening."

"How so?"

Rhoenne kept his focus on the plank floor.
Swishing sounds like those from fabric were barely
audible above the creaking noises throughout the
room, but his ears were fine-tuned to it.

"I shall need it to heat one of my blades."

"You want a heated blade?"

"Seals the wound.   Unless you are a hand at
sewing?"

Cassandra made another gagging noise.

"That's what I assumed," Rhoenne said
conversationally. "Ida? I was told you are a great
hand with a needle. You can also help me seal it?
Is she nodding?" he asked.

"You can look. I am once again fully-clothed."

The dress draped about her small form. It was still too revealing. Anything would be. He couldn't erase the memory of her womanliness no matter what she wore. Rhoenne glanced at Cassandra then away.

"May I have...the old dress?"

He put his hand out. Ida handed him a pad formed from a section of the material. Rhoenne thanked her with a smile, and replaced the used one. He was debating where to place it when Ida held out the bucket. He dropped the bloodied bandage into the bucket. Watched her take it to the door. Open it. He wasn't surprised to see Emin on the other side, either. It just seemed fated.

The eunuch handed Ida a dark bottle. Took the bucket.

"Your drink is here," Cassandra told him.

"It's na' just for drinking. It's for cleansing. I've got a line of Pict healers in my family tree...as well as trou...badours." He split the word into two distinct sections with a pause. It was getting difficult to concentrate.

"Who said anything about troubadours?" Cassandra asked.

Damn.

He was losing his sanity. Giving her all kinds of unnecessary ammunition. He knew women kept a constant log of things to use when it would cause the most embarrassment. Do the most damage. Hurt the fiercest. The best a man could do was keep ammunition out of their grasp. Hadn't he learned anything from being near

Aileen? Rhoenne scowled. If he didn't keep his mind focused, he didn't know what else he might reveal. He reached for a dagger. Checked the front of his belt. Sides. Back. He'd used all his knives? And, if he didn't miss his guess, most were on their way to the bottom of the sea.

The effects of this night just kept getting worse and worse.

"Cassandra? You still have the little dagger. I... need it."

He pushed from the cot to the floor, knocking his knees into the wood with the fall, and even that hurt. He felt light-headed. Woozy. It didn't help that the floor rocked.

"Emin! Help!"

He heard Cassandra's frantic call. Wondered about that. Everything was dark. Blurred. And spiraling insanely. He couldn't place his fate in the hands of two women and a eunuch. Not him. The Dark One.

And then his head hit the floor.

CHAPTER FOURTEEN

TERROR WAS DEBILITATING. Shock weakened. But panic was the undoubtedly the worst.

It had been a fairly normal day. Evening. Although the cabin had swayed more, and the sound of wind had risen, nothing had been different. Ida had been combing through her hair, making soothing sounds whenever she chanced upon a snarl, and then the door burst open. They'd used Emin's body as a battering ram. The man wasn't conscious.

Terror hit like a wall of black. It iced her blood and froze her actions. Then Ida jumped before her, and all manner of chaos happened. Cassandra screamed. Grabbed the dagger. Faceless men poured into the room, pushing, shoving, yelling. Some were even salivating. Emin groaned. She did the only thing possible. She turned the dagger on herself. Held it in front of her heart.

And that stopped them.

They'd seen her blade. Saw where it was pointed. Emin lumbered unsteadily to his feet. Moments ticked by. Somebody snarled. Guttural yells emitted from the crowd. And then the immense form of Rhoenne vaulted right over the top of them, smacked into the deck with a loud thump, and without hesitation, started slashing and hacking, and killing.

Annihilating all of them.

All.

Cassandra couldn't move. Breathe. Blink. Couldn't do anything other than watch as one after the other they fell to Rhoenne's actions.

And then it was over.

Seconds later the shock took over, coloring a section of time with a wash of red. All those bodies. And parts of bodies. Cassandra had never even seen men fight. She'd never witnessed violence. She'd never even seen an animal butchered. The sight was gore-filled. Nauseating. And somehow impossible to look away from. The floor was awash with what had to be blood. Entrails. Deck sway made trails of dark wet shine slither along the floor. And at the center of everything was Rhoenne. Wild-looking. Clothing ripped. Muscles heaving. Wet. Big. Strong.

Solid.

Fright and shock were consuming forces, but he was a beacon of security. A rock of shelter. She'd barreled into him without thought, clung instinctively, and sobbed with an abandon she'd never experienced before. Being cradled by Rhoenne Ramhurst was the safest place in the world, while listening to his words the most soothing sound ever. She'd been protected. Calmed. The weak feeling had just started to subside.

And then he'd collapsed.

Panic sent her heart racing furiously, her breathing gasped and rapid, motions frenzied and useless. Panic wasn't just debilitating. It incapacitated. Lantern light continually swayed across the cabin, lighting on Rhoenne sprawled at her feet, facedown, then showing Ida at his side, attempting to turn him over. And all Cassandra managed was bouncing in place atop the bed, stifling back a choked reaction with both hands to her mouth. She didn't know what to do. She couldn't think.

And for the first time in her life, she was at a complete loss.

Emin burst through the door, sword drawn. The wound on his head sent a trail of blood down his cheek. His glance met hers before he nodded, then dropped the weapon. It clattered on the planking. The next swing of the light showed him kneeling at Rhoenne's side alongside Ida.

"Highness? What has happened to His Excellency? Highness!"

His words started as a query but ended sharply. The next swing of light showed he'd rolled Rhoenne rolled onto his back.

"He is injured?" Emin continued. "How badly?"

Another swing of light caught Emin squatting, an arm wrapped about Rhoenne's lower legs as he swiveled him, placing his boots on the cot beside Cassandra. The next bit of illumination caught an expression she'd never seen. The man looked severe. Angered. And intense.

"Why did he not tell his men? Highness!"

Emin's voice was authoritative, and sharp. The light had swung back to the door, leaving him in dimness. And then he smacked his hands together, making a cracking sound just like a horsewhip.

Cassandra started. Emin's actions startled. Frightened. But somehow, they halted the discordant helplessness she'd been mired in.

Everything perfectly focused and cleared.

The light swung back to Rhoenne and Ida. Emin was again crouched at Rhoenne's side.

"Highness. Forgive me, but you must help. Now. Right now."

Cassandra nodded. She didn't know if he saw it. The next bit of light, showed Emin lifting the bloodied pad away from the wound. He'd put it back in place before being illuminated again. The next showed him pressing so hard that blood oozed from between his fingers.

"What did he say? What does he wish?" Emin asked.

"We need to get his man...Henry," she whispered.

"Is that what he wants?"

Cassandra would have answered but Ida was at Emin's side handing him another wad of material and the woman was emphatically shaking her head. The swing of lamplight made it impossible to miss.

"He does na' want his men?" he asked Ida. Cassandra heard rustling that could be anything. "What does he want?"

Ida gestured, lifting the bottle of spirits, then pointing to the light above them.

"He wants the drink for the candle? He wants to start a fire? In here?"

Ida gave a disgusted-sounding grunt. Cassandra heard a smack sound. She could only guess what had happened, because the light had swung away again.

"No." Cassandra answered.

"What does he want, then?"

"We have to get his man," she said.

"Highness. This man has just saved your life. The life of this woman. And me. He saved my worthless life. You had not been granted the sultan's favor yet, so you were not required to accept the true faith, but you must know. There is more at work in this world than chance and fate. It is a great power. You call it God. I name it Allah. They are the same. And I do not know why Allah granted me the blessing of service to this man, but I recognize the hand behind it. You understand? Serving this man is Allah's will. I will not go against his wishes. I cannot."

She swallowed. "He could die."

"Allah will not let that happen. We must help. So. Assist me. What does he wish of us?"

"He said something...about cleaning the wound. That is what the drink is for. And then he wants to heat a knife blade. He said it seals the... wound." She didn't gag, but it was willpower that stopped the reflex.

"He wishes to sear the flesh. Very smart."

"He also spoke of Ida sewing——." Cassandra

stopped. Shuddered. Fought the rising bile to her throat. She couldn't finish.

"I see. Very well. Ida? The bottle."

He held out his right hand for it. Light intermittently gave Cassandra a view of how Emin peeled back the pad to pour amber-colored liquid onto a wicked-looking, finger-length gash. Rhoenne jerked. The boot beside her tapped at her hip. The bleeding started up again almost instantly. With the next sway of lantern light she saw that Emin had a new wad of material onto the gash.

"Here. Hold this."

Ida took Emin's place, pressing on the bandage so that Emin could stand, lift the lantern from its hook and hold it out to her.

"Highness. You must hold this. Steady. We need the light."

Cassandra held the lamp on her lap, watched Emin open the little access window, pull a dagger from his belt and insert it into the candle flame. He swiveled and dropped to his knees returning to Rhoenne's side. Peeled the bandage away again. Poured more liquor on it. Rhoenne groaned and jerked again. The boot struck her thigh again. Emin had another wad of material in place. Pressing. And then he did it again. Cassandra's hold on the lantern kept light on the scene. She kept moving her glance from their ministrations to the blade, watching as the metal turned red, then yellow, then almost blue.

"Is it ready yet, Highness?" Emin asked.

"What?"

"The dagger."

"It's bluish," Cassandra replied.

"Ida?" Emin asked the figure on the opposite side of Rhoenne. "Can you hold him?"

Hold him?

Ida shook her head.

"Then you'll have to do the burn."

The woman nodded. Emin handed her a wad of cloth before he moved to Rhoenne's head. He pulled head and shoulders onto his lap, leaned forward to wrap both arms about his torso. Cassandra didn't see Ida take the blade, but she got a perfect view of the fiery hot blade touching Rhoenne's skin. As well as his instant reaction. Rhoenne jerked, arching up from the floor, even as Emin held him. An agonized cry filled the cabin. Bass tones overtook everything, even the sound of sizzling flesh. Tears instantly sprang to Cassandra's eyes. Blinking sent them down her cheeks.

Rhoenne was no longer unconscious, either. His blue eyes were open. Wide. And crazed. And then he started struggling. She'd already seen him fight. A boot hit her arm, nearly toppling her. Cassandra didn't know how Emin held him. The eunuch strained, muscles bulged as he held Rhoenne and the eunuch was losing. His grip on Rhoenne's was flung aside.

"Your wound, Excellency! You must cease! Cease this! You will break it open again!"

Rhoenne twisted. Grunted. Snarled. The knife used to sear him clattered as it slid across decking. Ida was shoved away. And for some reason, Cassandra knew exactly what to do. She slid down onto her knees, somehow choosing Rhoenne's uninjured side. She set the lantern on the floor with one hand and held it. And then she reached out, wrapped her free arm around him, put her nose against his throat, and just stayed there.

Rhoenne's thrashing instantly ceased. He dropped them to the floor. Emin huffed a relieved sigh. Cassandra blinked more tears into existence. Trembled. And then she felt a hand at her back. Fingers dug at her dress, pulling it tight against her ribcage.

"Aileen?"

The name was as unfamiliar as his tone. Raw. Tormented. Ugly. Cassandra shook her head, tickling her nose with his beard.

"Don't you *ever* come near me again. I warned you."

He flung her, using the hold he'd grabbed on the dress. Cassandra hit a wall, shoulder first. Scrambled upright. Shook her head to clear it. She was dazed. Stunned. Amazed she'd actually kept her grip on the lantern. It had smacked into the wood beside her. The glass was cracked, the flame flickered ominously, but miraculously the candle stayed lit.

"Excellency!" Emin's voice was curt. It carried a clear warning.

"Emin?" Rhoenne answered. He sounded confused. Guarded. Extremely wary.

"Yes. It is I."

"What...? Where...? Why...? How...?"

He didn't specify either question. Emin answered with a synopsis of events.

"We are on a ship. In the cabin. With the women. There is a storm. There was a battle. You received a wound. We have just sealed it. You reacted...," the eunuch paused and glanced at her before he finished, "badly."

"Cassandra?"

Rhoenne lurched as if he'd rise. Emin put a hand on his chest to stop him. It no longer looked difficult.

"She is here," the eunuch answered.

"I did not...hurt her?" Rhoenne asked.

Emin looked at Cassandra for confirmation. She shook her head.

"She is unharmed."

Rhoenne's chest rose visibly with his sigh. "The wound?" He touched his injury as he asked it. Lantern light slithered across him. Wet smears on his fingers were impossible to miss.

"As I said. You reacted badly," Emin remarked.

Rhoenne held his breath. Everything on him looked taut and angered. "Heat the blade again," he said.

"It is still mostly sealed, Excellency. Perhaps we should try Ida's skill with a needle first."

"That sounds worse, Emin," Rhoenne remarked finally.

"Yes, Excellency. Yes, it does."

"Ida?" Rhoenne turned his head. Ida was already at his side. "Go. Get your weapons."

"Weapons?" Emin asked.

"Needle. Thread. Trust me. These are a

woman's weapons. And right now, they are frightening ones. Do we have any of the captain's spirits left?"

Ida proffered the bottle. Rhoenne took a healthy draught before handing it back to her.

"Pour some on the wound. Bathe the needle, as well."

"Highness? Bring the light. Please."

Cassandra had never seen a flesh wound, either. This one was open and raw. Blackened with a burn. Oozing blood. She'd never seen anyone stitch under such conditions, either. Nor could she seem to shut it out despite holding her hands to her ears and keeping her face averted. Emin held the light while Ida stitched. Rhoenne's every groan sent a stab of tears to her eyes. Each time he sucked for breath a pain went through her breast. And through it all, her mind was continually drawn to the name he'd called her.

Aileen.

Cassandra didn't have to ask.

She knew Aileen. Intuition told her. That was the name of the woman who'd hurt Rhoenne, turning him into a black-heart that hated women. Cassandra tried to erase the name, but the opposite happened. It was solidified in her mind. She'd practiced it for too long. All those years in the harem. Listening. Learning. Memorizing. A whispered name, an observed gesture, a chance encounter – any and all information could be used.

Because knowledge was the real power.

It always had been.

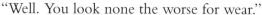

"Well. You look none the worse for wear."

Rhoenne looked over at Henry. He'd left the cabin. Ostensibly to survey damage, but it was more to gather thoughts. Breathe fresh air. And gain some distance – not only from the effects of battling and attending to his wound, but from Cassandra. The cabin wasn't big enough to escape awareness of her. No matter what he tried, he'd felt her.

Felt her.

Waves still rocked the ship, but the rain had stopped. The clouds moved away. Blue sky hovered on the horizon. And now they faced the aftermath. The situation didn't look promising. Leagues of ocean faced them. A skeleton crew. Disabled ship. He shrugged at Henry's observation. The shirt he wore concealed the gesture. Emin had pillaged clothing articles from somewhere on the ship. Of bright blue silk, the tunic was almost a match to his eyes, but destined for someone much portlier and a lot shorter. It was a poor fit through the shoulders, didn't cover his loins, and sagged in the mid-section. The last was why he'd selected it. The garment hid the wrapping Ida had insisted on winding about him.

"A night and morning spent in a cabin with two women must be agreeable. You must regale me with the tale some time."

"And a eunuch. Do na' forget about him," Rhoenne answered.

"Jaded. That's what it is," Henry remarked.

Jaded?

Rhoenne had spent most of the hours watching the others sleep.

The cabin did resemble a prison cell, although the lone ones he'd ever seen the inside of were those in Castle Tyne's dungeons. There wasn't even a window. Cassandra and Ida had the cot, their heads at either end in order to fit. It only worked because they were both slender and they were probably exhausted. They'd been overwrought. The aftermath of battle and horror and fright was usually physical exhaustion. He knew. Maybe Ida did, as well.

Emin and Rhoenne had taken up opposite sides of the cabin. Emin dozed with his knees tucked up and his head pillowed atop his crossed arms. Rhoenne had reclined for the most part, his legs taking up floor space, so he could lean against a combination of bedding and clothing to make it more comfortable, and the wound more bearable. He amended that. It had been to make what they'd done with the wound bearable. Finishing the contents of the captain's bottle had helped.

He'd been imbibing *Aqua Vitae*. It wasn't quite they quality of MacTarvat whiskey from home but it was a prize. Before they'd been lost, the crusader states had brewed a fine beer. Some of the ale had been aged in barrels to create this drink. It was close to whiskey and it numbed exactly as well.

The storm had raged. Raindrops pelted the ship. Everything rocked. Wind whistled through the walls. And for once, Rhoenne didn't assume responsibility. He could have, but he daren't chance it. He didn't want help. He didn't need pity or compassion. He'd never accept coddling. He was paying penance, all right. He had been since he was sixteen. His absolution depended on it.

And Henry pondered what all these night hours were for?

Guilt. Regret. Self-punishment. And they were his, alone, to deal with.

But keeping his injury secretive only worked if it stayed hidden. He'd have to trust Henry to handle their fate. Rhoenne didn't have the choice. For once, his body hurt too much. And no amount of the captain's *Aqua Vitae* altered anything.

He could ponder why. He didn't want to. He was afraid it was the woman lying atop the cot, snuggled on the far side of Ida. Cassandra. He'd fought feeling anything for her. Tried ignoring how his heart swelled every time he thought of her. Or looked toward her. Or closed his eyes...

Rhoenne wasn't delving any further. He guessed the reason for his affliction, but he'd rather deal with a wound that ceaselessly pained. Eyes that scratched from lack of sleep. A head that pounded in cadence with the throbs of ache emanating from his wound. Drunkenness sounded better.

At one point, the ship had rocked so markedly, Emin had stirred to wakefulness and the women almost rolled off the cot. That's when Rhoenne had scooted over, leaned back against the cot, and used his shoulders as a buffer to keep them abed. Henry had been right about the bruising that might occur. But Rhoenne wasn't tying her.

And then he'd actually done the unthinkable. He'd fallen into a sound sleep.

"So. You want the complete list of issues? Or a short version?"

Henry's question brought him back to the present. Rhoenne blinked his eyes and shook his head slightly to clear it.

"Of what?"

"Our situation."

"Have you ever been short with anything?"

Rhoenne regarded his man as if he hadn't said something witty. Henry was the one who smiled.

"Would you like the good first? Or the bad?"

"Bad."

"We have a ship that requires several crewmen to man. Luckily the sails were pulled in afore the storm. Otherwise—."

"We might have capsized. I know that. I reefed the sails."

"Yes. Well. If you notice, the canvas is still in that condition. We are basically adrift."

Rhoenne's shoulders sank. He hoped the shirt hid it. "I need to put sail out? Is that what you infer? And yet, you let me sleep?"

Henry considered him for a bit. "Not really. We don't actually need wind speed. Not at the moment."

"What? Why?" Rhoenne asked with just a hint of the surprise that flooded him.

"You asked for the bad first. I am complying."

Rhoenne gazed down at Henry without expression. The man returned the look. The deck rocked. Wood creaked. Henry finally spoke.

"Would you like me to continue?"

Rhoenne nodded.

"The crew is...mostly gone. Most taken in battle with you. The others were chucked overboard by Euan, myself, and the eunuch. Or perchance, they jumped. There are four left of the original crew." He shrugged.

"Four? Are they prisoners?"

"*Nae.* They do not appear to have been in on the plot."

Rhoenne narrowed his eyes. His headache was in danger of returning. "Plot?" he finally asked.

"The attack was planned, my laird. The fish stew tainted. These four ate it along with our clansmen. Everyone who partook is retching and ill. Except for Euan, and I have no explanation for that. We have three men down...along with the four crewmen."

"Go on," Rhoenne prompted.

"We may have to exist on salt biscuits and dry meat for a span. Euan is trying his hand at fishing. He has not had much luck. Oh. And the captain is deceased."

"The stew?"

"*Nae.* He bedded in the galley. Pots and pans... tend to shift, even in a small storm. His head got bashed. I do na' think he felt it."

"Small storm?"

"I am *nae* expert of storms at sea. This one did a bit of damage and moved on. The crew may have known this one would na' be bad, which could explain why the attack happened when it did."

Rhoenne frowned. He knew exactly why it had happened when it did. He wasn't speaking of it, however. "So. The captain is dead?" he remarked to get Henry back on subject.

"Aye. Already buried at sea. Or pitched overboard. You may select whichever one you like."

"How is that bad?"

"Oh. 'Tis not, really. I am heading into the good portion."

"And...?" Rhoenne waved a hand.

"We now have a goodly amount of goods to salvage. And a ship, such as it is."

Rhoenne grunted.

"You are well. I am well. Euan is well. The ladies are unharmed and well. The eunuch, also?" Henry finished.

Rhoenne nodded.

"All good. And we have seven crewmen once they recover."

Rhoenne grunted.

"Oh. We also have freshly-filled rain barrels for water. And here is the main thing, although I am undecided whether to label it good. Or...not so good."

"Well. What?"

"We are in sight of a port."

"What? Where?"

"Starboard side."

Rhoenne rushed to the side, grabbed a line,

jumped atop a rail, and grunted with pain. There was a definite dark mass in the distance. He couldn't see through an instant film. He blinked it back rapidly.

"Do we know which one?" he asked.

Henry stood on deck, his head level with Rhoenne's lower leg, looking up. His face was expressionless.

"That is the reason for my indecision, my laird. I can't tell yet. This ocean is full of options. The *Domini de Mar* is large. The Venetian Republic controls many domains of this sea. It might be Crete. Rhodes? Malta? We might be lucky and it is Sparta, or another part of the western mainland. Or...we may be facing the enemy again. It could be Persia. Or even Cyrenazi. Somewhere else in the Levant. *That* is why we do na' need or want wind speed at the moment."

"I see."

Rhoenne stepped back to the deck. "I'll go up. Get a look. Keep this quiet."

"Have I ever done other?" Henry replied.

"You don't really wish me to answer that, do you?"

"Well. Then consider. Even if I was a rumor-monger, I have few options to spread any information at the moment. Euan is otherwise occupied. I am not allowed to visit your women. And everyone else is prostrate."

Rhoenne's lips quirked. Henry was at a full grin. He was still smiling and shaking his head as Rhoenne started up the pole.

CHAPTER FIFTEEN

H E WASN'T CERTAIN until his third trip up to the mizzenmast, each immediately followed by pretending he didn't have a newly cauterized wound that wasn't shooting pain through him, oozing fresh blood through the newly stitched flesh into his bandaging, and making each indrawn breath hurt, following a bitten-off oath, or a stream of them. And it only worked because there weren't any witnesses.

On his third trip, he'd tacked the mainsail, taking advantage of the breeze. With luck and the right headwind, they'd reach the tide and get pulled into port without much effort. It was a far better option than the aimless drifting they'd been doing throughout the day. If anyone with knowledge had witnessed it, they'd have questioned the captain's sanity. As if they still had one. But the deck remained empty. Even Henry had gone below.

Closer and closer they'd drifted. The dark mass on the horizon became recognizable as a hill, then a harbor backed by a town. Dun-colored structures cluttered the shoreline before climbing toward a fortress at the hill's crest. Worry warred with hope within him as the day wore on. Although unfamiliar, it didn't appear to be an Egyptian or Islamic-held town, but it certainly wasn't the seaport in Cyprus where they'd departed for the crusade. That particular piece of land was flat.

Euan had given up fishing and followed Henry into the ship's bowels. They were welcome to it. Rhoenne would rather be out in the air and sunlight.

And solitude.

Mid-afternoon, he'd grabbed a meal of salted meat and dry biscuits washed down with fresh water, taken a slow walk around the ship, using the time to bolster and prepare, and then he'd braved the climb. Each movement had pain attached and every breath carried the same. But it was then he'd caught a glimpse of the flag. Narrowing eyes and focusing for long moments showed a color scheme that might mean safety. Despite straining however, he could barely make out colors. Red and yellow. That was his second trip. On the third one, he knew. Whatever the port, it was part of the Venetian Republic's maritime possessions called the *Domini de Mar.* There was no mistaking the yellow Lion of St. Mark on a red background.

Safety. A return to civilization.

And that meant it was decision time.

"See this one? 'Tis called a *lemniscate*. It's simply two loops, looking akin to a snake swallowing its own tail. This is the symbol for eight. And this one——."

Both women looked up as the door shut. Rhoenne's entrance sifted some of the powder they'd sprinkled on the floor. Cassandra jumped to her feet as if caught in some perfidy. Rhoenne glanced down as she tried to erase her work with the bottom of her slipper.

"Wait."

She stopped her efforts. Pulled her foot back under her skirt. He walked in another step. Looked down at her scuffed-over etching. Spoke in his language.

"You ken numbers?"

Cassandra shrugged. She kept her head bowed.

"Do na' bother hiding it. I can see. You know how to work with numbers? Count? Add?"

"Yes," she whispered.

"How did you learn such?"

She shrugged again.

"Oh, come now. Speak up. You know several languages. And now I find you ken numbers? How is this possible?"

"There were many long hours...in a day," she answered. "And many teachers."

"You were in a harem."

"Yes."

"There were teachers in there?"

Cassandra glanced up at him, her look enigmatic. Carefully blank.

"What is it?" he asked.

She shrugged yet again. Rhoenne sighed. "Cassandra. I asked you a question. I expect an answer."

She tensed oddly. Then spoke. Her voice was nearly inaudible. "Many women lived in the harem. From many walks of life...and all manner of lands. To an eager student, they were wondrous teachers. The eunuchs taught, as well. Even some of the slaves."

"What did they teach?"

Cassandra glanced up at him, then away. "All manner of things. Music. Dance. Medicine. Writing."

"You can write, too?"

"Yes."

"Which scripts?"

"Most. Arabic. Chinese. Phoenician."

He whistled lightly. "I do na' understand. Why would you hide this?"

"I am a woman."

Rhoenne tensed at the reminder. It was involuntarily. And vicious. A sharp pain went through his sewn flesh. "I am verra much aware of that," he finally answered.

"Knowledge is of little value for a woman. Some of it is forbidden. And punished."

"Punished?"

She nodded.

"I see. Yet you pursued it?"

"There are many hours in a day. Life can be tedious. Especially in a gilded cage...with naught to do."

"I heard they practiced...things. Like being

beautiful."

She snorted something that sounded like amusement. "Beauty is not practiced. It is a blessing. And a curse." The last was whispered.

Rhoenne grunted. "Then perhaps they played at enhancing beauty?"

She kept her head bowed. It was impossible to see her expression. "One can only spend so many hours looking at one's reflection in a mirror. Although there were some that thought it of benefit."

"What of the lessons in passion? Creating desire? And the orgies?"

"Orgies?" Cassandra flashed a glance at him. She looked as shocked as she sounded.

"Those happened. I've heard the tales. All those women. One man."

"You jest," Cassandra returned.

"*Nae.* I told you. I've heard tales."

"The tales are lies, I assure you."

"They didn't have orgies?"

"One thing I have learned since my escape... is that everything I thought true is open to question. Either my teachers were uninformed or the world has markedly changed."

"The sultan had dozens of women, yet you expect me to believe he didn't participate in orgies...or even more horrendous sins?"

"Hundreds," Cassandra returned.

"Hundreds of sins?"

"No. He kept hundreds of women."

"Good Lord. What did he do with that many women?"

Cassandra shrugged again. "Fed them. Clothed them. Ignored them."

"Ignored them? No. I do na' believe it."

"The sultan is an *auld* man. And portly." Cassandra shuddered visibly before continuing on. "He already has children. Many sons. From many wives."

"Many wives? So...that part is true?"

Cassandra nodded. "He was also...ill. He rarely visited the harem, even to choose a favorite from among his concubines."

"You?"

"Oh. No. No. Not yet, Thank God. I was lucky."

"You're na' Muslim?" Rhoenne asked.

Cassandra shook her head. "No. Had I become his favorite, however, conversion would have been forced upon me."

"This is unbelievable, Cassandra. How could he na' spot you? Was the man blind?"

She sniffed and this time he was certain it was amusement. "In a crowd of hundreds, all veiled, each with her beauty enhanced...and most vying for his attention, 'twas easy to escape notice. Besides, I was usually reading. Or studying. I was good at hiding both."

"Because of the punishment involved?"

"And I did not wish the sultan's favor. I was interested in escape."

"Oh. Well. Looks like you succeeded with that."

"Yes. But I didn't know what I would face! The things I had been taught? The knowledge I gained? None of it is true! Nothing I was told bears any resemblance to what the world is truly like!"

"You speak of last night?" Rhoenne asked.

"And the mercenaries," she whispered and shuddered again.

"Cassandra. Not all men are like that."

"Yes, they are."

Rhoenne regarded the top of her head for a span. "I am different," he replied.

She cast a glance up at him. Gave a tiny smile. His knees actually quivered. Rhoenne physically fought the reaction even as he denied it. Blamed it on his injury.

"You are a man," she finally answered. "And men seek to own. Control. And punish."

"You have a jaundiced view."

She snorted. "As do you."

Rhoenne regarded at the top of her head since she didn't look up. He had no rebuttal to what she'd just said. "I would na' punish you," he informed her.

"You punish every woman."

She sucked in a gasp after the words, and bent her head slightly lower on her shoulders as if he'd react. Long moments passed as he wondered what to reply, or even if he should. She cleared her throat. The sound was loud, yet frail.

"Forgive me. I spoke out of turn."

"There is naught to forgive. If I am honest, I earned the comment."

She looked up at him, surprise staining her features. Her shoulders straightened. She stood taller.

"I surprise you?" he asked.

She nodded.

"I do na' see how. 'Tis obvious you do na' fear punishment. At least, na' from me."

"You speak of the men you killed...on my behalf?"

"Actually, I refer to this." He stuck his boot atop the figure eight she'd drawn. "If knowledge of numbers is punishable, isn't it the same for Ida?"

The woman started at mention of her name. Cassandra touched her arm with a reassuring gesture. "A slave with needle skills has value, but one who can work with numbers is rare. It might afford her a better chance at...avoiding the horrors of her station."

"She is na' a slave," Rhoenne answered. "I'm Christian. We do na' keep slaves. Which is the reason I came here actually."

"You are freeing Ida?"

"I never owned Ida. She has ever been free. As are you."

Her eyes went wide. The liquid gold color darkened. "What...are you saying?"

"You have what you wanted. Escape from a harem. And freedom."

"No! Please. You must reconsider."

Cassandra leapt toward him, wrapped a hand around his upper arm. Rhoenne fought reacting to her touch. Sweeping her into his arms again like he had just last night. And holding her there.

"You should na' touch me," he warned.

"Please! Please! I will do anything. Do not discard me!"

"Discard you? What the devil? I can na' discard you. I never *had* you."

Cassandra's voice sounded like it filled with tears. "Please. I do not know this world but I have learned much. There is only one safe place for me. And for Ida. And it is...with you."

"No," Rhoenne returned.

"Please?"

"I do na' keep women. I just said as much."

"Please!"

"You realize what you ask?"

"I beg of you."

"Cassandra. Calm yourself. Now."

He removed her hand from his arm and held it within his fingers. His were massive. Warm. Hers were delicate. Finely-boned. Untouched by labor. And ice cold. She was also shaking. Ida wasn't silent, either. The woman was clueless to what had transpired, but she'd wrapped her arms about herself and was rocking in place and moaning loudly. Rhoenne looked heavenward, gave a heavy sigh, and looked back down at Cassandra. As he watched, she blinked tears into existence down her cheeks. Licked at them. He glanced there, then looked up and over her head.

"Stay here."

He didn't mean to sound angry. He didn't know what he was, anymore. He released Cassandra and swiveled, opened the cabin door, nodded to Emin, stepped out, and walked away. From her. Taking long strides. Purposeful. He winced with every other one. He was about to do something he'd never done.

Never even considered.

Reaching the door to the hold seemed to take forever. Rhoenne pulled in a breath, bent forward, stifled the agony of the accursed wound, grabbed the iron ring, and yanked the door up, opening a large black hole. And then he bellowed into the aperture.

"Henry!"

"Ramhurst?" A groggy-sounding voice answered.

"I need...help."

Moments later, four men poured through the opening, one after the other, all bringing swords. The first two stayed on their feet. The last two crawled.

"Well. Where are they?" Henry cried.

"I requested you, Henry," Rhoenne answered. "Not all of you."

"We are na' under attack?"

"Of course na'. Graham? Iain? You can na' even stand. Get back to your cots. Rest."

"You have never asked for help, my laird," Henry answered.

"'Tis na' that kind of help."

"What other kind is there?" Euan asked.

"I...need to talk," Rhoenne admitted.

"You need words? With Henry?" Euan hooted.

"Graham, Iain? Get below. And Euan, assist them."

"But—," Euan began.

"Now," Rhoenne commanded. It wasn't

optional. He already regretted his rash behavior. It sounded in his voice. He waited until the hatch closed before speaking again. "Come, Henry. Walk with me."

Henry sheathed his sword. "Yes. Well. I stand prepared, Rhoenne. For battle...or an ear for the listen. But I must say, I am surprised. You have never asked for my words."

"I have never done a lot of things. And most are happening since that woman came into my life!"

Rhoenne walked slowly, favoring his injured side. Henry walked alongside. If he noted Rhoenne's gingerly-taken steps, he didn't speak of it.

"What woman?"

"Cassandra!"

"Well...you do have two of them. I just wanted to be specific."

"Things are completely backwards, Henry. Up is down. Down is up!"

"Because of Cassandra," the man remarked.

"Aye!"

"What has she done?"

"She is beautiful."

"So you continually tell me."

"No! It is so much worse than that. She is too beauteous for belief. There is no comparison. Of any kind! I do na' have much time. Once we dock, her fate will be set."

"What fate? Why?"

"That is no heathen shoreline, Henry. 'Tis civilization. Christian civilization. Keeping slaves is a sin. And *nae* nobleman keeps a lady in his household...na' without besmirching her name."

"Besmirching her name? Cassandra? Are we speaking of the same woman?"

"Henry," Rhoenne said warningly.

"I do na' ken this trouble. She came out of a heathen potentate's harem. How is anything you have or will do besmirching anything?"

"Call me a fool, but I actually believe she is an innocent. Still."

"*Nae!*" The man's expression mirrored his shock.

"Oh. Aye."

"Well. This is... I see. That is surprising, but it is hardly a problem."

"I face two options. Either I set Cassandra up in a household with Ida and Emin...or I place her in a convent."

"Or you leave her on the street and go on your merry way."

"Never!"

"Why na'?"

"I can na' just leave her! She has gotten under my skin! I do na' even ken how. Or why. Or when. But last night showed me."

"Ah. I see. You...have discovered a fondness for her, and that is turning you a little too human for your own peace of mind."

"Why did I think speaking with you a good idea?" Rhoenne bit out through clenched teeth.

"Forgive me, my laird. I could na' resist. Have you asked her what she wishes?"

"Aye."

"And what does she say?"

"She is na' amenable to either option. She wishes to stay with me. She begged it just now."

"My. My. Things must have been verra interesting in that cabin with just two women."

"And a eunuch! Damnation, FitzHugh! Would you be serious? I need advice. Not jesting."

"Forgive me, my laird. I mused aloud, and the levity was out of place. I just. Well. This is all so...surprising."

"My asking advice?"

"'Tis more the quandary you are presenting to me."

"Cassandra is—. She—. Well. It is na' what you think. She is na' accustomed to much of anything. And she is far too beautiful. 'Tis most unreal. She believes the lone place of safety is with me. She is verra persuasive with her words, too."

"I do see your issue. Well. I must say of the three options I have just heard, only one is truly safe."

"The convent?"

"Convents are na' safe. Priests are – forgive the blasphemous thought – still men. If she is as beauteous as you say, how will covering her in a habit, with scapular, cowl, and veil, keep her protected?"

"She would *nae* longer be my problem."

"Nor would she be if you set her up in her own household."

"I canna' set her up with just Emin and Ida.

'Twould be akin to leading a lamb to slaughter."

"That leaves one option. The one she already requested."

"I canna' keep that woman with me. Who is to protect her, then?"

"You."

"*From* me!" Rhoenne announced.

"Ah. I begin to see the real trouble here." It looked suspiciously like Henry was hiding a smile. His mouth moved rapidly behind his beard. But his voice didn't sound amused. "Your options are narrowing as you speak. Would you consider... matrimony?"

"Of course na'. I am betrothed. You ken as much. You were at the ceremony."

"A decade ago. More. She was na' even birthed, yet."

"She is a Plantagenet. Sister to our queen."

"True. But...loyalty to England grows ever tenuous. Some say even Baliol clan or Bruce may lay claim to the throne next. Should you fail to abide the betrothal, the most that will happen is you will lose a fat dower. Your fief is large. Her dower of little moment, actually."

"What of the curse?"

"Birthing a Ramhurst kills the mother? Complete nonsense. Wife's tale."

"What of...Aileen, then?"

"Oh. Rhoenne. Please. Just grant me permission to be there when they meet. I would die a happy man. I vow it."

"I am *not* speaking of matrimony, FitzHugh. Ever. There has to be another option!"

"You wish me to take on the responsibility...in your stead?"

Rhoenne growled menacingly.   His hands knotted into fists.   He even took an instinctive step toward the man before stopping it.

"Well," Henry remarked slowly.   "That sounds like an answer to me."

"I already regret asking advice, FitzHugh. Don't make me hit you, as well," Rhoenne returned.

"Must you make this decision now?   Perhaps yon port is a licentious city.   Or one of little note. Your passage may na' be noted."

"Me? Go unnoticed?"

"Hmm. True. My wits do desert me at times. Perhaps she can stay veiled?"

"And have it known I keep veiled women in my household, like some eastern heathen?"

"You can say she is your ward. 'Tis na' unusual."

"My ward?"

"Cousin's daughter. Sister-by-law. Something. None need ken the truth."

Rhoenne snapped his glance to his man. A glimmer of hope altered his frown. "Oh, Henry. I never considered that."

"I believe the idea merits a word of caution, Ramhurst."

"Yes? What?"

"She is of marriageable age. And beautiful. If you are her sponsor, and she is as you say...then you will most likely face a fourth option."

"What?"

"Her marriage to another."

Rhoenne's step faltered.   He caught the

motion. Resumed walking. His torso twisted. The wound twinged unmercifully. He stifled the pain. But nothing stopped the other pain. The one that shot through his chest without a hint of warning. The one he refused to acknowledge.

Not in this lifetime.

And never because of a woman.

CHAPTER SIXTEEN

HE SAW HIM twice in the next eleven days. Twice.

The rooms she'd been escorted to were large and richly furnished, as befitted a city in the *Domini de Mar* of the richest most powerful trading empire in the world. Rhoenne had secured housing within the walls of Castle Kaza, the regional seat of power for the Dukedom. The castle was a hive of activity, housing many noble households, most attempting to secure financing for a personal matter or business venture. That would have also been Rhoenne Ramhurst's mission, save he'd arrived at the city in possession of a ship and a cargo hold full of luxuries.

The city was called Sitia. A massive structure called Fortress Kazarma overlooked the harbor from the crest of the highest hill. Part of the Realm of Candia, and controlled by the Venetian Republic, the fortress was a symbol of power and protection. Sitia's markets were awash in luxury goods. Rhoenne's cargo fetched monumental prices. His coffers were said to be bursting, even without the addition of her jewelry. Not that she worried over it, but Emin never mentioned what had happened with it, and she didn't ask. The ship was being repaired and retrofitted for an ocean journey, somewhere past the Island of Malta. A crew was being hired and trained. And if it hadn't been for Emin's information, she'd have known nothing.

Cassandra and Ida had been left aboard ship the entire first day and into the night. Before dawn, the women had been escorted under heavy veiling to a covered donkey-drawn cart, driven over cobblestoned streets for some distance uphill, then rushed through a maze of halls that echoed. A lone torchbearer had lighted the path, hooded, his face in shadow. Cassandra hadn't known who led their progress, but Emin had been the man behind them the entire way.

Candelabra had been lit throughout the three rooms of her new chambers. Emin had followed the shadowy man out. She'd heard the door closing, and then the definite sound of a lock being engaged. She'd tried the door since. It was always locked. Emin was the lone one allowed through it, and he knocked before every entrance.

Apparently, she'd just exchanged a small enclosed prison cell for a palatial one.

It didn't take long to have every bit of this one memorized. The main room held chairs, stools, and a large circular table. There was a fireplace along one wall, used only at night, for the light was welcome. It also warded off chill that pervaded the rooms. One antechamber was adorned with hooks, and shelves. Another one contained cots that she and Ida slept on. The largest antechamber held a large bed with three enclosed wooden sides and a thick velvet drapery to pull down for further privacy. That was the one Rhoenne used.

When he used it at all.

She could count the times he might have slept in it on the fingers of one hand, as Ida clicked her tongue and smoothed the coverlet. Cassandra would have helped her, but Ida was adamant, and would move any helping hands aside. Ida shared the incarceration, but the woman spent most of her time in measuring and fitting and working with the fabrics and items that Emin brought in and took out daily with the information that she was being fitted with a wardrobe. He didn't say why. And she didn't ask.

It was enough that Rhoenne hadn't discarded her.

So, Cassandra stood idly while Ida pinned fabrics. Cut them as needed. Sent them out with Emin. Finished, almost-ready to wear garments were brought back in. Cassandra's wardrobe grew to include ankle-length smocks of thinnest flax linen in varying shades, from ecru to one so white it shone light blue. Some smocks were crafted in gossamer silks, in rose, blue, and yellow tones. They were folded and set neatly on the closet shelves, alongside pairs of hose that had been crafted in every shade and from all manner of yarns. Some woolen. Most silk. As time passed, a multitude of sleeveless tunics joined the smocks, hanging from the hooks, all crafted

from colorful expensive fabrics: silks, linen,
velvets, brocades. The bodices were intricately
embroidered around slits for the lacing, in various
materials: satiny ribbons, thin leather cording.
Gold wire.

  She had three girdles as well, two worked in
gold, one in silver. They'd been fashioned in
a latticework fashion, making them not only
delicate but much less weighty. There were
matching headdresses, and she had a selection of
light-as-air veils to attach, each one exquisite.

  The days were full. When she wasn't sewing or
reading from the eight precious tomes on a shelf
in the main room, or partaking of wonderful
meals of varied and delicious items, she was
meditating - using the skills she'd been taught by
a woman from the Indus valley. But the nights
had become a morass of unease. Dream-filled
sleep intermixed with wakeful fretting. Ida had
no such issues. The woman fell asleep almost
the moment her head touched her cot, and she
didn't stir again until dawn. Such a thing must
be a benefit of long work hours, and a clear
conscience.

  Cassandra's wakefulness was the only reason
she'd seen him. She'd been fetching a cup of
water from their pitcher when the lock had
sounded. Cassandra barely had time to turn
about before Rhoenne walked in. The door shut
behind him. She'd been in her night-rail of thin
linen, silhouetted in the firelight. The fire glow
had illuminated him. She'd seen his lips tighten.
His teeth clench. And then he'd given a heavy

sigh. And narrowed his eyes.

"I...was...getting water," she stammered.

Without a word, he'd turned and walked out. Shut the door softly. Re-connected the lock. Cassandra had returned to her cot, but it had taken a long time to get back to sleep.

The second time they'd met had been deep into the hours of another night. She'd been restless. Apprehensive. She'd fallen from her cot, awakening abruptly from a dream. She'd heard male voices in the hall, raised almost in anger. Or entreaty. This time, before she left the chamber she shared with Ida, Cassandra had taken the time to don a hooded surcoat of velvet that trailed to her feet. She'd just raised the hood when the lock clicked. The door opened. She heard bits of conversation.

"...swear to you, Excellency!"

"She has na' been out?"

"No."

"And no one has been in?"

"None. I have let no one through this door."

Rhoenne had stepped in. Shut the door behind him. And then he'd looked over and seen her. He'd gone taut. His face blank. Completely emotionless.

"Where is it you think you are going?" he'd asked in a truly frightening voice.

"No...where," she whispered through cold lips.

"I left orders. You were na' to leave. Or be seen."

She nodded.

"Emin swears my orders were followed."

Cassandra nodded again.

"So...how is it you escaped?"

She'd frowned. "I did na'."

"So why are you dressed?"

She swallowed on a dry throat. Her heart was hammering. "I did na' think you wished to see me...undressed."

His lips pursed as if he might consider believing her. Or, it might be that he completely disbelieved her. She couldn't tell, and she'd always told herself she was good at reading expressions. He took three steps toward her, closing the distance between them, then lifted a hand and peeled the hood back. She couldn't meet his gaze. It would help if he wasn't so tall. Or so masculine. Or so close.

Cassandra kept her focus on the center of his chest at her eye level. He wore a sleeveless blue jerkin over a tunic of wheat-colored linen. The lacing was a thin black cord. It wasn't tied properly, or the shirt was sewn to gap, revealing chest. It didn't disguise any of his size. Or form. Or handsomeness. He needed to wear a lot more for that to happen.

She trembled with something indefinable. It wasn't with chill. She was completely covered. The surcoat she'd donned was concealing blue velvet with a gold stitched border. Beneath it was an ankle-length linen nightgown, fastened with a tie at her throat. Ida had done her hair in a loose braid down her back, like always. Nothing about her attire had felt remotely sensual. Or illicit. It did now.

"This was na' a good idea," he said.

"What?" she asked his chest.

"Keeping you."

Cassandra's eyes widened. Her heart raced even faster.

"You are much too beautiful."

"No, please. I will do anything. Cut my hair. Disfig—"

He touched a finger beneath her jaw, interrupting her as he lifted her chin. "I was accosted with a rumor tonight. In a tavern. By a complete stranger and two of his companions. They'd heard about the beauty I keep hidden away in my chambers."

Cassandra gasped, her eyes widened. She glanced up, got an impression of his frown. Looked back down again. She wasn't brave enough to look higher.

"*Nae* man can keep you hidden away safely. I am surprised the sultan managed it."

"Please?" Cassandra whispered and moved her gaze to his.

Her heart immediately stopped. Time froze. Firelight quit flickering. Even the air held still. She'd forgotten the effect of his intense blue gaze.

"You should probably stop me," he whispered.

"From...what?"

"This."

His head lowered to hers, while she went up onto tiptoes, the move instinctive. Perfect. Lips met. Hearts fused. Eons passed. Heat and light whooshed through the chamber. She saw it from behind closed eyelids. Felt it with every fiber of her being. She'd thought their first kiss touched on the divine. This one was even better. Her every breath matched his. Their blended moan swelled and filled the chamber. And then he lifted his head. His eyes were tightly scrunched shut. His entire frame was trembling. He opened his eyes and the look he gave her was haunting. He looked beyond pained. He looked tormented.

He lowered her to the floor. She hadn't even felt him lift her.

"Go," he ordered, motioning with his head toward the room she shared with Ida. His voice was low. Gruff. Commanding. "Now."

Cassandra ducked her head and rushed to the room. Shut the door. And launched onto her cot. Facedown. Nearly swooning with a sensation of bliss she hadn't known existed. She told herself he meant nothing by it. It was late. He may have over-imbibed. He didn't care for her. He never would. But nothing stopped the rapturous shivers that continually flew her skin. Over and over.

And over.

"Hurry, Highness! He approaches."

Cassandra turned at Emin's words. Smiled. The eunuch was acting like a mother hen with a chick. There wasn't anything more she could do to enhance her appearance. His wide grin and wider eyes showed he agreed.

They'd been under orders all day. Emin had repeated them to her that morning, along with a pot of *caffe*, and a meal of porridge with figs, kidneys with eggs, and blackened bread covered with melted butter and dusted with cinnamon. One of the *Consiglieri* of the Dukedom controlled the city of Sitia. He'd granted Scotland's Earl of Tyneburgh an audience. This evening. Rhoenne wanted Cassandra at his side, dressed in her finest ensemble. They would be accompanied by the men who made up his Honor Guard. She was to be ready and waiting before sundown.

Cassandra had been beset with excitement that grew apace with the day's ministrations. Wasn't this proof that he wasn't discarding her? He'd ordered this wardrobe for her presence at court. That must be the reason. Wasn't that proof that he wanted her with him! He was making certain the world saw and recognized it. The glow that suffused her every fiber was almost uncontainable. It was an aura of happiness. The entire day of preparations only enhanced the feeling.

Ida and Cassandra had worked almost non-stop. Every lantern and candelabra had been lit, the fire stoked. First they'd covered Cassandra's body with oil before scraping off any body hair using a sharp obsidian knife. That was followed by a fine-sand scrub. Next had been her bath. Emin had brought in a tub. He'd then delivered buckets of heated water, filling the chamber with moist steam. The water had been perfumed with *Cyprinum,* a mix of cardamom, cinnamon, and myrrh, adding aromatic essence to the steam. Once she'd dried, the same fragrance had scented the oils that were massaged into her skin. A lighter version of the same oil was then laboriously rubbed through her hair, coating nearly every strand. Ida had then worked her hair into dozens of tight braids while it was damp, before stoking the fire and setting Cassandra in front of it. The woman had then spent a good portion of the afternoon intermittently fanning Cassandra with a large ostrich fan to make certain the braids would be dry in time.

Ramhurst clan had a color scheme. They wore a *plaide* of gray and white with smaller bands of black and vivid blue through it. Emin had been given swatches of colors that Rhoenne wanted Cassandra to wear. That was no hardship. She had several dresses and kirtles in those colors.

Cassandra had mixed talc and a tiny drop of oil into kohl for her eyes. Ida had emphatically shaken her head, so Cassandra hadn't used much. A slight dusting on her lids, a dark line about each eye. Ida worried for no reason. Cosmetic enhancement was one thing Cassandra had been taught to do with precision. Ida's expression when she'd finished was all the proof needed. The maid not only smiled and nodded, she clapped her hands. Red wine was mixed into a tiny drop of whipped oil. Cassandra spread it on her lips for color and moistness. And then she was ready to dress.

Almost reverently, Ida helped her don each garment. They'd chosen a pure white linen smock for her under-garment. Her hose were pulled into place next. This pair was woven of gray-shaded silk and fastened just above the knee using black ribbon garters. Over that she wore a kirtle of ice-blue silk with silver embroidered bodice and hem. The same metallic thread decorated the edges of the elbow-length sleeves. Her sleeveless overdress was fashioned in heavy silk, dyed an intense blue shade. The neckline dipped beneath her breasts putting the silver embroidered kirtle bodice on display. Silver-edged, black ribbon cord laced her dress beneath her bosom, cinching the waist. Lastly, she wore the silver girdle, fastened low on her hips to define more of her shape.

Then Ida turned to her hair. Every braid was unfastened carefully, and finger-combed, leaving the ripples intact. The mass was then pulled back from her face with more silver-edged, black ribbon. Ends of that were arranged through her tresses. Then Ida brought out the matching silver lattice headdress. The headdress covered Cassandra's forehead and crown of her head. An attached gossamer gray-colored veil fell down her back. The veil did little to conceal her hair, and it fell short of her waist, leaving the ends of her hair displayed. There were blue silk slippers with leather soles for her feet, and she was ready. Ida walked slowly around her twice. She smiled and nodded as though pleased. Cassandra's reflection in the large polished silver mirror mounted on the wall seemed to agree.

She struggled for a calm her entire body belied. She wanted to look serene. Confident. It was such a difficult task when inside she was jumble of anticipation. Alight with excitement. Jittery with eagerness.

They had just finished when Emin warned her of Rhoenne's imminent arrival. He gave her a quick glance, and then that big swift smile of approval. Her heart instantly ratcheted to a faster beat. Her hands grew icy, her breathing quick and shallow. Her throat went dry. She had never been so excited in her life. Nor as frightened. Vastly thrilled, and yet scared at the same time.

She so hoped he'd be pleased.

She heard Rhoenne's deep voice first. Emin's reply. Rhoenne's words to his men. And her heart kicked into an even faster, stronger rhythm.

"Emin? Is she ready?"

"Yes Excellency. Her Highness waits within."

"Gentlemen? Wait here."

Emin opened the door. Rhoenne took two steps into the room before looking toward her. He stopped dead. His jaw dropped. So did hers. His was especially easy to note...because he'd shaved.

Oh, sweet heaven!

Cassandra tried to force her mouth closed. When that didn't work, she lifted a hand to her lips to hide behind. She'd thought him handsome before. There were no words. The man was beyond swoon-worthy. Especially since he'd pulled his hair back into a queue and shaved, revealing a thickly muscled neck, extremely chiseled jaw, and full lips. Their outfits were a perfect match, as well. He wore a large-sleeved tunic of pure white. Atop that was a sleeveless silk blue jerkin, laced together with silver-and-black

striped cord. A silver embossed belt rode his hips.
He had a short sword strapped to one side. Two
knives tucked into the front of his belt. Gray
trousers covered lengthy, muscled legs. There was
no escaping the fact that Rhoenne Ramhurst
was a physically perfect specimen. Masculine.
Virile. His attire clung to every bit of him as if
to showcase it.

He crossed the distance between them with a
few strides. Then just stood above her, breathing
hard enough it ruffled the veil atop her head.

"You are...pleased?" she asked, addressing the
cord laced across his chest.

He didn't answer. She dared a glance upward,
gasped, and looked down again. His eyes were
hooded. His lips pursed. His jaw set so tightly,
a nerve jutted from the back of one cheek. He
didn't look angry. She was afraid to decipher
what his expression signified. It was enough that
it sent a lightning charge rocketing right through
her. She trembled in place. Locked her knees.
And somehow kept from falling.

"I did na' think it possible," he finally remarked.

"My lord?" Cassandra asked.

"For you to get...any more beautiful."

There was a distinct pause in the middle of
his words. Ida gave a rapturous sigh. Cassandra
ducked her head, smiled widely, and suffered
through a series of blushes that sent heat all the
way to her hairline. She hadn't tinted her cheeks
with the red wine mixture. It wasn't needed.

"Turn around. Please? Don't turn back until
I say. Fair?"

"My lord?" Cassandra repeated.

"I am going to bring my Honor Guard in to meet you." His voice was filled with merriment. "And I think this may be one of − if not *the* - most enjoyable moment of my adult life. You ready?"

Cassandra pivoted to face the fireplace. She heard the door open.

"Gentlemen? Please. Come in. I have someone for you to meet."

This was scary and exciting. She heard the sound of boots. Clanking of metallic objects. Some of the candles flared and wavered before remaining lit.

"Ramhurst. Is na' this a bit dramatic?" She recognized Henry's voice.

"Oh. Aye. It is. Most definitely." Rhoenne's voice was filled with merriment. "Gentlemen. May I present the lady Cassandra? Cassandra? Please. Turn around."

She did, lifting her eyes to find Rhoenne first. And then she looked at the assemblage of men. There were five of them, all smaller than Rhoenne. All dressed in the same color scheme, although their attire and accessories varied. Most were shaved, and all stared wide-eyed, and open-mouthed. Choking, gasping, and a cut-off oath sounded. An older man with gray-streaked brown hair stumbled back two steps and stared. He was scholarly looking, with pleasant features. She pegged him as Henry. Two fellows dropped to a knee. A gangly one that had to be Euan dropped to both knees, his mouth open and gaping as he looked up at her.

"Well, gentlemen?" Rhoenne voice was loud. "Did I lie?"

Henry shook his head as if to clear it, then physically turned to address Rhoenne. "You need much better words, my laird," he remarked, almost beneath his breath.

Rhoenne snickered. Cassandra wasn't the only one staring before he sobered. He was still amused, however. It sounded in his voice.

"Cassandra?   May I first introduce Henry FitzHugh, commander of my Honor Guard? Henry? The lady Cassandra."

Henry turned back to her, met her eyes for a moment, bowed his head, and then went down onto a knee before her. Cassandra's eyes widened.

"This is Iain Montvale, and his cousin, Graham, also of Montvale."

Rhoenne went to put his hands on the shoulders of the two men who'd already kneeled. One was blond. The other had reddish brown hair. The blond wasn't shaved, and his beard had been fashioned to a point. It was a definite red-orange color, like sunset hues on the Egyptian desert.

"This is my cousin, Grant. Grant? The lady Cassandra."

Grant was large. He had dark hair. He might have had blue eyes, but he didn't look at her long enough to verify it. But there any resemblance ended. He nodded, bowed his head, and also went down onto a knee.

"And this lad...is Euan FitzHugh."

Rhoenne stepped to stand behind the gangly one she'd already pegged. Rhoenne patted the smaller man's shoulder. He had a definite grin on his face as he met her gaze over the five bowed heads.

"My men are swearing fealty, Cassandra. A vow to protect and honor you. I did not expect this. Nor did I require it."

She nodded. Intercepted a few peeks from the men. More than one reddened as their glances caught hers, before quickly moved away. She'd never experienced anything like this. Her heart was pounding. Warmth infused everything. The entire chamber felt abuzz with it.

"Rise gentlemen. We have an audience to attend. Surely you do na' wish to be late."

The men stood. Rearranged weaponry. Several cleared throats.

"I need a swift dram from my sporran," one of them muttered.

"If we had a sporran," another one remarked.

"I only hope I don't run into a wall," Euan said.

CHAPTER SEVENTEEN

HEY PROGRESSED DOWN massive halls
and through seemingly endless corridors,
passing tapestry after tapestry, going beneath arch
after arch. The thump of boot heels on stone,
the slightest swish of her leather slipper soles, and
an occasional rustle of weaponry were the only
sounds heard. Cassandra kept her right hand
atop Rhoenne's forearm. Her fingers tingled at
the contact. She should have had trouble keeping
up. She didn't. She practically floated.

They neared a mass of humanity. The halls
opened up, became a huge space crafted of stone
with large pillars that supported the numerous
vaults of the ceiling. Lit candles in globes dotted
chandeliers hung to just above Rhoenne's head
height. If he'd been any taller, he'd have to dodge
them.

It felt odd without Emin, but he'd been assigned
to guard Ida and the chamber. Cassandra hadn't
known until then that Rhoenne had turned his
room into a treasury, stashing *ducati* coins, and
all manner of jewels – including the ones she'd
brought.

Even without the eunuch, the Ramhurst clansmen made an impressive retinue. Euan and Henry Fitzhugh led. Rhoenne followed with Cassandra at his left side. She kept her focus on where Henry's queue ended on his back. The red bearded Montvale guarded her left side. The other Montvale and Rhoenne's cousin, Grant brought up the rear. Cassandra couldn't see much over the men. She didn't truly want to. And she didn't have to. She sensed the impact they created. She could hear conversation halting. Hear gasps. A thunk, then a large crashing noise, was followed by a flash of laughter that was almost instantly quelled.

"You see? It is na' just me. One peek at your lady and people run into poles."

Euan remarked it over his shoulder. Rhoenne grunted humorlessly. Cassandra dipped her head further. Fought another blush. They stopped at a massive set of doors. Time seemed to slow. Sound went mute. Her fingers tightened on Rhoenne's arm. She felt him lean toward her. Cassandra tipped her head, lifting an ear toward him.

"Do na' fash. All is prepared," he spoke softly.

Cassandra's gaze flashed to his. "Prepared?" she asked.

He didn't answer. His lips tightened and he looked away. His expression was grim. His mouth set. That look didn't bode well. She didn't know what he'd prepared. Her heartbeat pulsed. Breath grew rapid and shallow. Her fingers went icy.

"Are you certain you wish to do this?"

Henry had turned, met her glance before looking up to the man at her side. He spoke softly, yet earnestly.

"Aye," Rhoenne answered.

"Absolutely certain?"

"'Twas your plan, FitzHugh," Rhoenne replied.

"That was afore I met her!" Henry hissed. "And saw you two together!"

"FitzHugh," Rhoenne said with his warning voice.

"More specifically...when I saw *you* with her!" the man whispered.

"She understands Gaelic," Rhoenne replied, the words said through what sounded like clenched teeth.

Henry gave an oath beneath his breath, and turned away. Cassandra hadn't just understood their words. Her eyes were so wide the pressure of air hurt. Her mind stalled. Thoughts jumbled. Reaction wasn't far behind. An unpleasant series of shivers flew across her skin. Her lower lip trembled. And her heart fell. They had to wait to speak of a plan now? Without one hint of warning?

There wasn't time to say more. An older man dressed in a floor-length white-and-gold robe and wearing a high conical hat stepped toward them. He carried a long staff. The outer Cassandra watched as they conversed. The inner woman was awash in emotion. Terrified. Worried. Anxious. She was left to guess at the plan. It wasn't a difficult task. Rhoenne Ramhurst had never wanted her. He was ridding himself of an unwanted complication. A woman he didn't need. That was the purpose behind her wardrobe. Her preparation. This presentation.

She'd been fooling herself all day. Her mouth and throat felt as if she'd swallowed ashes.

The man with the staff cast a glance her direction and jerked as though startled. Cassandra barely noticed. He shook his head, then walked to the doors and rapped on the wood with his staff. An echo rippled through the room behind them. The doors opened inward. Cassandra got a glimpse of a lengthy red carpet, a crowd of elegantly dressed men and women behind waist-high barriers. Armored soldiers lined both sides of the carpet. Torches were lit in sconces, shedding light throughout the room. And everywhere was the glint of gold.

And if she could have been back in her chambers, she'd have raced there.

She kept her focus on the spot between Henry's shoulders. Stared without seeing. Unblinking. The spot blurred with emotion she forced back. She'd never cried in the harem. She'd silently chided anyone else who wept. Tears never solved anything. They were for the weak. The spineless. The foolish.

She'd been so naïve. Stupidly judgmental. Because she hadn't met Rhoenne, experienced what the world really was. And she hadn't fallen in love.

Oh dear God.

Her knees wavered. Her hand clenched Rhoenne. She felt the muscles in his forearm tighten beneath her fingers.

It wasn't possible.

It wasn't fair.

It wasn't smart.

But just like that, she knew. Despite everything against the notion, she loved him! It wasn't a pleasant feeling, either. It was harsh. Scalding hot, yet ice cold. Soft as a twilit breeze, and hard as stone. Immense. Soul-altering. She knew now why she'd begged to stay with him. Why she'd been so excited all day. Why his glance made her heart race, and his kiss had sent her spirit into sleepless rapture.

She loved him!

Cassandra stumbled. Rhoenne's arm went taut again. His steps stopped. He didn't look toward her. And curse her stupidity in checking for that very thing! The man in the long robe and conical hat stepped into the room and pounded the floor with his staff. It was unnecessary. Everyone seemed to be waiting for his words. He spoke. It was obvious why he had the occupation. He had a large projecting voice. Notes bounced off the walls and ceiling as he announced their party.

"Your Excellency, Councilor Angelo Moroseni! May I present Lord Rhoenne Guy de Ramhurst, Fifth Earl of Tyneburgh, from the Kingdom of *Scotia*?"

"Ready?" Rhoenne asked her.

To lose him?

Never.

Cassandra managed to nod. She didn't look up. She didn't dare. She put her mind on mundane things. The carpet was a thick pile. It sucked up any sound of boot heels or the leather soles of her satin slippers. Rhoenne and the others adjusted their gait to hers, waiting to take one step to her every two, their movements smooth and evenly spaced as though practiced. Cassandra noted the men kept their right sides free, their hand resting on sword hilts. Soldiers gawked, and stood straighter as they neared and then passed. The walk seemed interminable. The room enormous and chill. But that wasn't odd. The entire world felt the exact same. Vast. Frightening.

And cold.

They stopped at a circular section of carpeting. The Honor Guard fanned out, Henry and Euan moved to Rhoenne's right. The other three moved to Cassandra's left side, forming a slightly curved line with Rhoenne and Cassandra at the center.

The carpet hadn't ended. On the opposite side of the circle, it changed back to a long panel and climbed up a series of steps before disappearing beneath a row of chairs. Cassandra's glance upward saw the carved lions on the legs of gold-embossed chairs. She quickly looked back down. The shiver that rippled over her wasn't pleasant. Rhoenne lowered his left arm, releasing her. Cassandra moved her hand, clasped it with the other, and held them at the top of her lacing, just beneath her breasts. And she started praying. Silently. Fervently.

Please God! Let me stay with him! Please?

"My Lord Ramhurst. Welcome to Sitia!"

"Your Excellency."

Rhoenne bowed. His men all followed. And Cassandra surprised herself as she remembered how to accomplish a formal curtsey from somewhere in her past.

"I have been informed that you and your men just returned from the Seventh Crusade?"

"Yes."

"I have heard rumors. Bad ones. What tidings have you brought?"

"Dark ones. The cause is lost, Your Excellency. *Outremer* overrun. Acre is the lone outpost still holding. France's King Louis is being held for ransom. There are...few survivors."

"The pontiff must be inconsolable. I shall draft a missive to Pope Innocent IV."

Rhoenne nodded. Nobody said anything for a few moments. Cassandra continued her prayer, almost chanting the words.

Please God. Please.

She glanced up again toward the chairs. Quickly looked back down. A man and woman were in the center, sitting in the largest chairs. She assumed the man was Councilor Moroseni. He was part of the Great Council of Candia. There were several official-looking gentlemen on either side of the couple. In their purple robes lined with ermine, the councilor and his wife looked regal.

"I have heard you are a ship owner," the councilor continued.

"Yes, Your Excellency."

"And you prepare for a journey back to your

native *Scotia*?"

"That is my plan."

"I have also been informed that you are funding your own voyage."

"That is also correct," Rhoenne replied.

"And yet, you sought an audience with me? Are you desirous of capital for a business venture perhaps? You wish to expand into shipping? You wish sponsorship on a trading route?"

Rhoenne's lips twisted. Cassandra's heart made the same motion. And then he said the words she feared.

"I do wish sponsorship, Your Excellency. But not for me."

He held his hand out for Cassandra. She almost balked. Her feet didn't want to move. Her limbs felt leaden. Her blood frozen. Somehow, she gave the direction and her hand moved. She put her fingers within his. His hand was so warm. So strong.

Rhoenne drew her forward, separating them from the line of his men.

"This is Cassandra."

More detested tears pricked her eyes. She shoved them back. Hardened her mind and begged the same condition for her heart. Her chest felt like a burning piece of coal centered it, sending out bursts of fiery flickers. Each beat throbbed through her, sending pain.

"Cassandra," the councilor repeated.

She curtsied again and then looked up. The councilor's eyes widened and his brows rose. All of the men on the dais sat taller, as if in concert.

The councilor's wife's eyes narrowed and her lips pinched.

And then a loud thumping interrupted everything. It resounded from the entrance doors, sending the same echo as happened from the other side. The officials above her all looked over their heads in that direction. Rhoenne swiveled, moving her with him. His men also turned.

"Your Excellency, Councilor Angelo Moroseni! The Dowager *Duchesse* Lucia Zecchino begs an audience!"

The man with the conical hat announced it. There was a small wizened lady beside him, leaning on a cane. She was dressed in pale pink silk, while her headdress and kirtle were ablaze with diamonds. The same stones glittered from about her neck and wrists.

"*Signor* Pietro. This is highly irregular."

The councilor spoke. He wasn't speaking in French, the recognized court language throughout western civilization. He spoke in Venetian. Cassandra hadn't heard it since she'd learned it as a child. From her mother.

"It is of utmost importance, Your Excellency!"

"Very well. You may proceed."

The woman started toward them, the announcer fellow at her side.

"My Lord Ramhurst," the councilor spoke again to Rhoenne in the language they understood. "I beg a moment to hear this woman's words. She commands respect. She is the sister of our *duca di Candia,* Stefano Guistiniani. You...understand?"

"I have no objection," Rhoenne remarked. "If you wish, we can return at a more opportune moment."

Cassandra's spirit soared. Her heart raced. Her entire frame sagged with relief. And then the old woman ruined it.

"No! He must stay. They all...must!" The woman may be aged, but her voice was strong. Autocratic. The old woman smacked the announcer fellow with a finger, then spoke to him in Venetian as well. "Stop fussing, Pietro. I'll get there when I get there. You may count yourself in luck that I hadn't gone into supper yet."

Titters of amusement wafted through the chamber, and were almost instantly silenced by her next words.

"And bring some guards with you."

A line of soldiers formed behind the old woman and the man named Pietro. Cassandra saw Rhoenne and Henry exchange glances. Hands tightened on sword hilts. Rhoenne's jaw clenched. A nerve pulsed out one side of his cheek. He dropped his gaze to hers. His look sent a whoosh of emotion straight through her that stunned. Frightened. Electrified. And completely spellbound.

"Lord Ramhurst?" the councilor asked.

Rhoenne released her gaze. Looked back up at the dais. That's when Cassandra noted his men. They'd closed ranks, surrounding her and Rhoenne. Facing outward. They were already an impressive group. The threat they presented without a word of instruction was even more so.

"Excellency?"

Rhoenne answered him without a speck of emotion. He accompanied the word with a move to shift Cassandra behind him, holding her at his back with his left hand. His right hand never left his sword hilt.

"You...would stay to speak with Her Grace?"

"This is a request to converse?" Rhoenne asked.

The old woman came to a stop before Rhoenne, planted her cane into the carpet between them with a sharp gesture. And then she used the support to lean back and glare up at Rhoenne. Pietro was at her side. A dozen or more soldiers backed her. She was almost exactly Cassandra's height.

"Your Grace, please. You are creating an international incident."

"There may be an incident, Angelo. But it will not be of my making."

The woman didn't sound intimidated. Cassandra peeked around Rhoenne's arm, caught the woman's glance, and the look that crossed her face instantly nullified any threat. Cassandra had never seen anything so inquisitive and suspicious. But then the expression disappeared and she was once again glaring up at Rhoenne.

"Who is this man?" the *duchesse* demanded.

"This is the Earl of Tyneburgh. From the kingdom of *Scotia*."

Rhoenne recognized his name and the country. Cassandra felt him shift slightly. Straighten. His hand pulled her closer to his spine.

"Are you certain? Did you verify it?"

There was an audible gasp at the insult. Then murmurs and twitters from the listeners. Cassandra was grateful Rhoenne didn't speak the language.

"What, by the saints, would make you say such a thing?"

"I'll say a lot more than that, Angelo. I hear he just came from the east!"

"Yes. He was crusading."

"So he says. Did you verify that?"

The outcry at that outrageous statement was louder than her earlier one.

"Your Grace!" The councilor was no longer calm. Or remotely amused. "You will keep your comments civil."

"Why does he have my granddaughter? Did you at least ask him that?"

There was a swell of noise at the statement. Shocked cries. One might have even come from her. Cassandra's knees buckled but Rhoenne's grip held her upright. She snaked an arm about his waist for further stability. Focused on the carpet beneath them. Breathed in with quick gasps. Exhaled just as rapidly.

"Your...granddaughter?" The councilor's voice seemed a pale reflection of the surprise throughout the room.

"That is a Votten. I would recognize her anywhere. Tell me I am wrong."

"I don't see how—?"

The councilor spoke, but the old woman interrupted him. "My daughter wed a Bulgar prince, Philip of Vottenavia. A very handsome man...with a particular color of hair. Pietro recognized it at a glance and came to fetch me! You must remember the wedding. You were there! I visited them once. They had three daughters. Some years back, we were informed the principality was overrun...by murderous savages. The entire family was reportedly... killed." The woman's voice trembled more than once. She sniffed, pulled her head back, and then continued. She had her accusatory tone back as well. "And yet now, this man walks into your audience chamber with my granddaughter, Perina, and you don't even ask him how he came to possess her? No! Wait. Perina would be older. Madalena, perhaps?"

"Her name is Cassandra," Rhoenne answered.

Oh, sweet Lord!

He knew the language? He'd heard the insults the old *duchesse* had been hurling? And he hadn't shown the slightest hint of it?

Cassandra already knew how debilitating panic was. She recognized the symptoms. There was no Emin to smack his hands and shock her out of it. But there was the strong sturdy support of Rhoenne's hand at her back, holding her against him. The heat that emanated from his body. The chill hardness of his belt against her forearm where she still held him.

"But, of course." The *duchesse's* voice warmed markedly. "My youngest granddaughter. Cassandra Alexandria. Wait. You know her name?"

Rhoenne nodded.

"Then why is it you didn't bring her to me the moment your ship docked?" She had her insulting accusatory tone firmly in place again.

"I was not aware of her lineage," he returned.

"And now that you are?"

The entire room seemed to be waiting for his answer. Cassandra lifted her head. Snuck a peek at the *duchesse*.

"I believe I'll be requesting a private audience with the Councilor," Rhoenne remarked. "And I may even allow you to attend...Your Grace." He added her title after a moment, as if an afterthought.

Oh my.

Cassandra couldn't keep the slight smile of pleasure to herself. Her lips failed at hiding it. She knew he was confident and forthright. Beyond bold. She watched as the woman claiming to be her grandmother regarded him.

"Angelo!" The woman announced the name loudly, without taking her eyes from Rhoenne.

"Yes, Your Grace?" The councilor replied from the dais.

"You heard the man. Do you have time on your schedule for a private audience?"

"Right now?"

There was a general outbreak of hilarity through the room, some laughter. Chuckling. A swell of whispering. All of it almost immediately calmed. As if no one wanted to miss hearing what might transpire next. It seemed to relieve the tensions of moments before.

"Don't make me complain to my brother," she replied. "You know how he hates that."

More rumblings of amusement filtered through the room.

"Oh. I believe we can fit it in. Gentlemen? We shall repair to the green room." There was a murmured remark, barely audible. "Yes. I know it only fits thirty. That is the point."

Soldiers moved around the duchesse and Pietro, giving a wide berth to where Rhoenne and his retinue stood. Their boots were perfectly cadenced as they stepped across uncarpeted floor at one side of the dais. Cassandra heard what sounded like doors opening. Shuffling that could be the officials on the dais departing. She stepped closer to Rhoenne and tightened her arm about him. She didn't mean to. It wasn't planned or orchestrated. His fingers pressed slightly against her back as he felt it.

And her heart stuttered with joy.

Stupidly. Unreasonably. It still happened.

"Your Grace? You may bring Pietro. Lord Ramhurst? You will bring your men."

"And the lady Cassandra," Rhoenne responded.

"I wish to escort my granddaughter," the *duchesse* announced.

"I beg to differ," Rhoenne responded easily. "The lady Cassandra will be attending with me. As I just specified."

"Angelo! Do something!" The *duchesse* smacked the floor with her cane.

"This is my requested audience, Your Grace," Rhoenne spoke up. "*Not* yours."

The woman narrowed her eyes at Rhoenne. Her lips pinched tight. Her lined face even more aged-looking. And then she looked down at where Cassandra was hugged into him. Sighed. And nodded. She tapped Pietro, put a hand on his arm, and slowly shuffled past them, following the soldiers' path.

"Lord Ramhurst? If you will?"

Rhoenne looked up at the dais to where the councilor must still be situated. He regarded the area for long moments. Then nodded. "We will be with you shortly."

"You won't precede us?"

"I said...we will be with you shortly. You have my word," Rhoenne replied.

Crowd noise started up. There was a buzz of sound as people discussed and gossiped over what had just occurred. Cassandra recognized it. The harem had just such a reaction whenever something momentous occurred. The sultan had ordered them to prepare. A woman had discovered she'd been blessed by Allah and was carrying the sultan's child. A woman gave birth. Or if a truly handsome man was visiting the sultan.

And then Rhoenne pulled her out from behind him, lowered his head, and matched his forehead to hers. All so he could look right into her eyes.

And the entire world halted.

She knew they were the center of attention. The crowd all about them watched. Listened. Scrutinized. It didn't matter. There could have been quakes ravaging the earth, sea waves overtaking shores, landslides obliterating whole villages, and she'd have missed them. Cassandra was ensnared. Afloat. Rapt.

"What the devil is going on?" Euan asked.

She thought it was Henry shushing him. Nothing mattered save Rhoenne. And the question deep within his vivid blue eyes.

CHAPTER EIGHTEEN

"**M**Y LAIRD! DO you know what you are doing?"

Henry's hissed whisper wasn't loud, but enough to break Rhoenne's eye contact with her. His eyelids closed. Small lines crinkled at the edges of his eyes. His breath deepened. His upper lip lifted in a snarl. He raised his head from her and turned to Henry. Annoyance crossed his face. He looked grim. Cassandra should have matched the emotion, but she still trembled in place, encased in a blissful aura so vibrant, she could almost see it.

"What?" he finally asked from between clenched teeth.

"That woman is the sister of their *duca!*" Henry still whispered, even with an adding emphasis.

"She is?" Euan sputtered.

"We need to take this into the hall," Rhoenne replied in a soft, deadly serious tone.

"Agreed," Henry replied.

"But...we speak in Gaelic," one of the Montvales spoke.

"That does na' matter, Iain! You are in a place

of governance. No language is safe. And this is an audience room with great sound quality. Add to that the surfeit of listeners about us!" Henry still whispered, but it was rapid and intent.

"Oh," someone answered.

"Are you ready?"

It took a moment to realize Rhoenne spoke to her. Cassandra jerked. Shook her head to clear it. And looked up at him again.

"Do na' make me carry you. Please? I have created enough court scandal for one evening," Rhoenne remarked beneath his breath.

"One evening?" Henry huffed. "I think you've earned that position for the next year or so, my laird. Mayhap longer."

"And isn't that your fault?"

Henry looked up at Rhoenne. Rhoenne looked at his man. Cassandra looked from one to the other.

"The hall," they both said in unison.

Rhoenne put his arm out for Cassandra. The moment she put her fingers atop his forearm, they were moving. He was so big. So solid. So intense. She skipped beside him without thought.

They were expected. Soldiers lined both sides of the door. More stood in the hall outside. The door to the audience chamber shut behind them. Henry approached the man wearing the biggest hat.

"Is there an antechamber we may make use of? For a moment or two?"

The man tipped his head slightly. Considered. Then turned and opened the door behind him. The group filed in. Henry and Euan first. Rhoenne bringing Cassandra. The others followed. Henry started speaking the moment the door closed behind them.

"I do na' ken your issue, Ramhurst!"

The words were not whispered. And they were angered.

"His issue with what?" Euan asked.

"That woman!"

"Which one? The *auld* crone?"

"Mind your tongue! She is the sister to the *duca*!"

"So? What does she want with us?" Euan asked.

"She does na' want us. She wants Cassandra," Henry retorted.

"She does? Why?"

"Because she is her granddaughter!"

There was a collective intake of air from several of them. "Her granddaughter?" someone asked.

"How do you ken this?" Euan asked.

"Because I listened!"

"You understand their tongue?"

"Of course. 'Tis na' that difficult. We've been selling and trading on the market, Euan. If you do na' ken the speech, you do na' get good prices. You get poorly treated, *and* disrespected. The *Cretan* Greek they also speak is the harder one to pick up. If you spent time with trade rather than filling your belly and flirting with women, you'd ken the language, too."

"I do more than flirt with them," Euan replied defensively.

A couple of the men chuckled.

So, that's how Rhoenne knew Venetian.

Cassandra's gaze strayed up to him. Her fingers still rested on his forearm. He hadn't removed them. And she wasn't willing to release him at all. He wasn't watching the men conversing before him. He was watching her. He had his eyes narrowed. His lips pursed. She glanced back down before her blush showed.

"You are telling us that *auld* woman is Cassandra's grandmother?"

"Aye."

"Doesn't that make Cassandra, uh...what? Niece to the ruler, the *duca* fellow?"

"Grand-niece," one of them interposed.

"It gets worse," Henry continued

"How is any of this bad?" Euan asked.

"Cassandra's father is—I mean *was* – a Bulgarian prince!"

"Truly? She's a...princess?" Euan voice was an even higher pitch than normal. "But this is astounding. Is there a reward somewhere for her return?"

"We can na' be cousins. I vow," Henry replied. "Do na' you see? She has been living here as Rhoenne's ward! I'm a-feared 'twas on my advice, too."

"So?"

"She was in his household, Euan."

"Aye. I ken."

"Ramhurst is na' wed. Cassandra is na' wed. There is *nae* wife to see to the proprieties."

"She came out of a harem. Why would a harem

harlot need those?"

Harem harlot? That's what they'd thought? Cassandra didn't know whether to be angered, insulted, embarrassed, or amused.

"Because everything we thought is wrong! She's *nae* harlot, mon. She is a lady! An... innocent lady."

"*Nae!*" Several voices chorused it as one.

"But...what of Rhoe–? Oh."

Silence followed Euan's cut-off remark. Cassandra couldn't meet anyone's eyes. She dipped her head. Suffered a series of blushes. There was no disguising them.

"Henry," Rhoenne injected. "That is enough."

"Enough? When you just spoke words tantamount to a declaration of war?"

"He did what?" Euan sputtered.

"Your cousin speaks in poetic phrase. I did na' declare anything," Rhoenne said.

"You desire a sponsor for her! That was what you requested this audience for!"

"He wants a sponsor for Cassandra?" Euan asked. "Why?"

Henry ignored him, and continued speaking to Rhoenne. "Is na' the perfect sponsor her own grandmother?"

"I said that's enough," Rhoenne replied.

"I do na' ken any of this," Euan spoke in the silence that followed. "Don't you want her, Rhoenne?"

Rhoenne stiffened. She felt it.

"That is na' the question, Euan," Henry answered. "You can na' simply *keep* a princess!

This sort of arrangement will require marriage. If it is na' already too late."

Somebody whistled. Cassandra's eyes went wide. Her heart stopped. When it restarted, it pumped vicious amounts of heat through her face. Down her body. She swore she could feel it in the toes of her slippers. But that was followed by such an icy sensation, she felt faint. Dizzy. The room began a slow rotation. She locked her view on the carpeted floor beneath her. Silently begged the room to solidify again. *Marriage?* He was being forced to consider marriage? Oh. He would hate it.

And her.

This was her fault. She'd begged him to keep her. But she hadn't known!

"Well...is that so bad? I mean...I would gladly take your place. If you, uh...did na' wish marriage," Euan said.

"The Ramhurst is betrothed. His bride-to-be is sister to Scotland's queen. Henry III's daughter. England's king."

"Is that why you said Rhoenne just declared war? He can na' wed? Well. Perhaps I could be an option here? I am unencumbered by things such as betrothals."

"I already offered that solution, whelp," Henry said.

"Sounds like you FitzHughs are related after all," Rhoenne remarked, sarcastically.

"Enough of this foolishness, my laird! We've wasted time, gone round in circles, and I still do na' ken why you fought the *duchesse*! You

were just about to ask for a sponsor before her
grandmother arrived! There is *nae* better sponsor!
She clearly wants Cassandra, while you do na'."

"I never said that."

Rhoenne's voice matched the tautness
throughout his entire frame. Even his arm felt
like she touched iron. Cassandra's body wasn't
far behind. She felt like a statue. She couldn't
swallow. Her throat had closed off. Her back
ached from standing stiff and straight. She had
her knees locked, her fingers pinched on his
forearm. And still it felt like the room rotated.

"Ah. So, you do want her," Henry mused.

"I did na' say that either."

"I'm confused," Euan said.

"You are na' the lone one, lad."

That comment came from either of the
Montvale men, Iain or Graham. Cassandra didn't
have their voices pegged well enough to specify.

"Rhoenne. I ask it again. Do you ken what
you are doing?"

"Not really," Rhoenne admitted.

There was a shocked silence. Cassandra was
afraid to breathe.

"Finally...we get to the heart of the matter."

"Strange you should bring that up," Rhoenne
remarked.

"What?"

"Hearts."

Someone cleared their throat. It covered
Cassandra's gasp. She was afraid she'd heard it
wrong.

"I'm listening," Henry prompted.

"You ken I will na' force a woman."

"That was a long time ago," Henry replied.

It didn't seem possible to go stiffer than the stance Rhoenne had already engineered. But it felt like he managed it.

"Is this about your step-mother, Aileen? I mean—*oof*!"

Euan's comment was cut off as if he'd taken a blow. Cassandra didn't see it. And she didn't care. Her entire being was centered on what Rhoenne had said. Whoever Aileen was, and whatever her position, she didn't matter. Nothing mattered except Rhoenne. And what he might be inferring.

"We ken what you mean, Euan. Just do na' let it cross your lips."

The voice sounded like Rhoenne's cousin, Grant. But it could have been any of them speaking. Henry cleared his throat.

"I think I begin to see the quandary. I do. I have been dense. Extremely so, now that I think on it. But...I now have another word or two for you, my laird."

"With you, FitzHugh, it's never just one."

"You speak of force. But what if...there is *nae* force involved?"

Rhoenne grunted.

"What if...there is a proposal offered? And it is accepted?"

"Henry."

"Too late, my laird. I told you. I see your issue. So. Would you like me to handle this? Or are you going to ask?"

"I was working up to it," Rhoenne replied slowly.

Oh, dear God!

Cassandra's mouth gapped open. Tingles hit her nose and cheeks. Shivers containing giddiness flew over her limbs. She forced herself to calm. Think. He might be asking. But he'd been trapped. He'd hate her for it.

Someone chuckled.

Rhoenne pulled in a heavy breath. Audibly blew out the lengthy sigh. And then he put his right hand beneath her chin, and lifted her to face him. She'd never seen anything like the glow in his eyes, making their color exactly match the center of a flame. She barely heard him speak through a flurry of bubbles that continually popped, sprinkling the scene with sparkle.

"Cassandra. Alexandria. Votten."

He spaced out each of her names. Then gave a slight smile. Cassandra held her breath.

"Princess of Vottenavia. Grand-niece of the *duca de* Candia, and whatever other titles you carry...would you be willing to solve this entire mess...by marriage?"

"But...you hate me," she whispered.

He sobered. Tipped his head to one side. Regarded her. Cassandra didn't breathe. Didn't even blink.

"*Nae,*" he finally answered.

"You don't?"

He licked his lips. Then shook his head.

"But I thought—?"

He lowered his chin toward her, stopping her

words. "I have never said these words to a woman afore, Cassandra. And you are na' making it verra easy," he told her.

"Oh."

Someone snorted, bringing her back to reality that was an ornate room. The five listeners.

"Should I begin again?" he looked over her head to ask it.

Henry answered. "*Nae*, my laird. You are doing well. Continue."

He looked back at her. Caught her gaze. It wasn't difficult. She hadn't moved it. "Cassandra. We are in a bit of a bind here. And I would na' force your hand."

"But you would force yours?" she asked.

He regarded her for long, heart-thumping moments. Humming filled her ears. The candles flickered in their sconces. Everything seemed to pause along with him. And then he smiled. Her heart flip-flopped.

"*Nae* man has ever forced me to do anything, sweet. Not even my da'," he replied.

"That much is definitely true," Henry remarked. "I can vouch."

Oh my.

He'd just called her sweet! The humming dissolved into a symphony of sound, each note coming at her in rapid-fire fashion. Pinging sensations hit every limb, while some sort of effervescence bubbled through her veins. It was difficult to keep still.

"May I continue?" he asked her.

"Please!"

She answered so quickly his lips twisted. As if he withheld a smile. And then he cleared his throat and spoke again.

"Cassandra Alexandria Votten. Would you consider accepting marriage? To the laird of the Ramhurst Clan, from the Kingdom of Scotland? Right now. Becoming the Countess of—?"

"Yes!"

She interrupted. She couldn't help it. She'd started bouncing up and down, using his arm for stability. It looked like he was having a hard time staying serious. There were sounds of hilarity coming from the others behind her.

"Cassandra. I am trying to be official here."

She nodded. Somebody guffawed. It sounded like Henry.

"You agree to wed with the Earl of Tyneburgh? Become his countess? Here and now, you accept matrimony and—?"

"Yes!"

She interrupted him again. Tears were going to obliterate him and she didn't want to miss a moment of this. It might also make the kohl lining her eyes run. Cassandra sniffed. Tilted her head higher and blinked rapidly to clear them.

"Oh. Verra well. Me. Do you agree to be wed with me? Right now? Cleave only unto me? Honor and obey me? Until death?" he finished.

"I already said yes!"

Cassandra launched into his arms, and was enfolded in an embrace resembling heaven. She put her nose and lips against his throat. She'd thought it perfection when he'd held her in the little cabin. She'd been mistaken. This was so much better.

"I believe you have just earned yourself a bride, my laird," Henry said from behind her. "What do you gentlemen say? Did that look like agreement to you? Euan? Grant? Iain? Graham? Have I missed anyone?"

There was a burst of 'ayes' throughout the room. And a round of chuckling. Rhoenne lifted his head. Spoke firmly. Her nose vibrated with the words.

"Verra well. My turn. I, Rhoenne Guy de Ramhurst. Fifth Earl of Tyneburgh. Laird of the Ramhurst Clan. Do hereby wed this woman, Cassandra Alexandria Votten. I vow to honor, protect, and cleave only to her...also until death."

Cassandra listened to his words as they rumbled around her, experiencing thrill after thrill as he pledged his troth.

"Well? What say you, FitzHugh? 'Tis sufficient to our law?"

"Unquestionably. You have wed yourself a countess, my laird. And I am honored to be the first to offer congratulations. May your union be long and fruitful and all the other platitudes women say in times like this," Henry answered.

Cassandra pulled away from Rhoenne. Lifted her head. Turned to look out at the group, but focused on Henry. "Our union?" she asked.

Henry had a wide grin on his face, and no beard to hide behind. He wasn't the only one grinning, though.

"There is a dearth of clergy in the Highlands, my

lady. Marriage by Declaration before witnesses is done all the time. 'Tis na' only lawful...but unbreakable."

"We just wed? Truly?"

"Aye. Legally. And permanently. *Nae* man can put it asunder. Nor can any grandmothers with pointy canes...regardless of court position."

She looked up at Rhoenne. "You are my *husband*?" She couldn't even say it without blushing. Several chuckles greeted her words.

"Aye." Rhoenne leaned toward her and matched his forehead against hers again. "And you are my wife," he told her.

"Oh *my*!" The last word was barely voiced. It was also said in a much higher octave.

And that's when Rhoenne put his head back, gave a triumphant shout that resounded through the chamber, rattling several items of décor, and making the lanterns flicker. The door opened swiftly. Several soldiers peered in. They may have entered. They might have threatened. They might have been simply checking. Cassandra didn't notice or care. She was enwrapped within a blanket of happiness, vibrating with absolute joy.

The door shut. Henry spoke again.

"Well, my laird? And...my lady? Lads? Now that we have finished conducting a bit of quite enjoyable business, we should go and gird the dragon."

"Dragon?" Someone asked.

"Aye. Her Grace. The woman terrifies me. I am rather grateful she is na' my new in-law."

Rhoenne lowered Cassandra slowly back to the

floor. It took some time to feel her feet on a solid surface. She slipped a finger beneath each eye, testing for any residue of black before she looked back up to him. She'd thought him the most handsome man birthed. With the twist to his lips, and the light behind his eyes, it was impossible to look elsewhere. And then he winked.

Her belly roiled. She lurched oddly. He caught her to him before she floated off, and it actually sounded like a possibility. This time she didn't look away. She met his look boldly. She didn't bother hiding her interest. He was her husband. And soon! *Soon!* She would find out exactly what the harem teachers had left out of her studies. Cassandra licked her lower lip and pulled it into her mouth.

Rhoenne's chin lowered and his brows rose as if he read her thoughts.

"My laird! And my lady! Please. We stand ready to accompany you. We have officials awaiting us! A private audience to enjoin. One that you requested, I might add."

"I hadn't just wed, Henry."

"True. We will make it brief. Or as brief as court proceedings can be. Now that you are wed, it should na' be too difficult. We have the upper hand. Euan? Make yourself of use. See to the door."

'I hadn't just wed....'

The words repeated through her head. Just wed?

Dear Lord.

She might truly faint.

CHAPTER NINETEEN

H E'D NEVER DONE anything as gut-wrenchingly difficult.

The fact that he'd gone through it unscathed was not only staggering, it was too unbelievable to consider. He couldn't describe the sensation pumping through him. Despite denial, it was too exquisite. It grew with every beat of his heart, every continued second of his existence...and each time his new wife's fingers trembled in his.

Wife?

Oh. Dear Lord.

The thought actually made his knees wobble. He disguised it with a large step, and then had to adjust again to her small ones. Her arm wasn't atop his forearm as they walked the hall, surrounded by Ramhurst Honor Guardsmen. He hadn't offered his arm. He'd held out his hand. And he'd closed his fingers about hers – trapping her, the moment she'd touched him. It hadn't been optional.

She wasn't getting a chance to escape him.

If he pondered it, he had a few comparisons to this sensation. One, in particular, occurred to him. His near-drowning in Loch Grantham had been close. His father had given him orders not to try to swim the loch. To the fourteen-year-old Rhoenne, that was akin to a challenge. It had been a gray morn. Heavy with rain. The water icy. The waves topped with white caps. Rhoenne had sunk beneath the water more than once, the last time without a hint of energy left to fight. He'd actually given his final words to God. Sent the prayer on a winged thought. And if he hadn't touched shore with his toes, he might never have been found. No one would have known what happened to him. He still recalled the triumphant taste of air as he'd lurched out of the water. Collapsed onto shore. Sucked in breath. And fought tears.

Come to think of it, that wasn't even close to how he felt right now.

Handing responsibility for Cassandra to another had taken every ounce of courage he possessed. His innards had ached all day at the prospect. He'd prepared in the tower with his men, surrounded, yet alone. He'd ignored any fare that was brought. Drink as well. He'd bathed in cold water, shaved by feel, and dressed without speaking to anyone. He'd had to draw on every ounce of his hard-hearted reputation. Hide behind the 'Dark One' façade. And when the moment arrived, it felt like he'd been ripping his own heart out.

He hadn't known until the interruption by her grandmother that he'd fail. He couldn't do it. He wasn't letting Cassandra out of his sight for fear he'd never see her again. Who would protect her then? That was why he'd pressed her to his back in the audience room, and the reason he held her hand now.

Cassandra thought he hated her?

He was terrified of what he did feel. Literally. *Terrified*.

"Ah! Here they come!"

Signor Pietro blurted the words. He was the first official to spot them. He stood beside an open door, flanked by guards. Rhoenne sent a quick glance about the hall. There were a lot more soldiers than had been in the audience room. Henry noted it as well. He clicked his fingers twice. Honor Guard shoulders went back and hands sought sword hilts.

And then Cassandra's fingers trembled within his again. Rhoenne's knees did the exact same quake motion, followed by another stumble, and another overly-long step.

Signor Pietro rushed through the doors, and started an announcement so loud it was painful to hear.

"Your Excellency, Councilor Angelo Moroseni! The Earl of Tyneburgh, Kingdom of—!"

"Cease that, *Signor* Pietro. The room is not that large. We can all hear you." The councilor waved his hand dismissively.

The Ramhurst retinue stopped at the portal. The space supposedly fit thirty? It looked capable of holding twice that. The room glimmered with every flicker of torches in their sconces. They'd covered the walls with mother-of-pearl, or something as iridescently green. Overhead, a large painted span with a colorful Christian-themed fresco in more green tones plastered the ceiling. Long wooden rails lined the walls. At the moment, observers were behind rows of guards. A line of chairs stood across the back of the room, opposite the door. All the men who'd previously sat on the dais were there. The councilor's wife was the only one missing. In the right corner was a high-backed chair. Large. Gilded with gold. Set atop a step-fronted pedestal.

It held the *duchesse.*

And she didn't look amused.

"Finally!" she announced crossly.

She probably would have stabbed the floor with her cane, but she was up too high and the platform sides were the exact dimension of her chair. Rhoenne watched dispassionately as she settled with placing her staff across her lap and glared across at him. She sat almost at his eye level. That was contrived, and rather amusing. He didn't smile, however. He didn't allow any reaction to show at all.

Euan and Henry walked in first and separated, moving to either side of the doorway. Rhoenne and Cassandra were next, and they approached the councilor, his officials, and the *duchesse* as a front of four. The other three clansmen followed, but they'd turned around and walked backwards. For exactly ten steps.

They stopped as a perfectly cohesive unit. Rhoenne nodded his head to the councilor. He ignored the woman glaring at him from his right. He lifted his chin slightly to project his words.

He knew he had a stirring voice. He used it.

"Excellency? I wish to thank you for granting me this private audience."

"That you finally realized you'd have to attend!" the *duchesse* inserted with an acidic tone.

Rhoenne tipped his head toward her, regarded her unblinkingly for long moments, and then returned his attention to the councilor.

"I gave my word, Your Excellency. I keep it."

"We are wasting time, Angelo. You know what you have to do."

Rhoenne pulled Cassandra closer to him with a jerk. He heard her surprised gasp. Glanced down. She had a smile hovering on her lips. And he had to look away before he returned it. Or something even more basic. He wasn't known for a gentle nature. When he took a woman, it was because lust was a primal need and he'd failed at stifling it. He was almost vindictive. It didn't warrant pleasure. The act of mating was almost brutal. He didn't care. They were paid and they were told what to expect. All of them seemed to relish it – or they were excellent actors.

But he didn't care about that, either.

He'd wed with Cassandra because the other option had been a black pit of despair that opened up before him. He couldn't handle the thought of any other man being with her. Keeping her safe. Touching her...

The thought alone sent a heated shudder pulsing through him, made his gut clench into a tight knot, and sent a wash of red over his vision. He looked back to the councilor before it worsened. Lifted his chin to project his words.

"Afore we speak much further, Your Excellency, I wish to state that I find the *duca di* Candia's sister, the *Duchesse* Lucia Zecchino to be a staunch champion and worthy adversary. But I am at a loss...as to the reason for her apparent aversion... and open antagonism toward me."

"Unhand my granddaughter, young man, and I'll explain it to you. This instant. Cassandra? You are to step away from him."

"You see? She does not even grant me the time to speak."

"Guards!" the old woman yelled.

Swords came out of scabbards around him. Grant's shoulders bumped into his as they closed ranks. Rhoenne was the lone man who didn't pull his weapon. He lifted Cassandra's hand to his lips and kissed her fingers with a lingering gesture. He looked across at the *duchesse* as he did so. Watched her eyes narrow, her lips tighten, and she had a definite snarl that revealed dark-colored stubbed teeth. He moved their hands to his chest and turned his attention back to the councilor.

"Perhaps I should have been more specific earlier, Your Excellency...when my party was first introduced. This is not simply the lady Cassandra at my side. This is my lady wife, the Countess of Tyneburgh."

Exclamations followed his announcement. Murmurs that contained astonishment. The change in officials was instantaneous. Expressions cleared. Smiles wreathed faces. Cassandra's grandmother wasn't as quick. Her head lifted.

She gave Rhoenne a long considering look. Rhoenne didn't show any expression. He heard his men putting swords back into their scabbards. As a unit. Without direction. Their regimentation truly was impressive.

"Why didn't you say so earlier?"

The *duchesse* didn't ask. It was a demand. Rhoenne smirked. She hadn't lost an ounce of imperiousness.

"Because no one asked," he replied.

"Why doesn't my granddaughter speak? Cassandra?"

Cassandra was trembling. Rhoenne moved their conjoined hands to his right shoulder, bringing Cassandra even closer against his left side.

"She has been sequestered in a monastery, Your Grace. Consequently, she is...rather reserved."

Her expression altered slightly. "A monastery, you say?"

"Aye."

"In a heathen land?"

"There are Christian enclaves throughout the world, Your Grace. I was lucky enough to find one...and beyond lucky to have secured your granddaughter's hand therewith."

"Yes. You are definitely that," she returned.

The councilor clapped his hands. "Well. Your Grace? Lord Ramhurst? This audience has certainly been interesting, your information of great importance to the *duca di* Candia's family, and the entire realm. 'Twas also...timely rendered."

"Timely?" the *duchesse* snapped. "If you please, Angelo."

"I believe we have finished the audience. We can adjourn."

"Wait."

The *duchesse* spoke up. The councilor looked heavenward for a moment. Several of the other officials looked down at their laps.

"Yes, Your Grace?"

"I would request a visit from my granddaughter... if it pleases Lord Ramhurst, of course."

It probably cost her to say that with a modicum of respect. Rhoenne lifted a brow. He didn't alter his expressionless demeanor.

"I would like to offer hospitality...to his entire retinue. Tonight. At my home. So that I can... converse with my only remaining relative."

"Tonight?" Rhoenne asked.

She nodded.

"Sincere apologies, Your Grace. But tonight the countess will be otherwise occupied. I personally guarantee it."

Euan snorted. Started into a coughing fit. The Montvale backed against him smacked him, the motion so quick, it was almost undetectable. Rhoenne had said it mostly for the Honor Guards' benefit - to entrench Cassandra's position as their lady. He'd have to come up with something beyond drastic and soon. If he managed to somehow keep from consummating anything, Cassandra would not only remain ignorant of his darker nature.

But he'd keep his vow.

"The morrow, then," she continued. "I shall send an invitation."

Those must be prized. The reaction from the officials certainly showed there was something extraordinary about her words.

"You do that," Rhoenne answered. "And now. Your Excellency? Gentlemen of the court? Your Grace?" He bowed his head. "We bid *adieu*. Henry?"

Henry clicked his fingers as Rhoenne pivoted with Cassandra. They started toward the door. Iain and Graham Montvale had the front now. Grant dropped back to Cassandra's left side. Henry and Euan were the two walking backwards. It was perfectly set-up. Planned. Practiced. And executed. They didn't turn forward until they were halfway down the hall.

"Oh my."

Cassandra's whisper wasn't loud. It carried a trace of awe. Rhoenne experienced such a swell of pride he had to clear his throat. He wasn't the only one. Grant cleared his throat as well. And the Montvale men before him flushed, turning a rosy shade that reached their ears. It was especially noticeable on Iain's freshly-shaved neck. But they were moving at a snail's pace when he knew they needed urgency. He studiously kept their steps slow despite how his shoulders itched, while the hair on the back of his neck whispered. As soon as they turned the first corner, he swung Cassandra up into his arms. And they started down halls at a much brisker pace.

They'd passed the audience rooms and were at

a jog before Euan spoke.

"Um. Somebody want to tell me why we are rushing? What we are doing?"

"Getting the laird to his chamber, of course. 'Tis his wedding night," Henry answered in a low hint of voice.

"Oh. Right."

Cassandra gasped slightly and pushed her forehead into his throat. That was starting all manner of ills he didn't wish to name, and hadn't much experience dealing with. It was better to ignore it. But he hadn't any idea how. It didn't take long before they reached the chambers he'd secured.

Emin was standing with his back to the door, arms crossed, the image of security enforcement. He gave them an inscrutable look as they jogged toward him, and then slowed to a brisk walk again. They converged in the area outside Rhoenne's chambers, circling Rhoenne and Cassandra. Breathing hard, but otherwise nonplussed. Graham was the lone one facing outward, vigilant. Rhoenne didn't set Cassandra down. Her weight didn't hamper him in the slightest.

"All right. The truth. What are we doing... really?" Euan asked.

"I think he might be related to you after all, Henry," Rhoenne remarked.

Henry huffed an affirmation. Lowered his head. And his voice. "There is something afoot. 'Tis an undercurrent. I don't know what it is. And that has me...a bit uneasy."

He sent a glance toward Cassandra before

finishing. Rhoenne knew he'd downplayed the words for her sake.

"Uneasy?" Euan asked.

"Perhaps we should speak...elsewhere. With more privacy."

"I'm not letting Cassandra from my sight," Rhoenne announced.

"The grandmother?"

Rhoenne shrugged.

"You don't trust her?"

"The Dark One does na' trust any woman," Grant replied.

"With one exception, please," Rhoenne remarked. "I've got a wife now."

"You willing to trust her?"

Rhoenne tightened his arms, lifting her closer to him. It wasn't planned. Or considered. It just happened. And the resultant blast of warmth that filled him was beyond worrisome. His arms trembled before he staunched it. "Aye," he finally answered.

Cassandra gave a murmur. Rubbed her cheek against him. Rhoenne bent his knees slightly and tensed to keep the annoying waver throughout his legs unnoticed. He cleared his throat. Lowered his vocal range. "How much time do you reckon?" he asked Henry.

"High tide. Mid-day. We do na' want to miss it."

"We sail tomorrow? Is that what we're about?" Euan asked.

"We're ready. Have been. We only awaited Ramhurst's order."

"Consider it given. Tomorrow," Rhoenne inserted.

"What of the dragon? I mean the *duchesse....* and her invitation?"

"You can stay and attend to her if you wish," Henry told him.

"Oh. No thank you. I prefer my women a lot younger. And a lot less demanding. No offense intended. To you or your lady wife."

"None taken by me," Rhoenne replied. "Cassandra?"

He lifted her, brought her forehead to his. Got snagged, then hooked by the golden glow of her eyes. Despite the lock he had on his reactions, he gave the slightest of groans. Involuntarily. He was afraid it was audible. The chuckling about him made that official.

"I am not offended in the slightest," she replied.

Euan whistled. "It figures her voice is as beautiful as she is."

"It appears you have another conquest," Rhoenne told her.

She smiled. And blushed. And he nearly groaned again.

"Yes. Well. There is a long night ahead of us, gentlemen. We mustn't waste it," Henry spoke up.

"Us?" Euan asked.

"What do you need?" Rhoenne asked.

"Emin. Graham."

"Emin?" Euan asked.

"The man has an extraordinary ability to ferret out things. Procure items. Move about almost unseen. And he's rather handy with a blade. You hadn't noticed?"

"Well. Aye. I am na' dense."

"I shall also need coins...for bribing and what-not."

"Use what you need," Rhoenne replied.

"And...Ida."

"The mute? What the devil for?" Euan queried.

"She'll make a great addition to a randy fellow out on the town, such as I intend to portray. I am also giving our laird and his new lady a bit of privacy...unless he wishes witnesses to his consummation. In which event, we can all stay, and...?"

Rhoenne growled deep inside his chest. Why was his body failing to obey anything? The sound rumbled through the area.

"I rather thought that would be the answer. Euan, Grant. Iain. There is a fortune to be transported. And guarded. Euan? Fetch a cart. And a donkey."

"A cart and donkey?"

"You do na' wish to carry the chests to the ship yourself. Gold is verra heavy. You'd regret it."

"Cart. Donkey. Aye." Euan trotted off.

"The rest of you. Come. We've got some work ahead."

"We do?"

"Am I the lone one with wits here? We're moving those trunks from the laird's chamber to this foyer. Otherwise our laird and his new lady can na' have privacy. I do na' think they wish us... interrupting. But I could be wrong."

"Oh. Aye."

"Moving trunks."

"Got it."

More than one man answered, through not-so-subtle chortles. And guffaws. Cassandra was trying to meld into his chest. Rhoenne experienced another tremor. More vicious than before. Perhaps he should change things. Keep at least one witness in the chamber. Something that would keep him from Cassandra.

And what he might do to her.

He'd vowed to never wed. Perhaps if he kept repeating that silently, it would help. He had a vow.

A vow.

Worse, he'd never had a maid. That would require gentleness. Calmness. The ability to rein back hellish desire. *A maid.* The thought heightened tension, and sent fear.

They made quick work of emptying the bedchamber of chests filled with *ducati,* gold and silver items. Jewelry. He'd set Cassandra down on a stool beside the table to help heft chests. Snacked on handfuls of figs. Dates. Nuts. Downed a tankard of ale. And one of water. He stopped them from taking the bag that held her harem jewelry. He didn't know why. It just felt right.

Cassandra had spoken with Ida. He heard snippets. Told her she had a mission. The woman looked uncertain until Cassandra whispered something in her ear. Rhoenne had a very good idea of what it was, especially as the woman simply beamed up at him then clapped her hands. She hugged Cassandra. Made chirping noises. And wiped at what looked to be a tear or two. Then she set about packing Cassandra's wardrobe for them to tote out as well.

Women.

The chamber emptied. Ida blew Cassandra a kiss as she pulled the door closed behind her. Rhoenne walked through every room. Twice. Then he lowered the bolt across the door, sealing them in.

CHAPTER TWENTY

SHE'D BEEN SEQUESTERED in this chamber for days. Knew every nook and cranny of every room. Had helped Ida straighten them. Done all manner of things to escape the boring reality of stone walls about her. Slept. Daydreamed. Read the books, two of them twice.

But the space had never felt like it did right now.

Fireplace coals still smoldered, platters of nuts and breads, dates and figs sat atop the table, lanterns and torches were all lit, sending wavers of light pulsing through the area. It looked like the same chamber, but it felt so different. The very air had developed a tensile quality. Moister. Heavier. Loaded with tension. A barely-there hint of excitement. A goosebump-lifting sensile touch, enough to alter temperature.

As if the entire chamber had the ability to breathe and had it held.

Hovering in wait.

A sudden thud reverberated through the chamber. Cassandra jumped. Rhoenne still faced the chamber door, his shoulders heaving with large breaths. He had both hands splayed, palms flush to the wood. And then he moved his head back and smacked it into the door again. And held it there despite her gasp.

"Cassandra?" He hadn't moved his head from the door as he spoke.

"Yes?"

"We have to talk."

Talk?

Wasn't she ever going to learn what came after a kiss?

Cassandra took a couple of breaths, working to calm the instant ire before she answered. It would never do if he knew how much she wanted this. And him.

"I...am listening," she finally said.

"What was said in the chamber....at our wedding? 'Twas na' entirely accurate."

"Which part?"

"The wedded part."

"What? So we're not wed now?"

He huffed something that sounded like amusement. "Oh. *Nae*, sweet. We are definitely married."

"Then...what? I don't understand."

"You are a lot like me, I think. Oh. Na' in stature. Or gender. Or such things. It's more... our nature."

"Our nature." Cassandra repeated it automatically. She started working at the clasps of her headdress after her answer. Without Ida it was tedious work, but the silver pinched her forehead, and he wasn't watching anyway.

"I am na' fond of...crowds. I rarely speak with others. I do my own study. My own exploration. Figure out my own truths. I prefer my own council. That is the part we share. Am I wrong?"

She'd removed the metal headdress and was wrapping the scarf about it. Her fingers stilled as he finished. Surprise flowed across her like a wash of cool water. No one had shown insight into her most guarded sanctuary. Her place of safety and protection. Her inner self. How was it possible for Rhoenne Ramhurst to know it?

"I just told you how," he answered as if she'd asked it aloud. "You are a lot like me – the part of me that none ever get to see."

He took a deep breath, pulled his head from the door, and smacked it against the wood again. Cassandra jumped.

"Why do you do that to yourself?" she asked.

"Because 'tis better than the alternative."

What happens is that *bad?*

Maybe the harem instructors had been trying to help with their inept lessons. Cassandra straightened. She hadn't thought of that. "Go... on," she managed to reply.

"Our union is na' unbreakable."

Was he saying he wanted freedom from her? Already?

"With enough gold and a willing magistrate, any union can be put aside. Divorce is na' an impossibility."

Oh, so now he wanted a divorce?

Her breaths ramped up. Her heart rate kicked into a faster beat. Her throat felt like she'd swallowed a piece of bread that was now stuck.

"But 'tis easier still to annul it...*if* there has been *nae* consummation."

And then he smacked his head again.

"Would you cease that?"

Cassandra wasn't using a shy retired voice. She watched his shoulders lift again with a heavy sigh.

"Why?"

"Because you'll hurt your head."

"I'm hard-headed, sweet. Did na' I specify that when we first met?"

"No."

"Well...consider it added."

"You said a lot, Rhoenne. A lot. You're emotionless. Feared. Reviled. You take. Maim. Kill. Without regret or remorse."

"That's just the things I admit to," he told her.

"Well! I thank God in my prayers nightly for it! Especially when I think of those horrible men...on the ship!"

Her voice broke. *Is this what he wanted?*

He swore. "I can na' even get this right. 'Tis one of the reasons I avoid speech. I am not a man of honor, Cassandra. Our wedding is proof."

Oh. So now he was going to tell her he didn't want or need her?

After the looks he'd been giving her all eve?

Cassandra's eyes narrowed. She was walking toward him with the intention to help him slam his head into the door when he spoke again.

"I made a vow."

She stopped. "Oh. You speak of your betrothal?" she asked.

He shook his head. "She's a child. Should she

make it to the ceremony, I'd be an *auld* man. One foot in the grave."

That didn't look likely even if it were to take place a decade from now. The man was a perfect specimen. Virile. Manly. His vest was stretched at the shoulders showing their width. It had been cinched to his midriff showing he hadn't an ounce to spare there, either. His shirt sleeves clung to his arms in a vain attempt to obscure muscle and strength. The way he'd lifted his shoulders had raised the hem of his attire. He possessed some very nice legs and muscled buttocks, and the gray trousers were giving her a nice view of that, as well.

"I vowed na' to take a wife at all."

"Rhoenne. If you don't want or need me, just speak it."

The cry he gave was deep and guttural, filling the room with sound. It lifted shivers all along her skin.

"I am trying to do the honorable thing here, Cassandra. You are safe now. None can slur your name."

"You wed me to protect my virtue? Is that what you're saying?

He shook his head.

"Then cease avoiding my question. Tell me you don't want or need me."

He took another heavy sigh. Lowered his forehead to the wood without banging it. And addressed his next comment to his boots.

"I've been stifling want since our horse ride, Cassandra. 'Tis more than want, actually. Much more. As for need? That was my bane on the ship. I can na' think for wanting you. Can barely function due to need. My entire existence has become a hellish one. I have little left to fight this with."

Oh my!

Cassandra stepped next to him. Put a hand out toward his forearm that was level with her eyes. The same one she'd clung to for their first audience...and she'd felt shy then! It was nothing to how this felt. She had to reach out twice before she dared touch him.

An instant shudder ran him when he felt it. "You do na' want to touch me! Did you hear naught of what I've just told you?" He gave two huge breaths. Held the last one. Spoke through set lips and clenched teeth. "You may wish to run from me, Cassandra. *Now.*"

"But I love you," she answered. Then she gasped and slapped her free hand to her mouth.

His arms dropped. His head swiveled. His eyes were opened as wide as his mouth. His look of complete astonishment probably matched the one on her face. Then he gave the biggest smile she'd ever seen, pushed away from the wall, shoved his head back, and roared so loudly several torches sputtered and wavered.

The next moment she was in caught up against him. Held. His arms enwrapped her, sealing her against his chest. And his lips pummeled hers. Ungently. Fervently. Stealing breath.

"Oh no! No! I can na'! I will na'! I must go gently here! Calmly! Ah!"

The words didn't match how he sucked his way across her chin, licked the skin beneath an ear. Cassandra squealed. Hunched her shoulder in defense. Hard, quick breaths, pushed by passion, rushed across her skin, raising a storm of shivers.

"Cassandra! You have to stop me. Cassandra! You have to stop me! Cassandra! You have to *stop* me!"

Shudders accompanied the words that grew louder and more vibrant with each repetition. She put her lips to his throat in response and sucked on the shaved skin. He gave a yell that vibrated his skin against her tongue.

"Ah...sweet! You have to stop me! I am na' gentle! I will be a rutting beast! You have to stop—! Ah!" This cry was deeper. Longer. It pulsated through the chamber, sending primal tones that shot sparks through just about everything.

"You do na' understand!"

He tossed her over a shoulder. Raced for the chamber that held the bed. Brought her down into his arms a moment before launching onto the mattress. They bounced twice. Her hair cascaded about the coverlet beneath them. Her legs split. He filled the space with his lower body while his mouth again seized hers. He wasn't intent on gentle calmness. He stole her every breath. Replaced it with his, creating a siege of want. Desire.

And absolute need.

Cassandra helped. Jostling for position. His lips marauding. Taking. Laving and licking. Hers trembling. Absorbing. Learning. And thrilling.

Large hands rubbed up and down her sides, moving sections of skirt. Ripping seams. Deep-throated groans blended with her moans. Cassandra wasn't remotely passive. She grabbed the sides of his vest and hauled the thing apart, pulled at the ties of his shirt. Yanked material up from where it was secured beneath his belt. He lifted to help her. The bed swayed and bounced as he rotated and shimmied, yanking the mass of vest and shirt over his head and then chucking it somewhere outside the bed enclosure.

She'd seen his upper body that first night. In the tiny tent. She'd peeked at him with awe and admiration. She'd been tipsy with beer, but still recalled every nuance. But now, feeling the goosebumps lift under her fingers as she explored was an entirely new experience. Erotic. Sensual. Intense. He was hot. Hard. Strong. All manner of motion rippled beneath his skin. And then he went taut. Sucked in a quick breath.

"Oh. Your wound," she whispered. Her finger pads touched minutely on what had to be Ida's stitches. "I forgot. I'm...so sor—."

She didn't get the rest of her words out. He slammed his lips onto hers again, his lower body shimmying with jerked motions from between her still-clothed legs while holding his body weight from her with a push-up. She couldn't think. She could only experience. Her entire sphere was awash with sensation.

Taste. Touch.

Sound.

His kiss stole her voice. His breath meshed with hers. His hands burned everywhere they touched. She didn't know where her sleeves had gone. Nothing hampered how he moved her up and down, using his hands on her arms and shoulders in a kneading motion while he pushed his hips up against hers. Down again. Back against hers.

His palms created friction. His loins engendered wonder. His lips slid to her throat, tongued her skin just below her ear, tickling with the pressure and then cooling with his breath, while Cassandra gave vent to a cry that keened with emotion.

Her cry wasn't remotely soft. Or calm. It didn't even sound like her.

"Oh love. Oh, sweet! Oh, love. Oh, sweet! Oh, Cassandra!"

The front of her kirtle was shoved down, his hand closed about a breast. Smashing. Lifting. Kneading. Fingers touched her nub, and Cassandra launched upward. An intense spear of light flashed through her. She swore she saw it. Cries of pleasure ricocheting about the three-sided enclosure, blending with the growling sounds he was making.

The exquisite stitchery of her bodice tore.

He found her other breast.

Fingers rubbed at her peak with quick strokes, every motion sending electrified shafts rocketing from there. His breath went deeper. More harsh. He pushed himself down, his mouth searching and then latching to a nub, and at the first hint of suckling, Cassandra went absolutely wild. She grabbed his head. Pulled hair from his queue. Alternately bucked and writhed, panted and shook, gasped and cried, until she ran out of breath. Then she started it anew.

She moved to clench fingers at his shoulders, clawing at the muscle while her legs enwrapped and then gripped his torso. Tears flooded her eyes. Got blinked into trails to her ears. More material tore. He lurched back into view, rocking the mattress with his move. His belly was a wall of moving muscle as he pushed her dress apart, separating her skirt. Tearing the kirtle open. Delving beneath her shift. His fingers were hot. Hard. Intent. He touched a thigh. Slid up her leg.

And touched her core.

Cassandra went rigid with surprise and shock, and an instantaneous impression of sensatory pleasure. She pulled in a shaky breath, only to lose it as he slid a finger into her most private depth. Touched her core again. Slid within. And then he did it again. And again. Quicker. Deeper. Over and over.

And again.

The hint of ecstasy grew. Slivers of immense pleasure spliced. The sensation growing stronger and larger. And still he touched and rubbed, moistening. Warming. An entire whorl of delight opened right up before her. And then it swallowed her. Cassandra screamed. Soared. She ran out of breath. Sucked in another. And screamed until that one ran out, too.

"Oh, Cassandra. Oh, love."

Hard hands seized her hips. Yanked her to him, matching the spot he'd just brought to such incredible sensitivity, the entire area was afire and pinging with flashes of sensation almost too intent to bear. She felt his rod. Large. Rigid. Hot. Quivering. He slid it along her core, making the world sway with his motion. Up and down. Over and over. The bed rocked with him, the wood creaking and groaning with the same rhythm.

"Oh...Cassandra? You are a maid? Yes?"

The words were panted. Harsh. Incredibly deep-toned. She nodded.

"I am...so sorry! You must...forgive and—! I can na' wait...another—!"

He pulled in a breath, dug his fingers into her hips, and rammed into her. His deep groan ruptured space. Time. Sanity.

Cassandra jerked, absorbing pain that rippled across her belly and shot down both legs. His groan covered over the cry she gave, but not the sobs that followed. He arched upward, gaining leverage, only to shove deeper, and sent even more agony shooting through her lower region.

"Rho...enne? Rho...enne?"

The name came out in sections, each syllable filled with pain. And still he pushed into her. Rupturing her most sensitive place. Holding her in an inescapable grip so he could impale her and send torturous twinges. Agonized shoves. He wouldn't stop. And once he was fully sheathed, it grew worse.

He wasn't content with splaying her apart,

turning the experience into one of pain and agony? He needed to pound domination into her? Cassandra's pleas didn't stop him. Her tears hadn't any impact. So she tried fighting. She pummeled him. Arched up against him. Fell. Lunged. Twisted. Nothing worked. Everything on him grew even more taut and tensed. And ever more lethal.

"Put...your legs...about me," he panted between his shoves into her. "It may...ease pain."

She tried, but he wasn't any help. His body was a force of muscle and will, his face a blend of pain and pleasure. His lips were pursed to send angered, large gusts of breath that rippled over her. The bed frame creaked and rocked. The mattress bounced and shook. The space rotated. Spun. His lunges got faster. Went deeper. All of it meshing into an experience of blood and pain and sweat. The world careened about her in a pulsation of motion and sound. The bed joined in with an accompanying rhythm. And still Rhoenne pumped into her. Each thrust stronger. Faster. And accompanied now with a slight grunt as he continually pummeled her body with his.

And then something changed.

The agony she'd undergone warped somehow... became a throb of pain. Then it ebbed into ache. Soreness. Tenderness. And then the oddest sensation slithered across her experience, sending a glimmer of something. Something spectacularly...different. Completely new. Awesome and encompassing.

It was then she started helping, her movements changed from fighting against to matching with. He may have sensed it, for his thrusts grew even longer. Stronger. The pace got ever faster. Guttural grunting accompanied each one. He thrust into her, held in a fraction of time before pulling out. Thrust in again. Held it longer. Did it again.

"Cassandra! Sweet!"

And with the next shove, a riot of sensory delight ensued. It poured through her, gripping her with fulfillment that hovered on the exquisite. She barely felt him push up into a back-cracking arch, his mouth stretched wide to yell the loudest, longest, most heart-pounding and vivid yell she'd ever heard. He stayed in that position for pulse-pounding long moments of time, throbbing in place, his loins continually twinging against hers, while everything else on him was taut and unyielding, as though sculpted from stone.

And then it was over.

Rhoenne fell atop her, and rolled to his back, holding her against him, taking her with him. She rose and fell with his every breath. Each inhalation large. Lung-expanding. While the exhalations were slow and lengthy, dropping her several inches. Where they were still adjoined was jumping with little bursts of pleasurable sensation that slowly ebbed...yet still tender with barely-remembered trauma. The rate and depth of his breathing altered. His entire frame followed, changing from a taut pounding wall of strength to a trembling mass of male that sent fresh tears to her eyes. The room settled back to normalcy. The air lost its warm, moist, weighty feel, and turned slightly cool. Ripples of hair that had been stuck to skin slowly drifted off her, down to the covers.

Cassandra lifted her head, settled her chin on his chest, just below his throat. She slid a hand up his side, ran her finger along the slight scratchy feel of his chin, across the fullness of his lower lip, and then smoothed a lock of black hair from his forehead. He truly was gorgeous. Handsome. Excessively manly.

And all hers.

That's when she knew. Either the sultan was a failure at this act, or the ladies who'd been responsible for instruction at the harem hadn't any notion of what happened between a man and a woman. For one, they hadn't mentioned pain. For another, they'd never brought up sensation. They hadn't told of tenderness that enveloped the most private area, nor had they mentioned anything about the absolute bliss that could be attained.

She'd guessed they were the leftover concubines of the former emperor; the women who hadn't chosen sacrifice and burial upon his death. She hadn't known they were probably old maids. They'd never experienced mating. The passion. Sense of urgency. The violence. She'd been told to lie passively. Accept the sultan's staff. Put the mind to something pleasant and not on what was done to her.

What nonsense.

What had just transpired was so vast, Cassandra was still vibrating to it, reliving the width and scope of pleasure...almost forgetting the pain.

Rhoenne opened his eyes. Caught her gaze. His eyes were such an unworldly-blue shade! Especially right now, with warmth radiating from them. Her heart jumped. She gasped. He smiled. And her entire being flooded with a sense of happiness so massive, it brought tears. She sniffed, blinked them back, but more took their place.

"Oh, Cassandra," he whispered. "That was—." He cleared his throat. Dropped his voice an octave. "I hurt you."

"I—." She blushed. *Blushed?* Still joined with him, skin to skin, and she blushed? She couldn't seem to find her voice, either.

"Forgive me. I was na' gentle."

Cassandra dropped her gaze and shook her head.

"You will na' forgive me?"

"It's not that," she whispered.

"'Twas my speed, then? I was...um. A bit rapid. Brutish? You should forgive me for that, as well. I told you I had nothing left to fight this with." He dropped his head and spoke his next words to the canopy above them. "And here you asked if I wanted and needed you. Ha. I believe I proved both."

"Rhoenne?" she said.

"Aye?"

"There is nothing to forgive. That was...unlike anything I was taught. I was told to lie passively.

How was I to do that?"

"Oh. You dare try, and we'll have issues."

Cassandra giggled. "I love you. More so than before, I think."

His arms tightened around her. His tremor shook her with it. "You should na' say such."

"But it's true. And...I think you have feelings for me as well."

He sighed heavily. It was an interesting prospect from atop his chest. She rose, hovered at that level for a span, then fell back down when he exhaled.

"I am na' certain of the emotion, sweet. But if there is such a thing, then I am most likely... heavily invested in it as well."

"You love me, too," she translated.

"Love is a curse," he finally answered.

Cassandra actually managed to answer with a word said in a noncommittal tone. "Curse?"

"Aye. You should seek some sleep, Wife. You will have need of it."

"I will?"

"Most assuredly." He lifted his head again, looked at her, and gave her such a heart-melting smile a wash of moisture blurred him for a moment. "I told you. My existence has been a nightmare of hellish denial. The level of my want and need was..." He rolled his eyes before continuing, "Let's just name it vast."

"Vast," she repeated.

His head dropped back.

"Oh. Verra well. 'Twas uncontrollable. But... with a bit of rest. I may be able to hold back long enough...to at least undress next time."

"Oh, you may, may you?"

He gave the same growl she'd heard him use with his men. It was endearing. The timbre echoed through his chest when she rested her head on it. His hand brushed strands of her hair aside. Cassandra had never felt more secure. Protected.

And loved.

CHAPTER TWENTY-ONE

———❧———

"WHERE ARE YOU going?"
    Cassandra had a leg out, preparatory to rolling from him. His hand snagged her thigh almost instantly, stopping her. She'd seen his reflexes. They were still surprising. Especially when she thought he slept.

"To...wash."

"Wash."

The word reverberated through the chest she lay atop.

"I—. It's...sticky. Unclean."

He grunted and lifted his hand from her leg. She rolled from him, wincing slightly at the tenderness of her woman-area. Her legs were shaky, her fingers felt odd. Her shift and kirtle slid into place down her legs as she stood, stooping slightly. She had to hold her bodice together. A quick peek showed he wasn't watching. He was still focused on the canopy above him.

There was a pitcher of water in the main chamber. Cassandra poured some into a mug and tiptoed into the wardrobe room. It looked vacant and austere and cold without her clothing. There was a pale yellow ensemble still there, however. And a night-rail hung from one hook.

Heaven-sent.

That's how the garment looked. Once she'd shed the beautiful blue dress, white and silver kirtle, and shift, washed every trace of blood away, and had donned the nightgown, she knew it was heavenly. It not only covered her, it hid all the blushes. Especially over the small dark spots at her hips that looked like finger marks.

She fashioned a loose braid with her hair to keep tangling to a minimum. Opened the door. And nearly slammed it shut again.

Rhoenne looked up from the fireplace. He was crouched, poking at logs. His hair was unbound, hanging to mid-back, spilling over massively muscled shoulders. His side was to her, and there wasn't but a small towel or some other nondescript bit of material about his hips. He rose slowly and turned to face her. Firelight glanced off him, highlighting one side, while the other was hidden in shadow. He probably heard her sigh and assigned the correct meaning, if the way he glanced upward and turned a bit rosy was any indication.

He lifted arms then, pulling his hair back as if he'd tie it. The gesture put definition to both arms as well as all the roping of muscle through his torso. It also reflected on a thin trail of blood oozing from his knife wound. Cassandra was at his side moments later, without a hint of how she'd gotten there.

"Oh, Rhoenne. Your wound? We broke it

open?"

He gave a half-smile. "If we did, 'twas totally worth it."

"It doesn't hurt?"

"I did na' say that."

"So, it does hurt."

"I did na' say that, either."

Her shoulders fell. She gave him a deadpan look. "What did you say?"

"I said if what we did broke my wound open, it would have been worth it. Actually, we could have broken open all these scars, and it would have been worth it, lass."

"You have a lot."

"Scars?"

"Yes."

"Comes with the territory, lass."

"Fighting?"

He shrugged. All kinds of muscle moved throughout his frame. That was visual and stirring and altogether interesting.

"You should have been more careful."

"You didn't see the damage to my opponents."

Her brows lifted. "What is this one from?" She reached out. Hesitated for a moment, and then traced a line that undercut one of his nipples.

"Blade," he answered.

"And this one?"

He had a stripe along his upper left arm. It followed the line of muscle, as though it needed definition. The scar was large. Jagged.

"Hand axe," he replied.

"Oooh."

His lips twisted as if he hid a smile.

"And this one?" He had a line across his belly. It was a lighter shade than his skin.

"Sword."

"How about this one?" She touched a "v"-shaped one just beneath his elbow.

He smirked. "Fish hook."

"Fish hook," she repeated.

"I was na' born an expert fisherman. Such a thing requires trial and error."

"Oh. I see. What about this one?"

He had a puckered circular one on his lower belly, a hand-span lower than the one from the ship attack. He stiffened slightly as she touched the circular one, as if it still pained. Cassandra glanced up at him. He wasn't looking at her. He was looking over her head. And his jaw looked locked.

"Arrow."

"Oh my. That one must have really hurt. Is there another wound...where the arrow...exited?"

She went around to the back of him, searching. Exploring. Skimming her hand along even more scars. She didn't ask their cause. They appeared mostly like the sword or knife ones. The main reason she stayed silent was because his skin lifted with goosebumps beneath her fingers, and that was a truly divine sensation.

"Oh. Here it is. This is the hole. From the arrow. Yes?"

He nodded.

The other arrow hole was just above his waist. Same side.

"Is this where the arrow exited?"

"*Nae.*"

He was definitely tense. Cassandra traced the puckered scar with a concave center. "I don't understand."

"I was shot in the back," he replied tersely.

Cassandra came back around him. Stood before him. Waiting for him to look down at her. Establish eye contact. He glanced down at her, then away. He was definitely tensed. Every striation of muscle was prominently displayed.

"In battle?"

"No. Far worse. But 'tis na' something we'll be discussing. And definitely na' in the midst of our wedding night. With a large bed awaiting us. And completely privacy."

Cassandra regarded him for long moments. "You are very good at avoiding questions, Rhoenne."

"You...overly tender?" he asked instead.

She stepped closer. "That depends on what you have in mind."

He bent his head to look at her, lifted his eyebrows, and speared her with the intense blue of his gaze . "Plenty."

"Well. In that event..." Cassandra went onto tip-toes to wrap her arms about his neck. Reach his lips with hers. "I think we can work with it."

And the next moment she was in his arms.

———∞∞∞———

Cassandra truly was a beautiful lass.

Rhoenne smoothed a lock of hair from her

face and off her shoulder, regarding her at some length. He reclined on his uninjured side, his head propped with a hand, watching his new wife sleep. She'd rolled and changed positions at least thrice without waking. At the moment she was snuggled at his side, breathing deeply and rhythmically against his chest. He was naked. She again wore her night shift tied clear to the neck.

She looked incredibly young. Innocent. Ethereal. No one would guess she was a tigress. He had a couple of scratches to add to his collection now. From her fingernails raking him along his shoulders and upper arms. They weren't deep enough to scar, although he wouldn't have minded.

Rhoenne smirked. He'd been protective and possessive of her before. Now, she'd be lucky to seek her privy without him hovering. He was a very lucky man. This woman was so beautiful. So sweet. So loving. So wild. So intense.

So different from Aileen.

Damn it.

He wished Cassandra hadn't gone over his scarring. Bringing up anything from his past was not a good idea, especially with so many dark hours ahead of him. Dark, quiet hours made the memories harder to stifle. Especially Aileen.

Aileen was a beautiful woman...but she'd pale in comparison.

He still remembered his first look at her. He'd been sixteen. Spoiled as only the eldest son and heir to an earldom could be. Tall. Raw-boned.

Not yet the stature or weight of the fourth earl, however everyone had known he'd reach - if not surpass - his sire. Rhoenne was the image of Caillen Ramhurst, save for their eye color. Caillen had the usual Ramhurst brownish-green eyes. Rhoenne was a throwback to their ancestor, the first earl. The Norman – his namesake.

His mother had come from the Balliol clan. He'd never known her. She'd died at his birth. His first step-mother perished almost three years later at the birth of Rhoenne's half-brother, Bhaltair. Bhaltair took after his mother. She'd been MacDougall clan. He'd had a mop of burnt-orange-colored hair. Lots of freckling. Was short, and prone to fat.

After his second widowing, their sire, Caillen put his time and energy to protecting his fief, extending and enlarging his castle, and training his two sons. Along with their cousin, Grant, Rhoenne and Bhaltair spent their days on all manner of masculine pursuits. Hunting. Fishing. Riding. Fighting. Combat. Weapons training. Rhoenne was mentored and trained by the clan champion, Henry FitzHugh. At sixteen he was already, a force on Castle Tyne's list, nigh unbeatable by any except his father's Honor Guardsmen. The nights were devoted to study. Caillen had to continually hire and replace tutors from Edinburgh as his son, Rhoenne outpaced them. Grant kept up with the physical pursuits, but avoided most lessons. Rhoenne's half-brother, Bhaltair failed at just about everything.

And then her carriage had arrived.

Rhoenne's experience with the fairer sex was a bit of play with hoydenish lasses who chased him for kisses, and a few stolen moments behind the stables with the head groom's oldest daughter that had to be followed by a brisk swim across Tyne Castle's loch. He hadn't known women existed that looked like his second step-mother.

Father had given them a fortnight to prepare. He'd come back from a trip to London-town, after spending several months there. He told them of the young woman he'd met. How he'd fallen instantly in love. He'd returned home by himself, but they'd been told she would soon follow. Her name was Aileen. She was from the south, the daughter of a baron. The earl was a score and sixteen. Aileen was half his age. His da had described her as delicate. Lady-like. Her hair as brown as Scots Pine bark, her eyes as mercurial green as a pond on a mist-filled day.

Rhoenne had just given a hearty blow to a man from his father's Honor Guard when her carriage and two baggage carriages complete with outriders had entered the inner courtyard, stopping at the stables. It was a rain-filled day, the castle grounds sodden and slick. The list was a quagmire of mud. He'd been covered in muck. Hair plastered to his skull. Muscles heaving. The castle chamberlain rushed out along with a battalion of servants to meet the carriage. Rows of menservants held lengths of wool *plaide* over her path. A step-stool had been hastily brought and plunked down.

Aileen had stepped out, a vision in pink

garments. She'd looked over the mass of males in the vicinity. Lifted her chin. Jaws were dropping, his included. He'd also dropped his sword and his guard. And ended up on his arse from a blow that took his breath as well.

He didn't meet her until days later. Father told them the reason. Aileen was *Sassenach*. English. Her constitution was frail. She hadn't taken well to the journey. Or her marital status. Or her new home. Or the clime. Or the lack of feminine companionship...

The list was lengthy.

It had been a family sup. At Castle Tyne that meant it included the earl; Tevin, his younger twin-brother by a half-day, and the lads; Grant, Rhoenne, and Bhaltair. Rhoenne had dressed with particular care, as had the others. He'd walked into the Great Hall. Aileen had been wearing a pale green ensemble. It set off her beauty. She'd been holding to her new husband's arm. And the moment she'd looked up into Rhoenne's eyes, he'd been knocked sideways. Completely smitten.

He'd also been damned.

But he didn't find that out until later.

He took to swimming almost daily. The loch never froze, but at times ice crusted the waves near shore. Breaking through them actually helped with the emotions. He fought and trained with a vengeance. Rode every horse they owned, while breaking in new stock. He was working through the frustration, as was right. Rhoenne hero-worshipped his father. He'd never dishonor the elder Ramhurst. That meant his feelings were unrequited and they always would be. It was his secret. He'd drafted love poems to Aileen, only to burn them all in the fire. Composed songs, and sang them to flocks of sheep, herds of horses. Occasionally a salmon-filled burn composed his audience.

A year went by. Another. Jealousies and odd rages flashed through the ranks of the men throughout the castle. He didn't know then why. Life-long friends would challenge and fight as though bitter enemies. Rhoenne got stronger. Harder. Tougher. During the same time frame, Aileen's temperament grew more mercurial, her womb remained barren, their retainers became surly and unhappy, and the earl took to drinking heavily. Rhoenne didn't know anything about the last four issues. He avoided anything to do with the countess and her household.

And if only he'd tied himself to his bed that fateful night, things might have progressed naturally!

It hadn't seemed necessary. He'd rarely sleep-walked. He'd thought the episodes a childhood issue – a malady that he'd outgrown. He'd gone to his chamber late, collapsed on his bed, every muscle spent and sore. And the next thing he knew, Aileen was unclothed, screeching and crying, pointing and accusing, and his father was screaming with rage.

And Rhoenne was in their bed.

He hadn't been fully awake before the earl started beating him. He hadn't any chance to defend, even if he'd wanted to. Caillen thrashed Rhoenne nearly to death, and would have if Henry hadn't stopped it. The man had discovered him missing, mounted a search throughout the castle and out into the grounds. It was Henry who'd slammed through the doors of the chieftain's bedchamber, got between father and son, and held Caillen back long enough for Rhoenne to crawl from the room.

He'd left a blood trail. It hadn't gone to his tower. He'd gone to the stable, taken a Clydesdale, somehow mounted it, and ridden out into the night. Directionless. To hide. And heal. And hate.

The last one was directed inward.

He'd gone missing three days. If he hadn't been so gravely injured, he'd have left Tyneburgh and all it meant. It was Henry who found him. Rhoenne had holed up in a cave near the standing stones erected by ancients. Henry was the man who gave him the tidings. His father had suffered a seizure that same night. He'd never awakened.

Henry was his support. The shoulder he needed to cry on. And his nursemaid. The man was his conscience as well. It took a fortnight to heal enough to move without an assist. Throughout, Henry pleaded with Rhoenne to go back to the castle. Assume the title. Tyneburgh was his responsibility and his birthright. Rhoenne couldn't leave administration of the Ramhurst clan to his uncle Tevin, or his cousin, Grant. Tevin had always coveted the title. Giving him such power fomented discontent and revolt. Nor could he hand it to Bhaltair. His half-brother was barely fifteen, the lad ignorant and inept. And Henry begged Rhoenne not to leave it to that malevolent termagant Caillen had brought into their midst with his third marriage.

Those words were Henry's. He only said them one time because Rhoenne only warned him once. Rhoenne thought he knew the truth. Aileen wasn't wicked. She was the innocent here. This was his fault, and his alone. There was no loch deep enough to hide in. No place dark enough to mute the guilt. The remorse. The regret.

And the utter shame.

Rhoenne hadn't known he had a dark side until then. He was a man who could ravish his own step-mother. Cause his father's death. Fracture the core of the Ramhurst clan. There was no penance with enough breadth for what he'd done.

But he'd returned.

From that moment on, Rhoenne was changed. He no longer composed anything, poem or not. He ceased singing. He didn't josh and tussle with the others. He kept his own counsel. His manner became withdrawn and introspective. His mood pensive. He didn't move from his lone tower, either, refusing to take over the chieftain's rooms. Despite how Henry counseled against it, Rhoenne was not sleeping in his father's bed. Such a thing felt unsanctified and wrong. He didn't care if Aileen stayed there. He rarely sought sleep anyway. And out on the list, he was a true terror. Few men walked after a challenge. Most weren't conscious. He was rarely at any castle function, especially if it included women. Those, he avoided completely. It was in the tower that he fought sleep, training himself to achieve a state of wakefulness he could maintain.

Each day followed the next. Became weeks. Then months.

He'd reached his nineteenth year when Aileen started showing up in unexpected places. She'd cross his path as though inadvertently, and walk away giving him glances over her shoulder. Those looks didn't look afraid. Or prudish. They sparked interest that wasn't just wrong, it was evil. Her every move fomented a lust that just added weight to his penance. Once, when he'd been roaming the halls at night, she'd stepped from her chamber. She'd worn a simple robe. Nothing beneath. And she'd tipped her shoulder to make the garment gap, allowing a peek into the well of shadow between her breasts. Rhoenne had turned away and stalked off.

And then came the eve she'd visited his tower chamber.

Rhoenne had annihilated two Honor Guardsmen, swum the loch, and done a jog back around it. Exhaustion accompanied his steps to slog up the wheel stair, hoping he'd reach the tower room before his legs gave out and dropped him. And then he heard them.

"...any man in the castle. But keep your hands off him. I'm warning you. I'll toss you in a bog. They'll never find you."

It was Henry. In Rhoenne's room. For what reason, he didn't know.

"I can have any man I want." Aileen answered with snide tones Rhoenne had never heard from her before.

"You can na' have me."

"Who wants an old man?" Aileen answered. And then she'd laughed.

"You can na' have the laird, either."

"Surely that's for him to decide."

"I ken what you are, Mistress," Henry replied.

"Oh really? And what am I?"

"A serpent. Of Satan."

Rhoenne didn't hear Aileen's reply. Rage and anger sent fuel to his limbs. He'd reached the chamber swiftly, approached Henry, demanded an apology, and when it wasn't forthcoming, he'd slammed a fist into Henry's jaw. Followed up with a challenge to meet on the list. The very next day, he'd given Henry his first defeat.

And Aileen a clear field.

That's when she'd come to Rhoenne in his tower. Arriving one night when he'd been sleepless, just lying atop his bed, watching where the ceiling slats joined to form the vaulting. Her presence had startled. She'd brought a lantern. Set it high on his wardrobe. And she'd approached, opening her robe, and dropping it, revealing feminine perfection he'd never imagined. He'd gotten to his feet before she reached him. Stood looking down at her in disbelief, shock, and a horrifying stab of desire, which, since he slept with just a *plaide* draped about his hips, hadn't gone unnoticed. And then she'd touched him, right in the belly, just above his groin.

The contact hadn't sent anything lustful. Far from it. Her fingers sent a cold wash of shivers. He'd felt physically ill. He'd run from her, taking the tower steps two at a time as if pursued by a banshee of Scot lore. A swift swim in the loch hadn't cleansed him. Nothing did.

The episode started his sleep-walking again, too. He'd taken to barring himself in his tower with the bolt down. Tied to the bed. Suffered all manner of fitful trouble. Dealt with lust that wouldn't quench no matter how long he swam the coldest part of the loch, or how many trips he took to town, and how many women he paid to tupp. That's the reason he'd been outside the chieftain door one night when the lock clicked. He'd barely stepped into a shadowed doorway when clansman Lachlan MacDuff came through the portal, turning to kiss and fondle the same naked form that was turning Rhoenne's life into a whirlpool of craven desire. MacDuff had adjusted his attire and jauntily strode down the hall barely missing Rhoenne's hiding spot.

The bile was difficult to swallow. The disgust was impossible.

She'd bedded Lachlan MacDuff? A stable hand of low birth? The man had the odor of horse manure permanently attached to his frame. He was rough-mannered Unkempt. Barely civil. And the next night it was a different gent. And the next. And the next... And a fortnight full of them to convince, then revile. It conquered every emotion for her save disgust. But then she'd accosted him in the chieftain study. Alone. Wearing little. He knew now she went without underclothes in order to tempt and titillate. And stoke jealousies and rages. Working her wiles and spinning a web. Henry had been wrong. She wasn't a serpent.

She was a spider.

Cassandra stirred, jerking him from the insanity of such recollection and introspection. It was his wedding night. He'd been blessed beyond imagination. He'd wed a truly amazing woman. Beautiful. Chaste. Trustworthy. He didn't deserve her love. Nor did he deserve to love her. But that didn't stop it. He'd never felt anything like this. Ever.

Rhoenne shook his head slightly, lowered his lips to hers, and kissed her until she stirred. Stretched. And finally opened her eyes. She gazed up at him with such emotion within her glowing golden eyes, his heart thudded in response. She smiled sleepily. And the earth moved.

I...thought I'd dreamt you. And...this," she whispered. She was nestled against him, her palm flush to his chest. And then she blushed.

Rhoenne tensed and looked up rapidly, blinking at moisture that hovered atop his eyes for long suspense-filled moments before it dissipated. He couldn't disguise the tremble, however. He should tell her of his love. And someday – if he deserved it – he would. But, not now.

"I have na' been called a dream afore," he remarked finally.

"Yes. I know. I heard all about your accolades."

"Accolades? I guess I was na' succinct enough."

"I am still looking for the emotionless part you claim."

Rhoenne grunted a non-answer.

"That's what I thought," she told him.

"Are you...tender, sweet?" he asked.

"And if I am?"

Rhoenne cocked his head. "Well..." He sighed heavily, moving her with it before continuing, "It is my wedding night. I suppose I could forego—."

"Oh. Just you dare try."

She interrupted him with words, then pulled his head down for honeyed kisses that stopped any thought of speaking words. Her nightgown was reverently lifted over her head as she rolled back and forth to make it easier. Her body displayed for his adoration. Her skin responded to every touch. Each kiss. When he entered her, it was with gentleness and care. Each stroke lengthy and slow. His body poised and primed, and ready, but working only to pleasure her. At length. And multiple times. Until he couldn't hold it back any longer.

The bed rocked and creaked with each thrust. Her legs clung. Her arms hugged. Her sighs sounded. And fulfillment brought more than pleasure and release.

It brought sobs.

All this time, Rhoenne thought the act between a man and woman was evil. His needs were base and savage, and undeserving of tenderness. He hadn't known love made all the difference.

Well.
He knew it now.

CHAPTER TWENTY-TWO

T HE KNOCK WAS slight.   Barely a tap.
Rhoenne was on the floor, his sword in his
right hand, tunic in the left, and at the chamber
door before the knock came again.

"My laird!"

The words were hissed through wood but still
audible. Rhoenne lifted the bolt, opened the
door a crack. Henry slid through. Slammed it
behind him. He was breathing hard. Rhoenne
pulled the tunic over his head. Down his torso.

"The *duchesse*?" he asked.

"Worse.   Greek nobles...with anger in the
blood."

"Greeks?"

"These are difficult times. Crete is a conquered
land.   The Greeks...do na' take kindly to...
Venetian overlords. I do na' blame them. I feel...
the same about the Sassenach."

"'Tis a revolt?" Rhoenne grabbed up his trews.
Rapidly slid them on. Knotted his crotch tie.
Pulled on socks. Shoved his feet into his boots.

"Aye. Without one hint of warning. 'Tis na'
the first one, either...although the last ended

badly."

"Would that they'd waited just one more day!" Rhoenne remarked.

"Where is your lady?"

"She sleeps within." Rhoenne gestured with his head toward the bed chamber.

"No, I don't. I'm right here."

Cassandra spoke from right beside him, slipping her hand into his. Rhoenne glanced down. Imprinted her needs in an instant. She wore her nightgown. She was barefoot. She'd need a covering. Transportation.

"How many do we face?" Rhoenne asked.

"Countless."

"Armed?"

Henry nodded.

"Where are the others?"

"Aboard ship. I told you, there was not a hint on the street for warning! 'Tis verra well planned. And executed. Why...if I hadn't heard a strange bit of words earlier and pondered it through, I'd have missed it completely. They've taken the night guards out. The halls are besieged as we speak."

A swell of sound filtered through the door as though cued.

"We fight?"

"They are na' taking prisoners," Henry retorted.

Rhoenne nodded. "Verra well. You have a plan for my lady?"

"Of course. I was na' chosen as commander of your Honor Guardsman simply for my good looks. Emin awaits without."

"By himself?"

"Amazing fellow. He blends in well. We, unfortunately, will not. We do na' look like conquered impoverished Greek nobles. We do na' even look Greek. *And* we reside in the Venetian palace they attempt to overtake."

"The *duchesse* Zecchino?" Rhoenne asked.

Henry nodded.

"Get Emin."

"Oh, no. No. Please. You are not sending me to her," Cassandra objected from his side.

"We need a cover. And her jewel bag," Rhoenne spoke to Henry before pulling Cassandra into a hug. He held her close as he whispered in her ear. Snuck in a kiss. "'Tis only a precaution, my love. We will be right behind you. I swear."

"Then why can't I stay with you?"

"I can na' risk it. You are too precious."

"Please?"

"I can na' keep you safe and fight at the same time. We would both perish."

"Rhoenne—."

"You promised to obey me," he stopped her.

"That's unfair," she replied.

"Who mentioned fairness? Perhaps I should add that to my list. I am the Dark One. I maim. Kill. I am emotionless. And unfair."

She regarded him for heart-stopping moments. "You will be right behind me? You promise?"

"Only death would prevent it, sweet."

"You die, and..." Her voice stopped. Her eyes filmed over with moisture that made the golden color glow. "I cannot finish the thought."

Rhoenne swallowed. His throat was too tight to speak.

Henry walked back into sight, tossed him the bedcover and the jewel-filled bag. Rhoenne handed the bag to Cassandra. She took it automatically, and held it to her belly. He started swaddling her, just like he had back in Egypt. A glance told him she had the same thought.

"Why didn't those fools in the harem teach me something of value? Swordplay, for instance! *That* would have been useful."

"Well. I, for one, do na' rue anything. Your lessons did na':..ahem. Go to waste," Rhoenne teased.

"Wretch," Cassandra replied.

"Excellency?"

Emin materialized behind Cassandra. Henry held the door open a gap. Sounds of fighting were easily heard and deciphered. Swords clanged. Thuds resounded. Groans and cries split the gloom, interspersed with blood-curdling screams.

"If we separate, you must get my lady to the *duchesse* Zecchino."

"The grandmother. Yes, Excellency. I shall see it done."

Rhoenne bent his head to Cassandra. Matched his forehead to hers for the smallest moment.

"Cassandra?"

"Yes?"

I love you.

He almost said it. She nodded and smiled through her tears as if he had spoken aloud. Then

Emin hefted her over his shoulder, and settled her, looking like he'd pillaged castle property. It was reminiscent of when the man had first toted Cassandra into Rhoenne's life. Only now, it looked like he was toting her from it. Rhoenne shoved the thought aside.

"We wait. Or storm?" he asked Henry.

"Unlike you, I have na' had a good fight in some time," Henry replied.

"Storm," Rhoenne agreed.

They didn't get the chance. Armed men raced into the hall, filling the space with bodies. Emin's first attempt to leave got pushed back, into Henry. Rhoenne roared, and started hacking. He'd always had lightning reflexes. He used them, cleaving a way through adversaries, hacking through combatants with his sword arm, while shoving others aside with his left fist and elbow, and more than once, his shoulders. The attackers were all smaller men. Less well-trained. And his ferocity sent more than one man running from him.

He reached a wall. Rhoenne smacked into it, and pushed off, missing a head blow by a hairsbreadth. That assailant lost his arm. Rhoenne kicked him aside and watched Emin dance over the falling body without losing footing. Rhoenne caught a glimpse of the eunuch's back as he raced around a corner, then had to rejoin the fight. Henry went down. Rhoenne shoved and hacked and sliced and killed his way to his man. And from the other direction, enforcements finally arrived. Heaven-sent. Fresh. Trained. And disciplined.

The new men forced the angry melee down the hall in the direction Emin had taken, leaving fallen bodies and a lot of blood and gore behind.

Henry had taken a blow to the lower belly. His tunic was gashed and bloodied. The man groaned and tried to stand. Fell back to his haunches. Rhoenne crouched beside him, pulled Henry's arms and legs over his shoulders, took a deep breath, and heaved to his feet.

"You are na'…carrying me," Henry complained.

"Hold your tongue. For once."

Rhoenne tried to jog the entire way. The castle was built on the hillside making it a downward trek. Streets were deserted for the most part. A slight wind ruffled his hair. Moonlight gave him the path. No one would have guessed the turmoil happening in the palace behind him. But it took forever to reach the docks. Henry wasn't speaking, or groaning, or giving indication that he still lived. That added impetus to Rhoenne's every step. He didn't stop. He didn't flag. His chest was on fire, every breath labored. His legs and arms and belly joined the fray, but finally he reached the dock.

He had to stand huffing, grabbing enough breath to yell at someone to assist. Iain was on duty.

"Ramhurst…clan!"

Rhoenne's shout wasn't loud but Iain heard him. The man lowered the gangway and raced down it.

"Is that Henry? What happened?"

"Get a bottle of whiskey. And Ida! Tell her to

bring her needle and thread."

"Ida? And her needle?"

"Aye. She's got a patient. And get my cabin prepared." Rhoenne shuffled Henry's weight and started up the ramp.

"Where is your lady? And the eunuch?"

"Later," Rhoenne answered.

The cabin had been furnished for a voyage with a lady onboard. Now it was turned into a sick room. Henry hovered between life and death for five days after Ida sewed his innards back into him. Alternately fevered. Chilled. Incoherent. At one point they thought they'd lost him. Rhoenne had taken to napping on the floor. Ida woke him with a sharp smack to his shoulder. Grunted and pointed to the bed he'd bought for Cassandra to sleep in. Henry was tossing and mumbling, his skin hotter than ever. Ida ran for another bucket of water to bathe him with while Rhoenne shook his man.

"FitzHugh!"

"Rhoenne." The invalid's lips were cracked and dry. The voice croaked.

"Do na' speak!"

"*Nae!*" The man grabbed his arm. Opened eyes that looked wild and disoriented. And intent. Focused on Rhoenne. "These are...my last words on earth."

"Do na' say that!"

"Listen to me! Guard your back...Ramhurst. Always."

And Henry had collapsed.

"Oh, *nae*! You are na' dying on me!"

Fear drove Rhoenne's actions. He shook Henry, yelled at him, and then gave the man a blow to his chest that made Ida screech from behind him. And then he did it again. Tears blurred his vision. He was poised to hit him again before Henry gave a cough, a series of moans, and grabbed at a slight and labored breath. And then he took another. And one after that. And more. Rhoenne stood. Strode past Ida. Shoved his upper body into the rail, leaned on his hands, and gave vent to the sobs.

No one saw. No one would ever know.

For the full five days the ship stayed at anchor, Ida and Rhoenne alternated duties; bathing Henry with water when he fevered, covering him with blankets when he shook. Ida even shared body warmth, holding the man through the worst of his shudders. They spoon fed him water and then broth. His breathing grew less labored, but the fever wouldn't relent.

Throughout, the revolution continued, turning Sitia into a smoke-wrapped city. It hovered in pockets as the palace and other structures were sacked and burned. The destruction reached the marketplace. Then they even torched the tavern district. Rhoenne's every moment was filled with thoughts of Cassandra. Worry.

And yearning.

He wanted her back...at his side and in his arms. But Henry hovered too near death. Rhoenne daren't leave.

And that's why he sent his cousin, Grant to fetch her.

Grant snuck back onboard ship in the midst of the night. Silent. Surreptitiously. As if Rhoenne wasn't awake and alert, and watching from atop the mizzenmast as he awaited that very thing. The man was alone.

"Where is she?"

Rhoenne swung down into the space in front of Grant. Rose from his crouch and took a heavy step forward. His posture was intimidating, poised for violence. And Grant wouldn't meet his eyes.

Rhoenne heart stalled. "I asked you a question."

"My laird. I—" He stopped. Blinked rapidly.

"Where is my lady wife?"

"Rhoenne. I—" The man flicked a glance at him, then looked out toward the open ocean again. He shook his head.

"What is it? What?"

Rhoenne grabbed his cousin and shook him.

"'Tis...na' good," Grant managed to reply.

"What?" Rhoenne opened his hands, releasing the man. He'd experienced terror. Fear. Rage. And panic before. Never like this. And never in this combination.

"She is na' there."

"What?! *Nae!*"

Rhoenne's cry brought the Ramhurst clansmen out of the bowels of the ship and two of their hired seamen. He could hear a reaction on the waterfront, as well, as shouts and yells answered his outburst.

"I do na' ken how to say it differently. You...

heard me."

Rhoenne was shaking. His hands knotted into fists. His heart rupturing. His entire frame tensed and ready to erupt. Each breath came hard and fast. Grant backed from him.

"What? What happened? What did you say?" Euan said.

Euan was taking command?

"I was sent to the dragon's palace. To fetch her."

"Cassandra?"

"Aye. And she is na' there. No one has seen her."

"Oh, no. No," Euan answered. "Somebody. Go. Check."

"You can't. No foreigner can walk the streets at night without being accosted. They'd spot you at a glance."

Euan swore.

"There is more," Grant offered.

"Well? What? Speak up, *mon*."

"I overheard...something. I need to check. In the market."

"The market?"

Oh God!

Rhoenne was looking up now. His vision blurred with useless tears, while his entire being filled with something worse than pain. Far worse.

"...need funds," Grant continued.

"Done. Iain? Get him a purse."

The man took off at a run. Dove through the hatch door. He was back moments later with a bulging bag. He tossed it to Grant.

"Now, go. Find her," Euan ordered. "Report

back as soon as you can. Go!"

The silence was broken by the sound of running footsteps across the wooden deck. Rhoenne blinked tear trails into existence. They reached the hairline at his ears.

Please God. Please? Bring her back to me. I will do anything. Pay any price. Serve any penance. Please!

That silent prayer was just the first. It continued unabated throughout the night. He didn't stay aboard ship, either. He covered over with a cloak, and went to check himself. And found an empty structure. In ruins. Still smoldering.

He'd thought he knew pain. He'd experienced it often enough. He'd dealt with it and moved on. He thought he knew how. But nothing in his existence could have prepared him for soul-shattering agony that filled, overwhelmed, and destroyed.

And that was before Grant returned the next morning, bringing a jeweled armband he'd purchased from a market seller. On a tip that it came from a harem girl. She'd been a sultan's favorite, her hair a distinctive shade. And there was a lock of hair that proved it.

They were out to sea before Henry was well enough to leave the cabin. Euan had taken over Rhoenne's place in tending him. The lad had matured without warning, and not one of them had noted it. He was the man behind everyday orders. Settling of issues. Parsing out drinking water as it grew scarce. Doing the same with the rare fish they brought up for stew. The reason for the shortage in stores was due to Rhoenne. They'd lingered another ten days in port while Rhoenne spent a small fortune in *ducati* coin prowling the markets, the taverns, the docks. Anywhere he could think of. Interrogating. Threatening, and more than once coming to blows. All for a hint of anyone who knew about a harem girl...or the jeweled band he wore on his right wrist.

All for naught. No one had seen her. No one had spoken to her. She'd disappeared.

Exactly as he'd feared.

They'd finally sailed. Euan handled most administrative duties. Ida tended the invalid. Rhoenne attended to the rigging. Navigating. Observing the stars. Checking the horizon. Watching for signs of bad weather. He kept constantly moving. Avoiding anything to do with normal human needs. No one saw him eat. Or drink. Or sleep. If anyone chanced upon him, he'd look aside and brush past them.

His entire focus was on the chore he faced. The one he'd run from five years past. He was ridding the Ramhurst fief of the venomous Aileen. For once, he knew he'd succeed. He was empty inside. Completely inhuman. And absolutely emotionless.

Henry found the laird sitting atop a rail at the stern, watching dolphins cavort in their wake. The older man walked gingerly, wincing every so often, his gait slow. Rhoenne heard his approach. He didn't turn. He had his fingers wrapped about the pouch Ida had sewn for him. She'd slid it across the floor to him when he'd last checked on Henry. Days earlier. Her sobs had colored the scene.

Rhoenne hadn't shown any emotion.

The little pouch hung from a cord around his neck. He usually had it tucked beneath his tunic, hidden. Safe. It was stitched from golden colored silk, with almost invisible stitching. It contained a lock of hair. The golden jeweled band that never left his wrist reflected light if he moved it. Henry finally reached him. Rhoenne didn't react. He didn't turn from contemplation of the scene before him.

"Ramhurst?"

Rhoenne put out his free hand, palm outward, giving a silent command for silence. It didn't work.

"I just heard. They kept it from me. I am... abjectly sorry, my laird."

"Don't. Just....don't," Rhoenne replied.

"But if I had na' taken an injury, this would na' have happened!"

"'Tis na' your fault. 'Twas God's will. I have many debts, my friend. One is now paid."

"You had *nae* debt to me."

"I did na' say it was to you. Some things we never cease paying for. *Nae* penance is enough."

"Bhaltair's death was na' your fault! 'Twas a just penalty for attempted murder!"

"Say one more word and I will reinjure you."

"Rhoenne—"

"My façade only works if it is na' cracked. You ken?"

Despite the hold he had on his emotions, his voice broke. Rhoenne grabbed a sail line and started climbing. Hand-over-hand. Fully breaking open blisters and accepting easily what he used to consider pain. He'd reached the mizzenmast and straddled it before looking down again. Henry was nowhere in sight. The day before him was glorious. Sunlight dappled the waves. A breeze lifted strands of hair.

But inside he was dead.

CHAPTER TWENTY-THREE

"ANY WORD?"
Cassandra looked up hopefully at Emin's entrance
. The sewing hoop fell to her lap. It was a senseless effort anyway. She wasn't paying the slightest attention to her project, despite how *Nonna* lectured. Each stitch was more haphazardly sewn than the last.

"Much apologies, Highness. I have returned bereft. Once again. There is no message from Sitia."

Cassandra stood, walked with small mincing steps in her pointy-toed heeled shoes over to a window. She looked out over the rocky hillside forming the demesne of Zecchin Castle, the seat of the Zecchino duchy. The castle was constructed of buff-colored stone, completely impregnable. Safe and secure from any uprisings that might take place in any city of the Candia Duchy. Impossible to breach for a small group of Highland clansmen hailing from someplace called Scotland - a place that didn't just sound like the outer edge of the world, it probably was.

Her pale peach silk skirts rustled with each step. The binding about her midriff made breathing difficult. But *Nonna* insisted she dress as befitted her station. The woman had ordered and paid for an entire new wardrobe.

"You gave them my armband? And...the lock of hair?" she questioned.

"Yes, Highness."

She sighed. "Then why doesn't he come for me?"

"Forgive the impertinence, but is it possible he has...lost interest?"

Cassandra smiled to herself. Reminisced. "No."

"I have seen it often, Highness. The sultan... was a difficult man to keep entertained. Many were the woman he set aside through the years."

"That's because women are property in that culture. It's very easy to set aside a pair of shoes, or a new jewel. It's much harder to set aside someone you love."

"You are certain of his love?"

"Oh, yes." Her voice warmed. And she placed her hands atop her womb as if a child would already show.

"Then he will come. You must just be patient."

"Something is wrong. He didn't get the message. Otherwise he'd have come as soon as he found we'd moved!"

"They are still at their war, Highness. I am told the Greek rebels are in possession of Sitia. Armed Venetian warships are in the harbor at anchor. It may not last much longer."

"It's been a month! I cannot be patient much

longer. You don't understand. Yesterday, she introduced me to a Venetian count!"

"Yes," Emin responded with a noncommittal tone.

"She lives in the past! I don't even think she sees me!"

"Your own grandmother?"

"She doesn't want me, Emin. She only wants to use me! Rhoenne knew it instantly. He gave her such a difficult time! You should have heard him. But he knew. Somehow, he knew. She's not a loving grandmother. She's more like the sultan's mother!" She spun on her heels. "You remember her? We saw it often in the harem, especially among the old ones. All they do is manipulate and play with other's lives. It must be addictive. They want power. And once they get it, they want more of it. The *duchesse* thirsts for an alliance between the Zecchino house and the House of Dandolo, something that will give her enough power she'll eclipse the Morosini family. They politick for governance once my grand-uncle retires. It's a long confusing story that I do not care about...but it gives me insight to what she's doing – and why. I can see through her designs."

"These designs you speak of. They concern you?"

"Most assuredly. But she is forced to play a waiting game at the moment. The same one I am losing."

"A waiting game?"

"She wants to wed me to that count. Or –

should he balk, another member of the Dandolo family!"

"But you are already wed."

"I know! She disregards it, though. To her, marriage is only a means to gain power. I think she believes my marriage to Rhoenne is of such little value it can be set aside with a wave of her cane and a bribe to the right hands. Especially if he fails to come for me!"

"Ah. I begin to see."

"What are we to do?" She was wringing her hands now. A poor sign.

"We shall escape, of course."

Cassandra slanted a glance at him. "Again? You truly think it possible?"

"We are very successful at it, Highness."

She smiled with him. "True. Can you make it soon? Before my loss in this game is obvious?"

"You speak in riddles."

"Rhoenne has given me...a child."

His eyes went huge. And then he fell to his knees. "Oh, Highness. This is the greatest gift! The most wondrous event. He will be most pleased. As am I. Worthless though I am, I hereby pledge my life in service to your unborn son."

"You are so wrong, my friend. Not only about your worth, but this babe could easily be a daughter."

He looked her over for a moment. Considered it. Then shook his head. "No, Highness. That man would not sire a girl."

"Girls come from somewhere, Emin. And they are just as precious."

"Oh. They are much more so, Highness. Are not our vows to protect and serve proof of their value?"

"I am not being protected, Emin. This is just another prison."

"But Highness, it is the duty of every man to protect women. How are we to do that if we can't secure them?"

"Secure them. Apt words, my friend. That's it, exactly."

"Well. It will not concern you yet, *Princessa*. This child is not a girl. You carry a son. And I vow to do all in my power to protect and serve him, just as I do you."

Men.

Cassandra smiled to herself.

"I shall require another piece of your jewelry, Highness. Perhaps an anklet? Or some stones from a bigger piece?"

"Of course. Here." She reached beneath her mattress, pulled out the bag. "You have a plan?"

"We are just outside the city of Chania, Highness. It is a busy port. There are many ships in the harbor. Large ships. Ocean-going ships. It should not be difficult to secure you a berth. The more difficult task will be yours."

"I know. My every move is watched. Except when I'm locked away in my cell. I cannot imagine what might happen if they knew you were in here!"

"You can find some excuse to visit the markets? Stay a day or more in the city? Perhaps pack some of your beautiful new clothes?"

"If I agree to her plans, she will allow anything, I think. *If* I can do it without alerting her to my true purpose."

"You can do this?"

"I shall start tonight. At the dinner...if the menu does not cause my belly to revolt. That is why I suspected actually. What shall I do? What can I say? Should I portray anger at him for not coming for me? No...I shall be saddened. Weepy. That may be the more believable performance. And it will be true."

"You would not agree to wed this count?"

"I will agree to wed the devil himself if it will get me to Rhoenne! Here. Is an anklet enough?"

Emin took it. Bowed and slid back out the window. The sides of the castle were smoothed. Hard to grip. Her room was on an upper floor. Yet still, Emin managed to get to her. It was also why he visited at dusk, when the guards changed. Cassandra was at the window watching as he climbed the rope and disappeared through a crenel of the battlements. A moment later the rope slithered out of sight.

He couldn't use the door.

It was locked.

Subterfuge became her life. She'd practiced for years. A week went by without a visit from Emin. Then another one. The days passed with excruciating slowness. Cassandra got very good at acting. She was required to visit with her grandmother every evening, just before the dinner. That's when Cassandra would be told what was expected of her. Her continued failure at stitching would be pointed out. She didn't argue. She rarely spoke up at all. Every night was a repeat of the night before. *Nonna* required formal dress. Cassandra had gained the slightest bulge in her lower belly. Nothing noticeable. She could still fit into her tight dresses although it cramped. One of the maids looked at her sharply one night, however. That decided Cassandra. She hadn't survived eight years around power-hungry women without learning what they'd do.

And who they'd use.

Her sewing knife was sharp enough to slice a small cut at the top of one thigh. It was painful. She'd winced as she smeared blood on wads of cloth that she then left atop the waste in her bucket for disposal. That way the silent maids could note and report to her grandmother. Afterward, she dribbled wine onto the cut, gasping at the sting. And she'd watched them pour *aqua vitae* onto Rhoenne's gash? She didn't know how he handled pain so well. It had to have been agonizing.

During the third week since Emin's visit, she finally received the proposal. Count Dandolo wished an alliance with her. Nobody asked her. The proposal was given to her grandmother. He was offering for her hand. Cassandra wasn't even consulted before the offer was accepted.

And she'd thought harem life was restrictive and controlling and overbearing.

What a horrid life the *duchesse* was busily

constructing for her!

Cassandra couldn't even say with certainty what the count looked like. She'd never looked into his eyes. She daren't. The revulsion might be impossible to hide. She'd only addressed him if it was absolutely necessary. Most likely, he'd been told of her supposed time in a monastery. He probably thought her shy and retiring. The man was short, barely taller than she was. He was full of his own importance, dressed in vivid colors and costly fabrics. He wore a sword with a silver hilt at his side that looked incapable of slicing dinner bread, let alone protecting anything. He had a thick belly his attire failed to hide, a pointed beard with streaks of gray through the black, and his touch made her tremble with distaste.

But she didn't demure or protest. Instead, she started whining over her lack of attire. Despite the rows of dresses and kirtles in her wardrobe chamber, she needed new clothing, fashioned in the Dandolo colors of burgundy and gold, of course. Surely her grandmother knew how important it was to 'The Family'. She'd need to personally select the newest fabrics at the markets, freshly arrived from the east. And when *Nonna* balked, Cassandra did the best acting of her life, screaming and sobbing and tossing items with a fair degree of accuracy as though insanely enraged. She'd seen this type of behavior before in the harem. Surprisingly, it was quite enjoyable. She was hard put not to laugh as all four of her maids scurried from the room.

She didn't know what they reported. But it

worked. She'd succeeded.

Before dinner the very next evening, she was told she could have a short visit to the city. The Zecchino family owned a small villa for just such things. Cassandra would be escorted there under heavy guard. She'd be sequestered in the house, which meant she'd be imprisoned. She was not to visit the market. The tradesmen would bring their wares to her. It wasn't much, but it was enough...as long as God listened to the prayers she winged heavenward almost ceaselessly. Silently and desperately. And if Emin somehow knew what had transpired and came in time. There were so many variables at play; so many things that could go wrong. It got harder and harder to keep her tongue silent. She was so very tired of living a lie!

The trip from the castle took most of the day, traveling in a small carriage pulled by a donkey. The path wound back and forth through countryside of arid dirt interspaced with vineyards. Chania was a bustling city. She could hear it long before they came into sight. They skirted the thriving portions of the city, ending on a quiet street. The Zecchino villa was a single story structure, the walls adjoined to neighboring homes that probably had the same layout. She'd seen buildings like this before in Alexandria, Egypt. This was an ancient Roman design, the buildings still in use. There was one entrance at the front, another in the rear for servants and the like. Other than the large wooden entrance door, the entire front was a windowless wall of sand-colored stone. It looked more prison-like than anyplace she'd yet been.

Cassandra couldn't escape the feeling as the door closed shut behind her. The inside was cool, and quiet. The sleeping chambers were at the back of the house. They were spacious, and each had a small window opening high in the walls. It would be difficult for her to fit through, however. The home was designed with an atrium at the center, open to the sky. A fountain bubbled and frothed in its midst, creating rainbows of mist that sparkled in the dying sunlight. It would have been restful if she wasn't on edge every moment. Watching every shadow. Jumping at every sound. This was their only chance, and she didn't even know how to contact Emin! And even if she did, how would he manage to get to her? And if he did, how was he to fit through the window aperture?

She needn't have worried. The moment the last maid left the room, followed by the click of a key turning in the lock, Emin stepped from the darkest corner of her room. Relief made her knees sag while tears smarted at her eyes.

"Oh, Emin. Thank God."

"Allah willed it. I am here. You are prepared?"

Cassandra looked down at herself. She was in her night gown, dressed for bed.

"We need to be onboard ship within the hour!"

"What?"

"We must move quickly, Highness! You need a cloak. Some shoes. They did not unpack this trunk. We will take it." He hefted a large leather-bound wooden chest onto one shoulder as if it didn't weigh much more than she did.

"An hour?" Cassandra pulled on stockings. Pushed her feet into pointy-toed boots.

"The next ship will not leave until tomorrow night. They leave with the tide each eve! We dare not miss this one!"

"Can we get on it this late?"

"Of course. I paid passage this morn. When your carriage first arrived. I have been waiting that very thing. Highness, please. There is no time to dress."

She'd pulled a kirtle over her night gown. It barely fit. She looked lumpy and it was uncomfortable. She didn't care. It hid the bag of jewelry she'd slung over her shoulder, and that now rested at her hip. She snagged a dark green velvet cloak from another hook, and tied it on as she moved to the window. The aperture was small, and high up on the wall.

"We won't fit through there! What will we do?"

He smiled down at her. "Highness. There is another door. The key was in the lock. It leads to another room, where I have been waiting. There is another room beyond it. And then we will be outside. Come. I will not be able to carry you this time. I will have this trunk."

"I have legs, Emin."

"Yes," he replied. "I have seen. You will hold to my belt? Stay close at my side? And forgive the lack of respect, but...will you cleave to me, as if I am your man?"

"I would be honored to cleave to you, Emin," Cassandra said. "Any woman would."

He halted. His back straightened lifting the trunk enough it tapped the door jamb. "Highness?"

His voice trembled. Then he turned his head and stared at her for a moment as if he couldn't have heard correctly.

"Yes, Emin?" she replied.

He shook his head slightly and turned back around. "We must hurry."

She was so lucky to have him! So very lucky. She didn't realize the extent of it as they scurried along streets, dodging brightly-lit taverns and nefarious places of business, until a group of men stepped from an alley, bringing them to a stop. Cassandra saw a half-dozen men, maybe more. She quickly looked back down before anyone got a good look at her.

"Ho there! That is a nice big trunk you have there."

"And looks like you've got a nice little lady, as well," someone else spoke.

"Move out of my way," Emin returned.

His tone was low. Threatening. She should have known he'd speak the guttural Venetian lingo they used.

"Where is it you think you are off to...in such a rush?"

"Move. Now."

"Oh-ho. Look who thinks he is in charge?" one of them retorted.

"You do not wish to challenge me," Emin

answered.

"On the contrary. That is exactly what we wish. Isn't it, men?"

Cassandra couldn't breathe. Blink. Think. React. Her eyes were wide. Her heart hammering with instant panic. And a scream was stuck in her throat, choking her. Emin seemed immune. He lowered the trunk to the street before twisting to grasp her upper arms and lift her. He set her atop the trunk just above his eye level. The lid had a slight slope. Cassandra wobbled for an instant. Her gaze never left his.

"Do not move," he warned in a soft tone.

Move?

She was locked in place. It was a chore to nod, and that was accomplished with quick little gestures. He pulled his swords as he spun back to the group. Cassandra looked above them toward the star-filled sky. Silently prayed. She heard grunts. Squeals. Thuds. Something glanced off the trunk she stood atop, jostling her so she had to rebalance. The look down showed it had been a severed head. She couldn't prevent the gasp. Or the ice-cold shock. The scream that followed was a choked sound. She slapped her hands atop her mouth to stop it. Then slammed her eyes shut. Would that she could cover her ears as well!

"Highness?"

Emin's voice was the most steadying solid sound in the universe. Cassandra swayed, then fell. He caught her. She kept her eyes closed, working to control the hysteria, although nothing stilled the tremors that ravaged her entire body. He put her onto her feet beside him again. He wasn't even breathing hard.

"You are...unhurt?" he asked.

She nodded.

"Do you wish me to take the trunk? Or leave it?"

"What?"

"If I carry you, I must leave the trunk. What is your wish? It is no great issue. I can get more clothing. You and your unborn son are of the most import to me. The trunk is nothing. What is your wish? Can you walk?"

She nodded.

"You are certain?"

"Yes," she whispered from between frozen lips.

She heard him heft the trunk back onto his shoulder. She didn't open her eyes.

"Highness. You need to hold to me now. And... do not look down."

Cassandra slit her eyelids open enough to find his arm, and saw a lot of carnage. She gagged, turned her face away, and forced step after step. That's when she got a full appreciation of how truly lucky she was to have this man protecting, guiding, and assisting her. Unshed tears blinded her for several streets. She couldn't believe he called himself worthless. His worth was more than she could calculate.

As for her grandmother, she didn't spare the *Duchesse* Zecchino another thought.

The ship was at least three times larger than the one they'd sailed from Egypt. With three masts, a lot of sailors, and an entire deck partitioned for paying passengers. The gangway was a long wooden plank, too narrow to walk abreast. Emin strode up it with confidence, Cassandra holding to his belt. They were just in time. The sound of wood sliding on wood could be heard behind her. They'd barely been shown to her allotted space when the ship started moving.

Her newest prison chamber was twice the size of the cabin on Rhoenne's ship. It had a wooden platform with a straw-stuffed pallet atop it, and a mass of blankets. Two stools. A table. Some pegs in a wall. A small mirror. And a window. Cassandra untied the cloak with fingers that didn't feel like hers. She tried twice before she managed to hang it from a peg. Emin settled the trunk onto the floor in the center of the cabin and bowed, as though he'd depart.

"You are...not leaving?" Cassandra whispered. And then she embarrassed them both by barreling into him, wrapping her arms about his torso, and hugging him.

"Highness, please. You are safe now."

She shook her head and desperately fought new tears.

"Highness—."

"Why...is it like this? Why? We are not even in the east anymore! This is a Christian country!"

"Bad people exist in all walks of life, Highness. In every land. At every level."

"But, you—! They—!" She couldn't finish. The words were choked and incoherent. She couldn't even finish them.

"Ah. I understand. Forgive me. I have spent

many years training for just this type of event. In the sultanate they pitted me against opponents and we used real blades. I had to survive. Or perish. Only the best became sultan's guards. I am very good with swords and knives, Highness. But I had forgotten how it...sickens."

Cassandra swallowed. Nodded.

"You will be all right now?"

"Please don't leave me."

"I would keep you from the savagery that exists if I could. You have seen much of the world since leaving the harem. You will need to put some of it aside. Rest will help."

"Please, Emin."

"I will be right outside your door. You have my word."

Cassandra shook her head again. Sniffed loudly. And then tears began in earnest. She shook anew with the tempest. He sighed hugely, lifted her, and carried her to the pallet. He sat, holding her on his lap. Smoothed a hand down her braid along her back.

"I think there is more to this, Highness. You have been under great strain. This is a release."

His words only made her sob harder.

"*Princessa.* I am not a young man. I have lived my entire adult life in the harem. I have seen much. Understood more. You have been living a lie. It is especially difficult to do for so long. Guard every word. Pre-think every gesture. Pretend to be something you are not and fool others into believing it is so. It is very taxing. It wears on the soul. But you did it. Your lie is over.

No one will harm you while I am here. You are safe. Your unborn son is safe. I will let nothing happen to either of you."

She sniffed. Nodded.

"You do understand what I tell you?"

"I...love you, Emin. You are a treasure. Never forget that."

He stiffened. His arms tightened for a moment. And then he moved, setting her on her feet before standing beside her. He looked like he was flushed. It took several moments before he would look at her again.

"You are...recovered?" he asked.

She nodded.

"And I may go?"

"As long as it's not far."

"I will be just outside your door. You have my word."

Thank you," Cassandra replied.

"We will not speak of this night again," he said.

"If that is your wish."

"It is."

"Very well." Cassandra smiled at him. "Good night, Emin."

He nodded and left her, softly shutting the door behind him.

CHAPTER TWENTY-FOUR

I T TOOK ALMOST three months to reach
Scotland. Three months. Of mind-sapping
time when every day limped by slowly, and every
night was filled with memories of Rhoenne...
and the tears that ensued.

The journey slowed even more once they'd
docked at what had been described as a bustling
port city of the North. It looked neither bustling,
nor did it resemble a city. Cassandra had looked
out at her new home and shivered. Not just from
emotion, but it was much colder and wetter than
even London-town had been. She'd thought that
place the ends of the earth.

But she'd remember it.

Always.

It was at London-town that her baby had first
moved! She'd been standing at the rail holding
to Emin's arm, patiently waiting to disembark,
when the slightest flutter had stirred within her.
Her gasp, and the instant touch to her womb
earned Emin's glance.

"The child...moves?" he'd asked.

The emotion she'd experienced was too

vast. And warm. It overwhelmed with beauty. Cassandra had blinked away tears and beamed a smile. Emin cleared his throat, then returned her smile.

"Ah. That is good. He is strong."

And active.

She learned just how strong and active on the voyage to reach the Scot port city of Leith. Located just north of their capital Edinburgh, Leith was even more uninspiring than London-town. Low clouds hung over a motley collection of buildings. Everything was gray or brown, or the color of earth. Mud-covered. And wet. Anyone roving the streets wore plain colors or plaids in the same color scheme. It appeared residents simply wore garments made from whatever color the sheep had been when it was shorn. It shouldn't be a surprise. She'd had exposure to this in Rhoenne's small tent.

But that seemed like it had happened a lifetime ago.

She thanked God daily in her prayers for Emin. The man was a large, imposing presence at her side. He'd ceased scraping his body hair off, showing he had a full head of gray-speckled curly hair and facial hair that grew down his cheeks. Other than the slight dark tone of his skin, he looked exactly like a Scot vendor, or like member of the merchant strata of society. She'd portrayed his wife more than once, but even keeping her head covered and her eyes averted, it still created comment. Once, among a roomful of men, he'd even needed to threaten with the short swords he carried.

Once in Leith, he'd acquired a length of wool they called a *plaide*. Draped over the body and looped around the waist, it ended at his knees. It left the lower portion of his legs bare, but the shoulder section could be lifted over his head to protect from the elements. They were woven from wool. It seemed everyone wore woolen garments. For good reason. The fabric was thick, handled the damp well, and it was warm even when saturated. She had a length of it wrapped about her at all times.

The lone trunk they'd brought from Sitia had contained everything needed for a short stay in a sun-filled villa and little for warmth. Cassandra wore the beautifully woven silks and linens of her shifts for an inner layer. She had to. Her skin could not handle the wool. It itched and chafed and raised a rash when she'd tried. Two of the exquisite silk gowns, a set of stockings, and her two girdles had been traded for loose, floor-length woolen dresses, soft leather boots, and more. Emin was a master at procuring and bargaining, demonstrating a knack for making a deal, and a natural ability to understand and be understood, regardless of language barrier. He'd demonstrated that talent not only aboard the first vessel, but at the markets of London-town, and again on the trading vessel they had sailed north. She had first-hand knowledge of his skills, because she rarely left his side.

But nothing could have prepared her for what they'd endure once they'd docked at Leith. Emin bargained for two horses, one a short shaggy beast, the other a large workhorse with a wealth of hair at the base of its legs. Called a Clydesdale, they were told that horse would handle the path, the clime, any load, and wouldn't bolt at an attack, in the event of wolves. Emin procured a small cart that was attached to the small horse. It held the trunk and an assortment of items that passed for food. Ancient-tasting oat cakes. Dry, smoked meats. Old, shriveled berries. Small squares of hardened honey. A bag of oats and another of barley. At least her belly no longer revolted at the fare he provided. She'd had difficulty keeping anything down aboard the first ship, and again in London-town. Once she passed her third month, however, any illness disappeared. And then Emin couldn't keep her fed. She was always hungry. She was large by the time she'd entered the fourth month of carrying Rhoenne's child. But that was to be expected. The man was enormous. He would be even amongst his countrymen. He wouldn't sire a small babe.

It was at Leith that they finally got a positive answer about Rhoenne. Cassandra had listened intently as the man described it. Near everyone remembered him, but Emin chased down the fellow who'd actually dealt with the Ramhurst. The earl and his party had landed a sennight or so earlier.

A week!

She'd missed him by a week?

He'd spent a nice sum at the markets equipping his party for a journey, the man believed they'd gone west to Castle Tyne, the seat of the earldom. Cassandra had held to Emin to keep from bouncing as thrill after thrill coursed her body... and that just from listening.

They set out to follow. It rained more often than not. The air chilled exposed skin. And then raindrops turned into thick flakes, blanketing everything with a layer of white that melted once the sun came out again. She'd seen snow long ago. In Vottenavia. Emin was the one who looked stunned even after her explanation.

They lost the cart on the fourth day. The track had narrowed to a path. It covered hilly terrain, clung to the sides of a gorge, and went through a rock slide that upended the wheeled vehicle and sent their stores flying. Despite Emin's stricture, she'd helped him gather up food. The babe hampered her only slightly when she knelt and reached. The trunk was secured atop the small horse. The bags at the horse's sides bulged with items. The reins were attached to the Clydesdale's saddle. Then Emin pulled her into his arms to mount the bigger horse. Their journey got even slower.

And on the fifth day, they were accosted.

"Halt!"

Cassandra had been dozing, curled into a ball atop Emin's lap, wrapped in her blanket. She hadn't known it was snowing again, until the command stopped their horse, waking her. She sat, slit the blanket open, and peeked out over the horse's head.

Snowflakes were fluttering down, dusting

the band of men standing before them. She counted six. Each was armed with a bow at his back. Short swords strapped to their sides. And a plethora of knives tucked into their belts. One had an animal carcass over his shoulders. Behind her back she felt Emin moving. Reaching for the swords he carried on both sides. And then she noticed something.

"Wait! Emin wait! They wear gray and white with smaller stripes of black and blue! I have seen these colors." She turned back to the band and spoke in Gaelic. She had a foreign accent, but that couldn't be helped. "You are...Ramhurst clan, yes?"

One of them stepped forward. Cocky. Handsome. He had vivid blue eyes reminiscent of Rhoenne, but this fellow was a blonde. But he was definitely wearing the colors she'd mentioned.

"What of it?" he said.

"Oh! Thank the saints! Are we near Castle Tyne?"

"What business would you have there?"

Cassandra took a couple of seconds. Debated options. And then she just told them. "I...am the countess."

They erupted in laughter. Loud. Visual. Unrestrained. The man with the deer carcass even tossed it down so he could join in.

"Silence, you dogs!" Emin was off the horse and threatening enough they stopped laughing. But then they had knives pulled out, and more than one held his sword.

"Wait! Please. Gentlemen! There is *nae* cause for this! Rhoenne Ramhurst is my husband. I swear. We wed in Sitia! He was on a crusade. You know this, yes?"

Everyone stopped as she maneuvered her legs to the side so she could jump down. Emin forestalled her.

"Highness, please!"

"Highness?" one of them asked.

"I was a princess afore I wed. 'Tis of little import. What is important is Rhoenne. And his band. They have been this way, yes?"

The men looked at each other. Shook their heads.

"We've na' seen the mon in years," the first fellow announced.

"I heard rumor that he'd come back, recent-like," another man spoke up. "I discounted it."

"Trust me," Cassandra answered. "He is back. He may already be at the castle. Is it near?"

"How do we ken you speak truth?" the leader asked.

Cassandra reached up beneath the blankets, peeled the sides of the blanket apart in front of her face, and lifted it from her head. She looked down at him with the haughty expression she'd gleaned not only from the harem but her grandmother. She discounted snowflakes that dotted her cheeks and melted on her lashes. His eyes widened, and then his jaw dropped. The others had similar expressions.

"Verra few question me," she finally said.

"Oh. My lady."

The first man went to a knee. The others followed suit. Cassandra put her blanket back over her head.

"Rise. Please. The elements are *nae* place for this. We are near the castle?"

"My croft is nearer," an older fellow spoke up. "'Tis just over that drum. Come. We'll take you there. My wife will have a fire. And sup."

Emin took up the reins and walked at her side, behind the others. She knew why. He kept his other hand on his sword hilt. Just in case. Such a staunch champion he was. So protective. So dependable.

What they called a drum was a long sloping hill. It led down into a valley with a stream at the bottom of it. They crossed that, and went behind an outcrop of rock. A croft turned out to be a rounded structure built into the hill, using one side of the rock outcropping for a wall. It was protected from the elements, covered over with grass, and nearly invisible. And the inside was a dark moist haven of warmth.

"Angus! You home so soon?"

A large robust woman engulfed the older man in a hug. She wore an off-white cap on her head, and the braid peeking out the bottom was red-streaked gray. There were at least two other women inside the home. Cassandra couldn't see much else, because men filled the space and Emin was at the back, with her in his arms. Their clothing started steaming up the interior, making it even more difficult to breathe and see.

"We have a healthy stew on the fire, Meggie?"

he asked.

"Of course. Do na' I always?"

"Good. Serve it up. We've got the laird's new wife to feed."

"What?!"

The woman squealed, fell backward, and dropped. She was lucky there was a stool behind her, stopping her fall. Her husband slapped his thigh and chuckled.

"I could get fond of this," he announced.

"Go away with you, Angus! Who do you have with you, really?" The woman was back on her feet. She gave him a healthy smack in his chest. It didn't do much. He still had a grin within his gray beard.

"I told you. The laird's back. He's gone and wed. This here is his wife."

Emin set Cassandra on her feet. This was probably her prompt to unwind the mass of blanket about her and show them. She did so.

"What's this you say?"

An old stooped woman came from the shadow or a back corner, her eyes narrowed to see, hands gnarled with age. Everyone turned toward her.

"Now, Mother. Do na' pay us a mind. Go back to your daydreams."

"You say this is the laird's wife? Caillen's lad? Our Rhoenne?"

Everyone stepped back except Emin. He hovered behind her like a worried mother hen with a chick. The old woman came close. Walked around Cassandra. Came back into view.

"How far along are you, lass?" she asked.

"Mother!" Angus said.

"Get the woman a chair, son. She's increasing. Any fool can see that. I would na' wish to have any harm come to the lass. Or her wee bairns."

Cassandra gasped. She wasn't the only one.

The old woman cackled. "Do none of you ken your history? Our last laird, Caillen was a twin. 'Tis the meaning behind the name of his brother, Tevin, God rest his soul. You think it rare? Ramhursts have sired twins off-and-on since the first earl wed his Pict bride. 'Tis also helpful with the birth...if you ken what I'm saying."

Twins?

Cassandra swayed an instant before Emin caught her.

———

"Now, that there is a right bonny lass. Trust that Rhoenne to outdo his sire...even in that."

"Mother."

"Do na' tell me you did na' note it, Angus. You've got eyes that work, same as everyone else. Oh, good. She's waking."

Cassandra stirred back to consciousness, opened her eyes, and blinked the latticework of beams above her into focus. She was on her back on a cot along one wall of their house. She turned her head. The old woman was on a stool near her head, Angus's wife behind one shoulder, wringing her hands. The old woman had just lifted a damp cloth from Cassandra's forehead. Emin sat on the floor before her. A strange sound filtered into existence, emanating from outside. Cassandra wrinkled her forehead.

"You all right, lass?"

She nodded.

"Here. Let me help you. Margaret. Get the countess a drink."

Angus's wife disappeared from view. Cassandra turned onto her side and struggled to sit up. Another woman came close. Younger than Margaret. She maneuvered a mass of blankets behind Cassandra's back, propping her up.

"Thank you," she said. The woman smiled and tipped her head.

"That is my grand-daughter, Nessa. She's wed to the man who first accosted you. Brodie, by name."

"Ah. The handsome one," Cassandra answered and watched Nessa blush. She accepted the tankard with a smile. Swallowed cool refreshing water that had been splashed with ale.

"Thank you," she answered.

"What is your name, lass?"

"Cassandra Alexandria. Ramhurst."

"They tell me you are a princess?"

"My father...was a Bulgar prince. It was...a long time ago."

"You are a verra bonny lass, Cassandra. But that Rhoenne is a verra handsome fellow. Manly. Little surprises me anymore. A union between you two...well. The moment you two set eyes on each other, it should have been a fore-drawn conclusion."

Cassandra looked down for a moment. *If they only knew...*

"The men told me you spoke of the laird's return. And that he had a band of men with him."

Cassandra nodded.

"Many?"

"Only five."

"Five!" Angus stepped into sight.

"Now do na' upset her, son. I'm warning you."

"Please tell me Clyde Blair is one of them."

Cassandra shook her head. "The only men with him are Henry and Euan FitzHugh—."

"Euan? The lad?" he interrupted.

"Yes. The others are Iain and Graham Montvale....and his cousin, Grant Ramhurst."

"But *nae* Clyde?"

"No. I am sorry."

The man went to the door. Ran a hand across his eyes. Opened the door and left. A wailing of musical notes filled the room before the door closed.

"What is that sound?" Cassandra asked.

"Bagpipes," the old woman answered. "They are calling the clan."

"Bagpipes?"

"'Tis a Scot instrument. Verra difficult to learn and play. That Brodie is one of the best. He's full of hot air. Makes for a good piper."

"Grandmother," Nessa smiled as she said it.

"How long will they play it?" Cassandra asked.

"Until we get the clan here."

"But it's snowing."

"We are Ramhurst clan, my lady. Loyalty to the laird is supreme. There is trouble at the castle. You will need clan backing."

"Aileen?" Cassandra guessed.

"He told you of her, did he?"

"Na' much."

She nodded sagely. "I see. Smart man. Are you hungry?" she asked.

"Yes. But, please? Could my man have some, as well?"

"Of course. Margaret?"

"Thank you," Cassandra replied.

"Oh, *nae*. Thank you. I am an *auld* crone with little value. But look here. Ever since your arrival, I can order my daughter-in-law about with impunity."

"Mother."

Angus's wife was smiling as she came near, toting two bread bowls filled with a hearty stew of mutton and barley along with some thinly sliced carrots. She handed one to Cassandra. The other to Emin. He accepted it with a nod.

The old woman cleared her throat. "About this...man with you. Well. I do have a bit of a question about that."

"Emin? He is not my man. He is...a most loyal champion and friend. He is the reason I am alive and well and here right now."

"But you've been in contact with him...for some time. Alone?"

Cassandra nodded.

"Will na' the laird have an issue with that?"

"Emin is my personal guard. He would never harm me. Ever. He would give his life for me."

"Do all princesses have...personal guards?"

"I do na' know about other princesses. I only

know that I have been blessed to have him."

"I see. Well. You eat your fill, my lady. Rest. You are safe. Among clan. We will have you at the castle on the morrow. And then. Well. I only wish my bones were up to the trip. I will just have to wait to hear how that witch takes to your arrival."

"Mother!"

This time Margaret sounded shocked. The old woman cackled delightedly. "I'm *auld*. It's a gift. I can say what I think. The rest of you...? You just have to think it. Rest up, my lady. Please. If we can get you anything, you just say it. As for your man? Emin. Does he sleep...near you?"

"Emin?"

"I will na' leave her side," he replied.

"Well. We'd best get the man a pallet, then. And a blanket or two. Ladies?"

The fire was kept stoked all night. Figures flitting across the light occasionally. Cassandra snuggled into her blankets, lost in thought. She listened to the continual sound of bagpipes playing. Held the mound of her babe as it moved often. Pondered the idea of twins. Rhoenne hadn't felt so close in weeks.

Nor so far away.

CHAPTER TWENTY-FIVE

"**H**IGHNESS? YOU MUST awaken soon."
Emin's whisper at her ear was soft, but
still Cassandra jerked awake. She grabbed for his
arm and stared at him wide-eyed while the babe
added a flurry of movements.

"You are safe, Highness. I am here."

She collapsed back, waiting for her heartbeat
to calm. She'd been dreaming of horrifying,
frightening things. Swords. Blood. Decapitated
heads. And been startled into wakefulness in a
strange place. Save for Emin, nothing was familiar.
It took long moments to puzzle it through. She
recalled meeting up with Ramhurst clan. They'd
been taken in. Fed. She was abed now in a croft.

Cassandra darted a glance around. There
weren't any windows. The lone light source was
the fire. It sent shadows across a latticed span of
boards above her. Smoke from the fire tickled her
nose, mixing with a combination of unfamiliar
smells. The woolen blanket atop her scratched
and itched against her cheeks. It was heavy. And
had an odor she couldn't place...something floral,
and yet with an undertone of musk. She'd spent

eight years imprisoned, dreaming of life outside the luxurious walls of a harem. Wondering how it would feel to wake up to a different view than a span of curtains, incense-wafted decadence, drapery-bedecked walls. Pillow-strewn chambers. The idea of freedom had been intoxicating. Thrilling. Exciting.

She'd been so naïve.

Just then her babe gave a series of hearty kicks. And everything felt right.

"My lady?"

The middle aged woman approached. Put a hand on Emin's shoulder. Aside from the slight flinch he made, he didn't move from it.

"It's...Margaret? Yes?" Cassandra greeted her.

"Ah. You remembered my name." The woman's face was wreathed in a smile that included her eyes. "Will you be wanting...a repast? And for your man as well?"

"Breakfast?"

"We've fried up kidneys, cooked a big kettle of porridge, and toasted some black bread that was fresh-made just yesterday. My other daughter, Maysie – over at the fire? She just brought it."

The woman at the fire turned and bobbed a curtsey, before taking up stirring again. That explained the myriad of smells.

"Is there...a privy I can use?"

Cassandra sat up. Emin helped her arrange the wad of blankets she'd used for a pillow into a backrest. The old woman sat in a rocking chair back in a far corner.

"Oh. Heavens. Of course. We use the stream

outside...but you can na' do that. Na' this morn. I'll have a bucket fetched. Nessa?"

The grand–daughter went to the door, and opened it. A loud rumbling sound filled the croft and was muffled the moment the door shut again. Cassandra frowned. Considered. Margaret correctly guessed her expression.

"Brodie was verra successful with his piping. The clan has gathered for you. All morn they've been arriving. And soon, we'll be escorting you to the castle. All of us."

"All...of you?"

"Except for Mother, of course."

"Is it far?"

"Oh my, *nae*. The castle is a league...mayhap a league and a half. Na' much of a walk, really. Especially when the sun comes out, and the snow melts."

"The castle is...that close?"

"Angus could ha' taken you there last eve, but he's got a bit of smarts to him. And I do na' say that simply because I'm proud to be his wife. He used to be one of the castle stewards, afore that—." She pinched her lips together at the last second, stopping herself.

"Witch," the old woman inserted, making the rocking chair creak as she stood. She hobbled over to them and settled onto the same stool she'd used the night prior. "Tell it true, Margaret."

"Well. That is a-tween her and the Lord. 'Tis na' my place. All I ken is that once the laird left... well. That woman does as she wishes. She up and dismissed my Angus. And my girls. With na' a word of warning! She does it to all she takes a dislike to."

"And she takes a dislike to many," the older woman added.

Cassandra exchanged glances with Emin. They both nodded. This Aileen sounded as if she wielded power like the Great Wife had. That woman was vicious and cutthroat. Rumor had it she'd poisoned every male child born until she'd had her own son, and even then a male babe was in jeopardy. Cassandra had only crossed her path once. She didn't doubt any of the rumors.

"Angus sent a mon last night to the castle."

"He did?"

"We...needed the lay of the land, so to speak."

"And Rhoenne?" Cassandra's voice betrayed her excitement. Margaret shook her head.

"I am so sorry, my lady. The laird has na' arrived as of yet."

"Oh." The instant deflation colored the word.

"Worry not, my lady. He is on his way. They just recent-like received word to expect him."

"But...where could he be?" Worry filled her words. She was close to wringing her hands.

"I wish I had an answer for you, my lady. But, we should soon. Angus sent a man to Leith. And our youngest is on his way to Edinburgh."

The croft door opened to admit Nessa, bearing a bucket. Her entrance brought even more noise before the door shut.

"We've got an army gathering, Mother."

"That's well and good. We'll be a-needin' them. Now, my lady. We'll just get you a bit of victuals on a platter, and then allow you a bit of privacy. Is there anything else we can get for you?"

"Could I get my trunk?"

"I'll see it fetched. And...dare I ask if you'd like some clean water for washing? And we've a bit of heather soap."

Cassandra couldn't contain the joy.

"I thought as much. And I'd like to offer Nessa's assist? As I told you, she used to work at the castle. She's done many a maids duties. She's got an artist touch with hair, as well. Come Maysie. We've a breakfast to provide, and chores to see to. Mother? You'll na' be in the way?"

"Go away with you, Margaret. I'll assist. And do a bit of checking on the wee bairns."

"You truly think...I carry more than one babe?" Cassandra asked.

"How far along are you, lass?"

"A little over four months."

"You certain-sure?"

Cassandra nodded.

"When were you two wed?"

"That same night." Cassandra couldn't stop the blush.

The old woman cackled delightedly. "That Rhoenne is clearly a Ramhurst! And that means you most definitely carry twins, my dear."

"Mother!" Margaret expostulated.

"Oh, go on with ye. You'd think I didn't birth seven of you, myself."

"Emin?" Cassandra asked.

"I will be just outside, Highness."

"My. What a manly fellow. You ken...my

Maysie has been widowed many a year now. And she is an excellent cook."

Margaret was still speaking as she followed him out. And for the first time, Cassandra watched Emin flush bright red.

———∽∽∽———

It took an hour to prepare. The ladies helped. The men were banned. All save Emin. He stood just inside the door with his back to the proceedings. Arms folded. Feet apart. Watching the closed portal.

After her washing, Cassandra donned a white linen shift with a dark blue kirtle. Atop that, she wore one of her two formal silk gowns. Sewn from sky blue satin, it was the perfect color. It had been fitted to her shape from months earlier however, when she'd been lithe and slender. Margaret and Maysie worked miracles, cutting and basting and working so that the dress flowed loosely just beneath the bodice, looking not only beautiful and elegant, but refined.

Nessa really did have an expert touch with arranging hair, too. Cassandra's mass of hair had been twisted on either side of her head into ropes that were looped and pinned atop the crown of her head. The remainder of her tresses flowed loosely down her back. It was Emin who brought out the finishing touches, however. He pulled the harem headdress piece and breast collar from the bag at his hip, to loud gasps and murmurs of awe. The jeweled pieces were settled atop her last, the gems sparkling every time she moved.

Emin opened the door a fraction and peeked out. Crowd noise assailed her. He turned, and lifted a brow. "Are you ready, Highness?"

"Yes," Cassandra answered.

He held his fingers to his lips and sent a shrill whistle. They both listened as calls for order were shouted, followed by a series of drumbeats, accompanied by loud bursts from bagpipes. Then the drums stopped. The area quieted. And someone started speaking in a loud voice.

"Ramhurst Clan! We've called you together this morn...to provide an escort!"

"To who?"

"For what?"

"We leave for the castle!" the announcer informed them. "The laird has returned!"

"He has?"

"Truly?"

"I heard the tales," someone shouted. "But I discounted them!"

"Well. 'Tis true!" the announcer continued. "And there's more! The laird has wed. He has brought us a princess from across the sea! Do you wish to meet her?"

There was a loud chorus of 'ayes'. Cassandra felt like butterflies flitted about in her belly, while the bairn did antics alongside them. She didn't think of her baby as more than one yet. She couldn't. It was too unreal. Maybe, once she reunited with Rhoenne...

"Highness?"

Emin held out an arm for her. Cassandra took it. He was such a large specimen, easily a head taller than all the others. Large. Fit. But she knew all of that. He ducked beneath the door jamb, taking her with him, but then he surprised her completely by gripping her waist and hoisting her atop one shoulder, his open palm beneath her buttocks to stabilize and hold her.

"Emin!"

"Trust me."

His whisper was soft and accompanied by what actually looked like a wink. Then he walked around the rock outcropping and she could see the reason for his action. The entire area was a sea of people, standing with mouths agape, and then almost as unit, the men went down to one knee, while woman held their skirts and dipped into curtsies.

"Behold! We bring you the new Lady Ramhurst, the Countess of Tyneburgh!"

That's when she saw the announcer. He was short. Stout. Red-haired and bearded. He possessed a great projecting voice. The entire area erupted with cheers. Shouts. Clapping. Angus brought the Clydesdale over to her. The horse had been groomed and curried, and wore a flat saddle on his back. Emin set her on it. Someone handed up a length of gray and white plaid, woven with intersecting black and blue lines. Emin helped drape it, almost fully enclosing her.

"You don't ride with me?" she asked, trying to hide the concern.

"We walk. Do not worry, *Princessa*. I will be right here. You will not come to any harm."

He meant it, too. Emin walked beside her over

the low hill they'd traversed just yesterday. Angus FitzHugh walked at her other side. A younger fellow had the Clydesdale's reins, controlling the horse. They reached a large plateau covered with a slight crust of snow. They crossed it. Tackled another hill. There was a footpath beneath her. The horse followed it. The mass of clan spread out on both sides of her. The sun rose higher. Snow melted. Mist hung at ground level turning everything into a sparkling wonderland that gradually dissipated. Throughout the pipers played, drums kept a steady beat, and several people raised their voices in song. Emin kept his right hand at her back the entire trek. His left rested on a sword hilt.

Just after mid-day, Cassandra got her first view of Rhoenne's castle. She hadn't voiced any misgivings she'd harbored, but the sight of Castle Tyne not only salved every bit of apprehension, it obliterated them. Rising atop a hill, it lorded over the large valley about it. The castle was impressive. Large and imposing. Castle Tyne was a massive fortress of black stone in a jewel-like setting of lush verdant green. A deep blue loch lapped at the back of it, spawning two rivers that threaded around the castle's base, forming a large moat. The castle got larger as they neared. More awe-inspiring.

And then the drawbridge started lifting.

Angry shouts erupted. Orders rang out.

"Clan! Get down there and cancel that nonsense!

"This is *nae* invading army! 'Tis a homecoming!"

Clansmen raced for the castle gatehouse, women and youngsters at their heels. From a distance, Cassandra watched them arrive. The gate stopped lifting. And then it slowly started descending back to bridge the moat.

"Well. It appears the woman still has support in the castle. That is unfortunate, but na' surprising. There are too many she can blackmail." Angus spoke up. His wife Margaret marched at his side.

"It better na' be a member from our family," Margaret muttered.

"Well. If 'tis, we'll be disowning them."

"Forthwith," his wife answered.

Cassandra's brows lifted. She looked over at Emin and exchanged another glance.

"You are na' to be off-put by this, my lady," Angus commented.

"Off-put?" Cassandra turned to him. "Oh Angus FitzHugh, if I didn't know better, I'd swear I'd spent years being trained for just this event."

The drawbridge was wide. Lengthy. The crowd thinned as they started across, the wood echoing with their passage. And then they passed beneath the arch in the gatehouse, walked across another span of bridge, and beneath the arch built into the barbican wall. The stone wasn't as black as she'd suspected. The castle was actually dark gray stone with black and light gray marbling. She got a good look at just how thick they'd fashioned the outer wall. The entry appeared to be at least four times Emin's height. There wasn't a soul who spoke out or challenged them. The area was deserted. A portcullis was lifted high into the arch, its long spikes sharpened and lethal. The crowd quieted as they crossed the first courtyard. Cassandra sent her gaze up high stone walls that contained slits for archers, murder holes for pouring down hot liquids, and uniform crenellation at the top to hide more defenders.

They went beneath another archway, entering a long passage between the barbican wall and inner wall. The stone on both sides was constructed to such a height, it felt like a tunnel. The path curved around the outside of the castle, eventually opening into a large outer courtyard. She could see stables at one side, a great volume of horses, but no groomsmen. At the back of the courtyard, they were finally met by clansmen. A group of at least forty men, all beefy, bearded, and armed, stood in a semi-circle blocking the entry to the inner courtyard.

The crowd of clan that accompanied Cassandra fanned out, easily outnumbering any opposition. Her mount was led forward, walking through them, until the young man with her reins halted. She sat atop the horse, approximately twenty paces from the guards. They were all large men. Even sitting atop the horse, she was just slightly taller. She would have intercepted several glances if she wasn't covered over in Ramhurst plaid. Nobody looked amused.

"Stand aside, Calum! We're escorting the new countess!"

The stout announcer fellow shouted it. She noted he didn't step from the ranks of the masses, showing he might have a large voice, but not much bravery to back it up. The man at the forefront of the guards stepped forward. He had a wealth of dark reddish-brown hair that ended in curls at his shoulders.

"Cease that, Gawain MacDuff. We do na' need the *bladier*. I wish to speak with Angus! Angus FitzHugh! Show yourself."

That was fairly silly. Angus hadn't left her side. He walked forward a few steps. And then he shouted as if they were courtyards apart.

"Calum Montvale!" Angus yelled.

"Angus FitzHugh!" Calum yelled back.

That was interesting. Calum must be related to Iain and Graham. He did resemble Iain, and she should have recognized the shade of hair.

"Did you na' get the message?" Angus shouted.

"We allowed ye to enter, did na' we?"

"Then, stand aside. Cease this!"

"For what reason?" Calum answered with a belligerent tone.

"You heard the *bladier*! We are escorting the countess! Now, stand aside, or I'll be challenging you."

"I do na' war with *auld* men!" Calum announced, using a belligerent tone.

"Who you callin' *auld*?" Angus returned with the same kind of bravado.

Men!

Oh, why did men always act so foolish? This wasn't going to get anything accomplished. Emin's fingers tensed at her back. Cassandra stiffened. Held her breath. Calum must have decided the same, for his next words held a conciliatory tone.

And he didn't shout them with quite the same volume.

"Come along, FitzHugh! We have orders. You ken we will na' disobey!"

"This is the new countess, mon! Newly arrived from the east! Any orders you have...are hereby cancelled!"

A slight whine from a bagpipe in the crowd interrupted them, followed by a flurry of hushed voices. That was the only sound for long moments. And they truly didn't have to continue shouting. The entire area was teeming with people, but it was quiet enough to hear her heartbeat as it picked up tempo.

"You say you bring the new countess?"

"Aye! We do."

"And we are to accept this? On your word? Without authority?"

Calum Montvale tossed his head up, clearly addressing his words to her. Cassandra took a deep breath and lifted her hands. She pinched the plaid at her forehead between her fingers and thumbs, and slowly peeled the garment back, making a grand gesture of it. The material dropped onto the horse and Emin's hand behind her. Her act displayed not only her features and elegant attire, but the headdress and jeweled collar couldn't be missed. Her heart was hammering. Her hands icy. The babe even gave several sharp kicks as though displeased at the situation.

Several of the men behind Calum exhibited the wide-eyed, open-mouthed expression she'd come to expect whenever anyone saw her. Cassandra swallowed to still any tremor. She needed to speak loudly, confidently, and imperiously, using exactly the same intonation she'd heard from the Mamluk sultan's Great Wife and the *Duchesse* Zecchino.

"Angus FitzHugh speaks on my behalf." Cassandra spoke. "I am Cassandra Alexandria Votten Ramhurst." She announced each name loudly and succinctly before continuing. "I am the grand-niece of the *duca* Guistiniani, ruler of the kingdom of Candia, in the *Domini de Mar* of the Venetian Republic. I am a princess of Vottenavia in the Bulgar Kingdom. And I am the lawfully wedded wife of your lord and liege, Rhoenne Guy de Ramhurst, the fifth Earl of Tyneburgh. I understand my husband has not arrived as of yet. He will...shortly. And I doubt he will understand the manner in which my arrival and identity are being questioned."

The man's mouth opened and closed several times as if he'd speak, but he didn't say anything. Angus chuckled.

"You may wish to swear fealty about now, Nephew," Angus said.

Nephew?

Cassandra's lips twitched at the relationship, but she'd stilled any expression a moment later. Calum pulled out his sword, put the tip into the ground before him, nodded to her, and then went down onto a knee. His head bowed. One by one behind him, the others did the same. A murmur of reaction went through the crowd. The announcer Gawain quieted them.

"You and your men may rise, Calum Montvale,"
she said when she could again be heard.

CHAPTER TWENTY-SIX

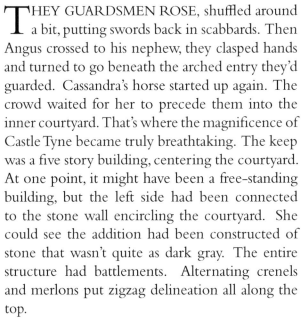

THEY GUARDSMEN ROSE, shuffled around a bit, putting swords back in scabbards. Then Angus crossed to his nephew, they clasped hands and turned to go beneath the arched entry they'd guarded. Cassandra's horse started up again. The crowd waited for her to precede them into the inner courtyard. That's where the magnificence of Castle Tyne became truly breathtaking. The keep was a five story building, centering the courtyard. At one point, it might have been a free-standing building, but the left side had been connected to the stone wall encircling the courtyard. She could see the addition had been constructed of stone that wasn't quite as dark gray. The entire structure had battlements. Alternating crenels and merlons put zigzag delineation all along the top.

It looked more than impressive. It looked like a royal residence.

The bottom floor of the keep hadn't any access that she could see. There was a long flight of stone steps that led to a double-wide door in the second story. The two floors above that had crucifix-shaped window slits for archers. And the top floor appeared to have large windows. With real leaded and glazed glass in them.

Here? In the farthest reaches of the civilized world...they had amenities such as glass in their windows?

Cassandra felt a faint stirring of something that she wanted to believe was a sense of belonging, but she knew it was probably relief. She didn't know why she'd worried. Rhoenne's home was the perfect backdrop for the man. Unfortunately, nothing about the castle felt familiar or home-like. It was too massive. Entirely imposing. And impressive. Emin felt some of that, too. She could tell. His brows rose as he looked up the front of the keep and then he touched his gaze to hers.

"My lady?"

The guardsman, Calum, was speaking. Cassandra tipped her chin down and looked across at him. He stood beside Angus. He wore the *feile-brecan*, as they all did. His emphasized a strong, well-defined physique. And he was a good half-hand shorter than Emin.

"Yes?" she answered.

"Allow me to escort you into the castle."

"My thanks...but I have a personal guard," Cassandra told him. "Emin?"

She swiveled toward him, and was swept into his arms. That wasn't what she had in mind, but the courtyard did look muddy, and the flight of stone stairs was daunting. She didn't argue it. He stood with her in his arms, facing Calum. Angus thought it was highly entertaining if his grin was an indicator.

"You may lead us," she said.

Calum regarded her for a long moment, before swiveling on his heel. Eight of his men accompanied him. Calum's back was stiff. His manner offended. Cassandra didn't give it much thought. Just because he'd apparently capitulated and sworn fealty, didn't mean he was in her good graces. For all she knew, he was firmly in the enemy camp. He deserved any loss of honor to his status. She'd been a little off on height comparison, too. Emin was almost a head taller.

The guardsmen started up the steps, Emin at their heels. They took the steps with a regimented cadence, their boots making a sound akin to drumbeats. She didn't know how many of the others followed. She kept her gaze forward. Any expressions to herself.

It was dimmer once they went through the portal. Cassandra blinked and refocused. They passed through a short hall and entered a chamber so enormous, it echoed. It was probably the length of the keep. The walls were high spans of dark gray stone with small window slits along the top. The ceiling was groin vaulted, and looked to be at least two stories high. Wheel-shaped chandeliers hung from the vaulting, unlit at the moment. Torches rested in sconces along the walls, also unlit. Massive fireplaces were centered along each wall, each capable of burning a small tree. Benches and tables intersected the room. At the far end was a raised platform holding a long table and a row of high-backed chairs.

Along the wall to her left was a stone staircase, constructed into the wall. The banister was carved wood. It led to a circular landing that had a door behind it. The door opened, a woman came out. And everything came to a complete halt.

Cassandra had been around beautiful women her entire life. She was used to the vagaries of nature that gifted some women with amazing coloring, perfect features, and voluptuous forms while others received imperfections: pocked faces, small eyes, crooked noses, thin stringy hair, and figures that needed all manner of enhancement.

Nature hadn't cheated the woman that stood on the landing. She was stunning. She was at the height of her beauty. And she was well aware of that fact. It wasn't just apparent in the way she held herself. It was demonstrated by every step she made as she slowly descended the stairs. She'd be an instant success in any harem...if the reigning favorite didn't poison her first.

"Captain Montvale!" the woman spoke just before she reached the bottom of the steps. Her voice didn't match the image. It was sharp. Angered. Discordant. That was jarring.

"My lady." Calum stepped forward and tipped his head.

"You were na' to disturb me."

"The new countess has arrived, my lady. Her authority...transcends yours."

"New countess? Says who?" The woman responded using an even more abrasive tone. She sounded like she spat the words.

"I need a perch."

Cassandra leaned up to whisper it.   Emin looked to the right, then left before walking to a near table.   He tilted, lowering her feet onto one of the stools, facing her toward the woman.   Then he walked around her and stood just behind, hovering.   Resolute.   Backing her.

"Why...the new countess, of course," Calum continued.

"And just why would you assume that to be true?"

She'd reached the plateau at the base of the steps, placing her level with Captain Montvale. She was completely ignoring where Cassandra stood.   Now that she was closer, Cassandra could see further details.   She had a wealth of dark hair. Her skin was pristine.   Her lips were reddened. Her eyes were lushly lashed, or enhanced with something like kohl.   She was wearing a purple-hued dress, in varied shades.   The color was the most costly dye to produce.   The manner of shading had to have been not only expensive but time consuming.   Her kirtle was white, as was the cap atop her head. There were pearls in all shades and sizes affixed to her cap, as well as her bodice.

"He did not assume anything.   I informed him of my identity upon my arrival," Cassandra announced loudly, and then she waited.

Oh my.

Aileen gave Cassandra the same exact look Selique once had.   On both instances, warning ripples cascaded over her.   This time, even her unborn child reacted. The woman started toward her, the crowd parting for her passage. It didn't appear a respectful move. It looked more as if they didn't wish to touch her. Men leaned away, and women pulled their skirts back. She stopped several feet shy of where Cassandra was situated. Looked up at her with set lips and an expression that demonstrated distinct displeasure. Poor woman. She obviously hadn't been around other women as physically gifted. She thought beauty was her venue alone. Absolute. Unchallengeable. And unassailable.

"You are actually claiming to be the new countess?" the woman spoke in an aggressive tone.

"I do not *claim* anything," Cassandra replied. "I *am* the new countess. Rhoenne Ramhurst is my husband. And I carry his heir." She rested a hand atop her belly in the event Aileen missed the inference.

"So you say," came the reply.

"We have not been introduced, but you must be Aileen. Rhoenne's...step-mother," Cassandra prompted.

"My. My. Aren't you misinformed."

Cassandra's brows rose.

"I am not anyone's step-mother. I am the laird's sister."

Sister?

Cassandra's eyes went wide. Her heart dropped. Her belly roiled unpleasantly. She hadn't known she'd swayed until Emin stepped forward to stand just behind her on the left side. She didn't see him. She felt his presence like a reassuring wall to lean against. She lifted her chin but didn't move her glance from Aileen.

"Angus FitzHugh?" Cassandra called out.

"My lady?"

He trotted toward her, making a semi-circle about Aileen, clearly avoiding her.

"You were a former steward of Castle Tyne? That is what you said?"

"Aye. That I were."

"Explain this woman's status to me, please."

"This is Aileen Ramhurst. She was brought here as wife to the fourth earl, Caillen Ramhurst. After his passing, she...uh. Well. She up and wed with the laird's younger brother."

That was distasteful. Borderline incestuous. Angus said it with a hint of disgust. Cassandra's nose wrinkled. She couldn't help it.

"Didn't that make him her...step-son?"

"What does that matter?" Aileen snapped out.

"I am not speaking to you, Aileen," Cassandra addressed her. "You will hold your tongue until I do."

"Well!"

Aileen's exclamation was loud. Scandalized. Cassandra ignored it to look back at Angus.

"Tell me, Angus. This brother. Does he have a name?"

"Bhaltair."

"Where is Bhaltair?"

"He was murdered!" Aileen inserted.

"I will repeat myself. Once more. I am not requesting any information from you, Aileen. You will be given an opportunity to speak when

I allow it," Cassandra replied.

"So, I am supposed to just stand by and—?"

"Silence!"

Emin's command was loud, shocking even Cassandra. She started. His hand immediately touched her back, holding her in place. Cassandra watched as Aileen evaluated that. And knew she put a wicked interpretation to it.

"Allow me to introduce my personal guard." Cassandra spoke loudly. Succinctly. And with a bit of amusement coloring her tone she didn't even bother hiding. "This is Emin. I should probably warn you. He is from the east."

Aileen looked Emin over, her gaze slow and lingering. Akin to a touch. Cassandra watched her dispassionately. She didn't know what expression Emin had, but she could guess. Aileen was very good. Her method of enticement practiced. She had a frown when she'd finished and tried locking gazes with Emin. It was obvious she hadn't received the response she expected. That was even more amusing.

"Angus FitzHugh!" Cassandra called out, as if he wasn't standing directly before her.

"My lady?"

"How old was Bhaltair when this wedding took place?"

"He was a man grown!" Aileen burst out.

Emin stepped from beside her, two daggers in his hands, poised to throw. Cassandra actually wasn't certain of his intent. Aileen's eyes went huge. She took a step backward.

"Calum Montvale!" Aileen called out.

"My lady?" the captain of the guards responded from behind her with a nonchalant cant to his voice.

"You will stop this man from threatening me."

"Apologies...but I obey the countess's orders now."

"You would allow this man to harm a woman?"

" I do na' see any harm."

There was a rumble of reaction from the crowd, instantly quelled. Aileen gave a choked sound, sent through clenched teeth. Her expression was not a beauteous one.

"The lad was sixteen, your highness," Angus supplied in the silence that followed.

"Highness?"

Aileen's shocked exclamation was gratifying. Cassandra decided to humor her.

"I will allow your outburst this once. And I shall answer. I am a member of the ruling families of two kingdoms. Princess is one of my titles. Do not interrupt again. Angus?" Cassandra tilted her head toward where he stood, but her focus didn't move from Aileen. "I return to my query. You are telling me this Bhaltair was sixteen at the time of his nuptials. But now...he is dead?"

"Aye."

"Was this death...recent?"

"Five years past."

"Oh. So...sad."

Cassandra wasn't thinking of the heartless woman before her. She was thinking of Rhoenne, and his younger brother. Barely a man. Wedded to this manipulative woman. Perishing so young.

"Lady Aileen is twice widowed, then? Is that correct? Or are there are further Ramhursts she might have... also wed?"

"How dare you!"

Emin flung the blades. They smacked into the wood floor pinning the bottom of Aileen's skirts to it. It forced her to hunch forward slightly. He had two more knives out before the first two ceased wobbling. There was a collective gasp from the assemblage. Cassandra almost pitied the woman.

"I did warn you, Aileen. Emin is...from the east. I am not addressing my questions to you. You need to hold your tongue until I do. Angus FitzHugh?"

"Aye?"

"How old was Bhaltair when...he died?"

"He was murdered!" Aileen burst out.

"Emin!"

Cassandra's cry wasn't in time to stop his throw. These two blades hit the floor right next to the first two. The hilts clicked against each other in the silence that followed. He had two more ready to throw. This time the collective gasp about them was stained with awe. Aileen paled significantly. Cassandra had to re-evaluate her first impression. Aileen wouldn't have lasted a day in the harem. She hadn't even the sense to keep silent.

"He is going to kill me!" Aileen shrieked.

"Aileen. Please. Emin would never harm a woman. He is an expert marksman. He could shave an eyelash if he wished. He is simply enforcing my request for you to hold your tongue. Perhaps I should see you sequestered while I finish questioning my new steward. Angus?"

He still possessed a mouthful of white teeth. They were on full display with his newest grin. He stood taller, as well. "Highness?" he replied.

"Are there chambers in this castle for the reigning countess?"

"Aye. With the earl. Chieftain's chambers. Right up those stairs." Angus pointed, but Cassandra had already guessed.

"The ones Aileen used?"

"One and the same."

"I am confused. Didn't Bhaltair have an assigned chamber?"

"Tower. East wing."

"And the Dowager Countess? Where would she be situated?"

"Hmm. Well. There has na' been a dowager since Caillen and Tevin's mother. She used the east wing as well, though na' the tower."

"I see. Well. Aileen? I am speaking to you now. It appears you have chambers for your use in the east wing. Which is your preference? Tower or lower rooms?"

"Neither."

"How...unfortunate. If you do not wish to select a new domicile, I shall do it for you."

Aileen lifted her chin, and attempted to look down her nose at Cassandra. That was amusing. She was tall. It would have been easier if Cassandra wasn't atop a stool. Aileen's upper lip lifted in a sneer. She obviously wanted to do more than glare, but she kept glancing toward the blades in Emin's hands.

"Your choice, please?' Cassandra prompted.

"I have been in the chieftain's chamber since I came here. For over a decade now," she finally answered.

"Well. That is over. Angus? Is there a place for Bhaltair's widow to...rest...while the chieftain's rooms are cleared out?"

Aileen almost burst an exclamation out. Whatever impression Emin was demonstrating stopped her.

"The ladies solar should suffice,"Angus supplied.

"Good. That is where the lady Aileen will be taken. Captain Montvale?"

"My lady?"

"I have an assignment for you and your men. You are to escort Lady Aileen to the solar. She is not to leave it until her rooms are ready. Is that understood?"

He nodded. Aileen was looking inordinately pleased at Cassandra's order. That would change.

"Oh. And Captain? Could you retrieve Emin's knives for him?"

Montvale knelt down. The blades didn't look easy to pull free. Cassandra watched Aileen and Calum exchange glances. It was precisely as she'd suspected. They'd been lovers, or still were. Aileen was exactly the type to use men. It had soured Rhoenne. She didn't know how many others Aileen had favored and then used. Or what they'd do for her. But for now, Cassandra would have some of them gathered into the same area of the castle. They'd be much easier to deal with.

The captain handed the blades to Emin. Bowed toward Cassandra, then turned and offered his arm to Aileen. The eight men who'd entered the castle with him moved to accompany. The rest of his original guard unit were either still outside, or didn't step from the crowd. They formed a small retinue of men surrounding Aileen. They walked to the back of the great hall, and entered a dark space to the left. The crowd parted for them. Cassandra waited until the sound of their boots faded before speaking again.

"Angus?"

"My lady?"

"Do we have any men who could keep an eye on the area around the solar? Make certain my orders are not...countermanded?"

He nodded sagely. "I will personally select them."

"Excellent. And do we have...trustworthy staff to assign the chore of cleaning out the chieftain's chamber?"

"We brought them with us, Highness. 'Tis why we came."

Cassandra looked over the myriad of smiling faces. Wobbled slightly.

"Ah. I see you are the perfect steward. I have just a few more items, please. Is there a chamber that Rho—Rho...enne used?"

She stammered on his name. Her heart gave a mighty series of thumps, the babe kicking in harmony. And then Emin was at her side, placing his hand at her back again as if he knew she'd need it.

"Aye. He had the west tower."

"Can someone see me to it?"

"Of course. My womenfolk will be honored. Margaret? Nessa? Maysie?"

The ladies came forward.

"Thank you, Angus," Cassandra responded.

"Oh. My lady. Thank you. The clan has been needing a cleaning out for some time. 'Tis honored I am to have been able to assist. Clansmen! I need volunteers to keep watch on my nephew and his men! Any takers?"

The chorus of 'ayes' was loud. Emin opened his arms. Lifted his brows. Cassandra nodded, and he swept her up again. Good thing. Her legs were too shaky to step down.

"You did well, Highness," he spoke softly as they left the great hall, following the same path Aileen had just taken.

"Because of you," she answered.

He shook his head. "No. You are strong enough by yourself. I, but shortened the event."

He thought her strong? Tears hovered just beneath the surface. She felt drained. Exhausted. Weepy. Bereft. She needed Rhoenne more than ever. Missed him with every fiber of her being. The baby must have felt the same for the amount of movement was ceaseless and massive. Emin felt the kicks against his abdomen, if the glance he gave her after a spate of them was an indicator.

"Your sons are strong," he told her as he mounted circular steps, following Nessa. "His

Excellency will be pleased."

"Sons?" Cassandra queried.

"I believe the old one's words have merit. You carry two sons. He will be most pleased."

"If I only knew where he was."

"He is not far."

"If...only I could believe that."

"Highness. Please. He is close. You will be together. Soon."

"Oh, Emin. What makes you so certain?"

"Allah. Faith. And knowledge of the man. You wed well, Highness."

He gave her a smile that she returned. And then they reached Rhoenne's old chambers.

CHAPTER TWENTY-SEVEN

"WELL. THIS MARKS another day with naught to show for it."

Euan's remarks preceded him into their chamber. He shoved into a chair with the same aura of discontent that colored his words. The chair almost upended. Someone chuckled. Rhoenne sent him a glance before ignoring him again. Euan's remarks didn't rancor. They didn't even disturb. Nothing broke through the shell around him.

They didn't understand.

No one did.

Rhoenne lived with constant pressure about his heart. It burned. Squeezed. Pained. It was always there. Every waking moment, and if he managed to sleep, it seemed worse when he woke. It accompanied every heartbeat. Unyielding. Never easing.

He touched the little bag that held the lock of Cassandra's hair. It remained hidden beneath his tunic. He silently regarded the fire brightly burning in this chamber he'd been given. Words ebbed and flowed about him. He didn't truly listen. He might be present physically, but that was the extent of it.

"Well, I suppose if I was a lad of thirteen and king of the Scots, I'd probably spend my days in hunting, too," Iain remarked.

"I can na' blame King Alexander his preference. I am sorely tired of this court, too. Already. So. Looks like we've an eve of feasting and a bit of revelry ahead of us, men," Euan remarked.

"As happens most every eve here in Edinburgh Castle," Grant piped in.

"Yes. Well. Who is for attending?" Euan continued.

"Are they serving tripe?" Graham asked.

"And haggis?" Iain spoke up.

"Well. Come along. We'll check."

"And if things begin to pall, we can always start a fight. Who's with me?"

"Grant. Please."

"None of this is getting us any nearer an audience than we were four days ago," Henry spoke up.

Rhoenne huffed slightly.

"You find it amusing?"

"I do na' find anything amusing anymore, Henry. Anywhere. At any time." Rhoenne answered the fire.

"Then why can we na' go and find non-amusing things at your own castle, rather than dance attendance on the king's court? Especially when the king even avoids it?"

"Because I need to see him afore I can leave."

"But not the regent?"

"You ken MacDougall detests the sight of me. Despite being a relation."

"Most men detest the sight of you, Ramhurst. *Nae* lady will even look their direction after being soured by a glimpse of you. They can na' compete."

"Cease." Rhoenne gave a desultory wave of his free hand.

"Well." Euan spoke with a forced bright tone. "Let's off to join the fest then. We ken they'll have tripe tonight. Who's with me?"

The room emptied. Rhoenne didn't note it. Or care.

He wished they hadn't brought up the king's regent, Laird Allistair MacDougall. The MacDougall clan was one of the most powerful in the Highlands, their antecedents going back beyond recorded time, their land holdings immense and fruitful, the relations with the crown solid. They were the clan Bhaltair's mother hailed from. Laird MacDougall had the same carrot-red hair as Bhaltair and looked to be the same size Rhoenne's younger brother would have achieved...if he'd lived into manhood.

Staring into the fire brought it back vividly. Blame for what had happened to Bhaltair was squarely at Rhoenne's feet. Aileen had given him the clue.

He just hadn't listened.

It had been when she'd accosted him in the chieftain's study. The last time she'd touched him. Rhoenne had stood near the desk, looking over a Latin tome, one laboriously hand-lettered by monks in the prior century at the Jedburgh Abbey. Aileen had loudly coughed, interrupting him. Rhoenne had looked up, and instantly known that she'd gone to a bit of trouble with her attire. Her hair had been plaited into braids behind each ear and pulled back. She'd worn a white linen dress, and a tiny lace-edged caplet to match. It should have looked pristine and pure. It hadn't. She didn't wear undergarments, and the opacity of the linen wasn't strong enough to disguise it. She looked like the material had been poured onto her.

She'd approached where he stood, holding the book aloft, trembling in place. The same sensation of cold washed over him as she neared. He'd thought it was revulsion. Now he knew it was deep-seated fear instilled in him years earlier by his father's beating. He couldn't conquer it. He'd swallowed nervously as she neared.

"Ah. Rhoenne. Here you are," she'd said. "I have been looking for you."

He remembered asking what she wanted. She'd lowered her eyelashes and stepped close, slanting her chin in order to glance up at him. She'd put her hand atop his, and squeezed. Rhoenne had recoiled back a step, breaking the contact.

"Don't touch me," he'd told her. "Do na' ever touch me."

She'd laughed and done it again. And that's when he'd warned her. "You touch me again, and I'll break your fingers."

That time, she'd lifted her hand. Considered him for a long moment until he'd finally asked her what she wanted.

"I want to be your bride. So I can be countess again," she'd replied. "I should think it obvious."

"I'd sooner wed a snake."

The instant the words left his lips, her face had contorted into something ugly. Rhoenne had kept the revulsion hidden. And then, as if a film had passed over her face, she'd calmed. Laughed with a brittle sound. And shrugged her shoulders. And she'd left the study without once looking back.

It hadn't even occurred to him that she'd go after Bhaltair. `

———⁓⁓———

"So. Do you want to tell me what this is about?"

Rhoenne shook himself. Looked over his shoulder. He'd thought they all left. He should have known Henry would stay to be his conscience.

"I told you. I need an audience with the king."

"But you did na' tell why."

"Couldn't you just keep Ida company tonight?"

"She rests within."

Henry gestured to the bedchamber Rhoenne should be using. He'd given it over to Ida and Henry, who was still recuperating. Or he used that for an excuse. Rhoenne wasn't dense. Nor did he care. Henry laughed often and seemed spry lately, while Ida blushed whenever she glanced at Henry. She'd also put on some much-needed weight.

"I need the betrothal altered," Rhoenne

admitted.

"The lass is but eight."

"So? Alexander wed his queen when she was that age. They were both children."

"And have yet to be together as man and wife."

"True. But it gained our king what he needed. The same thing I need– England's King Henry III for a father-by-law."

"That poor girl."

"What poor girl?" Rhoenne asked.

"I'm just thinking of...the man she'll be getting for a bridegroom."

"I certainly hope you do na' refer to me," Rhoenne commented.

Henry took a deep breath. "Well. I—."

The door smacked open. Euan rushed in, followed by Iain, and Grant. "Be quick, my laird!"

Rhoenne lifted a brow.

"You must hurry! Now is your chance!"

"The tripe is that good?" Rhoenne remarked.

"His Majesty has attended! But he wearies of the fest. He has already spoken on it. He may leave at any moment!"

Rhoenne stood. He wasn't dressed for a court appearance. He had an old *plaide* draped about him. Boots. His short sword was in a scabbard attached to his belt. Daggers tucked around his waist. No shirt. No jacket. He couldn't remember if he'd donned socks. He grabbed up his claymore. Strapped it over a shoulder as they walked. Pulled his hair back into a queue. Henry handed him a cord. Rhoenne had his hair tied back as they entered the great hall.

There were a lot of participants for the evening's feasting. Rows of nobles sat at tables intersecting the great hall. The king and his companions were on the dais. The king was a good size for a young man. He still looked small. And he was standing. Allistair MacDougall was just rising to stand beside his monarch. Rhoenne took the situation in with a glance and started toward them. His group was instantly noticed. Conversation stilled. He strode purposefully, smacking his boot heels into the floor, making booming sounds. There wasn't anyone his size in the vicinity. It was obvious. People moved out of the way before they could be shoved aside.

"Your Majesty!" Rhoenne spoke loudly enough to stop them.

Allistair stopped mid-rise. The king turned and regarded Rhoenne from above him, due to the dais. Rhoenne stopped just shy of the platform, his men fanned out to either side. He pulled the claymore from his back. Put it tip down onto the floor, and then knelt on one knee beside it.

"Who is this, please?"

King Alexander spoke. The lad had a boy's changing voice, his vocal range moving over octaves as he spoke. The regent answered.

"This is your earl, Rhoenne Guy de Ramhurst. Of Tyneburgh."

"Ah. I have heard of you. Rise. Please."

Rhoenne stood. Grabbed the sword scabbard with his left hand and inserted the claymore back into it, sliding steel against steel. The claymore was a large broadsword, usually requiring two hands to wield. Rhoenne made it look easy. It was actually beneficial that he hadn't donned a shirt. He could tell it impressed. The king wasn't the lone one staring wide-eyed. But the lad did sit back down.

"Well. My lord Ramhurst. What can His Majesty do for you?"

The king wasn't talking. Rhoenne knew how Bhaltair's relations regarded him. It was reflected in the man's tone.

"I have requested an audience. It is a private matter."

"You can speak here," Allistair informed him.

Rhoenne considered Bhaltair's relation, and then moved his gaze back to the king. "Verra well. I am here about my betrothal."

"That is a matter for the crown?" Allistair challenged.

"My betrothed is the queen's younger sister," Rhoenne replied.

"Ah. That is where I have heard of you." King Alexander piped in. "Go on. Please?"

"I wish to have the wedding take place as soon as it can be arranged."

"She is a child," Allistair informed him.

Rhoenne ignored him, addressing his next words to the king. "And I wish to put forth a change of bridegroom."

There was a shocked sound rippling through the crowd behind him. It hit his men as well, although all that happened was a collective indrawn breath and straighter shoulders. Rhoenne didn't move his gaze from the king.

"You wish to...change the groom?"

"Aye."

"On what grounds?"

"I have just returned from the seventh crusade in the east. It was na' a victorious war."

"We had heard this already."

Allistair spoke, using the supercilious tone he always used around Rhoenne. The king glanced at his regent with a perplexed look on his features before looking back at Rhoenne and his men.

"All the crusader kingdoms have fallen. *Outremer* was lost."

"We heard that as well," Allistair interrupted him.

"Yes. Well. King Louis of France was taken. He is in bondage. The ransom amount will be extremely large. It will need to be raised."

Rhoenne watched them assimilate that information. Scotland was an ally of the French crown. Everyone knew where the funds were going to be required.

"The reason I request the groom to be changed is because...well." Rhoenne took a huge breath. "I am in violation of the agreement. I have wed."

"What?" King Alexander and his regent, Allistair said it in tandem.

"It was a diplomatic solution. One with potential benefit to the crown. If I may explain?"

"Please. Continue."

Alexander waved a hand. That was a kingly gesture coming from one so young. Rhoenne almost smiled.

"My bride is the daughter of a Bulgar prince,

Philip of Vottenavia. She is also grand-niece of the *Duca di* Candia, Stefano Giustiniani. As you may be aware, Candia is in the Venetian *Domini de Mar.*"

"Your wife…is related to the ruling family of Venice?"

"That is what I am telling you," Rhoenne replied.

"You have access to Venetian gold?" Allistair no longer sounded condescending and arrogant. That was a pleasant change.

"I did na' say that," Rhoenne remarked.

"Explain please?"

"I believe I have secured a venue for requesting gold from the Venetians. One, they will find difficult to decline."

"This is extraordinary. You are wed to a member of the ruling families of two kingdoms? Two?"

Rhoenne considered. Smiled to himself. Then answered, "Aye."

"How did you manage such a feat?" Allistair asked.

Rhoenne stood taller. Regarded the regent for long moments while twitters of amusement flit through the room behind him.

"I told them I was a Highlander," he replied, drawing out the words for effect.

The room erupted around him. MacDougall yelled for order. Someone beat on a large drum. The din gradually quieted. None of Rhoenne's men had moved. The king was smiling widely.

"Laird Ramhurst? I noticed you did na' request release from your betrothal. You asked to be replaced. True?"

Allistair spoke. Rhoenne addressed his reply to the king.

"Aye, Your Majesty. That is true."

"You have a proposed groom to offer? One who will be accepted by our king's father-in-law, England's king, Henry? Should he decide to sponsor your request?"

"I do," Rhoenne replied easily.

"And that man would be...?"

"My cousin...and – should there be no issue of my marriage – my heir, Sir Grant Ramhurst. Grant. Step forward, mon."

His cousin choked. Henry pushed him forward. Of the line-up of men before the dais, Grant was the only one approaching Rhoenne in height and bulk. He bore a distinct resemblance as well. Rhoenne watched as they also noticed it.

"Ah. This Grant. Can we grant him a title of some kind?" the king asked. "Maybe some land?"

"I will offer the land, Your Majesty," Rhoenne said.

"Excellent. And I shall award a title. Grant Ramhurst? Prepare yourself."

Grant dropped to a knee. The king stood and walked to the end of the dais, trailed by his regent. Once he'd reached the floor, it was apparent he was a slight lad. The entire line of Ramhurst men dwarfed not only him, but his regent beside him.

"Your sword, Grant Ramhurst."

He was handed Grant's broadsword. It took both hands to wield, but that was due to his size, not ability. The lad was young, but he wasn't weak. He tapped Grant's shoulders one at a time.

"Rise. Viscount of Tyneburgh!"

Grant rose. Accepted his sword back. And looked like a man who'd just taken a blow to the head. The king stopped before Rhoenne and looked up at him. He was about shoulder height, but wasn't finished sprouting. Rhoenne waited.

"I shall send a missive requesting a betrothal change from the earl of Tyneburgh to the viscount of the same clan. I will also ask that the marriage take place within the month."

"My thanks, Your Majesty."

"Is there anything else?"

"May I retire?"

The king nodded. Rhoenne dipped his head. Took one step back. Swiveled. And strode back out the way he'd come. His men did the exact same maneuver and were at his heels while they exited the great hall. People once again moved from their path. Nobody spoke until they were almost back to their chambers.

"Well, Viscount Tyneburgh! I think this calls for a celebratory toast. You have whiskey on you?" Euan spoke.

"Me? I did na' even bring a flask in my sporran," Grant still sounded like he was in shock.

Somebody smacked him.

"We'll just have to return to the fest."

"Aye. That we will."

"And now that we have a bit of notoriety, thanks to the laird, we should have *nae* trouble interesting a lass or two."

"I had *nae* trouble afore," Iain remarked.

"I was speaking on Euan's behalf."

"Oh. My thanks," Euan remarked.

"Go. All of you," Rhoenne remarked. They'd reached the chamber. He opened the door. Turned back to his men.

"You will na' join us?"

"I have things to plan," he told them.

"In that event, I shall stay," Henry remarked.

"They do na' include you," Rhoenne answered.

"You continually surprise me, my laird," Henry told him. "Continually. I am in awe at your ability. Privileged to be commander of your Honor Guard. And na' dense enough to leave you to plan your next move without a hint as to what it might be."

Rhoenne regarded his man. Henry returned the gaze. Rhoenne finally shrugged and walked into the chamber. Henry followed and closed the door.

He'd been successful. He'd gotten what he wanted. But the pressure around his heart didn't let up at all.

CHAPTER TWENTY-EIGHT

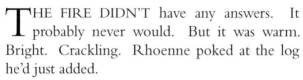

THE FIRE DIDN'T have any answers. It probably never would. But it was warm. Bright. Crackling. Rhoenne poked at the log he'd just added.

"I see you are determined to be unreadable. As usual," Henry joined him, yawning and rubbing at his belly. That was probably a mistake. He wasn't fully healed. The man caught his breath with a wince.

"Why do na' you join Ida?" Rhoenne returned.

"She has had enough of my company lately."

"That does na' bode well."

"For what?"

"Your future, of course," Rhoenne answered.

"With Ida? Hmm. Interesting thought. I may have to ponder it."

"Well, 'twas you talking of settling down. Gaining your own croft. Starting a family. Finding a comely wench."

"And you think I should choose Ida?"

"You could fill the day with talk and she'd never complain."

"Oh. She complains. Just na' in words."

Rhoenne smirked.

"So. I have been waiting, my laird."

"Truly? What for?"

Henry settled onto his haunches before the hearth beside Rhoenne. "An explanation."

"To what?"

"All manner of things. Your performance this eve for a start. You had me worried."

"About what?"

"The betrothal. And your part in it."

"Oh. That."

"You could have forewarned me. You did na' have to accept my words of reproof."

"You? Words of reproof?"

"You let me speak words about wedding the lass yourself. You could have told me you were requesting the change to your cousin."

"I was na' at all certain I would. I do a lot of pondering, Henry. You ken that. Some of my ideas are mere thoughts. Some are fully planned afore I put them into action. Some...I just jump and allow things to go as they may. I was na' sure what I'd say once I saw the king."

"Well. It was brilliant. You have to be the only man in Scotland that could violate a royal betrothal and na' just avoid royal disfavor, but the king may actually be indebted to you...should he need help raising ransom funds. 'Twas the perfect solution. But that is na' the explanation I speak for."

"You worry over my selection? Ponder Grant's abilities?"

"*Nae.* He is your next of kin. He has also

proven to be trustworthy. Loyal. A man could na' ask for better. 'Tis more the request for a speedy ceremony. That has me puzzled."

"Grant will make an excellent laird for the Ramhurst Clan." Rhoenne didn't turn from contemplation of the fire.

"You are the laird of the Ramhurst Clan," Henry finally spoke.

"True. But I will be...elsewhere."

"And where is it you intend to be?"

Rhoenne shrugged. "Wherever the path takes me."

"For how long?"

"As long as it takes."

"You are heading back, aren't you? To find her," Henry remarked.

Rhoenne sighed. "You are ever insightful, my friend. I have to return. I *have* to. She is na' dead. I ken it in my verra bones. And that means she is out there. Somewhere. Alone. Defenseless. And vulnerable."

Each word sent pain through his veins, a throb of ache through his skull, and the bondage about his heart squeezed, making each beat hurt. The combination had no salve. And then his eyes pricked with a suspicion of tears. The flames blurred. Silence wrapped about them for long moments while Rhoenne worked at controlling each breath, keeping the emotion at bay, and Henry unaware.

"You discount Emin," Henry finally spoke.

"One man." Rhoenne looked down, blinked until the jeweled band on his wrist came back into focus.

"I begin to see the reasoning behind your actions, my laird."

"Truly? That makes one of us."

Henry huffed a breath that contained amusement. "You are making certain Grant has enough backing to oust Aileen. The king of England as a father-by-law should suffice. That is why you need the ceremony completed quickly. So you are free to go."

"You are a smart man, Henry FitzHugh."

"I am na' captain of your Honor Guard due strictly to my good looks."

"So you continually point out," Rhoenne returned.

The chamber door opened. Grant walked in. He didn't look like a man celebrating his good fortune. He looked shame-faced and pale. Rhoenne and Henry exchanged glances. Henry stood to greet him.

"Grant? You return early. Has the fest ended, perchance?"

"*Nae.*"

"You have perhaps...over-imbibed already?"

"*Nae.*"

"You are feeling poorly?"

"I need a word with Rhoenne."

"Do you wish me to leave?" Henry asked.

Grant glanced at him, then back down. He took a deep breath. Let it out. It brought out his resemblance to Rhoenne even more.

"*Nae.* Privacy will na' make this any easier. I have earned whatever I reap herewith."

Henry and Rhoenne exchanged glances again. Henry's brows rose.

"Sit. Join us."

"'Tis better if I stand. I may need...the ability to move."

Rhoenne stood slowly. Walked to his cousin. Placed a hand on his shoulder. "Perhaps it should remain unspoken then, Cousin."

"Grant shook his head, then shook off Rhoenne's hand. "I have been silent too long already. 'Tis time you knew."

"Verra well. I am listening."

Grant walked to the shadowed area of the room. Turned around and came back to the lighted area. Did it again. He didn't look up from the floor.

"First loves are...verra special. You ken?" Grant started. "And I—. Well. I—. This is even more difficult than I feared."

Rhoenne stilled.

"Are you saying your heart is engaged elsewhere?" Henry asked before turning to Rhoenne. "This could be problematic, my laird."

"Na' really. 'Twould be a minor issue. I'll just request another alteration to the betrothal. The king has na' had time to draft his missive yet."

"Well. You do seem to have a talent for creating court scandal," Henry remarked wryly. "What is one more?"

"It's na' that," Grant interrupted them.

"You have *nae* issue with the betrothal, then?" Henry asked.

"Are you mad? I was just given a title. A royal bride-to-be. A dowry beyond my dreams! I will be the son-in-law of England's king! All without a hint of warning. I am simply...uh."

"Overcome?" Henry asked.

"Unworthy," Grant mumbled.

"You are a loyal clansman, Grant. I would na' have put forth your name otherwise," Rhoenne told him.

"Please! This is already difficult. You only make it more so. What I am about to confess will na' only earn me your hatred, but you may wish to punish me. With banishment or worse! And I will deserve whatever you decide."

"Wait."

Rhoenne walked to the table and started pulling knives from his belt. He placed them one-by-one on the table. Then he lifted a foot, pulled the *skean dhu* from his sock, and did the same with the other leg. He placed those daggers next to the other blades. His short sword was pulled from its scabbard and positioned atop the pile of weaponry already on the tabletop. He didn't wear his claymore. It leaned against a wall beside the fireplace. Once he had all his weapons removed, he moved to the door leading to the room Ida slept in, turned around, folded his arms and regarded his cousin. His mind reeled. His heart was in a pain-ridden vice, each beat sending fire through his veins. But his features were deadly calm.

Grant was the man who'd brought word of Cassandra. He'd been the one taking the *ducati* to the market place, supposedly to purchase the lock of hair and the jewelry piece. And no one had any information about any of it.

If his cousin had any part in her disappearance—!

Rhoenne couldn't finish the thought. He was already trembling. He knew his reflexes. He didn't dare have a weapon near. If Grant had anything to do with the loss of Cassandra, Rhoenne wasn't certain even Henry could prevent what he would do.

"Verra well," he said. "I am ready to hear."

"I...fell in love at fifteen," Grant began. "She was older...and so beauteous. So womanly. It was completely wrong. Dishonorable. But I couldn't help it. My every moment was filled with thoughts of her. I wrote sonnets to her. And when I gave them to her, she'd smile and laugh. I composed songs. She told me how sweet I was."

His voice took on a dreamy quality. Rhoenne straightened. Stared.

"And then. When I least expected it. She—. She told me she loved me, too. I was overcome. Ecstatic. And then...she even allowed me into her bed...oh! I cannot tell you how that felt. She...was my first. She made me a man. For eight days. Eight. I once thought them the most magical days of my life. We had to sneak about, of course. That added a thrill. Why once. Once! She let me tupp her...in the study. On the desk. When anyone could have interrupted."

Aileen.

He knew it as if Grant had already told them. Rhoenne set his jaw and moved his gaze to the fire. It was better than watching his cousin as he described some of the same sensations Rhoenne had experienced, and it was much better than meeting whatever expression Henry displayed. It was Aileen the man spoke on. Nothing to do with Cassandra. The agonizing pressure about Rhoenne's heart eased.

"And then. One night. We were uh. In bed. Fully...uh...you ken. *Engaged*. And the laird came back unexpectedly. I heard him on the landing just outside the chamber. I didn't have time for more than a leap to the hall door. I barely missed ramming you."

Rhoenne glanced at his cousin. Grant still looked down to the floor.

"Me?" Rhoenne asked.

"You did na' see me. You were in the midst of that walking you used to do while asleep. I raced past you, down those cold halls. Naked. I heard her behind me, talking softly. Soothingly. I heard the laird's shout of rage. It made me run even faster."

Grant paused. A log fell in the fire as if on cue, sending out a burst of light. Grant pulled in another large breath.

"From that moment on, though...things changed. The laird took ill. Then he died. The household was silent. You'd gone missing. I did na' ken that she'd placed you to take the punishment in my stead. I did na' find out until you returned to the castle, all bruised and battered. That's when I knew what she'd done. Mayhap she thought the laird would spare his favorite son and heir. I do na' ken her thinking. But I should have confessed it to you. I should.

That is where I wronged you. But I held my tongue. And as each day followed the next, it got harder and harder to speak. It has been a weight on my shoulders...for years now."

Rhoenne met Henry's glance again. Rhoenne sucked in his cheeks and returned to looking at the fire.

"Why didn't you speak up?" Henry asked.

"I was in love! I told you! Or – what I thought was love. You do na' ken what it is like. I thought—. I thought she loved me, too. It made me...special." Grant's voice lowered. It had a sobbed sound to it as well. "I thought...we might have a future. Once things settled down. And things got back to normal. But then—. Then—." His words took on a hard, ugly note. "I went to her chamber. The door was locked. I waited in the hall. Hidden in a doorway. And she had a guardsman in there! They embraced in the doorway. I saw it. I felt such a swell of hatred. And disgust. And anger! You can na' imagine."

Oh yes, he could.

And that was the exact moment when Rhoenne realized the favor Grant had actually done for him. If it hadn't been for the mental scarring inflicted from his father's beating, Rhoenne wouldn't have experienced a sick feeling whenever Aileen came near. Her manipulations could so easily have included him. And – if he was honest – they would have.

"I found her in the garden the verra next day. Spoke angry words. Ended with pleas. I am na' proud of that episode. That's when she told me she'd never be interested in a youth like me. She told me I was inept. I would never satisfy a woman. Because I was puny. And for years I thought it true."

"Grant. You are a Ramhurst. There is *nae* way you are puny," Rhoenne spoke up.

"I ken that...now! But back then, I was young. I had no one to speak to. What did I ken of it?"

"You've been around others your entire life."

"I've na' been around anyone when they're uh...primed! I am na' that dense. You do na' ken what she is like. She can plant a thought...and make it believable. She did it to me a-purpose. To belittle me. To make me worry. To unman me. To make me impotent."

"Your father should have counseled you," Henry said.

"My da?" Grant gave a humorless snort. "He took to drink. You wish to ken why?" His voice lowered. "Because the guardsman was na' the lone man I caught visiting her."

"Uncle Tevin, too?" Rhoenne didn't bother hiding the revulsion.

"And more. And then what happens? She up and wed Bhaltair? After calling *me* inept? He was na' even *auld* enough to shave yet! You saw him. He changed. He started getting all mean. And angry. Vengeful. And...then he's found with a knife in his chest? And no one knew what happened? Oh, Rhoenne. For all I knew, it had been my own da'!"

His voice broke on a sob then. Rhoenne tensed between his shoulders. A twinge went through the scarred flesh where he'd been shot in the back with an arrow. But he otherwise didn't move.

"There was no one to trust. No one I could talk with. Everyone was suspect. You'd disappeared. Both of you. Nobody knew where. My da was drunk more times than not. And then—. Then." He took another big breath. "She started anew with me. I'd find her blocking my path where I'd least expect. Wearing little clothing. Acting like I should na' care that she'd broken my heart and treated me like offal."

God damn Aileen!

"You did na' take up with her again, did you?" Henry asked

"I confess. I was actually considering it. You do na' ken what she is like. But we got the message to come serve you at King Louis's court in France. Oh, Rhoenne. That saved my sanity.... and my manhood. It was in France that I finally got up the courage to tupp a woman again. I discovered the truth. I'm *nae* slackard. And I'm na' puny, either!"

Grant took a deep breath. Exhaled it sharply. That was so like himself, Rhoenne couldn't help noticing again.

"Well, Cousin. That is the secret I was taking to my grave. And why I am na' the man you think. You can na' honor me with this title and the betrothal. I am unworthy of it."

"I truly...was na' with Aileen that night?" Rhoenne asked.

"*Nae.*"

"You swear to it?"

"Easily. I am the fastest runner in the clan and I barely had time to escape. I can na' believe the laird did na' see me. There is *nae* way you did anything. You were in the midst of a sleep-walk. You did it oft, you ken? You'd wander about, completely unaware. Sometimes we'd take your arm and set you on another path entirely. Once we put a ramp up to the dovecote to see if you'd actually walk it, and you did! And then you would na' come back down! I tried everything to move you, but you were dead asleep up there. And then came the warning shouts that you were missing. So. What could we do? We hid the ramp. And ran."

Rhoenne caught Henry's glance again. Henry eyes were twinkling. Rhoenne cleared his throat and walked to the table. First he laced his scabbard and sword back onto his belt. He replaced the knives next. Then he turned back to his cousin. Nobody spoke the entire time.

"I thank you for your words tonight, Grant. I would have wished them earlier, of course, but I do thank you for them."

"I ken 'tis too late to beg for forgiveness, Rhoenne, so I will na' ask. I am the lowest of wretches. I accept whatever punishment you deem deserved."

"Well. If I had na' met Cassandra and discovered that there is such a thing as true love, and that it is the most powerful of emotions...well. I admit. I would probably be beating you into the floor right now, Grant Ramhurst. You'd be lucky to be banished. But I have to tell you. Hearing this na' only lightens my heart, but assures me I have done the right thing in selecting you."

"What?" Grant's head went up, and for the first time he looked directly at his cousin.

"I can na' think of another man better placed to take on that witch. You na' only ken exactly what you are dealing with, you will na' be swayed by her feminine wiles, soft touches, and manipulative ways."

"Calling her a witch is generous, my laird."

"She may try her wiles on you again, Grant. You are a viscount now. She may even wish marriage."

"I'd sooner wed a snake," Grant replied.

Rhoenne considered him for some time, while a smile played about his lips. "Good word choice," he finally replied.

"Aside from which, she would na' have the chance. If the missive to England's king is successful, it will be too late. I will already be wed."

Henry whistled. Rhoenne knew why. The man had just gotten more answer to why Rhoenne requested speed for the nuptials. Just then, someone knocked on the chamber door. Not quietly. They all looked that direction.

"Your chamber appears to be a much desired destination this night, my laird," Henry remarked.

"Oh. That will be the others," Grant said. "I asked for some time afore they sought their pallets."

Rhoenne grunted. Grant opened the door a crack. Euan spoke from the hall.

"Grant. Apologies. We need entrance. Right now! I ken you asked for time, but—this can na' wait. A lad's just arrived."

Grant looked over his shoulder at Rhoenne. He nodded. Grant opened the door. Euan brought a slight fellow with him into the room. They were followed by the Montvale men, Iain and Graham. The lad with Euan was spare. Lean, but muscled. He was almost Euan's height. He wore Ramhurst gray and white plaid, with thin black and blue stripes. He had a shock of red hair. Blue eyes. He stared up at Rhoenne slack-jawed.

"This lad accosted us at the ale keg. Spotted the Ramhurst *plaide*. Claims Angus FitzHugh sent him. With an urgent message."

"Angus FitzHugh? My cousin? Is he a relation to you, lad?" Henry asked.

"Aye. My da."

"Oh. Of course. I remember you. LeRoy. Right?"

The lad nodded.

"You've grown. You must be...thirteen now?"

"I'll be sixteen next month," the lad replied.

Sixteen?

That sent a wash of anger. Rhoenne stiffened.

LeRoy looked so young. Not a lad. Not yet a man. Eager. Honest. And innocent. The same age he and Grant had been when Aileen came into their world, and upended it. LeRoy was a visual reminder of what had been done to them...and who was truly to blame. Grant may have had the same thought for he was watching for Rhoenne's glance before they turned back to their visitor.

"What is the message?" Henry continued.

Euan answered. "He would na' tell us. Says it's to be delivered to just the earl."

"Verra well," Rhoenne said. "You have reached me, LeRoy."

"You are him."

LeRoy spoke with awe staining the words. Rhoenne considered him for a bit. Then nodded. "Aye. I am the earl of Tyneburgh."

"The Dark One 'Tis said you never lose. You kill without regret. Or remorse!"

Rhoenne regarded him for a few moments. "I have been named such," he finally admitted.

"You are the scourge of the east! And every ocean a-tween!"

Rhoenne grunted. "I have na' heard those afore."

"I was told the moment I asked for you! Is it true you vanquished an entire ship full of pirates? All by yourself?"

Rhoenne glanced up at the ceiling. Fought the smile.

"Euan," Henry carried the tone of reproof Rhoenne knew so well.

"I only told one man! I vow."

"While at a table-full of listeners," Iain remarked.

"It does na' matter," Rhoenne told them. "The larger a reputation grows, the fewer challenges are tossed."

"But those that are received will most likely be from worthy opponents. Men who wish to add to their own reputations," Henry added.

"All of which is destiny, while an important messages waits undelivered. So. LeRoy? Speak up, lad. What is my message?"

"My laird."

The fellow went to a knee before Rhoenne. There was a series of coughs and throat clearing happening from the others. Rhoenne looked down at the lad's mop of red hair. Almost touched it before he caught himself. He spoke with solemn tones.

"Rise, Clansman LeRoy FitzHugh."

The lad got back to his feet. He had a huge smile on his face. He received like expressions from all the others.

"And now. Please. Deliver the message."

"You must come to the castle immediately."

"I am but recent arrived to Scotland. What dire event could possibly have occurred that needs my presence forthwith?"

"The wife has arrived."

"What wife?"

"Yours. The princess. I think her name is Cassandra. And she has a man with her."

Rhoenne's jaw dropped. His eyes went huge. His heart sent a lightning bolt through him. His throat closed off. His knees gave. He smacked his palms to his thighs for support. But nothing stopped the absolute joy. It was uncontainable. He sucked in a breath, shoved his head back, and roared with a combination of ecstasy and relief. The sound bounced off walls. Brought Ida to the door of the chamber. It ended with laughter.

And then he sucked another breath in, and did it again. Tears blurred his eyes. Sparks flew his veins. Cords stood out in his neck before he finished.

"Henry!" he barked.

"Open the door!" Henry commanded. "Someone. Anyone! Go, my laird! Run."

Rhoenne sprinted off.

"Grant? You're the fastest. Get going, mon! Stay with him!"

Emotion demanded an outlet. Intensity fueled his limbs. He didn't see stone walls. Any occupants. Guards. Any of the courtyard. Not a hint of the large arched gateway. He was racing down to the valley floor before he even noticed it was a moonlit night. He slowed, but it was to gather breath, bellow another loud yell into the night.

And then he was racing again.

CHAPTER TWENTY-NINE

GRANT CAUGHT UP with him at the beginning of the marshy *Nor Loch* area. Rhoenne had taken to pacing back and forth, jumping from boulder to boulder, laughing whenever he fell. He'd never felt so amazing. Energized. Joyful.

Alive.

Grant stumbled to a halt beside him. Fell to his knees, which had to scrape. Rhoenne smacked his shoulder. "Cousin! I see you finally got here!"

Grant lumbered to his feet. "Well, I did na' have a head start."

"True."

"And I did na' just find out that my true love that I thought lost to me, is na' only alive...but close!"

"I ken! Is na' it grand?" Rhoenne rushed his cousin, wrapped his arms about him and jumped with him. Twice.

Grant shoved free. "There are few men can lift me. And few still I allow to do it."

"Oh ho. That sounds like a challenge."

"Later," Grant returned.

"Why the glum face, Cousin? Is this na' the grandest of nights?"

Rhoenne leapt atop a boulder, gave a loud whoop, and finished with a burst of laughter. Grant moved to an adjacent rock and sat, placing his forearms on his thighs. He blew a sigh.

"I am happy for you, Rhoenne. Truly. I have never seen you so...happy."

"And it is wondrous!" Rhoenne flashed a grin.

"It must be. But...I admit. I am a bit jealous. Your love for her...'tis truly enviable."

Rhoenne jumped down. Sat beside his cousin. "You were soured by Aileen."

"Aye. Aileen."

"You do na' still harbor feelings for the witch?"

"*Nae.*"

"You swear?"

"If you want the truth, to me she resembles a mud puddle. Slimy. Dank. One I'd rather skirt than step into."

"Better words could na' be voiced. You obviously have the same troubadour in your lineage as I claim."

"I told you I wrote sonnets to her. Did you think they were *nae* good?"

Rhoenne sobered. "I think you wasted a dearth of talent and years on her already. But she did one thing for us both."

"What is that?"

"We sure ken what a witch looks and acts like now. And how to avoid them."

"True. Well, my laird. You ready to race again?"

"Where to?"

"Back up, of course."

Rhoenne grunted.

"We should na' waste a moment, you ken?"

"I celebrate and you call it wasteful?"

"I'm actually thinking things through."

"Ponder away, then! And allow me some happiness!"

"Oh, verra well. As long as the others have horses prepared and ready to ride."

"In the midst of the night? After a night of feast and drink? What sprite has stolen your wits?"

"A mud puddle."

"Look about you, mon! Everywhere you step is a mud puddle."

"You are na' listening. We need to leave, Rhoenne. As soon as possible. Think, mon! Even if young LeRoy rode nonstop, it takes three days from Edinburgh to Tyne. He's young. Fit. He still had to rest. So...I'm guessing it took four days, mayhap five."

"And this has meaning, why?"

"The wife is at Tyne Castle."

"Aye! And I still can na' believe it!"

"It will be three days afore we can reach it. If we get fresh stock and do na' rest."

"So?"

"The mud puddle is also at the castle."

Rhoenne shot to his feet. "Oh, dear God. She will be at Aileen's mercy for a sennight!"

"Exactly!"

Rhoenne didn't hesitate a second longer. He took off, racing up the moonlit path of castle rock. Grant passed him before they reached the summit. Rhoenne knew why. Joy had been an energizer. Worry was the exact opposite.

His Honor Guard were already assembled at the stables, packed. Ready. Henry handed Rhoenne his sword and a thick *sett*. He tossed it over his shoulders and pulled the hood over his head. They were good men. All of them.

"We have one stop afore we set off," Rhoenne told them.

"St. Margaret's Church?" Henry retorted.

Rhoenne smiled. "You ken me too well, my friend."

Thus it was that a band of seven men and one woman entered the chapel built in the last century in honor of King David's mother, late at night. When most souls were abed. The sanctity of the enclosure surrounded them. An aura of peace enwrapped them. Rhoenne strode up the aisle, knelt before the altar. Bent his head. All around him he felt the others follow suit. He spoke words, but there wasn't a prayer with enough gratitude for the blessing he'd just received.

And he knew it.

"*Princessa?*"

Cassandra turned from contemplation of the castle grounds directly below Rhoenne's tower. Emin stood just inside the door Nessa had opened. Emin made the woman look small. Rhoenne would dwarf her. But he did that with most women. Cassandra smiled at them both. She already loved this tower. She had since she'd first entered it.

The west tower was sturdily built of thick gray stone. Rhoenne's room took up the entire top and was at least six stories above ground. The tower was octagonal. Long narrow windows had been constructed into three sides, two facing outward, one looking over the inner courtyard. The view included what looked like an herb garden – if it received some care. The garden was located along the inner courtyard wall. Beyond the barbican walls was a vista of sky and water. Chill wind whipped white-topped waves along the loch's surface. Today the sky was gray and cloud-filled, promising another bout of sleet or snow. It looked damp. Cold. Bereft.

But none of that filtered through the thick glass at her nose.

The fire behind her burned brightly, its warmth chasing any chill into submission. There was a large shield and display of weapons on an inner wall. An immense wooden target hung on another, the multiple missing chunks mutely telling of Rhoenne's practice. The bed was enclosed on three sides, large and sturdily built. There was a stool. A small table. A low bench. Some pegs for hanging garments.

When she'd first seen it, the place had been filmed with dust. Disused. In need of a good cleaning and airing. But the FitzHugh women weren't the only ones who'd accompanied her to the tower. There'd been at least a dozen women at Emin's heels. Cassandra had waited with him on the landing while every piece of fabric was taken from the room. They'd hauled out rugs and tapestries and bedding. They'd even maneuvered the old mattress out the door. Nessa and Maysie had stayed behind, dusting and straightening and sweeping. Maysie definitely sent lingering glances in Emin's direction. Cassandra caught more than one of them. That was amusing.

Clanswomen had returned with buckets of water, newly woven rugs and clean *plaides.* And before the day was out, two clansmen had lugged a newly stuffed straw mattress up the steps. The chimney had been checked, a fire kindled in the fireplace. Everything smelled and looked clean and fresh, adding to the aura. The chamber had welcomed and soothed when she first entered it.

A sennight later, it still did.

Cassandra smiled at Nessa and answered Emin. "Yes, Emin?"

"The chieftain chambers are readied."

Cassandra made a face.

"Everything has been replaced, Highness."

"Everything?"

"Your people are most industrious. They possess great skill with woodcarving. I am quite impressed. They have crafted new furnishings for His Excellency and you. The wall and floor coverings have been replaced. Everything is new. I have been assured all is in readiness."

The baby kicked sharply. Cassandra placed her hand atop it. Nessa beamed at her.

"If you think it best," she replied.

Emin dipped his chin slightly. "I do not know how to reply, Highness."

"You don't?"

"None ask me what I think."

"Well...maybe it's time we started."

There was a knock on the door jamb behind him. He and Nessa turned.

"My lady?"

Margaret FitzHugh bobbed a curtsey. Angus FitzHugh was an excellent steward. He'd done wonders. Even before she'd reached Rhoenne's tower, he'd been changing things. The old staff had either retired to their own crofts, or undergone some manner of testing to assure loyalty. Cassandra hadn't needed to ask. Angus informed her daily of progress. There hadn't been but a handful of women in the entire complex. Very few clansmen had allowed their daughters to work at the castle while Aileen had been in charge. Now that Cassandra had arrived, things changed. It wasn't subtle. Angus's wife, Margaret assumed management of the household. She controlled an army of women, cleaning and refurbishing. Dusting and polishing. Replacing rushes. The entire structure was starting to sparkle.

"Mistress FitzHugh?" Cassandra greeted her.

"The seamstresses are ready for you in the ladies solar."

"'Tis time already?"

"They have a lot of work still to do."

"But, of course. And they do such fine work, so na' they?"

Cassandra lifted her skirt. She wore a light gray colored kirtle atop a linen under-dress. The kirtle had been woven from finely spun wool. It was

THE DARK CRUSADER   441

then embroidered all about the hem and bodice with satiny white stitching in a floral motif. It was ladylike and refined, and gathered beneath her bosom for fullness. A matching cap was atop the hair Nessa had just finished braiding.

"Aye. That they do. And Maysie has just baked sweet rolls. With cream-filling. Best get one while they're hot. They will na' last. And I'm to make certain you ken which ones are for you, Master Emin."

Cassandra flicked a glance toward him. Emin was studiously avoiding meeting it. Maysie had been put in charge of the kitchens, and seemed intent on sending the most mouth-watering dishes for each meal. The woman had her sights set on Emin. She wasn't keeping it secret. And they all got to enjoy her culinary artistry.

Cassandra followed Margaret down the wheel stair to the third floor. They left the spiral steps and entered a hall leading not only to the ladies solar, but it ended at the chieftain's chamber. She needed to move there. She knew it. Leaving the rooms open only gave ballast to Aileen.

She just wanted Rhoenne to be there, too.

The solar backed the great hall, sharing chimneys with one of the immense fireplaces. They burned a combination of dried peat with wood chips most of the time. The smell was distinctive and would take getting used to. The room had high windows that didn't let in much light, but the sconces held flickering flames, and there was a fire kindled. The room seemed filled with fabrics, sewing implements, the smell of fresh bread, and a quantity of chattering women. They stopped as Emin escorted her to the door, took a look over the room, then turned his back to the proceedings. After greetings were exchanged the chattering started right back up. Nothing was whispered. Nobody sent malignant glances. Occasional laughter rang. And the sweet rolls were divine. Cassandra ate two of them between fittings. It wasn't remotely reminiscent of the harem.

Emin knocked on the door.

"'Tis your steward, my lady."

"Ah. Angus. Please. Come in."

He looked impressive, wearing a new sett and full weaponry. He pulled the tam from his head before giving her a bow. Gave his wife a wink. That was a heartwarming gesture.

"You have an update for me?"

He nodded. "The widow has na' left her chambers. Still. We've added another guard."

"Another?"

"Three more men sit in the dungeons because of the woman."

"Good heavens. Three? Has she tried to get another message out?"

"Worse. Perhaps we should speak...elsewhere."

Cassandra nodded. All talk ceased as she walked to the door. Margaret was at her heels. Emin shut the door behind them.

"What has she done now?" Cassandra asked as soon as door closed.

"We caught two clansmen at the well. Another stood watch."

"The well?"

"Aye."

"Poison?"

"Monkshood."

Cassandra gasped. The baby reacted as well. She put a hand atop it protectively.

"Rest assured, Highness. They did na' do the deed. And she will na' get another chance."

"Was...your nephew involved?"

He shook his head. "*Nae*. Calum remains steadfast and loyal. I'd stake my life on it. My sister runs the alehouse now. Even if the lad were under a spell, he'd na' betray you. My sister has him well in hand."

"The woman has that much sway?"

"Well. Aye. She is his mum. He is her lone son."

Cassandra nodded and gave a small smile. "I see."

"We've got loyal clan guarding the well now. All the food stores. Every egress. And I've got men overseeing those men. Maysie has the kitchen under control. Everything is being taste-tested. You are safe. The bairn is safe. We will na' allow harm to come to you, or anyone in Castle Tyne."

The sound of boots interrupted him. They all turned to watch a group of guards approach at a trot. High slits in the wall brought the only illumination. The group was in shadow as they arrived. Panting. The foursome went to their knees before her in a flurry of plaide and clink of weaponry.

"This here is my brother, Rory, and some of

the men. Rory FitzHugh! He has assumed commander of the guards...until such time as the laird returns and can assign such duties."

"Rise, Commander FitzHugh," Cassandra replied.

The man stood. He was younger than Angus, bore a distinct resemblance, but he was a lot bigger. He was almost as large as Emin.

"Well?" Angus prompted loudly. "You have news?"

"Aye. We just got word. The laird's been sighted."

Oh, dearest God!

They spoke of Rhoenne!

A flicker of excitement shot through her at the instant realization. Her heart jolted. Her breath caught. The babe did all manner of antics. She was surprised she wasn't bouncing. Like magic, Emin was there beside her, placing a hand beneath her elbow. Protecting. Stabilizing. Supporting.

"'Tis the earl?" Angus continued. "You certain?"

"Aye."

"Well, speak mon! How close is he?"

"Apologies."

The man tipped his glance briefly to her, before looking back to his brother. There was none of the usual surprise she received whenever anyone got a good look at her. That was disconcerting. And slightly worrisome.

"We just barely heard the pipes. Pipers are relaying. And you ken how sound travels out on the moors."

"Can ye give us *nae* clue?"

"Well...he's on Ramhurst soil. But 'tis a large fief. Could be hours yet."

"Outset?"

"Evening. We've got men stationed. I'll apprise as soon as a rider gets here with a report."

"Verra good."

"Thank you, Captain," Cassandra said.

He bowed his head, turned about and the men trotted off.

"Oh dear," Cassandra remarked.

"My lady?" Angus queried.

"I look the size of a horse. What am I to wear?"

Angus looked startled. "Oh, please, Highness. You are a slip of a thing. Well. I mean—."

Margaret clucked her tongue. "Go on with ye, Angus FitzHugh. This is ladies work. Be off! We've got all manner of wardrobe almost ready... and it sounds like we've got all day to find just the right garment. No worries, my lady. We've got that well in hand.

"Verra good. My lady?" He nodded to first her and then his wife. "Meggie. I'll report back as soon as we receive word."

Angus clicked his heels, swiveled, and disappeared into the gloom at the end of the hall.

They spent horses only to exchange them for fresh mounts. Euan rode ahead, setting up the exchanges, paying for food, heat, extra woolens. He was the best horseman and the lightest. If anyone lagged, they'd be left behind. Iain,

Graham, and Grant kept pace. Henry and Ida had branched off the first night. Heading west would be easier going, but slower. Rhoenne and the others kept a northwest direction, over wind-whipped moors, through bog-filled forests, between icy passes of the Grampian Mountains. They were forced to shelter at a MacHugh croft for three hours. Sleet made the path impossible to decipher. Everyone slept. Even Rhoenne.

The moment they crossed onto Ramhurst fief, he heard the pipers. Saw a rider take off. The next stop gained him a lot of shoulder smacking and grins. More than one swept-away tear. More clansmen for escort, although most lagged almost instantly. And the most important - they had news from the castle. Angus FitzHugh was back as steward. Rhoenne hadn't even known he'd been dismissed. The countess was well. According to rumor, his wife had the witch well in hand. No one bothered sweetening anything. They all knew who the witch referred to.

It started sleeting again at the second-to-last stop. The men shoveled in stew. Fresh bread. Joints of mutton. Washed down with full foamed tankards of ale. Well-wishes abounded. Dry *plaides* were donned. Heavier woven setts were wrapped atop that. They even had a pair of boots that fit Rhoenne. All of it a God-send.

Snow blanketed the last league, plastering them with a coating of wet, slowing the pace to a slog, making it difficult to see and appreciate Castle Tyne even as they bore down on it. They didn't approach as a lone group of four. Rhoenne had at least a hundred clansmen with him, most on horseback, but quite a few bringing up the rear on foot. Rhoenne led across the drawbridges without breaking pace, the volume of horses with him making thumping sounds akin to drumbeats. They rode beneath the portcullis. Trotted through the corridor between the walls. Spilled into the outer courtyard. Past the priory. Stables. The place was awash with light. Pipers blaring. Drummers drumming. And clansmen yelling. Shouting. Gesturing. Swords high.

Clansmen lined both sides of a pathway straight through to the inner courtyard. Rhoenne raced along it, sped to the base of the front steps, reined his horse in at the last moment, jumped onto the stairs, and raced up them two at a time. Grant was at his heels. Iain and Graham right behind.

The plaid atop him was saturated. Cold. He shoved it off as he crossed the foyer, holding it out behind him. Grant took it without breaking stride, then passed it back. He felt Grant doing the same with his own outer *plaide*. No doubt the others followed. Rhoenne had his broadsword pulled before he stomped into the great hall. The place was lit up like a fest was in play, despite holding only a few occupants.

They had four trees burning, one in each fireplace. All of the torches, and even the wheeled chandeliers were lit. Light reflected from all the weaponry on display. Sound swelled as the pipers accompanied him gave a final blast. The sound hadn't finished dying out before he spoke.

"Where is she?"

Rhoenne's shout carried through the room, the words stained with pent-up worry. He didn't care. From the shadowy recess of a chair atop the dais, a woman stood. It wasn't Cassandra. Rhoenne sheathed his sword.

"Why...I'm right here, my laird. Rhoenne. To welcome you...home."

Aileen used extremely low, sultry tones. She'd obviously dressed with care. She wore a pure white ensemble, extraordinary pristine-looking. She did a beautifully executed curtsey, designed to show off her bosom, the perfect skin of her face and throat, the mass of arranged hair down her back. Rhoenne sneered across at her.

"Viscount Tyneburgh!" he lifted his chin to yell it. He didn't move his gaze from Aileen.

"Aye," Grant answered at his side.

"You are to handle the witch until I return." There was a collective gasp at his words. Rhoenne just got louder. "Use as many clan as you need."

"Aye, my laird," Grant said.

"You have any issue with my order?"

"Na' in the slightest," Grant replied, then added, "mud puddle."

Rhoenne smirked. "Angus FitzHugh!" he shouted next.

"He's on his way, my laird. Angus! Hurry up, mon!"

The man came running from the back corridor, crossing the room at a jog. He was clearly winded. Rhoenne's glance raked him.

"My laird! Welcome back! We were just awaiting word of—"

He probably would have said more if Rhoenne hadn't interrupted, barking his next words. "Where is she?"

"Uh...the wife?"

"Of course, the wife!" Rhoenne burst out.

"I believe she will be in...the tower."

"Which. Tower?" Rhoenne separated the words through clenched teeth.

"Oh. Yours. Of course."

Rhoenne was across the great hall before Angus finished.

CHAPTER THIRTY

NOTHING FIT RIGHT. Everything made her look large. And sloppy. And unattractive. Why – when it mattered so much – could she find nothing flattering?

Every outfit Nessa brought over looked more voluminous and cumbersome than the last. Her breasts even seemed larger, and strained against beautifully embroidered bodices that had just been fitted and stitched. Every color she tried seemed to turn her skin sallow and her hair dull. No one knew what she meant when she'd requested kohl. Cassandra had tried mixing a dot of candle wax, a smear of grease, and some dusty soot for an alternative. That failed abysmally. The result looked garish, worse than any done by the most inept harem slave. She couldn't remember having such trouble with her appearance. Everything felt wrong. She needed to enhance, not detract. And she hadn't much time. The last message she'd received alerted her that the laird would be arriving at any moment.

And just look!

She wore a shapeless linen shift, a kirtle of light

blue atop it that she had yet to fasten, and her hair in a long braid down her back that hadn't any definition to it. For the first time she was having issues with her appearance. She'd never felt so unattractive. She suspected why, too.

Aileen.

Cassandra was in competition, her rival was a stunning woman...and she resembled a large-bellied sow. She didn't know what else to try. She'd never been this worried over her appearance. Ever.

Nessa finished hanging the last dress Cassandra had discarded. It was a beautifully woven woolen dress, in a dark green color. Cassandra had felt like she wore a tent.

There was no help for it.

She'd just have to start over.

She splashed water onto her face, washed, patted dry, and then stared in consternation at what looked like an actual blemish on one cheek! This was disastrous. Even her skin was in rebellion? What mischief of fate would mar her beauty when she needed it most? But, perhaps the hand-held silvered mirror had the mark. Cassandra huffed a moist warm breath onto the mirrored surface, and rubbed it with her sleeve. The spot looked different. A little less red...

Was she imaging things now?

Her hand trembled as she set the mirror onto the table. She picked up the next option Nessa had brought for her. This dress was crafted of burgundy wool, the strands so thinly spun the material fell like water from her hands.

"Can I get you anything, my lady?" Nessa asked.

"Some...water?"

Cassandra watched Nessa pour her a mug from the pitcher. They spoke meaningless words, wasting precious seconds, when every moment added edginess she could almost touch. It was so hard to be calm and collected! Everything inside was alert and tense! Jumpy with anticipation. Alive with something that didn't just tingle; it sizzled as if ready to burst into flame. The babe experienced it, too. Cassandra caught a breath and put her hand to the mound as a series of vigorous kicks and shifting moves happened. The babe settled. She lifted the shoulders of the dress up to hers, holding it in place as she stuck out a leg, evaluating the drape.

"Cassandra!"

She heard his shout a moment before the door opened. Emin held it wide so Rhoenne could barrel past him. Nessa squealed and dropped the mug. Rhoenne flew past, breathing heavily and rapidly. Hair unbound and unkempt. Damp. Large. Raw. She didn't see more. The next moment she was in his arms, lifted and held in an embrace of iron and muscle. An instant film of tears filled her vision just before his lips swooped down to capture hers.

Light burst behind her closed eyelids, accompanied by absolute rapture. His groan combined with hers, the sound swelling outward until the walls seemed to pulsate with it. And then he lifted his head, nuzzled her neck, and murmured words touched with sweetness.

"Oh, Cassandra. My dearest! My lady. My only—! I thought I'd lost you!"

"Rhoenne!" Cassandra said.

"Oh, sweet. I was a-feared I'd never see you again. This is...almost too much!"

He lifted her closer. Put his nose to her throat and inhaled a huge breath. Blew it out his mouth. Did it again. The second time his exhalation carried more words.

"Oh, dearest God, thank you! There are *nae* words I can offer! Nae prayers or praises—!"

His voice stopped. His breath halted as well. He wore a shirt beneath his *feile brecan,* but it was damp. The material might as well have been painted onto him. She was pressed tightly against his abdomen. The babe made a healthy barrage of thumps against him. Rhoenne's head lifted. His gaze caught hers. His eyes went wide. He blinked and stared at her uncomprehendingly for a moment before looking down at where the mound of babe was pressed to him.

Back up to her face.

Down to the mound again.

Back to her face.

Comprehension brought a stunned, thunderstruck expression. "You carry...a *bairn?*"

The last word was a whisper, an octave higher than his normal vocal range. Cassandra pulled her lower lip into her mouth. Lifted her eyebrows. Smiled. And then nodded.

"Ah. Ah. Ah! Ah! *Ah!*"

He shoved his head and shoulders back farther with each repetition. His knees bent, his back arched. The cries grew in volume and timbre. The last one was roared until he ran out of breath. And then he just stood there. Trembling. His head flung back. Every bit of him taut. Defined. Sculpted.

He pulled in a breath, moved his gaze back to hers, and held it. His eyes weren't just the vivid blue she adored, they were much hotter. Much more intense. And filled with a heart-stopping emotion that touched on the divine. She'd never seen anything like the look he gave her. She didn't think anyone had.

He shook his head slightly, stood upright and shifted her in his arms, loosening his hold slightly. Then he backed to the bed and sat, holding her atop his lap. He was breathing hard, moving her up with each inhalation, dropping her with the exhalation. His right arm held her sealed to him, while he moved the other, tilting her chin up. And then he lowered his head and matched his forehead to hers, to gaze deep into her eyes.

Exactly as he'd done the night he'd proposed.

It sent almost exactly the same rush of emotion, too. Excitement. Enticement. Adoration. All amidst a flood of liquid heat. The door shut softly. Cassandra barely heard it.

"Oh, my sweet. Cassandra."

He closed his eyes. Lifted his head away. Several seconds passed as Cassandra looked him over. He was thinner, but that just made him much more defined. He'd shaved fairly recently, too. A slight growth of whisker shadowed his lower jaw and upper lip, giving him a rakish appearance. The man was entirely gorgeous... just so handsome. He possessed heart-stopping features. A palace champion physique. Memories of him had awakened her in the throes of dream-filled passion more than once. Moist with desire. Beset with yearnings.

The reality of being with him - actually looking at him - brought it all back. He moved his head down and caught her glance. His lips twisted and he colored slightly as if he knew her thoughts.

"I can na' believe this," he whispered. "I can na'. 'Tis a dream. I'm half a-feared if I move wrong, I'll awaken."

"My thoughts exactly," she answered.

"There are *nae* words...or my tongue cannot find them." His voice got hard. It matched how his chest tensed. "Na' three nights ago I was filled with such blackness! I was setting plans in motion. Changing destiny. I was going back to find you. No matter how long it took, or where the search sent me."

"Find me?"

He lifted his left arm. Her armband was on his wrist.

"We bought this at the marketplace. They said—! They said—!" He gave a sobbed sound before continuing, "I was told you'd been *sold*!" He scrunched his eyes shut and shook for several moments.

"Oh, no. No. Rhoenne, No." Cassandra cried.

Rhoenne took a deep breath, and opened his eyes. There was a definite film atop them, making the blue sparkle. "I can na' tell you what

I have envisioned. The nightmares I've had. I can't. There are *nae* words dark enough."

"I was never sold. My grandmother had me imprisoned! Emin was supposed to see that armband got to you...along with a lock of hair and my missive."

He sighed heavily. "Well. For once. It appears Emin failed."

"No. He wouldn't. He said it got to your man!"

"Whoever he gave it to, it was *nae* Ramhurst. Emin must have trusted the wrong man, and the blackguard sold it. And then disappeared. Not one soul knew where you'd gone! Or in what direction." He swiped a hand across his face. "I cannot finish with this. 'Twas absolute hell. Trust me."

"Oh, Rhoenne, no." She fought tears. A sniff betrayed it.

"'Tis nae time for tears. And it does na' matter who or what or how. Emin has more than atoned for any lapse. I owe that man everything. He kept you safe. In a world of dangers...I cannot even begin to comprehend."

He scooted along the mattress edge toward the headboard, turning so he leaned back against it, holding her against him the entire time. The coverlet bunched as it was pulled beneath him. The burgundy dress was still scrunched against her front. The kirtle gapped where it hadn't been fastened.

"This is too much to absorb. I am with you. You are right here. In my arms! And then. I find out—." He stopped. Swallowed audibly. His voice warbled when he continued, "I find that you carry...my bairn? Oh, sweet! There is *nae* homage for how blest I feel at this moment. I may...uh. I can na'—. I think I—. Can I touch him?"

"Why does everyone think it a son?" She teased.

Rhoenne's hand trembled as he held it above the babe for a few moments, and then he lowered it to her belly. The response was immediate. Several kicks were delivered with accuracy against his palm. Rhoenne's eyes glowed as though lit from within as he felt it. It was her turn to blink back tears.

Rhoenne cleared his throat. "He is strong, yes? Looks to be a...healthy size. That does na' bode well. We may have a new worry, love."

"I am very large for just over four months, but...Mother FitzHugh thinks it's because...there are two babies. Emin is in agreement."

His eyes went even wider. "Two? We are expecting...*twins*?"

"'Tis what is suspected."

He sucked in a shaky breath. Tilted his head back. Every muscle tensed. She waited several moments before he looked back down at her. The film atop his eyes was back. Her eyes filled in response.

"Oh, Cassandra. I can na' take much more," he whispered. "I can na'. My heart feels like it may burst."

Cassandra lifted a hand to smooth a stray lock

of black hair behind his ear. He blinked rapidly. Trembled even harder.

"I do na' ken how to handle any of this. I have been the 'Dark One' for so long. Emotionless. Heartless. I thought I was damned. There was *nae* salvation for me...so it mattered little what I did. I tried to kill everything. My conscience. My heart. And then my soul."

"Because of Aileen?"

He went still. When he spoke his voice was raw. Angered. Tormented. And he searched for words. "She—! You do na' ken! She—!"

"You needn't explain it to me. I knew the moment I met her. That woman is evil to the core. The harem was full of women just like her. They'd pawn their souls to gain and hold power. Why do you think I hid?"

He lifted her with a sigh. "Well. I thought that of all women."

"I know. You told me...even without words. But it wasn't your fault. You could not have been very old when your father wed her."

"Sixteen." The word was harsh.

"Well, I see the trouble already. She met you at sixteen? That is not much younger than me. You were no doubt big, strong, and handsome, for a-certain. Yes?"

Rhoenne sent a glance toward her. His lips twisted. "You think I'm handsome, do you?"

"Immensely. But I am not the lone one," Cassandra told him. "I completely understand why she set her sight on you. You did not stand a chance. But...whatever happened with her, it does not matter, Rhoenne. It is in the past."

Rhoenne smiled with a gentle expression that reached his eyes. "I have something to tell you. Something I did na' think I would ever be worthy enough to say."

"You? Unworthy?"

"Aye. Me. You see...," he gave a heavy sigh. "I had — I mean, I *have* an odd issue with...sleep."

He glanced away. A slight flush started up his neck. A beard would have hidden it. Cassandra's lips quirked. She barely caught the smile. "Really?" she queried.

"I sometimes leave my bed and wander. Move. Speak. Do things I have little to no recollection of once I awaken."

"Such as...our first kiss?"

Rhoenne moved his gaze back to hers. Regarded her for some time. His eyes grew even warmer, and supremely gentle. He smiled finally. "That *was* amazing, wasn't it?" he asked her.

"'Twas my first. And...very intriguing."

She ran her index finger along his lip. He nipped it. Shivers raced her skin. And a babe thumped against Rhoenne's hand where it still rested.

"You are still a vixen, I see." He gave another sigh. "Desirable. Passionate. Beautiful. I would like nothing better than to...hide in this chamber with you. Right now. But...alas. I am the laird. Newly returned. And I've run from the responsibility long enough. Why...the witch awaits me now in the great hall. I shall need my wits about me and a good number of guards."

"Guards?" Cassandra moved her gaze back to his.

"Aye. To keep me from strangling her."

Cassandra smiled. "I see. But...wait. You say she's in the great hall?"

"I did. And she is."

"She actually came out of her rooms? Now?"

"I was told she has given you little trouble. Was that a lie?"

Cassandra shook her head. "No. Thanks to Emin, she was no trouble at all. She just has not come from her area since my arrival. I didn't let it bother me. I thought it a blessing."

"But the great hall is her area. Her chamber is above it."

"Not anymore, it's not."

"She's na' in the chieftain chamber?"

"No. I had her moved to the east tower...the one your brother used. She is his widow. That is her station. I have had the chieftain rooms cleared and cleaned. And then I had them blessed."

Rhoenne considered her for a long moment. "That must have incensed her."

"One can hope."

He grinned. "So, the witch has been in the east tower. And she is now out in the open. Was she under orders to stay?" His voice hardened. As did everything about his frame. His muscles twitched.

"Not from me. She stayed of her own accord. It was an act. She portrayed suffering for those who still believe her. We've intercepted several missives to...certain men...as to her imprisonment and unfair treatment at my hands, as if 'twere true."

"Tell me the names. I'll round them up."

"No need. Angus FitzHugh is a verra good steward and his brother, Rory is a competent captain. There are eight men in the dungeons thus far."

Rhoenne grunted. "Only eight? She must be slowing down."

"That's...disgusting, but not surprising. You say she is in the great hall?"

"Aye. Under guard."

"Was she dressed and arrayed with care? To show off her slim perfection?"

"That witch? We can na' be speaking of the same creature."

"She is a beautiful and desirable woman, Rhoenne."

"Na' to me."

She put a hand to her breast. "Oh, Rhoenne. How I love you. But...look at me. Just look. I am already large and ungainly. I have never been so—so cumbersome. And I just found a blemish on my face!" She pointed to her cheek.

He held her closer and huffed something that sounded like amusement. "Cassandra. Love. You are the most beautiful woman I have ever seen. And now that you carry my sons—? Oh. That gives me such thrill to say! I may puff out my chest with pride. Just watch me." He licked his lips and took a breath that trembled. "I vow...this ungainliness you speak of? The size my sons have caused? It makes you even more beautiful than

JACKIE IVIE

afore...if such a thing is possible."

"You truly think so? I have been so troubled. Worried. Of what would happen when you saw me again...compared me to her. She is very interested in you. She will wish you back. And... she has a lot of—"

"Back?"

He interrupted, pulling his head away and regarding her for long moments. His eyelids narrowed. His cheeks sucked in. "Cassandra Alexandria Ramhurst. My lady wife. I do na' ken what she has told you, but anything other than complete disgust is a lie. I swear to you – on everything I hold most holy – that I never touched that woman."

"Never?" she asked.

"Ever. I thought I had. I believed I'd forced myself on her during a sleep walk. I have since learned that she placed me and acted a part...in order to be discovered by my own sire. 'Twas that which caused his death."

Cassandra gasped. "Oh, dear God. How...vile."

"Vileness is simply her beginning point. Grant said she is akin to a mud puddle. Ugly with filth. Dark with ooze. The man was na' wrong. Now that I think on it, strangling is too good. That woman plants destructive thoughts in men's heads." He hung his head. "I believed I was a brute. Capable of...vicious things. Bestial. And so, I lived accordingly...especially in regard to women."

"I hope you don't refer to our wedding night, Rhoenne Ramhurst, because that was fain perfect. I have often envisioned it..." Her voice took on a husky timbre. She lowered her eyelashes. "At night. Alone. In this big bed...that once belonged to you."

She flashed a glance toward him. Shied away. She felt a definite stir in the lap she sat atop. A blush slowly suffused her face and throat, sending warmth clear to her hairline.

He touched a kiss to her nose. "So beloved. So beauteous. And so desirable."

"You still find me desirable?"

He slid her against his groin. Back and forth. Lifted his brows. "You need ask?"

Her lips parted. He groaned slightly. Trembled. His arms tightened for a moment.

"Oh, love. You are so perfect. So totally... perfect. You make me forget all else."

"Good."

He shifted her in his arms, held her against his belly again, scooted to the mattress edge, and stood. He cradled her in his arms, looking down at her with a smile. "I thought you said you were large. Cumbersome."

"I am," she replied.

"You are a slip of a thing. Beautiful beyond belief. Beloved past all reason. And I will na' allow you to stay a moment longer in this small tower."

"But...I like it."

"You say the chieftain's chambers have been cleared? Prepared. And blessed? Well. I am the laird of the Ramhurst clan. Earl of Tyneburgh. Chieftain. I've run from my responsibilities long enough. Time to take my rightful place. With my lady at my side. Emin!"

He smacked the door with a boot. Emin opened it, and stepped back for them pass him. He was grinning, and looked flushed. But that could be because Nessa wasn't the only FitzHugh lass keeping him company on the landing.

She'd been joined by a flirtatious Maysie.

CHAPTER THIRTY-ONE

T HE MAIN DOOR to the chieftain room opened. The one above the great hall.

Emin stepped out first, put his fingers to his lips and gave a whistle. A solitary drum started up. The beat was thunderous. Loud. And necessary. Almost deserted earlier, the great hall had grown crowded in the interim. Rhoenne gave a quick glance below. A row of guardsmen hovered at the bottom of the steps, preventing access. Grant and the rest of Rhoenne's Honor Guard stood atop the dais, facing the crowd. They hadn't drawn their swords, but they were definitely in an aggressive stance. Rhoenne could just make out the top of Aileen's white caplet as if she cowered behind them.

Bagpipers started up next, sending a blaring sequence of notes throughout the room. The sound reverberated as it died away. Everyone looked up. Gawain MacDuff had been the clan *bladier* as long as Rhoenne could remember. The man stood two steps down from the landing. He had a massive voice, demonstrating why he held the position.

"Ramhurst clan! Listen, one and all! Just as you have heard! Our laird has returned and—!"

"Oh, Lord! I can na' believe it!"

A female voice interrupted, and then she punctuated her words with a squeal. A din of noise burst out. Voices yelled cheers, drums thumped. More than one piper put a long-winded whine into the mix. MacDuff yelled more than once for quiet. It took some time before the crowd complied. Rhoenne stood beside Emin in the shadow of the open doorway. Watching. Waiting. The circular landing he was about to enter had been designed with this type of presentation in mind. Despite it being mid-afternoon and a day filled with low-hanging snow-cast clouds, weak daylight managed to stream through two high windows, creating a spotlight on the landing. The chandelier above glowed brightly with candle-filled lanterns. Lit torches on either side of the door added to the effect. Rhoenne turned his head and winked at Cassandra.

She wore a burgundy dress atop a light-gray kirtle. A silver collar spanned her shoulders. A matching headpiece covered the crown of her head. Both pieces had been rushed from the Ramhurst treasury. She looked radiant. Cool and elegant. Refined. Rhoenne pursed his lips. Beneath lurked a woman of immense passion and ardor...and he couldn't wait to appreciate it. The cold water bath he'd taken in the cistern hadn't been just for cleansing.

As if she knew his thoughts, she lifted her fingers to her lips and blew him a kiss. Rhoenne's knees wobbled, some of his weaponry rattled. And then MacDuff started orating again. Rhoenne lowered his chin, and gave Cassandra a look that made her gaze shy away. If he wasn't mistaken, she blushed. And then he turned back and listened for his cue.

"Ramhurst clan! Behold! Just as you have heard! The Earl of Tyneburgh has returned! I present Rhoenne Guy de Ramhurst! Our rightful laird and chieftain!"

"Oh my."

Rhoenne heard Cassandra's awed words a moment before the cheers started up again. He stepped out three steps, entering the light, and stood looking over the gathering. He straightened even more. His throat closed off. His eyes stung. His heart filled. It was more than pride. It was honor and respect.

He pulled the ceremonial claymore from its scabbard at his back and lifted his arm. The blade was old, heavy, had been used in battle more than once. The sound of cheers swelled to a roar, especially with the addition of drums and bagpipes. Rhoenne's arm was trembling before sheathed his blade. The room quieted. He turned and held his hand out for Cassandra. Nodded at MacDuff.

"And I present to you our countess, the princess Cassandra!"

She stepped out, gliding toward him. And then every man pulled the tam from his head, put sword tips to the wooden floor, and went down onto a knee, while the women joined them. He lifted Cassandra's fingers to his lips, and pulled her to his side. Rhoenne took a breath.

"Rise, Ramhurst clan!"

His voice rang out, as loud as, yet even deeper then the *bladier*. The response was immediate and loud. Rhoenne didn't wait. He motioned MacDuff to precede them down the steps. Rhoenne kept Cassandra at his side, nearest the wall. She couldn't possibly see what was happening. Her head barely reached his shoulder. Her fingers trembled within his. Her glances were filled with something massive; Love, trust ... and pride. His throat closed off. His heart pounded. He blinked back the wayward emotion.

And his chest was definitely puffed out.

The guards made a corridor for them. Rhoenne moved Cassandra to his left side and strode firmly to the dais, his boots thumping with each step. The *bladier,* MacDuff was on Rhoenne's right side, making quick steps. Cassandra somehow kept pace effortlessly, as if she knew his intent. Rhoenne had a crowd to impress. He may be their laird by birth, but he was a leader on his own merit. He'd earned it. He was undefeated list champion. He'd been the largest back then. He was even bigger now. Save for Emin two steps behind at his back, few men neared him in height, and none had the same brawn.

At their approach, his four Honor Guardsmen moved as a unit to stand side-by-side at the front of the platform, swords held before them, hilts at their chests, tips down. They hadn't had an opportunity to bathe or change. It actually added to their impact. They looked more than impressive. They looked battle-honed, and ready. He could barely see the bottom of Aileen's skirt behind their legs.

The woman needed protection? Here, in the great hall of Tyne Castle? From Ramhurst clan?

That was interesting.

Rhoenne pondered it as he escorted Cassandra up the steps. He walked with her to his chair at the center. All the chairs were large, but the chieftain's was especially massive. Aileen stood beside it, giving mute challenge with her stance. She had her head flung back. Two spots of color stained her cheeks. Her lips were tongue-moistened. She wasn't much taller than Cassandra.

"Step to your place," Rhoenne told her.

"Good eve to you, too, Rhoenne."

Her voice was a sultry sound. Rhoenne felt Cassandra stiffen slightly.

"You are na' countess, Aileen," he informed her.

"Well. I would be, save that you are such a... poor lover," she lowered her voice on the last two words, using a huskier tone, alluding something illicit. Forbidden. Secretive. And shared.

He knew her intent. He recognized it. She didn't speak for his benefit. Nor was it directed to the Honor Guardsmen. The words were meant for Cassandra. Aileen was watching for any reaction from his wife. Cassandra must not be responding the way she was supposed to for a slight frown marred Aileen's forehead as Rhoenne narrowed his eyes and lowered his chin.

"It will na' work on me anymore, *sister.*"

Rhoenne couldn't prevent the sneer as he spoke her title. "I never touched you. That time, or any other. You know it. As do I." He lowered his voice to a throb of sound.

"You...disclaim it now, do you?"

"You wish to hear it from Grant, do you?"

She paled. He tried not to let the flush of success show, but it colored his voice. "Thanks to him, I now ken exactly what you did to me. And to my father. Exactly."

Something resembling fear flashed across her eyes, but it was instantly gone, replaced by a sheen of glass-like opacity. He realized Henry had been right all those year earlier. Aileen was definitely a serpent. He should have guessed what next she'd say.

"I suppose you'll next claim you did na' run from a charge of murdering your younger brother five years past?"

The four guardsmen stiffened. Someone gave a gasp. Cassandra's fingers tightened within his, but she didn't give any outward sign that Aileen had said anything shocking. Rhoenne kept his gaze on Aileen as he lifted Cassandra's hand to his lips. He gave her fingers a lingering kiss before letting go. And then he vaulted up to stand on the seat of the chieftain chair. He swiveled toward the crowd and pulled in a large breath.

"Ramhurst clan!" he bellowed.

There was an instant pause throughout the great hall. Rhoenne filled it with more yelled words. "I stand before you now. The fifth Earl of Tyneburgh! Chieftain by birth – but afore you accept me, I must tell you something that may change your minds!"

Silence greeted his words. Rhoenne continued.

"I left you five years back...na' because I wished to, but for a reason! A grave tragedy. This is about the death of my bairn brother, Bhaltair...and my part in it. I need to explain. Speak of things long buried. You see, 'twas a day like any other. Spent hunting. Fishing. What happened is—!"

A loud blast from more than one piper drowned out his words. The sound emanated from the entry and continued on unabated as if he hadn't been addressing his clan. Rhoenne wasn't the only one glaring as KilCreggar clansmen in black and gray *plaide* poured into the chamber. They spanned outward until they numbered several score. They had swords bared and spears lifted, looking exactly like a clan on unfriendly terms.

And then they hoisted his friend and mentor, Henry FitzHugh onto a table.

"Apologies, my laird! They would na' have been allowed through the gates, save for the man with them. 'Tis clansman...Henry FitzHugh!" MacDuff announced nonsensically.

Henry pointed across the room right at Rhoenne. "Greetings, Laird Ramhurst!" Then he swept his arms outward to include the room. "And may I extend greetings to all the members of Clan Ramhurst assembled herewith! I have brought KilCreggar clan to also...greet you! We've ridden non-stop to make it!"

"Why bring them here? You ken the consequences!"

"They told me a grand tale, Ramhurst. While they were sheltering me and the wife."

"Wife?" Rhoenne's outburst was joined by several voices simultaneously.

"Do na' be so shocked. Rhoenne Ramhurst is na' the lone man to return from the east with a wife. I have also just wed. Her name is Ida. Someday you may all meet her! But that is na' the reason I am here, nor why I have brought the KilCreggar clan laird with me! Laird Dughall, show yourself!"

A balding, red-bearded man stepped up onto the table beside Henry. The man was in fine shape for his age but had a definite paunch. He had his sword drawn, and planted the tip into the wood at his feet. Rhoenne regarded the duo for long moments.

"This is a surprise Laird Dughall KilCreggar! But I do na' ken the need for arms. We have na' been at actual war for years."

"We soon might be," Henry responded.

That comment got a lot of reaction. Several voices shouted for quiet. It wasn't until the pipers started up again that the room settled down enough to hear.

"What have you done, FitzHugh?" Rhoenne asked loudly.

"This is na' about me, Ramhurst! You ken exactly what it's about and why I have come."

Rhoenne's blood went icy. His heart dropped. "*Nae,* Henry. No. I forbid it. If you say one word—."

"You will banish me," Henry interrupted

loudly, finishing the threat. "After you flay me. I ken. You made it verra clear. Well. I accept the terms. And have provided for them! Should any of that happen, I have taken a new laird.... and a new clan." Henry opened his Ramhurst plaid cloak and dropped it, revealing he wore KilCreggar *sett* beneath it.

His announcement was swallowed up by an outpouring of angered voices that continued unabated until the pipers drowned them out again.

"You can na' change clan allegiance, Cousin!" Angus spoke when words could again be heard.

"Of course, I can. Any man can. 'Tis a free land!"

Rhoenne took a deep breath. Tried for calmness. A voice of reason. "Henry. Do na' do this."

"What choice have I got?" Henry replied.

"Damn you, FitzHugh! On the memory of my father, I beg it of you!"

"And you already ken...that is just why I must speak!" Henry's voice broke.

Rhoenne pulled his sword over his shoulder again and held it aloft. "I challenge you to a battle. Right now. Afore you say one word!"

"Verra well! I accept! But not until *after* I have spoken!"

"I will na' let you do this!"

He had to reach Henry. Pull him off the table. And throttle him.

Rhoenne leapt down, hit the floor of the dais, preparatory to launching toward Henry and the laird of KilCreggar. He didn't even see Grant's arm. The blow hit Rhoenne's midsection, and sent him reeling into a smaller chair. His sword fell with a clatter. The chair rocked backward precariously. And no one even noticed because Grant jumped up onto the chieftain seat and started his own spate of yelling.

"Wait! All of you! Wait! Afore we go to bloodshed, let me speak!"

"Speaking now is Grant Ramhurst, cousin of the earl!" MacDuff orated.

"I am Viscount Tyneburgh now! His Majesty awarded me the title na' three days past. Henry FitzHugh kens this. He was there."

Most of the crowd looked at Henry. He nodded.

Rhoenne was desperate. Almost panicked. He had to do something before the Ramhurst name and legacy was shamed forever. Yet the moment he thought it, Cassandra was there. She perched at the edge of the adjacent chair, reached for his hand and laced her fingers through his. Rhoenne lifted his gaze to hers and everything altered. His heartbeat. His pulse. His hearing. Even time.

Her eyes widened suddenly and she gave a slight gasp. He watched her place her free hand atop their babies. The beatific smile she gave him instantly pacified. Everything felt right. And warm. And completely peaceful. Despite the words that would soon be spoken. And what might ensue. Rhoenne blinked several times with the surprise.

"Verra well. Ramhurst clan! I present to you

Grant Ramhurst, Viscount Tyneburgh!"

MacDuff said it loudly in his official voice. Nobody cheered, making Grant's words easily heard.

"I want to hear what Henry FitzHugh has to say. I need to ken what this is about. As should we all!"

There was a chorus of 'ayes' throughout the great hall. The sound echoed through the room as it quieted again.

"Well, Henry. We await your words. Speak them!"

Grant ordered it. Rhoenne closed his eyes, tipped his head back, and forced each breath to follow the next in a calm, modulated fashion.

Betraying nothing.

"I want you to ken afore I start...that this is the most difficult thing I have ever done. I swore a vow of secrecy over this and I have always been a man of my word."

Rhoenne bit back an acidic retort about the keeping of vows. And how a man's word was his bond. Never to be broken. But then realization hit him worse than Grant's blow. He was guilty of the same. He'd violated a vow when he'd wed Cassandra.

As if to punctuate things, a stifled chortle sounded from Aileen. Rhoenne swallowed. He didn't turn to where she still hovered, on the other side of Grant. He didn't care what expression she'd have.

"Your banishment will depend on what you tell us. And if Rhoenne retains leadership of the clan once we hear," Grant said solemnly.

"Oh. He will."

"What makes you so certain?" Grant asked.

"Because I was there the day Bhaltair Ramhurst died. I ken what happened. I just did na' ken all of it until recent."

Silence descended on the hall. Rhoenne noted absently that Aileen was no longer chuckling.

"Go on," Grant prompted.

"Your laird was about to speak on how Bhaltair died. And what caused his death."

There was a collective gasp. Rhoenne's shoulders flinched.

"Rhoenne said it was a day of hunting and fishing. 'Tis true enough. He was successful, too. I was on watch. He had just killed a red deer and was dressing it out with a skean. That's when I saw Bhaltair. The lad was less than ten paces behind his brother. Ten paces! You ken how close that is! The lad had his bow pulled... with an arrow at the ready."

Cassandra's fingers clenched on his. Rhoenne slid his thumb pad along her finger.

"I was too far away to change anything. I shouted a warning. Too late. As I raced toward them I watched Bhaltair shoot his brother – right in the back. Rhoenne heard or mayhap he sensed something, for he moved. That is why the arrow did na' spear his heart. It went in about here. And it was sticking out...right here."

Henry pointed to the spots on his ribs, back and then front. There was another collective gasp from the crowd, several cries, and more than one woman sounded like she wept. Rhoenne didn't react. He knew where the scars were. So did Cassandra.

"You recall the laird had been using his skean on the deer, aye? Well. He did na' go down easy."

Rhoenne stopped breathing. His heart felt like it was in a vise. Getting squeezed. And Henry just kept talking.

"He twisted and launched his blade as he fell, and—."

"Ah ha! So he did murder his brother!" Aileen screeched it.

"Silence!" Grant hurled the command. It sounded like Aileen backed a step

"*Nae!*" Henry yelled. He sounded hoarse. "Rhoenne was bad hurt. His skean did na' look well-tossed. But I did na' actually see it." His voice lowered. "I am mortified to admit afore you all. Even now. I fell. Hit my head on a rock. Me. Castle champion. I was na' there to save my laird."

Henry paused. The man was a consummate storyteller with a flair for dramatics. It felt like the entire space held its breath. Rhoenne was on his feet again, eyes narrowed on Henry, listening intently. He'd pulled Cassandra up with him. He'd been certain his blade killed Bhaltair. He'd lived with the knowledge for five long years... only to find it might be false?

"Well? Go on! Tell us! What happened next?" Grant prodded, breaking the silence.

Henry stepped closer to the man beside him and put a hand on his shoulder. "This part is why

I brought KilCreggar clan with me. Laird Dughall KilCreggar? You tell them what happened next!"

Laird Dughall KilCreggar lifted his head to pull in a large breath, leaned a bit on his sword, rolled his head on his neck, exhaled, and then lowered his chin to regard those on the dais.

"Well. You see. A small band of us were about on the lands that day. Hidden."

"You were on Ramhurst land? Reaving?" Grant burst out.

"Na' exactly...although I will na' speak of our original intent. No one saw us. We were well-hid. We watched the earl take down his deer. Watched the younger lad approach. I can name the clansmen with me. I gave them orders na' to interfere. 'Twas exactly as FitzHugh says... but there comes a point when a man can na' sit quiet and allow murder. You ask who killed Bhaltair Ramhurst? Well. I confess. 'Twas me. I launched the blade. And I happen to have a verra good aim."

The man gave another healthy sigh before continuing.

"Henry FitzHugh came upon us as we reached the lads. We helped with getting the arrow out. 'Twas a right bloody ordeal. I did na' ken the earl failed to recollect this. He fought all of us mightily, raining curses down on our heads throughout."

"So, why did you run away?" Grant asked.

"Run away? You accuse a KilCreggar of cowardice, young viscount? Now? Afore so many witnesses?"

"'Twas na' cowardice. They were following my orders!" Henry was definitely hoarser. His voice was a scrape of sound.

"Why would you give such an order?"

Rhoenne asked it as he stepped between Euan and Graham. They shifted sideways to allow space. He kept Cassandra with him. Henry regarded him for some time before he gave the slightest nod.

"Two reasons. You were bleeding worse than a stuck boar. I needed their help. We were near KilCreggar land, leagues from any Ramhurst croft. You think it easy to heft you, Rhoenne Guy de Ramhurst? And get you up on a horse? It took four of us just to carry your arse. We had to take turns."

There were titters of amusement filtering through the crowd, releasing some of the tension.

"And then I had to make certain you'd live! You were at death's door for more than a fortnight afore I could see you moved. Is that na' true, Laird KilKreggar?"

"In my best chamber," the man replied.

There wasn't a hint of noise from the crowd as Rhoenne stepped nearer to the front of the edge of the dais. "So, what's your other reason, FitzHugh?" he asked levelly.

"This is na' easy for me, Ramhurst. Aside from the oath you made me swear the moment you were well enough."

Henry looked at him with the most heart-rending expression he'd ever received from the man. Rhoenne's eyes stung.

"I believe my reason is the same as yours. The reason you forced my oath of silence. Even though 'twas self-defense, to speak of it would sully Bhaltair's name. And he was a Ramhurst."

The last words trembled. Henry stopped. Cleared his throat. Looked up at the ceiling for several moments. Rhoenne blinked an answering emotion back. Cassandra wasn't as successful. She sniffed at his side. Her breaths were short and shaky. She swiped surreptitiously at her cheeks. Rhoenne squeezed the fingers of the hand he held. She responded in kind. Henry finally lowered his head and continued.

"Bhaltair would never have done harm to you... or anyone for that matter. Na' on his own. I saw his face. The lad was tormented. He looked like a man possessed. I can na' explain it other. I did na' ken how far the plot went, nor how many others might be involved. All I was knew was who was behind it all. It was *nae* hardship. There is but one person who wanted your death. So she could be countess again."

With these words, the entire room full of clansmen and women looked at Aileen.

CHAPTER THIRTY-TWO

———∾∾———

"**B**URN THE WITCH!"

The cry came from the back of the crowd, the speaker anonymous in everything save gender. It was a woman. She wasn't alone in her sentiment. The reaction was immediate as fists were raised. Shouts issued. Aspersions yelled. And a mass of angry clan rushed the dais.

Any question as to why his honor guard had been in an aggressive stance before Rhoenne arrived was answered. The crowd had an ugly side, and a target. Iain and Graham moved to protect his right side. Euan pulled his sword at the front. Grant strode across chair seats to reach Aileen's far side, blade drawn. He was joined by a number of guards as he stepped down. Rhoenne caught a glimpse of Aileen's white face. She was wide-eyed, and her face showed an emotion that might actually be fear.

Rhoenne kept Cassandra against him as he twisted and bent, pulling the ceremonial sword. Emin materialized before them. Rhoenne nodded, released her into the other man's care, got back atop the chieftain's chair, and held his sword high, twisting and turning it to catch any available light.

Drummers started up. Pipers injected a loud discordant whine into the cacophony. More guards filed onto both sides of the dais and filled the space directly before it, making a barrier that effectively stopped the crowd. The guardsmen then fanned out into a semi-circle, pushing clan back. Fists got unclenched. Angry expressions calmed. Some turned shamefaced. Drums and pipes halted. Rhoenne pulled in a deep breath and yelled for silence.

He only did it once.

In concert, as if planned, every Ramhurst went to a knee and bowed their head. A well of silence descended. Soundlessly, KilCreggar clansmen sheathed blades and stepped back to the walls. Laird Dughall put his blade away. Upon seeing that, Rhoenne slid the large broadsword into the scabbard at his back. As a unit, every guardsman did the same with his own weapon. Henry didn't move. He'd folded his arms and regarded Rhoenne from atop the table, his expression unreadable.

Then the *bladier* spoke, his voice altering the surreal quietness. His words sent a thrill up Rhoenne's spine. "Behold! Our true and rightful laird! The earl of Tyneburgh! Rhoenne Guy de Ramhurst!"

Rhoenne cleared his throat. "Rise. All of you! 'Tis na' the time for anger. Na' yet."

There was a rumble that could be agreement. He scanned the room before focusing on the entry door opposite him. He took a deep breath.

"If you accept me as your laird...you accept much. I am known as 'The Dark One'. Emotionless. Ruthless. Merciless. There are more titles. I earned every one. I lived them." He lowered his voice slightly. "Well. You'll need to bear with me. I have never spoken as I am about to."

There was another spate of rumbling from the crowd. Rhoenne took another deep breath and kept speaking.

"Like you, I have just learned...many things. I avoided any memory of that day. If I had recollection of what happened after I fell, it was of pain. Anger. And self-hate. All these years I thought it was my blade that killed Bhaltair. I'd thrown it in self-defense, but I wished it kept silent. *Nae.* I commanded it be kept silent! For a reason. Who among you wants a brother's memory tarnished...as it now will be?" His voice wavered. He cleared his throat before continuing.

"That is why I forced Henry FitzHugh to swear a vow. And he is a man of his word."

He looked directly across at Henry.

"So. I speak to you now, Henry FitzHugh. Your vow is na' broken. It should never have been required. I am rescinding my challenge as well as any punishment. I will na' fight you on the list. Na' over this. Nor are you banished. You are a true clansman, captain of my Honor Guard. Should you choose to again take up the Ramhurst colors, you will be welcomed."

Henry grinned and started stripping. Rhoenne

wasn't the only one with raised brows. It didn't take long to shuck a *feile-brecan*. Henry wasn't a young man, but he was extremely fit. In premium fighting condition. His actions displayed almost all of it. Rhoenne wasn't the lone one relieved to see the man wore a loin-wrap.

They all watched Henry fold and then hand the black and gray sett to the laird of the KilCreggars with a reverent gesture. Then he lifted his Ramhurst *plaide* of gray-and-white with smaller blue and black stripes. Nobody spoke as he wound it about his frame, tucked it beneath his belt, retrieved and secured several skeans. He said something to Dughall. The man nodded. Then Henry jumped down to the floor of the great hall and strode toward the dais. The crowd parted for him. Several men clapped him on the back as he passed. Behind him, the laird of the KilCreggar clan left the tabletop as well, and got swallowed up by the crowd.

Henry chose to access the raised platform using the steps nearest Aileen. Guards moved out of his way. Grant stepped back for him. When Henry reached Aileen, he made a large arc around her, never once taking his eyes from her until he'd passed. Then he reached Rhoenne and stood, although Henry's head was just level with the laird's thigh.

Rhoenne stepped down. Offered his hand. Henry clasped it and gave an iron squeeze. Rhoenne returned it until the man let up. And then they both grinned. All of it immensely satisfying. Rhoenne took another deep breath, and turned back to address the crowd again.

"Now! For my next duty, I will need my captain of the guardsmen! Show yourself!"

"Here!"

"*Nae.* I am here!"

The calls came from opposite sides of the dais. Rhoenne looked left and then right.

"Get down in front. Both of you," he ordered.

He recognized Rory FitzHugh easily. Angus's brother was a larger, younger version of the steward. The other man was clearly a Montvale. He resembled both Iain and Graham. The two men claiming captainship were a like height, approximately the same age, and appeared to have the same brawn, too.

"You both claim to be captain of my guards?"

"Aye!" they replied in unison.

"You!" He pointed to the Montvale. "State your name and your claim."

"Calum Montvale. I am the captain of the guards. I earned the position at the games three years back. I've held off all challenges on the list e'er since."

"And you?" Rhoenne pointed to Rory.

"Rory FitzHugh! I was assigned the duties a sennight ago. Called in by the steward."

"Who just happens to be your brother," Aileen inserted snidely.

There was a collective indrawn breath. Rhoenne turned his head toward her.

"Lady Aileen," he said each word with a promise of deadly intent. "I am ordering you to be silent. Should you speak again, I will toss you to the crowd. And I will na' stop them from burning you. You are warned."

Her eyes widened again. Her lips quivered. She clutched a hand to her bosom. None of it gave him any satisfaction. He turned back to the two men before him.

"So. FitzHugh. The steward recruited you. He must have his reasons. I assume the selection met with the approval of my wife?"

His voice reflected how much he liked saying the term. He didn't bother disguising it. He looked over to where Cassandra stood, Emin behind her, Graham and Iain at her side. She nodded and gave him a quick smile. He returned it but sobered before facing the men again.

"I have my answer. The countess approved your selection. You must have qualifications. Have you any wins in the games or on the list?"

"I did na' compete in the games. Nor did I challenge on the list."

"Why not?"

"I would prefer na' to answer that, my laird."

"Well. I am requiring that you do so. You look fit. You appear brave enough. You're a FitzHugh. You come from a family of warriors. So, I ask again. Why would you na' compete?"

"Because serving at the castle was na' a position of hon—." He caught the word, and cleared his throat as if it was a mistake. "I mean...'twas na' something I had any wish for. My mum was adamant about it. I was also betrothed...if you ken my meaning."

Somebody coughed. Rory was flushed, but he

didn't look away. Nor did he blink. Rhoenne considered the man's steady regard. Calculated his words. Rory was a handsome fellow. Strong. Manly. Exactly the type Aileen would have favored. The man had obviously been avoiding a lose/lose situation. Service meant more than guard duty, while denial meant he'd be shown the gates.

Or worse.

Rhoenne's lip curled with distaste. "Is this true of...other clansmen?" he asked.

"I do na' ken. You will have to ask them," Rory replied.

Rhoenne liked Rory's forthrightness. But there was tradition to consider, and Calum Montvale had earned the position.

"Angus MacHugh!" he called out.

"My laird?"

The steward was at the edge of the platform on Cassandra's side. He stepped down to the main floor, the row of guards let him through. He joined the two men before the dais.

"It appears we have a competition to schedule. Announcements to make. A plan to enact assuring every clansman hears about it. Not only do I need to replace fallen members of my Honor Guard, but I wish to oversee selection of guardsmen for Castle Tyne."

"Verra good, my laird."

"And I want the competition to start with a battle a-tween these two. Calum Montvale and Rory FitzHugh."

Calum and Rory looked at each other. Back

at Rhoenne. Both looked inordinately pleased.

"And now. I have an assignment for you, Rory FitzHugh."

The man took a step toward him.

"I understand we have eight men in our dungeons? Ramhurst clansmen?"

"Aye, my laird. We do."

"I want you to fetch them. Take as many men as you need."

Rory gave him a slight bow before trotting off, pointing to several fellows as he went. The crowd parted easily, letting Rory and at least a dozen others through to the door. As they left, new arrivals entered the same door, brushing snow from their heads and shoulders while stomping feet.

"Angus!" Rhoenne said.

"My laird?" the man asked.

"We seem to have a gathering on our hands of a sudden. And more arrive as I watch."

Ripples of amusement ran the assemblage at his remarks. It continued with the repeating of them.

"It is na' every day the true laird returns...and takes control of the clan."

Rhoenne nodded and rubbed his chin, hoping he looked august and sage. "Well. While we stand about, do we have anything we can offer our guests? Some ale casks to be tapped? Followed by roasted venison or boar...or even mutton?"

"I'll see to it."

The man walked back through the barricade of guardsmen. Calum Montvale watched him go before looking up at Rhoenne.

"Laird Rhoenne?" he queried.

"Calum Montvale," Rhoenne responded.

"I have ever been a loyal clansman," the man remarked.

Rhoenne regarded him for long moments. Then spoke. "Have you ever taken down a deer and found the meat inside was damaged?"

"My laird?" The man was obviously confused. His face was a match to most of those in listening distance.

"Surely you ken of what I speak. You cut your deer open only to discover unusable meat. Perhaps it suffered a past injury. Or perchance 'tis filled with cancer. You ever take down an animal like that?"

"I do na' ken what this has to do with me," Calum answered.

The man wasn't amused. He sounded aggressive and angered. Rhoenne wondered if Calum was the type to spark easily. A quick temper made a man especially easy to take down in any contest. Rhoenne regarded him again. Calum wouldn't meet his gaze.

"Once you open an animal like that – riddled with rot, there is little you can do about it save find the source and start carving. You cut as much and as deeply as you have to. There may be good meat there. You just have to look closely. Because some of it...may na' look bad on the surface."

Montvale straightened. His mouth thinned and a flush rose up his cheeks, visible above his beard.

"Do na' fash, Calum Montvale. I do na' hold

a man's past against him. The new viscount can vouch. You will be given a chance to prove loyalty. Every mon will. When it's time."

"And, until then?"

"Well, for now...you are to stay exactly where you are. I think we both ken why."

Calum flashed him a look that didn't just contain anger. It held apprehension. Rhoenne noted that both Iain and Graham were studiously looking above their relation's head. Rhoenne turned and took two steps to where Cassandra stood.

"You need to sit, sweet?" he asked softly.

She nodded. He held out his hand for hers, and brought her to the chair beside his. Waited as she sat. Leaned down, his words meant just for her.

"You are taking this exceptionally well, love," he told her.

"You would na' truly...let them burn her. Would you?"

He kissed the tip of her ear to whisper his reply. "As long as she thinks so."

"I knew it."

And then she smiled.

Rumbling sounds filled the front entryway, heralding the arrival of Rory FitzHugh, the guardsmen, and a contingency of eight shuffling souls with downcast heads. They all wore chains, adding to their burden. Their appearance stopped all conversation. The crowd parted to let them through to the dais, stepping away as if a touch might taint. Their appearance sent an obvious message. Any time spent in the Ramhurst dungeons was an unpleasant matter.

The semicircle of guardsmen opened to allow the prisoners through. Montvale stood to one side, clearly making a distinction between himself and the new arrivals. Rhoenne recognized most of them – if not by name, then by family representation. And he had no trouble picking out the stable hand Lachlan MacDuff – the first man Rhoenne had seen visiting Aileen's bed. He looked even worse than normal. The fellow always smelled of horse manure. Today it looked like he'd rolled in it.

The prisoners stopped. Rory walked among them, pulling them apart using their shackling. Then he stepped forward, lifted his head, and met Rhoenne's gaze.

"I have brought the prisoners, my laird," he loudly announced.

Two of them remained stiffly straight. A couple shifted back and forth, their movement rattling iron. One was extremely lean, or young. It wasn't possible to tell since he didn't look up. Rhoenne regarded the group for a few moments, absently wondering what quantifier linked them other than their gender.

"Is there any among you wishing to speak for the whole?" Rhoenne asked finally.

"I do na' eve ken why I'm here!" The largest man spoke, shoved his head back, looked up, and then his mouth fell open. "Rhoenne? Rhoenne Ramhurst? It is truly you?"

Some of the others looked up. Stared.

"Aye. 'Tis me. Your laird. Newly returned from

the seventh crusade. And I find na' a welcoming castle...but one infested with vipers."

The speaker looked puzzled. "I do na' ken your words. I did naught. My name is Camdyn MacHugh, my laird. I work at the smithy. I was asleep when I was seized three days past."

"Rory?" Rhoenne asked.

"He was sent a missive, my laird. Same as these other two." He motioned to the specified men.

"A missive?" The man looked at the others in confusion then back up at Rhoenne. "This is over a...message? I got *nae* missive."

"Rory?"

"He is correct, my laird. The messages were na' received."

"But we have them?"

"Of course. They were intercepted almost the moment they were written. Save for Lachlan, and...this...lad here."

Rory pulled the lean prisoner out of the line as he spoke. The fellow was young, resembling LeRoy FitzHugh in stature and age. Rhoenne heard Aileen's choked reaction. She sounded angered. Frustrated. And exasperated.

Rory continued. "Lachlan's message was na' written. He does na' read. His message was sent via this lad – who also works in the stables."

"What is his name?" Rhoenne asked.

"Arran."

The lad lifted his head and gave a head toss to shift hair off his face. His glance went toward the dais, then away. He didn't appear cowed. Quite the opposite. He looked to be a hot-tempered type, quarrelsome. His upper lip was even lifted in a sneer.

"Surname?" Rhoenne requested.

"He does na' have one. He's an orphan."

Rhoenne grunted. "What is his crime?"

"We caught him scaling the castle wall."

"Climbing walls is a crime?"

"'Twas the east wall, my laird."

"Hmm. That is na' an easy climb."

"Especially with how he managed it. The lad used skeans - two of them. He inserted blades into the smallest of cracks. We could na' believe our eyes, even as we caught him. He was given a message to deliver to Lachlan MacDuff, along with a small signet ring for payment."

"One, you took!" Arran burst out aggressively.

Rory yanked on his shackle. The lad stumbled but instantly corrected it. He gave Rory a belligerent-looking glare.

"The lad is correct. We have the ring."

"You are an efficient captain, Rory FitzHugh," Rhoenne told him. "But I am na' certain Arran's crimes warrant a stay in the dungeons."

"The lad is slippery, my laird. And the ring has...recognizable ownership."

Rhoenne grunted. "I see. Arran?"

The lad blew a desultory sigh through his lips before glancing at the dais.

"You like blades, do you?"

Arran shrugged his shoulders and moved his gaze to Rhoenne. It held the same antagonistic look he'd just given Rory. Rhoenne was hard-put not to laugh. It was too close to how he'd once regarded his elders.

"You appear to need a strong hand, young man. One, with an expertise in blades. Emin?"

"Yes, Excellency?"

The eunuch stepped forward, dipped his head in a bow before straightening back upright. If anything the lad looked even less impressed.

"This is my wife's personal guard. He's from the east. He is an expert with blades. Emin? Show the lad."

Emin rapidly tossed knives at Arron, pulling them one-by-one from his belt, alternating hands. The blades smacked into the wood floor at the lad's feet, advancing in a line that stopped where a toe stuck out the end of the lad's boot. Arran jumped backward. Emin's next toss was right in front of the same toe. The next knife landed right beside it, thrown so quickly, the two blades clacked together.

Arran's high-pitched cry didn't just hold fear. The lad was clearly awed. The crowd shared his reaction. Shocked sounds were followed by an instantaneous burst of applause. Arran was open-mouthed and wide-eyed, and looking up at Emin with a completely different expression than his previous.

"Emin?" Rhoenne called out when his words could again be heard.

"Excellency?" Emin turned and gave him another bow.

"How do you feel about gaining an apprentice?"

"You speak of the boy? This...Arran?"

Emin's voice held a hint of repugnance. The

lad's shoulders went back. And his upper lip lifted in a sneer again.

"I do," Rhoenne answered.

Emin jumped down from the platform. He was taller and a lot more muscled than most of the others. He crouched to pluck blades, stashing them in his belt as he advanced toward Arran. Emin stood after pulling the last two, looked down at Arran while twirling the blades in his fingers, and then he flung them right back into the floor where they'd been. Without once breaking eye contact.

To his credit, Arran flinched but didn't move. Applause rang out as the two stood regarding each other. Then Emin stepped back. Turned toward the dais.

"Excellency?" he addressed Rhoenne.

"Aye?"

"I accept responsibility for this apprentice."

Arran gave a whoop. It was immediately stifled. It didn't help. The lad had a rosy flush. And a smile that flashed across his face more than once as the audience hooted and clapped.

"Rory? Unshackle the lad. His apprenticeship begins immediately."

The sound of irons being removed was loud. Arran rubbed at his wrists when he'd been freed, then stepped closer to Emin. The eunuch put a hand on the boy's shoulder and directed him toward the dais. The platform was four steps above the main floor. It was a healthy jump. Emin made it look easy as he vaulted onto the platform. Arran backed up for a slight run, before accomplishing the same maneuver. Emin resumed his position at Cassandra's far side. Arms folded. Resolute. Arran stood beside him, and assumed the same stance.

Rhoenne's gaze dropped to Cassandra. His wife was looking at him with tear-filled eyes and a heart-melting smile. Rhoenne's heart stuttered before he caught it. He quickly moved his glance over her head, and regarded the chandeliers above them. The vaulted ceiling. The high windows. He had a somber demeanor back in place before looking back down at the prisoners.

"Well," he announced loudly. "I have sentenced one of you. The rest of you will na' receive the same leniency. You are na' here because you were a messenger. Your crime is that the sender chose you...and the why of it."

"Except the end three prisoners, my laird," Rory spoke up.

"They have a different transgress?"

"Aye. They were caught at the well early this morn. Afore they could poison it. With monkshood."

The reaction was a moment of shocked silence, followed by a swell of sound. Loud. Vicious. More guardsmen filled the space around the prisoners, pushing the swarm back. Voices shouted for order. Rhoenne turned to look at Aileen. Her eyes resembled opaque green opals. There wasn't one expression on her face.

It seemed the more rot he carved away, the worse it got.

He felt cold.

Almost sick.

And he'd thought her evil before.

The room quieted, showing the three men huddled together at the center of a number of guardsmen.

"Rory?   March those three back to the dungeon," Rhoenne commanded. "They will be tried at dawn. And then executed."

"Wait! My laird! 'Twas na' our idea! We were na' told it was monkshood!" One of the sentenced fellows screamed the words. He gestured toward Aileen. "Why must we pay when—?!"

"Silence!"   Rhoenne roared.   He pulled the broadsword as he went to the edge of the platform. "Or face a beheading right now!"

One swayed, taking the other two with him. Guards closed around them. Keys were produced. Locks opened. The three were separated, and then walked from the cleared area. One was mostly dragged. Sobbed sounds emanated from them. Rhoenne watched with a set jaw. His fingers tightened on the sword hilt. He sent one hard breath after the next as he regarded each of them in turn, including Calum. Every one of them stepped back. Rhoenne finally moved, to place the sword's tip onto the wood at his feet and then he leaned forward, using the weapon for stability.

"Listen closely. The four of you. I have determined a consequence for being a party to this. You may na' even find it onerous."

They looked surprised, but no one spoke.

"I have an offer to make. To one man, and one

man only. The first who accepts will be freed.
I will give you ten pieces of Scot silver. New-
minted, so they'll be nae loss with shaved edges.
Along with a horse. And safe passage from my
fief." Rhoenne paused after each item. "In
exchange you accept banishment...*and* the hand
of Lady Aileen Ramhurst. You ken my offer? You
will wed to her! Right here! And right now!"

Stupefied expressions greeted his offer. Shocked
silence. And Aileen screeched.

"How dare—!"

Rhoenne swiveled and flung the chieftain sword.
It caught the top of Lady Aileen's headdress, and
slammed her backward into a chair. She had a
definite expression on her face now. She stared
at him dumbfounded while the sword swayed
back and forth atop her head. And it wasn't just
swaying. Each swing sliced hair. Locks of it sifted
onto her shoulders as he watched. The sword
was planted through the chair nearly to the hilt,
holding her stuck in place. Any move cut more
of her hair off.

Rhoenne knew he had instant reflexes. A
perfect aim. But even he was stunned. So were
the faces of everyone around him. Grant and
the others moved back so the crowd could see.
Rhoenne threw back his head and howled until
he ran out of breath. Then he was laughing.

But it wasn't heard over roar of approval that
commenced throughout the great hall. That was
ear-splitting.

CHAPTER THIRTY-THREE

"GRANT!" RHOENNE HISSED it to his cousin.

"Aye?"

"I need your sword. Mine is...in use."

Grant chuckled and handed Rhoenne his blade. Rhoenne watched his cousin tap the guardsman beside him. Speak to him. That man also snorted his amusement. He then tapped the man beside him. And so, it continued. All of them were snickering. Aileen's response was a low grumble hurled through her closed teeth.

It didn't sound feminine.

It didn't even sound human.

Her lips were pulled back, baring her teeth. Her eyes narrowed to slits. Her nose wrinkled up. Rhoenne regarded her for a long moment, his face emotionless and hard; the exact countenance a man known to be 'The Dark One' would exhibit.

A rumbling happened at the front of the great hall. It snagged his attention. Immense oaken casks were rolled through the door and into the great hall, followed by small wheeled carts loaded with tankards. Angus waved at him from the foyer. Rhoenne lifted the borrowed sword in response before stepping again to the front of the dais. He looked over the remaining prisoners then began speaking again. His words were for them, but he projected his voice outward so it could be heard and repeated.

"Forgive the interruption, gentlemen. It appears I failed to restrain the bride-to-be afore I made my offer. I have since...corrected that lapse."

The crowd tittered. Some of the guardsmen smirked. A few gave outright grins. Calum Montvale had his head back, chin up, his arms folded, and his feet shoulder–width apart, looking clearly angry. Probably offended. His attitude exactly what Rhoenne would expect from a man whose trustworthiness was being scrutinized. The three shackled men didn't exhibit any response.

Murmurs filtered through the great hall, caused by kegs being tapped, ale poured out. Amid bits of conversation. Rhoenne started talking again.

"Well. You heard my offer, gentlemen. I need a groom for the widow Aileen's hand. But...it has just occurred to me that I have been short-sighted here."

He looked over his shoulder toward Aileen. Her head turned in his direction, shaving more strands of hair from her scalp. Her snarl got more vicious, her choked screams louder, and vivid red spots mottled her throat and face in stark contrast to the pristine white color she'd chosen to wear.

Rhoenne started pacing along the front of the

platform, speaking as he went. "I do na' think many ken how closely my family is connected to one of King David's abbeys. As you know, he constructed four of them: Jedburth, Dryburgh, Melrose, and Kelso."

Rhoenne didn't walk the full length of the dais. He turned at Emin.

"The abbeys are all magnificent edifices to the faith. Truly awe-inspiring. But the one I specifically refer to is Jedburgh. A Ramhurst helped in its construction a century past. We've continued our support ever since," he continued.

Rhoenne used his cousin, Grant as the other end point to his pacing. Then it was back to Emin. A return to Grant. Each time Rhoenne's glance would skim Cassandra's face, her eyes lit with something beautiful and pure. The area around his heart warmed pleasantly.

And then he'd catch sight of Aileen.

The first time, her ugliness paused his step. He couldn't believe his luck. So easily, he could have been one of Aileen's victims, his world one of betrayal and jealousy. Rage. Disgust.

'The Lord works in mysterious ways.'

From nowhere he recalled the priest's words from Batok. They were never more apt. He shook his head slightly before turning around at Emin.

"About Jedburgh Abbey...I completely forgot that it possesses a large nunnery. The prioress hails from Ramhurst clan, or she did five years past. 'Tis little matter, actually. What prioress would turn down a novice that comes with a donation sum of ten Scot *groats*?"

He'd reached Grant again. Rhoenne turned around. Started back.

"This is more than I thought I could offer. I hope you are listening, Aileen?" He paused for a moment before continuing. He didn't truly care if she answered. "You have three choices before you. Marriage and banishment – *if* I can find a willing man; a life of poverty as a nun; or you burn at a stake alongside the men I now have to hang...*because of you*."

He paused in front of Emin. Rhoenne's face must have mirrored the loathing that stained his last words. The eunuch gave him a solemn nod. It looked and felt like approval. Rhoenne took a deep breath, and swiveled.

"But first. Afore we continue this, I need a groom! I can na' seem to get any takers. Perhaps I should sweeten the deal. And open it to a wider group."

Rhoenne stepped at the center of the dais to face the assemblage again. He shouted, but it wasn't necessary. Everyone in the room was avidly listening. They weren't even pouring or drinking ale.

"Ramhurst clan!" he yelled. "I have an offer to make! To any unwed man here! I will give him ten—*nae*! I will make it twenty! You hear that? Twenty new silver *groats*! I now add two horses from my stable. Safe passage from the fief! All in exchange for accepting the hand of the widow, Aileen! Along with banishment, of course. So? Are there any takers?"

"What was that?"

Lachlan MacDuff stirred and lifted his head. The man lifted a hand and smoothed it over his hair and down his beard. The iron chain he wore rattled. He looked unkempt, disreputable. And absolutely perfect for what Rhoenne wanted.

"Did I hear you offer...so much? Just for weddin' with the wench?"

"Do na' even think it, brother!"

The words burst from the *bladier*. Titters, guffaws, and outright jeers ensued. The man had used his large announcer voice. It was impossible not to have heard him.

"'Tis a fortune!" Lachlan responded.

"I'll disown you!"

"I'd be banished anyway, mon. What is your threat over that?"

"Lachlan MacDuff?" Rhoenne inserted quickly. "Are you willing to wed the lady Aileen?"

"Will you look at her, mon! Have you lost yer wits?" Gawain MacDuff yelled, and the words resounded though the chamber.

Everyone did as requested. Rhoenne, included. Aileen's headdress was still stuck to the chair, but she was no longer pinned to it. A handful of hair strands were all that connected her head to her headdress. The entire top of her head was shorn. She'd always taken great care with her hair. She'd had lush, thick, lengthy tresses. He hadn't known how much it added to her attractiveness. Without it, she was colorless and plain. If he factored in her contorted features and how her skin was mottled and dark purple, she was absolutely abhorrent.

She slapped both hands to the top of her head, the move slicing through the few remaining strands keeping her in place. Her new expression was ludicrous, filled with shock, horror, and then mortification. He had a good guess at the cause. She was accustomed to being a much-vaunted and eye-catching beauty. She'd used it not just to manipulate and control, but also to scorn, deride, and mock. Now she was getting a notion of what it felt like to be on the receiving end. The room erupted with laughter, derision-filled hoots, and a massive thumping noise that came from fists on tabletops and stomping boots on the floor.

Aileen jerked at the scarf trailing from the headdress, held it tightly against her head, and looked down, cowering from a public humiliation. Unattached locks of hair sifted onto the floor at her actions. The crowd reaction was uproarious. Rhoenne gestured to get them quiet enough he'd be heard. Lachlan had his nose wrinkled. He looked indecisive.

"Now, wait a bit there, Lachlan MacDuff!" Rhoenne yelled. "Hair grows back, and I will sweeten the pot. How about I give you twenty-five silver pieces?"

"Will you add in a saddle?" the man queried.

"Aye."

"And whiskey?"

Rhoenne tipped his head to one side as if considering. "As much as you can heft."

"And a new sword?"

"You are pushing my good humor, MacDuff," Rhoenne replied.

The fellow grinned, showing he still had some teeth, but they were discolored. No matter who did the appraisal, Lachlan was a seedy, unkempt specimen.

"I was just checkin' on how badly you wished to be rid of her," the man responded.

"If that be the case, I can burn her at a stake without costing much at all," Rhoenne responded.

Surprisingly Lachlan showed he was a handy negotiator. He didn't alter his stance. He didn't counter-offer. He simply waited. He wasn't the only one. The entire crowd seemed to be holding its collective breath. Rhoenne finally took a heavy sigh.

"Oh, verra well. Lachlan MacDuff. I agree to the terms. I will add a sword. I will even toss in a scabbard. But that is my final offer."

"In that event, I accept."

Rhoenne shoved his head back and shouted. "You hear that, clan? We have an offer!"

Crowd noise rose again, radiating about the great hall in waves of sound. Rhoenne waved his arms once more. It didn't take long for quiet this time, as if they sensed blood being drawn...and nobody wanted to miss it.

Rhoenne turned to face Aileen again. "I assume you have been listening, Aileen? In a moment I shall give you a chance to speak. Do na' waste time with excuses. You are being removed from my fief. The only choice you have is how that takes place. Your actions directly resulted in the deaths of my father, my uncle, my brother...and you plotted mine as well."

He didn't bother controlling the disgust and repugnance.

"And now we ken you attempted to poison everyone in the castle!"

He stopped for a moment. Sent a growling noise from deep in this throat.

"You may think this harsh, but I am amazed at my leniency. I only cut your hair when I should have slit your throat. It must be because...at one point, my father – and then my brother – loved you enough to wed with you. They are na' the lone ones to offer you their hearts. And what did you do? You trod on them. All of them."

There was complete silence throughout the room.

"So. What is it to be? Your choice. You may wed with Lachlan MacDuff and leave; you can accept a life of service to the church at Jedburgh; or you will be burned at a stake come sunrise. Do na' make me wait overlong. I will na' hesitate to decide for you. Or...perhaps I should just let the clan choose!"

The crowd reacted. Voices hollered countless slurs. Yelled options. Descriptions. The thumping started up again, too.

Rhoenne regarded her with complete indifference, waiting and watching.

Aileen wasn't contrite. She speared him with a look of pure malice. Her shorn hair was ruinous to her attractiveness. Or perhaps it was just insight into the real ugliness she carried inside. Long moments passed. She finally turned her head away dismissively. Rhoenne turned back to

wave at the crowd again. They stilled as if they'd
been waiting for him.

"Calum Montvale!" Rhoenne called.

The man straightened.

"I need Lachlan MacDuff unshackled and—!"

"No!"

Aileen's screech stopped him. It snagged
Calum Montvale's attention as well. He gave
her a look of complete loathing. Aileen saw it
before looking away again. Rhoenne held back
his smirk.

"You have something to say, Aileen?" Rhoenne
asked.

"I will take...the convent," she whispered.

"Oh. Verra well. Montvale? I have new orders
for you. I want this woman incarcerated in the
east tower. Under *nae* circumstances is she to
have any communication. Do you understand?"

"Perfectly," the man replied.

"Take as many men as you need."

"Now, wait just a moment here! Wait! My
laird, wait! We had a deal!" Lachlan gestured
as he yelled, adding the clinking of iron to his
shouts.

"Oh. I hope you forgive me, Lachlan. Perhaps
when you are freed, you'll consider it proper
recompense?"

"We had a bargain! I said I will marry the
wench! And get the fortune!"

"Apologies, MacDuff. She does na' want you."

"She wanted me well enough afore!"

"She did?"

Rhoenne looked from Lachlan to Aileen and

back, doing his best to act surprised and slightly offended. Despite forcing the recollection away, long nights ago he'd wondered how he'd handle just this event when he returned to his fief. Of all the scenarios, nothing came near the enlightenment and enjoyment he was experiencing. He pointed at Aileen.

"You can na' possibly be referring to the widow!"

"Aye! That be the wench I speak of."

"Lachlan. Please. I've rarely known you to leave the stables. Or bathe, for that matter. And the widow does na' ride. Whatever would she have wanted you for?"

"Service a-tween her legs, mon! And she kens it!"

"No!"

Aileen's screech of anger held something close to embarrassment. Grant sounded like he gagged. Montvale shared his revulsion. Guardsmen throughout the ranks exhibited a like reaction. The crowd found it uproariously funny. Hoots and laughter rang out. Rhoenne was hard-put not to respond in kind. He had to look up to stifle it. He let the merriment continue unabated for several moments before waving his hands for quiet.

"Well. This is...surprising," he spoke, when it calmed enough he could again be heard. "I find your claim fairly...unbelievable. If 'twere any other woman, I'd be challenging you to the list over such a slur! But...I'd best ask her first."

"Why do that? She'll just lie!"

"This is a lot to...consider. We should at least allow a response afore we continue." Rhoenne turned physically to look at Aileen. "Well? You heard the man, Aileen. I am allowing you to speak again. Clansman MacDuff has accused you of – what is it, Lachlan – the sin of fornication? Or do you speak of adultery?" Rhoenne tipped his head toward Lachlan again.

"Both!" the man answered.

Aileen's wail was swallowed by crowd reaction. It wasn't an amused sound this time. There was an undercurrent of anger that permeated the outburst. Rhoenne added the tone to his next question.

"Well, Aileen? Do you have a defense? Is any of this untrue?"

She didn't answer. She didn't look up. She didn't act as if she'd even heard. More of her hair fell off her shoulders to the floor.

"Calum Montvale?" Rhoenne addressed the captain again.

"My laird?"

"Is it still snowing?"

"Snowing?" he repeated.

Rhoenne sighed heavily before looking across to the opposite end of the great hall. "Anyone near the door! Is it still snowing?" he shouted.

Several throats hollered back an affirmative 'aye'.

"My thanks!" Rhoenne yelled back before looking down at Calum again. The fellow was flushed with emotion. His hands balled into fists. Rhoenne regarded him for long moments before explaining. "Snowfall and darkness make journey dangerous. I would na' send any man or beast out in it. That being the case...I seem to have a bit of time afore I make a decision. So. Calum Montvale."

"My laird?"

"Your orders stand. Incarcerate this woman in the east tower. Do na' allow any visitors nor answer any of her requests. Use as many of your men as you need."

The man started pointing to guardsman on either side of him, and those on the dais.

A flurry of activity happened at the entrance again. Rhoenne looked up. Large platters of roasted meats and steaming vegetables were being trundled in, along with a assortment of enormous black kettles, and several carts containing what looked like bread loaves. And then he saw the KilCreggar laird at the doorway, an almost unrecognizable woman at his side. Rhoenne looked over at Henry.

The man grinned, then nodded.

"Ah! It appears the feast has finally arrived!" Rhoenne announced. "Just in time. And look! Sir Henry FitzHugh's new lady is also here. Henry?"

Henry FitzHugh rushed past Emin and his protégé to reach the floor. Rhoenne had been avoiding looking that direction for some time. With good reason. He was acting the part of 'The Dark One'. Looking at Cassandra might be his undoing. Her eyes lit up as she recognized Ida and then she turned to meet Rhoenne's gaze.

Rhoenne made a fist and put it atop his heart. The smile she gave him made her eyes glow. She truly was a beauty, inside as well as out.

"My laird?"

Calum was still below him, in front of the dais. Rhoenne dragged his attention from his wife with reluctance. The man gestured to where several guards hovered about Aileen's chair. She had her head turned aside and her hands gripped to the chair arms like claws. Rhoenne pulled in a breath before he approached. The guardsmen parted for him.

Aileen was no longer beautiful. She looked demeaned, and completely diminished. His gut wrenched slightly. He'd wondered sometimes at the level of satisfaction he'd experience when Aileen was finally punished. Oddly, any pleasure was missing. He didn't feel anything.

Vengeance was hollow.

That was profound.

He lowered his voice so only the closest could hear. It still throbbed with menace. "Aileen. If you do na' get to your feet and walk with these men, I will have you dragged off. I will na' care if you are kicking and screaming o'er it. In fact – I believe the clan will find it verra enjoyable."

She stood. Guards surrounded her, their height making it difficult to spot her shaved head as they moved off the dais. Calum joined them at the main floor, finally assuming the lead. If Rhoenne placed a wager on the first bout of the upcoming games, it wouldn't be on Calum. He waited until they disappeared from the hall before speaking

again.

"Euan? Iain? Graham?" The men were at his side almost instantly.

"My laird?"

"I do na' ken if you noted things, but my wife—," Rhoenne stopped on the title. His voice warmed. He glanced in her direction, smiled, and then cleared his throat. "She...uh. Carries my bairns."

Eyes widened and their jaws dropped. The three of them looked over to Cassandra and then back. Rhoenne met their return glances with a wide grin. He didn't bother hiding it.

"That being the case, she probably hungers. And thirsts."

"Oh. Aye. We will see to a sup," Iain said.

"We'd best fetch a table first," Euan added.

Rhoenne nodded, and turned back to the chair Aileen had occupied. He placed his hands to his hips. The chieftain sword pinned Aileen's headdress and strands of hair to the chair back. The dais was almost empty.

"That is going to take some work to get out," Grant remarked at his side.

"True."

He slanted a glance to his cousin. "I appear to have lost a commander to my Honor Guard. Henry mentioned retirement some time ago. He yearned for a wife. Bairns. His own place. Well. He must have meant it since he's gone and got himself a wife."

"Aye. 'Twas quite a surprise, too. He said naught of it three days past."

"Well...a lone man traveling about the Highlands with an unwed woman has few choices *if* he wishes her accepted. 'Tis obvious they wed by proclamation. Exactly as I did."

"But she does na' even speak!"

"A nod would have sufficed."

Grant nodded. "Fair enough, but...Ida?"

"The woman's changed. As have we all. You have na' looked at her recent-like or you'd ken it."

Grant grunted something noncommittal.

"So. Viscount Ramhurst. What do you think?"

"About what?"

"Assuming command of my Honor Guard. Until such time as the games are enacted and you earn it on the list."

Grant straightened enough he was almost Rhoenne's height. "My laird. Cousin. You do me yet another great honor. I will na' fail you. I swear."

"I ken. 'Tis why I spoke."

Grant cleared his throat and gestured back to where the chieftain ceremony sword was stuck. "We should get that out while we're alone. If I hold the chair, mayhap you can pull the blade?"

"*Nae.* I shall just leave it like that...for the time being."

"Trophy?"

"More of a gut feeling," Rhoenne said reflectively.

"Cousin?"

"I may have need of it in the morn. Oh. Here." Rhoenne pulled Grant's sword from his scabbard and held it to his cousin. "You can have this back now."

Grant took the hilt. Looked across to his cousin. "You are a verra lucky man, Rhoenne."

"Oh. Trust me, Cousin. I ken it. Fully." Rhoenne nodded, and moved to take the most desirable spot in the world.

Right beside his wife.

He'd raised emotions within her since she'd met him, but they were nothing compared to the aura of pure light that filled her breast. Stung her eyes. Made her quiver. Cassandra dabbed at her eyes as he settled into the chair beside hers. Caught a sniff.

"You ail, sweet?" he whispered.

She shook her head. Lifted her gaze to his. He gave her a smile that sent shivers. Her breath caught. Her knees knocked together. He held out his hand to her, palm-up. She blinked rapidly. Sniffed. The sight blurred momentarily as she put her fingers atop his. He raised her hand to his lips, touched a kiss to the tops of her knuckles, and sent a flood of warmth through her entire being. He moved their entwined hands to his chest and held them there. That's when she realized she wasn't the lone one trembling.

"I can na' believe...my life. How blest—." He and cleared his throat. "I do na' ken what to say. Or how to speak fully of it. My tongue searches for the right words...and fails."

"I love you," she replied.

He sucked in a quick breath and lifted his chin. Jaw muscles tightened. Everything about him went taut. Veins pulsed throughout his neck. Several heart-throbbing moments passed before he looked back down at her. The film of moisture that glazed his eyes made them resemble gemstones. Cassandra's heart pulsed. The world rocked sideways, then re-righted. She was amazed that she wasn't swooning.

"Oh sweet. I can na' comprehend the scope of this. 'Tis...too vast." His voice wavered. "I have spent so many years striving to kill off emotion. Harden my heart. I cared little what I did or whom it hurt. There are *nae* amends I can make. Too many to appease. That alone is worrisome. But. There is more. I have found something akin to heaven. Right now. Here with you." The words stopped. He swallowed audibly. "Na' only am I unworthy of such a thing....I am also frightened."

"Frightened? You?"

He tightened his fingers about her as he interrupted. "Oh, love. I am supposed to be 'The Dark One', but I must admit. 'Twas a façade. I have received a love so precious. So...perfect. I can barely absorb how it feels. Especially after the months just past...when I thought you lost to me. And now? Now that you carry my bairns? Oh. Lord above."

He stopped again. Pulled in a large breath that shuddered. His chest expanded outward, moving their entwined hands. He exhaled. Words came with it. "Oh, my love. If anything were to happen to you or to our bairns? I truly do na' ken if I could handle it."

Cassandra tightened her fingers within his. Received a slight pressure in return. "Surely, that is in God's hands. And thus far He has been very gracious."

"Beyond my ability to comprehend," he replied. "I believe I spoke earlier of my trouble with words this eve. Did you na' hear?"

"Trouble? Surely you jest."

He shook his head. Cassandra smiled.

"How old are you, Rhoenne?" she asked.

He snorted with surprise and possible amusement. "*Auld* enough."

"In years, please."

"A bit over a score and five."

"Twenty five? That's all?"

One eyebrow lifted before he answered. "I certainly hope you are na' calling me youthful, or inept, or some other slur. If so, I need warn you. I've taken umbrage for less. And your punishment...may last through the night."

She tipped her glance away from his for a moment and felt the blush sending warmth everywhere. It took an act of will to look back at him. "I merely ponder over your words tonight. And the wisdom you exhibited. Especially with regard to that woman."

"Aileen is na' a woman, love. She is a witch."

"Either way...how could you know?"

"Know what?"

"What she'd do?"

He stiffened. She felt it. "I do na' follow your

thinking," he finally replied.

"Whenever a sultan passes on, everything in the harem changes. Those who had power – his lesser wives, his favorites, even the lowest of concubines – they are given a choice. It's unspoken, but known. Those who didn't take it bore the punishment. They were treated as offal. Their value equal to a slave...if not less."

"What was their choice?"

"No one was forced to follow the sultan to the grave. They willingly take poison, or put their necks in the path of a blade."

"I see. And...this somehow relates to my words this eve?" He had a smile hovering about his lip and his eyes sparkled as he asked it.

"You are sentencing three men in the morn."

He went taut. His eyes narrowed. When he answered, his voice carried the anger. "They earned it. They tried to poison the well. Even if they did na' ken it was monkshood, there is *nae* defense."

"That is na' what I speak of. You ken the likely source of the poison, and that she probably has more of it."

"True."

"And you have sentenced her to be alone. All night. To relive what has happened. She has lost quite a portion of her beauty and her actions have been exposed. To all."

"You think she will take the monkshood?"

Cassandra shrugged. Then gasped, as the babes decided to be active again. She placed her free hand atop the mound beneath her bodice.

Watched as Rhoenne's eyes warmed to a cobalt blue shade. The man was beyond handsome. Truly. She barely kept a sigh from sounding. She had to glance away or her voice might not work.

"I cannot say what she will do. I simply think you have given her a fourth choice. One...she may take."

He lifted her hand to his lips again. Spoke the words to the tops of her knuckles. "May I ask you a question now?"

Cassandra moved her gaze back to his, but it was difficult. Blushes warmed her, nervousness flit about her belly, and still her heart dropped when she reached his gaze again.

"Just how *auld* are you?" he asked.

She smiled. "Some months shy of a score."

"You are nineteen?"

She nodded.

"Hmm. And she thinks I display wisdom beyond my years," he remarked. And then he moved their entwined hands to his chest and stood, lifting her to her feet beside him. "Come. Our chamber awaits."

"But—? The men? The table they've just gone for? Your fest? All...these people?"

"I've had a change of heart. I've just reunited with my wife. We have a chamber. A world of love afore us. And privacy," he answered.

And then he lowered his chin and took her breath away.

Again.

EPILOGUE

DOWNPOUR STOLE VISION and breath, quagmire slicked the path despite spikes driven through the bottom of boots for traction, and Calum Montvale's powerful hits continued to hammer Rhoenne's shield, sending it against his shoulder more than once. The man had gained strength, bulk, and arrogance since winning the competition against Rory FitzHugh. Enough of each that he'd challenged the laird to this contest.

They fought on the castle list, surrounded by clan while more gathered by the moment. This was a spontaneous event. Unplanned. Unprepared. Totally unscripted. Rhoenne could have postponed, but fighting Calum had sounded like a good way to pass the hours he'd otherwise spend with waiting. And pacing.

The rules of the contest were simple. No steel. No skeans. Each man claimed only a wooden shield and a club with a knotted tip. They weren't child's toys. A hit from these clubs could split a man's skull. Break bone. Split ribs.

Rhoenne peeked around his shield edge, saw an opening, and smacked his club end into Calum's thigh just enough it would sting. Calum's cry of rage heralded another barrage against the wooden shield. The man had great strength and power behind each blow, but he needed to work on emotion. That's why Rory held a position in Rhoenne's Honor Guard while Calum led the castle guards. Montvale man angered easily. Still. And anger could lose any contest.

Rhoenne timed Calum's next bout of hits against the shield. Blows came rhythmic and quick. Five...six...seven. On the eighth one, Rhoenne smacked back into the blow with his shield. The move lifted the piece high, obstructing the downpour so he could watch Calum's off-balance lurch backwards, before the man fell onto his buttocks. A spray of muck lifted into the mist about him. Hoots and hollers came from the crowd, barely penetrating the rain. Somebody started thumping on a kettle drum, sending a rhythmic throb through the scene. Rhoenne tauntingly hit his shield-front twice before resuming a defensive stance. He didn't have time for more. Calum had rolled and regained his footing quickly. He knew the man would. 'Twas how he'd defeated Rory. Calum Montvale was quick, and he didn't give up.

Both excellent traits.

The man appeared to have changed tactics. Moments passed as Rhoenne waited for another head-on attack , before he saw a blur of movement to his left. He deflected with his shield-covered arm and swiveled, missing the hit to his thigh by a hairsbreadth. Calum's counter-move with his shield smacked Rhoenne's right shoulder, knocking him sideways, and if his spikes had any grip, he'd have gone down. As it was, he made several awkward steps, keeping Calum at his front, his shield between them. Calum pressed his advantage, hitting with such jolts, the shield cracked, wavered against his arm, and then split. Rhoenne didn't watch as the bottom section separated, smacking his lower leg before it fell to the mud.

He barely felt it.

Heartbeats filled his ears, rain plastered his hair to his skull, each heave of breath fogged the air around him. He began moving his left wrist, rotating the half-circle barrier to counter blows where needed. Calum's advantage made him bolder. More intense. Speed of his movements flung raindrops. Grunts of effort fled his lips. Time and again he attacked only to find his blows blocked.

Rhoenne deflected and danced about, holding his club ready, waiting for an opening. He slid. Recovered. Slid again. This time his boots struck the half of his shield half-buried in muck.

"You are losing, Ramhurst!" Calum bellowed.

Rhoenne stepped onto the wood, his shoe spikes gripped giving him a fulcrum to pivot. He launched a blow around Calum's shield, striking into the man's unprotected mid-section. Calum launched backward, landing into a puddle with such force, mud-spray spouted upward before settling back.

The crowd reaction was raucous. Although

muffled, hearty cheers blended with hoots and whistles while the drummer sent a rapid series of beats that matched Rhoenne's pulse. He straddled the half-shield, teetering back and forth as he watched Calum roll to his knees, then lumber to his feet. It took longer this time. Rhoenne waited until the man was upright again.

"Why do you wait, my laird? You need an invitation?"

Calum yelled the taunt and finished by smacking his club against his shield. Rhoenne bent his knees. Started rotating his half-shield again. And then he heard his name being called.

"Rhoenne! My laird, Ramhurst!"

Rhoenne swiped a hand across his forehead and held it there so he could spot waving arms that belonged to Henry FitzHugh. The man was some way off, and at a run. The crowd parted at the back and he disappeared into their midst.

Rhoenne jogged to the list barrier, tossing his club to one side, the partial shield to the other. Calum Montvale was at his heels, similarly weaponless. The crowd went quiet, the drums silent. Rain continually peppered the world, making it difficult to see and hear and gain breath. It also lifted a skim of moisture on both men as it cooled. Calum caught Rhoenne's glance, huffed out a fog-wrapped breath, then grinned.

"Is this...a forfeit, my laird?" he teased.

Rhoenne's chin lowered. His lips twisted.

"Oh, verra well. Rematch?"

"Agreed," Rhoenne replied.

Henry appeared finally, spat from the crowd.

He bent forward and pulled in several panted breaths as everyone waited.

"Well?" Rhoenne prompted.

"You should na' run so, mon. 'Tis bad at your age," Calum offered.

Henry stood.   "I'll   show...you   *auld,*   you young—."

"Henry!" Rhoenne interrupted.   "Do you bring word?"

"Oh. Aye. I've word."

Several beards split with grins at Henry's reply. A lot of voices started up, hampering hearing. Rhoenne held up a hand for silence. The crowd quieted again.

"'Tis your countess! Her time...has started."

Rhoenne sucked in a breath. Held it. Listened to the hammering of his heart. Felt emotion he recognized flash through his belly and stop there, where it would solidify and gain heft. He exhaled. "How much time do I have?" he asked.

"The wife said it will be a spell."

"The countess said that?"

"Oh. *Nae.* I speak of my wife. Ida."

Somebody chucked. It was quelled instantly.

"I've   time   for   a   swim,   then," Rhoenne announced. "Come! I'll race you to the loch!"

Only the fittest men kept pace as Rhoenne ran for the loch shores, chucked his *feile-breacan,* and dove into storm-whipped water. Cold smacked him,   waves   alternately   tossing   and   assisting. Every   stroke   he   made   was   massive   and   strong. Rhoenne   swam   across   the   loch,   took   several chest-filling breaths on the far shore as he jogged in place, working his arms and shoulders. Then he dove back in and swam back. He crawled onto dark rain-soaked earth, flipped onto his back, and watched the tunnel of raindrops falling from above. He felt aware, awake, and alive.

And yet the worry he worked at conquering had solidified in his belly. He had no choice but to ignore it, and that meant he needed to stay active. He rose to his feet. Surveyed the scene.

No one could dry until they reached the shelter of a lengthy structure, constructed for just such a purpose. The solid wall of Castle Tyne loomed above the group massed about a fire. Someone tossed Rhoenne a warm, dry plaid. He rubbed his skin before donning it, knotting one end at his side before flipping the other over his shoulder. The enclosure was most welcome, providing shelter from the rain, drying warmth from the fire. Rhoenne settled onto his haunches near it. Someone had brought an ale keg and large mugs. The keg was tapped, tankards filled and passed out. Rhoenne snagged one and gulped thirstily. Once drained, he rose and addressed them.

"Men of my Honor Guard. Come with me. 'Tis time to check on the proceedings," he announced.

The chosen men stood, brushed sand and pebbles from their plaids, and accompanied Rhoenne up a flight of stone steps to the entry near the kitchens. Savory smells wafted through the halls as they walked in cadence, boots striking stone in a rhythmic fashion. Rhoenne entered the Great Hall just as shouts from above alerted him.

"Race you!"

"No! Wait! I get to go first!"

Two lads leaped atop the railing and started sliding. Rhoenne reached the base of the steps first, bumping into Emin who'd materialized at his side. Rhoenne snagged a black-haired lad with one arm. Grabbed the other's belt with his free hand. The boys squirmed a moment before realizing who held them.

"Da!" They shouted in unison.

"Good catch, Excellency," Emin offered.

Rhoenne started laughing as both boys climbed him, hugged his neck, then pulled away to look at him with matching blue eyes.

"You said you would show us how to fight with real swords!" one accused.

"I said that?" Rhoenne replied.

"Henry's right, Da," the other boy offered.

"Did na' I also say we'd start on the morrow?" Rhoenne asked his firstborn and namesake.

The younger Rhoenne Guy de Ramhurst was the calmer, quieter twin. He studied Rhoenne for a moment before nodding. "Aye. You did say that."

"But tomorrow is too far away!" Henry opined.

"'Twill be here afore you ken it, lads. We'll start tomorrow. But, tell me...what have you done with Maysie?"

"Well, we—," Henry began.

"Oh, there they are! Oh. My laird. The lads were just starting letters, and I turn my back for one moment, and they're gone!" Maysie explained as she came rapidly down the stairs.

"Lads?" Rhoenne asked with a firm tone.

"Book learning."

Henry opined it in disgust. His temperament wasn't the exact opposite of his twin, but if there was mischief afoot, it was usually Henry's doing. Rhoenne couldn't prevent a smile.

"Well, lads. What can I tell you? Every man needs book learning," he finally remarked.

"What about fighting? Euan told us you fought a whole ship full of pirates! All by yourself!" Guy said.

"Euan."

Rhoenne turned to look over the men. Euan stifled a grin before ducking his head. Rhoenne looked back to his sons.

"Now lads. You ken that sometimes Euan tells tall tales."

"But Emin said the same," Henry argued.

"How can we fight like you if we do na' train?" Guy added.

Rhoenne didn't answer right away. Being a father sent a massive dose of emotion. It weakened his knees and his heart felt as swollen as his tongue.

"The lads have you there, Rhoenne," Grant remarked from behind him.

Rhoenne cleared his throat. "Fair enough. We'll start on the morrow. You've my word. Now. It's back to letters for you both." He set them down and swatted rears as they raced back up the steps, Maysie right behind them. Then he turned to regard Emin.

"They nearly escaped you this time, Emin."

"Your sons are quick, Excellency. Strong-willed. But I do not slacken. They are safe as long as I breathe. I vow it."

"I ken as much, my friend. You'd best hurry though. Maysie may need an assist, and you know she only wants yours."

Rhoenne lifted his brows several times. Emin reddened, opened his mouth to reply. Thought better of it. Then followed the boys and Maysie.

"I guess that there is proof that where there's a will, there's a way—oof!"

"Leave gossip to women, man!" someone hissed.

Rhoenne turned to regard the group. Nobody spoke. He swallowed against the stone feeling in his gut. Despite how he ignored it, the sensation of worry grew. Got heavier somehow. He knew from experience that the lone thing that tempered it was physical motion.

And lots of it.

"Well, what are we waiting about for? I've got to check on the lady wife still. See how much more time I have."

He didn't wait for affirmation. He jogged across the Great Hall to the Chieftain steps, the sound of boots striking wood showed his men in tandem. They reached the alcove. Rhoenne stopped. Adjusted his attire. Took a couple of deep breaths.

"Do you ever think on the dark times?" Grant said at Rhoenne's side.

"Dark times?"

"Afore Aileen poisoned herself."

"*Nae.* Never."

Grant grunted a reply. The Chieftain's chamber door opened, Angus's wife Margaret and another woman came out, empty water cans in their hands.

"Ladies!" Rhoenne greeted them.

The women dropped curtsies. "Greetings, my laird. And to your Honor Guard, as well."

"Any word?" he asked abruptly.

The younger lass shook her head. Rhoenne's shoulders dropped visibly. The weight in his belly shifted.

"'Tis getting closer, though," the older woman offered.

"How much closer?"

She lifted her shoulders un-helpfully.

Rhoenne turned toward his men again. "Well. You all heard. I've time on my hands still. Come along, then. We'll gird the nursery."

"To the nursery!"

Someone called it and they set off down the hall.

Castle Tyneburgh nurseries were located on the third floor of the keep. To reach them required climbing a tower wheel-stair, taking a dogleg turn and traversing another hall. It wasn't the only way to reach the set of rooms, but it was the quickest. Arrow slits constructed into the tower stone sent gray-cast spears of daylight onto the spiral series of steps, but the upper hall was gloom-filled, lit intermittently with torches in sconces. Before they reached the nursery, Emin loomed out of the shadows. Rhoenne was the lone man who didn't come to a stunned stop.

"Ho there, Emin!" Rhoenne said. "I take it Guy and Henry are hard at work with book learning?"

"With three guards to oversee the effort," Emin replied.

"How did he get here afore us?" someone asked in a loud whisper.

Emin's lips twitched. Rhoenne's smile widened.

"Everything quiet within?" he asked.

The man nodded, reached to open the door. "The wee ones are asleep, both at the same time. 'Tis a rare event."

Rhoenne beckoned his men with a finger to his lips before turning to peek at the scene. The nursery was a large room, the walls rendered in a cream shade. The color warmed the space as much as the large fire in the fireplace. Rhoenne's heart swelled to a painful level with the rush of joy and pride. His life was so full now. So joyous. His existence centered in a love that just kept growing.

Five women were in the room, keeping a careful eye on his second set of twins. Their heads could just be seen above matching plaids. The younger lads were almost identical to their older brothers. Black-headed. Blue-eyed. Perfectly healthy. They'd just reached their second year. Finding a moment when they were both asleep was a rare event, indeed.

Ida smiled at him from a rocker, her arms full with Henry's pride and joy, a red-haired lass named Sandra. She wouldn't be able to hold the child on her lap much longer, as time approached for the birth of their second bairn. Rhoenne returned her smile and pulled back from the doorway. Emin softly closed the door behind him.

"I'll visit later this eve. When they're awake," Rhoenne said in a low tone.

Emin nodded.

Rhoenne shoved aside the weighty sensation in his gut, but it didn't cease. It was a throbbing issue he well remembered. He turned around, pulled in a couple of deep breaths. He'd heard this waiting and worrying got easier with each passing birth.

That was false.

"Well men," he addressed his Honor Guard. "What say we take a visit to the chapel?"

"To the chapel!" Iain announced from the back of the crowd.

The castle chapel was encased within an inner courtyard tower, its walls rendered with white lime coating. The windows were leaded stained glass. The east-facing altar was draped with a cloth worked in minute stitches by his countess, Cassandra, using real gold thread. The entire area was imbued with a sanctified reverent aura. Rhoenne and his men filled the aisle, spilling into the rows of carved benches. Rhoenne went to a knee. Bent his head. Prayed. All about him he sensed his men doing the same.

Rhoenne finished and stood, genuflected, then turned back to his men. They didn't speak until they were in the hall outside the chapel.

"It is in the Lord's hands now, lads," he told them.

"The Lord has certainly been heavy-handed with your blessings thus far, I would say," Grant remarked.

"True," Rhoenne agreed.

"Sometimes I envy you. Still."

"'Twill be your turn soon enough, cousin. The English king granted your entreaty a sennight ago. You heard the decree. Your royal wife is on her way to you."

"Aye. Finally. And that, under threat of rebellion."

"Well, Grant." Rhoenne clapped a hand to his cousin's shoulder. "The twists of love are ever harsh. But, oh! The rewards are mighty."

Someone groaned.

"What? You do na' like my prose? I'm told 'tis a family trait. I've a troubadour in my past." Rhoenne clapped his hands. "But come. Enough chatter. We should retreat to the Chieftain's chamber. It has a grand span of floor. We will have need of it."

Several men groaned.

"You ken I've got to keep moving. This waiting and worrying grows burdensome. Takes years off a man. And here I thought 'twould would get easier."

"You do na' appear worried, my laird."

"Trust me. I am."

"Na' so much as the first time though," Euan remarked. "You did na' slacken or allow any rest for hours!"

"You even had us race you around the loch!" another man added.

"And that after taking on all challengers on the list!" another man added.

"All right. All right." Rhoenne held up a hand. "You are right. I was a trifle overwrought. And to what end?"

"Soreness to every muscle I claim," Euan quipped.

Rhoenne considered. "In that event, we'd best order a keg delivered to us in the Chieftain's Room."

Cheers followed that statement before they started back to the Great Hall. The area had altered considerably since they'd just been there. Servants were at work, spreading rushes, pulling tables and benches into place, removing the partition around the dais, working without chatter or noise, as if the entire castle was also hovering in wait. Tense. Dogged with worry.

Rhoenne threaded his way around benches and tables, guardsmen in single file behind him. They were halfway across the room when a shout from above stopped everything.

"My laird! Rhoenne!"

"'Tis the bairns?" he shouted back.

The woman gestured for him and ducked back into the darkness. Rhoenne ran for the steps, took them two at a time, arrived at the landing before she'd reached his chamber door again. He didn't know if anyone followed. His pulse had overtaken his hearing.

"Well? Is it the bairns?"

She nodded, then shook her head.

"What the blazes does that mean?" Rhoenne croaked.

"I am na' allowed to say," she confided and just then the door opened.

Rhoenne shoved past her and raced across the floor to the bed. He leapt atop the platform to kneel beside where Cassandra reclined, propped up with pillows behind her shoulders. She was still. Her eyes shut. His heart stopped. But then she sensed him, opened her eyes, and gave him a smile.

And nothing had ever looked so sweet.

"Oh, Cassandra! Thank God! I thought—! Feared for a moment that—!"

His voice choked too much to continue. He plucked her hand from the cover and lifted it to his lips where she couldn't fail to feel his trembling.

Her smile warmed yet her eyes filled with tears, making the golden depths luminous.

"Oh, Rhoenne."

She looked up and blinked rapidly. His hand tightened on hers.

"My love?"

"Have you seen...the babe?"

"My world revolves around you, my lady wife. All else can wait."

She swiped at her lashes with her free hand, before speaking to someone behind him. "Would you bring the babe, Meggie?" she asked.

"*The* bairn?" Rhoenne repeated.

JACKIE IVIE

Cassandra nodded.

"We do na' have twins?"

"No."

"But...it is healthy?"

"Yes. And large."

"Then I do na' see the reason for tears."

She moved to adjust herself. Rhoenne was instantly on his feet and assisting. As soon as she'd settled, he sat on the mattress edge beside her. They watched a trio of women approach, Margaret in the center, carrying the babe. Cassandra opened her arms, and the swaddled infant was settled into her arms.

He'd rarely beheld anything as beautiful as her expression.

His wife hadn't been entirely accurate. To his eye, the newborn didn't look much bigger than the others. There wasn't much difference at all. It had the same amount of black hair. Small chin. Puckered lips.

Rhoenne touched a tiny hand with his finger. "Having just one will take some getting used to," he remarked.

"That's not the only difference, love."

One of the women giggled.

"Truly?"

"May I present...our daughter!" she announced.

"A lass? We have a lass?"

She nodded.

The rush of emotion slammed into his nose and rocketed off his head. Rhoenne gave a whoop that startled everyone except his baby girl.

"I take it you are pleased?" Cassandra actually

asked.

"Verra much so. I am beyond blessed. And thankful. And praise be to God she was na' our firstborn."

There was a collective gasp from just about everyone. Only Cassandra looked at him without expression.

"Cassandra. Love. Do na' you see? She will take after her mother. Thank God she has four elder brothers. I'm going to need all the help I can get protecting her."

THE END

OTHER BOOKS BY JACKIE IVIE

Highlander Series
LADY OF THE KNIGHT
TENDER IS THE KNIGHT
THE KNIGHT BEFORE CHRISTMAS
HEAT OF THE KNIGHT
A KNIGHT WELL SPENT
ONCE UPON A KNIGHT
KNIGHT EVERLASTING
THE KNIGHT AND WHITE SATIN
A PERFECT KNIGHT FOR LOVE
LAIRD OF BALLANCLAIRE
KNIGHT BEYOND BLACK (Highland Hunger)
FOREVER KNIGHT

Brocade Series
BRANDYWINE
MORGANNA
AVERILL
GISELLE
LINNA
BESSIE

Vampire Assassin League Series
KNIGHT AFTER KNIGHT
BE STILL MY HEART
DEARLY BELOVED

WE ARE GATHERED
TOGETHER TO JOIN
THIS MAN AND WOMAN
FOREVER AS ONE
SHOULD THERE BE
ANYONE HERE
WITH JUST CAUSE
WHY THESE TWO
CANNOT UNITE
LET THEM SPEAK
NOW OR FOREVER
HOLD THEIR PEACE
DO YOU TAKE
THIS VAMPIRE AS
A FOREVER MATE
TO HAVE
AND TO HOLD
TO LOVE
TO HONOR
AND TO CHERISH
FOR RICHER
AND RICHER
FORSAKING
ALL OTHERS
AS LONG AS
YOU BOTH
EXIST
WHEN IT COMES
TIME TO DIE
BE NOT LIKE
THOSE WHOSE HEARTS

Author Bio

Jackie Ivie lives in the beautiful state of Alaska with her husband and pets. She started her writing career in 2004 with a Highlander adventure romance series through Kensington Publishing. She's now working on at least one of the following:

ARE FILLED - #35 in the VAMPIRE ASSASSIN LEAGUE series,

ANNIHILATE - #3 in the PORTALS OF TIME series,

TRAPPED - #3 in the CHRONICLES OF THE HUNTED series,

or Book #2 in the new VALOR AND STEEL series

She can be reached at
PO Box 90226, Anchorage, AK
99509-0026

Connect on Facebook
www.facebook.com/JackieIvieAuthor

Made in the USA
Middletown, DE
03 July 2021

43580780R00321